Praise for Mary Daheim
and her Emma Lord mysteries

THE ALPINE ADVOCATE
"The lively ferment of a life in a small Pacific
Northwest town, with its convoluted genealogies and
loyalties [and] its authentically quirky characters,
combines with a baffling murder for an intriguing
mystery novel."
—M. K. WREN

THE ALPINE BETRAYAL
"Editor-publisher Emma Lord finds out that running
a small-town newspaper is worse than nutty—it's
downright dangerous. Readers will take great pleasure
in Mary Daheim's new mystery."
—CAROLYN G. HART

THE ALPINE CHRISTMAS
"If you like cozy mysteries, you need to try Daheim's
Alpine series. . . . Recommended."
—*The Snooper*

THE ALPINE DECOY
"[A] fabulous series . . . Fine examples of the
traditional, domestic mystery."
—*Mystery Lovers Bookshop News*

By Mary Daheim
Published by Ballantine Books:

THE ALPINE ADVOCATE
THE ALPINE BETRAYAL
THE ALPINE CHRISTMAS
THE ALPINE DECOY
THE ALPINE ESCAPE
THE ALPINE FURY

THE
ALPINE FURY

Mary Daheim

BALLANTINE BOOKS • NEW YORK

Copyright © 1995 by Mary Daheim

All rights reserved under International and Pan-American Copyright Conventions. Published in the United States by Ballantine Books, a division of Random House, Inc., New York, and simultaneously in Canada by Random House of Canada Limited, Toronto.

Library of Congress Catalog Card Number: 95-94545

ISBN 0-345-38843-7

Manufactured in the United States of America

First Edition: December 1995

10 9 8 7 6 5 4 3 2 1

Chapter One

THE FROST WAS on the pumpkin, and also on Leo Fulton Walsh's rear end. My new advertising manager had skidded on one of Alpine's icy sidewalks, landing in Front Street, across from the newspaper office. The accident wasn't entirely Leo's fault. He was from California, and unused to winter weather. If there was blame, it rested on me for hiring Leo in the first place.

The situation had been desperate. My former ad man, Ed Bronsky, had inherited a small fortune from an aunt in Iowa. His exit had evoked mixed emotions. Though Ed showed occasional flashes of enthusiasm, he usually acted as if he were being forced to walk the plank. Gloom had hung on Ed Bronsky just like his baggy raincoat. But money had done wondrous things, and Ed was now downright chipper.

He was also off *The Alpine Advocate*'s staff, which was why I'd hired Leo Fulton Walsh. Ed's abrupt leave-taking had put me in a bind. Leo had been available, and had come recommended by my son's father, Tom Cavanaugh. Tom is not and never was my husband, but he does own several small weeklies west of the Rockies. I've always had faith in his judgment. I'm not sure why, since twenty-two years ago he was the one who assured me I couldn't get pregnant. Adam's arrival nine

1

months later proved Tom wrong. I was beginning to think that Tom might be mistaken about Leo, too.

"He's drunk. Again." Vida Runkel, my House & Home editor, looked up from a sheet of contact prints taken at the Alpine Elementary School's Halloween party. "I'm afraid Leo is an alcoholic, Emma. You'll have to do something about him."

"I already did," I replied dryly. "I hired him. And he's *not* drunk." My tone turned defensive, though I wasn't sure whether I was defending Leo or myself. "It's really icy this morning. There's a snowstorm coming." I tapped the latest wire service forecast for the central Cascade Mountains.

"He's drunk." Vida's voice brooked no argument. Neither did her gaze, which didn't blink behind the tortoiseshell-rimmed glasses. As ever, she looked daunting, even sitting down. Vida is in her sixties, a big woman with strong shoulders, a formidable bosom, and unruly gray curls. She gave me her gimlet eye, then resumed squinting through a magnifier at the Halloween picture. "Is Bryce Bamberg wearing a mask in this photo? I can't tell."

I glanced over Vida's shoulder. I couldn't tell, either. Bryce Bamberg, fifth grade, was one homely kid. I shuddered, and dismissed Bryce from my mind.

"Leo may have sprained his ankle," I said, looking out through the small window above Vida's desk. Front Street was busy on this first Monday of November. That is, there were at least a dozen cars in sight. With not quite four thousand residents, Alpine, Washington, isn't inclined to gridlock. Indeed, the traffic was somewhat lighter than usual, due not only to the ice, but to the local economic crisis. The backbone of Alpine's industry is, as I once inadvertently said in print, rooted in trees. But logging has been curtailed by environmental restrictions, and as yet, the community hasn't been able to re-group.

Cars, including Sheriff Milo Dodge's Cherokee Chief, continued to trickle past the *Advocate* office. I gave up waiting for Vida's response. Maybe she hadn't heard me. But she had—Vida can hear people even when they don't speak out loud.

She had finished choosing the Halloween pictures for the Wednesday edition. "Give me something," she demanded abruptly. "I'm doing 'Scene.' "

"Scene Around Town" is our version of a gossip column. Vida writes it, but we all contribute. Rarely are these items juicy; only occasionally are they of interest. Still, Alpiners love to see themselves and their relatives and neighbors and friends in print. The column is the best-read in the paper, with the possible exception of the obituaries. When we have any.

"You could use Leo," I suggested. "Falling down always makes news."

"Not when it involves drunkenness." Vida looked both grim and prim. "So far, I only have three items: Tim Rafferty and Tiffany Eriks enjoying double-tall nonfat lattes at the new Starbucks; high school coach Rip Ridley losing his voice after the football team's 45–7 defeat in Sultan; and Dot Parker seeing sparrows ice-skating on her frozen birdbath. Give me something useful."

But Front Street looked very ordinary from my vantage point. Running east-west on the flat, the heavy frost which had turned to ice was almost melted by eight-thirty. The north-south streets heading up the mountainside were another matter. That was where Leo had slipped, coming down Fourth and crashing at the corner by the Alpine Building. He had walked from his apartment on Cedar Street because he was afraid to drive his new Toyota on the ice. Our office manager, Ginny Burmeister, and I had rescued Leo, guiding him the two blocks to the medical clinic where he was having his ankle X-rayed. Ginny was still with him.

My remaining staff member arrived just as I was pouring a mug of coffee. Carla Steinmetz is young, pretty, enthusiastic, and flighty. On this Monday morning, she seemed uncharacteristically withdrawn. Carla's step dragged over the threshold.

" 'Morning," she mumbled, not looking at either Vida or me.

Vida's mouth set, and her eyes narrowed. "Good morning, Carla. How are you?"

It wasn't a rhetorical question. Carla's gaze slid in Vida's direction, then fixed itself on the coffeemaker. "Depressed," my reporter answered in a bleak voice. She poured herself a cup of coffee and went into the front office, presumably searching for her soul mate, Ginny.

Vida was looking out the window. "Francine Wells is wearing new boots. Very smart, probably not suitable for this weather. The refrigeration repair truck is in front of Harvey Adcock's hardware and sporting goods store. Maybe his bait box blew up. Cal Vickers's tow truck needs washing. Ah! Cal's towing Fuzzy Baugh's Chrysler! The mayor must have gone into a skid." Vida shot me a quick look over her shoulder. "You see, Emma, even after going on four years, you still don't have the knack for picking up small-town news. It's the everyday occurrences that people like to read about. In Alpine, we don't need drive-by shootings and arson fires and drug raids to entertain us."

I managed to refrain from retorting that even callous city people didn't exactly consider tragedy a source of entertainment. At least most of them didn't. Vida knew as much; she was merely tweaking me for being an outsider. I probably wouldn't ever be anything else if I lived until I died in Alpine.

Vida was back at her typewriter, rattling off her three new items for "Scene Around Town." "I need at least four more," she announced, throwing the carriage of her archaic machine with a flourish.

"You've got until five P.M. tomorrow," I pointed out as the phone rang on Carla's desk. I picked it up. "Emma Lord," I said into the receiver just as Carla reentered the newsroom.

Ginny was on the line, calling from the clinic. She wanted Carla to help her bring Leo back to the office. According to Dr. Peyton Flake, my ad manager had suffered a slight sprain and was on crutches.

But Carla folded her arms across her chest and planted her booted feet squarely on the worn linoleum. "I'm not going to the clinic. I'm never going to the clinic, not even if my arms and legs fall off. Ginny can put Leo on a sled." She slammed back out of the office again.

I raised my eyebrows. "What did Leo do to Carla? Or is she mad at Ginny?"

Vida was editing her new copy. She didn't look up. "Carla isn't angry with either of them. She's broken off with Peyton Flake."

"Oh." Vida's niece, Marje Blatt, worked at the Alpine Medical Clinic. Like so many of Vida's kin, Marje was not so much a relative as a conduit. If Marje had ever taken an oath regarding patient confidentiality, there had been an asterisk excluding Vida. Had Vida been Catholic—perish the thought from her Presbyterian soul!—my pastor, Dennis Kelly, would have sent a note off to the Vatican stating the seal of the confessional did not apply when it came to my House &

Home editor. Doctors, lawyers, merchants, and chiefs acknowledged Vida as both source and repository. If any of them objected, they didn't dare say so.

I sat down on Vida's desk. Never mind that there were stories to write, proofs to read, and a newspaper to lay out. An unhappy staff is an unproductive staff. Leo was injured, Ginny was detained, and Carla was in a funk. I needed the facts if I was to cope with my personnel and meet a deadline.

"Dr. Flake is too big for his britches," Vida declared. "Since he came to Alpine last year, the clinic's practice has grown. Young Doc Dewey gives all the credit to his new partner for actively soliciting new patients from the Stevens Pass corridor. It's true, I'm sure. Young Doc is like his late father, competent, thorough—and passive. But Peyton Flake is, as you know, a maverick. Not only does he possess the latest methods in medicine, but he markets himself aggressively. He also considers himself a god. Carla is irked."

I didn't blame her. Carla isn't stupid, but she does a fine imitation. Peyton Flake might take advantage of what I considered her lack of focus. Maybe he belittled her, or at least teased too much. At twenty-five, Carla's self-esteem wasn't firmly rooted. At forty-two, my own was on shaky ground.

"Maybe they'll make up," I said. "They've been going together for six months."

Vida didn't reply; she was inserting a fresh sheet of paper into the typewriter. Using only two fingers, her hands danced across the keys. I retired to my office, wondering about our lead story.

It had been an uneventful week in Alpine, as most of them were. The icy streets would give us an extensive list of minor accidents. The annual spate of Halloween vandalism would fill another six to eight inches of copy, plus photos. The only out-of-the-ordinary event was the resurfacing of Highway 187, unofficially known as the Icicle Creek Road, between town and the campground. The project had begun in mid-October, with a rush date to finish before the first heavy snow. Maybe I could squeeze a lead story out of Big Mike Brockelman, the construction foreman. I dialed his cellular number.

"Sorry, Ms. Lord," said Mike. "No news here. We can't work this morning because of the ice."

"That's great," I said, then hastened to explain. "I mean, that's news. 'Weather delays highway project.' You see?"

"What?" Big Mike's deep voice went with his muscular build and imposing height. "Oh, yeah, sure, I guess."

I needed another three inches of copy. A photo of the idle road machinery would help. "What does the crew do when this sort of thing happens?" I inquired, delving for information to pad the story.

Mike snorted. "They stay home. Like I'm doing. You called me in Monroe."

"Oh." I was disappointed. For some reason, I'd thought that Brockelman and company were holed up in the Lumberjack Motel. Briefly I'd envisioned two pictures—one of the immobilized equipment, the other showing the six-man crew playing pinochle. "How soon before you'll be able to resume work?"

"Can't say. The stretch we're working on is just past the Petersen farm. Lots of big evergreens, no sun even if the clouds lift. Tomorrow, maybe. If it doesn't snow." Mike sounded as gloomy as the weather.

I asked a few more questions, the kind that people find stupid, because there are no real answers. Completion date, additional costs, possibility of further postponement—I knew Mike couldn't do anything except guess, but even ambiguity fills the front page. By the time I finished my interview, Mike was testy and his wife was yelling at him from somewhere in their Monroe-area home.

Twenty minutes later, I had finished my lead story. Carla, however, demurred at taking a picture.

"It's too dangerous," she pouted over a sugar doughnut she'd fetched from the Upper Crust Bakery. "My car may be old, but it's new to me, and I'm not risking it by driving up 187. Can't we use stock?"

We could, since she'd taken several shots of the road equipment when it had arrived two weeks earlier. We'd featured the six-man crew in the previous story; this time I'd run Big Mike, leaning on his steamroller. This was one of those weeks when there wouldn't be much drama on the front page. In a small town, that was often the case. There had, however, been a few issues in the past when I had wished for tamer topics. I shivered a little as I recalled the murders we'd had in Alpine. Some victims had been familiar; others were strangers. Either way, we didn't need news like that to liven up the paper. Vida could create readership with Francine Wells's new boots.

"Ha!" Vida had sprung out of her chair after rubbernecking through the window again. "Now, that's an item!" She plastered herself against the wall and peered out as if she could see around corners. She probably could. "Little Bobby Lambrecht," she whispered, as if whoever he was could hear through walls. "He's heading into the Bank of Alpine. My, my!"

"Who cares?" The small, desolate voice belonged to Carla, eating her third doughnut. "I've never heard of Little Bobby Lambrecht."

Vida had resumed her seat. "Of course you haven't. You're new in town." The gray eyes darted in my direc tion. "And you, Emma. You wouldn't know Bobby, either."

By Vida's standards, Carla and I were both babes in the woods when it came to Alpine background knowledge. I'd hired Carla four months after I bought the paper from the original owner, Marius Vandeventer. Having arrived as adults, fully formed by forces outside of Alpine, we could never truly belong. As usual, we endured Vida's smug, insider's expression.

"So?" I asked, feeling prickly. "Who's Little Bobby Lambrecht?"

Vida squared her shoulders, which caused the black polyester vest to quiver over the black-and-white print blouse with the pussycat bow. "Robert Lambrecht is Faith Steiner Lambrecht's son. The Steiners were great friends of my parents, Earl Ennis and Muriel May Woolrich Blatt. My father and Edward Steiner were among the first elders of the Presbyterian church in Alpine." Pride rang in Vida's voice. "Faith married a minister from our church. Years later, he was posted to Wenatchee. The family moved there when Bobby was a junior in high school. Bobby and Milo Dodge went through school together. I still hear from Faith—she's widowed and lives in Spokane—and Bobby is quite the bigwig with the Bank of Washington in Seattle. Now, why is he in Alpine?" Vida peered first at me, then at Carla. I flinched; Carla ate another doughnut.

"What difference does it make?" Carla was defensive. I thought she was talking about Little Bobby Lambrecht. She meant the doughnuts. "So I get fat and ugly and old? Who'll care? This town is a dead end. I'm going to die without ever having lived."

"Did you get glazed?" Vida was looking severe. "The Upper Crust does glazed only on Monday and Thursday."

I felt like snatching the white bakery bag from Carla's hands. Before I could move, Ginny opened the door and edged into the office. Leo Walsh was leaning on her. He looked sheepish.

"No ballroom dancing for a while," he said, hopping to his desk. "Sorry, Emma. I didn't realize the sidewalk was so slippery. Hell, up the hill by your house, you don't even *have* sidewalks."

It was true. At least one third of Alpine didn't have sidewalks. My street was paved, but it was lined with a thin trail of dirt. Or mud or slush or snow, depending upon the season. All my editorial efforts at putting a Local Improvement District bond issue on the ballot had been in vain.

"Black ice is hard to see," I conceded, pulling out Leo's chair. "How do you feel?"

If Leo truly had been drunk this morning, he was sober now. His face reminded me of tree bark—rough, seamed, weathered, indifferent to the elements but vulnerable to time. His graying auburn hair wasn't combed as carefully as usual, and his sharply pressed flannel slacks were rumpled.

"It's not serious," Leo announced, aware that all eyes were upon him. "Two, three days. That's it. Ace bandage, painkillers, crutches. No biggie."

Carla's sigh was elongated, trenchant. "You're lucky. Physical wounds heal. I'm emotionally scarred forever."

Having worked with Carla for three months, Leo wasn't disturbed by the remark. He ignored her, which, I realized, was his custom. I suspected that Carla reminded Leo of his grown children in California. I was aware that they were not a pleasant memory.

"Okay," I said in my most businesslike voice, "time marches on. We've got a paper to get out. Let's hit it."

Vida did, by putting on her coat and a wool pillbox

with earflaps. Without another word, she left the four of us staring at each other.

The silence was broken by Ginny Burmeister. At twenty-three, Ginny seems older and wiser. Certainly she's competent, not only running the office, but helping with the advertising. Ginny is one of those redheads whose sole claim to beauty is her hair. Still, Carla's recent attempts at a makeover had improved Ginny's appearance. Under certain circumstances, Ginny is almost pretty. On this November morning, she was plain as a post.

"The mail will be late," Ginny announced in a flat tone. "Marje Blatt says the post office doesn't want to chain up, except for the rural routes. If they hit a bare spot in town, the chains break and it costs the taxpayers money."

Leo emitted a growl. "What doesn't?" He busied himself with a layout for Stuart's Stereo. "I should get chains, I suppose. I never had them in L.A."

Ginny stared. It was obvious she couldn't imagine a Southern California winter. Judging from her expression, it was also obvious that she wouldn't want to live in a place where November through April didn't bring snow. Ginny left the news office on a trail of disapproval.

I had edged over to the window. The skies had lifted slightly, and pedestrians on Front Street were walking without undue care. They included Vida, who had just gone into the Bank of Alpine. No doubt she would return in half an hour with Little Bobby Lambrecht's life story encapsulated.

Vida was back in less than ten minutes. I was pruning my annual editorial on Halloween vandalism when she stomped into my little office and closed the door. "Bobby's in a meeting with Marv Petersen," she announced, undoing the ties that held the woolen hat under her chin. "I wonder why."

In the spring, there had been a rumor that Washington Mutual Savings Bank planned to open a branch in Alpine. There had also been rumors that Fred Meyer and Starbucks were coming to town. Fred Meyer had gone elsewhere. Starbucks had made its local debut in early September. Washington Mutual apparently had changed its mind. But perhaps their interest had piqued that of other financial institutions, such as the Bank of Washington.

I gave Vida a curious look. "A buyout?"

Vida was horrified. "Of the Bank of Alpine? Good grief, what next? Annexation to Everett?"

My remark hadn't been intended to upset Vida. I'd spent my first twenty years in Seattle and most of my second in Portland, where big-city mergers and acquisitions were common. I should have known better when it came to Alpine. The bank belonged to the town, in the same way that residents claimed Mount Baldy, Tonga Ridge, and the upper Skykomish River.

"The Petersens would never sell the bank." Vida was scornful. She was also still wearing the hat, the ties drooping on her brown tweed coat, the pillbox crown atilt, and the protruding earflaps giving her the look of a bespectacled bloodhound. "Why, the family's been in the business since the beginning, back in 1930, when Carl Clemans decided to keep his hand in after he'd closed the mill in 'twenty-nine. Originally, the bank was the company store."

Vaguely I recalled hearing how the Bank of Alpine had been created. Carl Clemans had shut down the original mill that had sustained Alpine for almost twenty years. He'd moved back to Snohomish, but lent his name and some of his money to the fledgling bank. It was a sign of faith by Alpine's founding father. The town would go on without him and his mill.

"For years, no money was exchanged in Alpine," Vida was saying in a huffy voice. "The millworkers were paid in scrip, which they used at the company store. If there was anything left when the season ended, Mr. Clemans paid off the difference in cash. Of course, he gave credit, too. It was paternalistic, but fair. People could be trusted."

Maybe. People were people. Still, it wouldn't do to say so. Vida was a realist, but when she got launched on the subject of Alpine's history, her judgment was sometimes clouded.

"So what's Bob Lambrecht doing here?" I asked in a mild tone.

Vida evaded my gaze. "Fishing. With Milo."

"At the bank?" My expression was droll. "Well, why not? Milo's always complaining that there aren't any fish in the river."

"It must be a courtesy call." Vida was frowning, speaking more to herself than to me. Abruptly her arm shot out in the direction of the news office and she threw me a challenging look. "Larry Petersen wants to talk to you. It's about Leo."

I blinked. "Leo? What now?"

Vida turned secretive. "I couldn't say. Do you think anyone at the bank would breach customer confidentiality?"

Of course they would if Vida asked them. Especially if one of her kinfolk worked there. Off the top of my head, I couldn't recall a connection.

"I'll go see Larry before lunch," I said. "I need to cash my check anyway." It was the first of the month, payday, and Ginny would distribute our checks as soon as she and I signed them. We were paid on the first and

the fifteenth of each month, a tradition started by
Marius Vandeventer. In almost four years, I'd given
three raises to Vida, two to Ginny, and one—not entirely deserved—to Carla. Maybe it was time to give
one to me. I'd already screwed myself once by paying
too much for *The Advocate*. No doubt I'd done the
same with the secondhand Jaguar I'd bought before
moving from Portland to Alpine. The monies had come
from an unexpected inheritance that had been nowhere
in the same class as Ed Bronsky's windfall. However,
the newspaper and the Jaguar had both brought me
great joy as well as various headaches.

It was ten minutes before noon when I entered the
Bank of Alpine. Back in the 1950s, Frank Petersen, the
original president and chief financial officer, had been
considered an old fuddy-duddy for refusing to cave in
to modernization of the lobby. Time had proved him
right. Though small, the bank's interior was replete with
Grecian columns, gilded grillwork, and a marble floor.
Pilasters ran halfway up the walls, and next to each pair
were medallions depicting the profiles of the bank's
founders. The three teller cages featured the original
brass bars and were faced in polished mahogany. Fir
would have been cheaper and more plentiful, but Carl
Clemans and Company wanted the best. In the depths of
the depression, it must have been difficult not only to
raise the capital, but to build such a handsome bank.

Larry Petersen represented the third generation of his
family to work for the Bank of Alpine. Grandpa Frank
had been dead for almost twenty years, and Larry's father, Marvin, had been president since 1960. Larry's official title was treasurer, but everyone in town
recognized him as his father's heir apparent.

"Emma!" Larry exclaimed, swiveling in his old-
fashioned chair behind his old-fashioned desk. He was

about my age, a tall, balding man with a wide jaw and slightly sunken blue eyes. "Payday, right?" He got to his feet and came over to where I was standing at the mahogany rail that separated the executives from the customers.

I shook Larry's hand. "Right," I agreed, inwardly wincing at his enthusiastic grip. "Vida said you wanted to see me."

Larry grimaced, then opened the grilled gate that led inside the office area. "Yes, about Leo." Larry was seated again, his hands circumspectly folded on the desk. "Well. Leo's a fine fellow, I'm sure of that."

Bankers, like brokers and bookies, put me on guard. I always sense that they want my money for the sole purpose of enriching themselves. Unlike plumbers and electricians and retailers, they pretend to have my best interests at heart. I suspect otherwise, and I'm always wary.

"Leo has increased advertising revenue by twenty-two percent," I said, which accounted for my on-the-spot decision to give the entire staff a raise after the first of January. I'd get one, too. But the newspaper's financial status was another source of resentment toward the Bank of Alpine. When it came to money, I had no secrets from Larry Petersen or anyone else who worked for the bank. "I'm Leo's employer," I went on when Larry said nothing but merely inclined his head in what I assumed was approval. "What he does in his private life is none of my business."

Larry had the grace to look embarrassed. "I know that, Emma. But he's new in town. His account here was activated just three months ago. Already he's had six NSF checks. We believe in personal banking, Emma. He claims to be poor at math, yet he must handle business transactions for the newspaper. I suspect he's simply careless. We try to help our customers, not hinder them. How do you think Leo would feel about a proxy arrangement?"

I frowned at Larry. "Proxy? By whom? Me?" The thought was appalling. I had enough trouble keeping my own books straight. I, too, was poor at math.

But Larry chuckled and shook his head. "No, no. I mean we handle his money. Manage it, I should say. Automatic deposits and withdrawals. We don't advertise the service, but we do offer it. Most banks and credit unions do. The fee is nominal—much less than he's paying for NSF charges. Of course, we waived the first three."

Leo's money matters weren't my affair. I started to say so, then realized I wasn't entirely correct. If Leo ended up in rough financial waters, his job performance could be affected. According to Vida, he already had other personal problems.

"I'll ask him," I finally replied. "Do you really do this for other customers?"

"Of course." Larry's expression became guarded. "Several, in fact. Naturally, I can't name names."

Naturally, I thought, mentally cataloguing likely candidates. Crazy Eights Neffel, local loony, sprang to mind.

Larry, meanwhile, had turned philosophical. "Most people don't realize it, but banking's a sacred trust. Yes, we want to make money—we have to in order to meet payroll and turn a profit—but our major concern is our customers. You know that ad we've been running?"

I nodded. I was well acquainted with the recent series, which showed a picture of a locked safe. The slogan, inspired by Leo, was *Your Money is Safe with Us*.

"It's not just a catch phrase," Larry said, very serious. "Our family and the bank are part of Alpine. We

both go way back. I was five years old the first time
Grandpa brought me in here." Larry gestured at the
lobby, as solemn as a tourist guide pointing out the trea-
sures of the Vatican. "It was the most beautiful thing I
ever saw. All the marble and wood and brass. In a way,
I never changed my mind." His slight smile was diffident. "I grew up knowing I'd work here someday. And
all the while, Grandpa and Dad kept reminding me that
we had a responsibility to the town. As far as I'm concerned, friends and neighbors are the same as customers
and investors. We care about them. That's why we want
to help Leo."

The little speech had been pretty, and I couldn't deny
that Larry was sincere. If he fancied himself born with
a silver dollar in his mouth, there was no harm in it.
Somebody had to run the Bank of Alpine, and it might
as well be a Petersen. It always had been, and probably
always would.

I rose, thanking Larry for his concern. Then, in one
of my rare and usually futile attempts to one-up Vida, I
asked about Bob Lambrecht. Larry's face closed as tight
as a bank vault door.

"Now, Emma, Bob's visit is strictly confidential.
Milo Dodge can tell you more than I can."

"Can or will?" I gave Larry my most ironic smile.

He chuckled again, a dry, mirthless sound. "Bob's not
here to make news. I can assure you of that."

I wasn't assured. I'm still surprised by people's opinion of what's newsworthy. Fifteen years ago, I covered
a four-alarm fire at a Portland warehouse. The owner
insisted that the story shouldn't run in *The Oregonian*
because the warehouse was empty, and besides, he was
insured. When we ran the article and a photo, he threatened to sue us for invasion of privacy. I kept waiting for
him to be arrested on charges of arson and insurance

fraud. It turned out that he was honest. But he sure was dim, at least when it came to news.

Since it was payday for many Alpiners, all three tellers were on duty. I stood in line behind Polly Patricelli, a fellow parishioner at St. Mildred's. Polly is small, with a wrinkled face and badly fitted dentures. She acknowledged me with a smile that dislodged her upper plate.

"I'm getting used to him," she whispered. "Are you?"

"What?" Andy Cederberg, the bank's manager and loan officer, had just left his desk behind the mahogany rail. I assumed that Polly referred to Andy, but I couldn't think why. He'd worked at the bank for years.

"Father Kelly," Polly said, still whispering, still not in control of her teeth. "You know what I mean. His *color*."

Dennis Kelly was black, not yet forty, and extremely personable. In an age when good priests were as hard to find as buried treasure, the parishioners at St. Mildred's were very lucky to get Father Kelly. Had he not been a Tacoma native surplussed from a recently closed seminary in California, we might still be suffering through haphazard liturgies performed by Sister Mary Joan and Buzzy O'Toole.

"Father Kelly is a miracle," I asserted. "He's well organized, frankly devout, and his homilies aren't bad." At least, I thought to myself, they didn't take place in a time warp as did those of our previous pastor. I had tended to tune out Father Fitzgerald whenever he began railing against bootleg gin and the Axis powers.

Now Polly's lower plate jutted. "He's nice enough," she mumbled. "But he's still *colored*."

"I think it's a permanent condition." My retort was a

trifle testy. Polly, however, didn't notice. She was being beckoned by Christie Johnston at window number two. Denise Petersen, Larry's daughter, was still waiting on Harvey Adcock. Maybe the hardware and sporting goods store owner had to dig deep into his reserves to pay for his refrigeration repair.

Rick Erlandson finally finished with a woman I recognized only vaguely. Apparently she didn't recognize me at all. We exchanged the faintest of nods as I approached Rick's window.

Rick is in his mid-twenties, and has let his unfortunate orange punk-rocker hair grow out into a normal style. Or more normal, I should say, since his head featured hair only in a close-cropped circular cut. He looked as if he were wearing a brown doily. Such reactions on my part make me feel older than forty-two and stodgier than Vida.

Rick was glum. Usually he's friendly; always he's sincere. His greeting was polite, but there was only fleeting eye contact. Wordlessly he cashed my check, made the separate deposits into savings and checking, then handed me my eighty dollars in cash.

"Thanks, Ms. Lord. Have a nice day." Rick looked over my shoulder. "Next, please."

Delphine Corson of Posies Unlimited greeted us both in her breezy manner. I darted a glance back at Rick. He was still glum.

On my way out, I saw Marvin Petersen, the current family patriarch, speaking to Linda Lindahl, his daughter and the resident bookkeeper. I intended to wave, but noted their serious expressions. I took one last look around the lobby—Andy Cederberg and Larry Petersen had both gone to lunch. Denise Petersen was closing her teller's window. Rick and Christie were still busy with customers. Marvin and Linda had now disappeared behind closed doors. With a shrug, I left the bank.

I could never have guessed that one of the people I'd just seen would be dead before the next payday.

Chapter Two

CARLA AND GINNY occupied a booth for two at the Venison Eat Inn and Take-Out. Judging from their sour faces, they didn't want company. My perverse streak compelled me to greet them. They reacted as if I'd rung a bell, announcing a virulent strain of leprosy.

"Well?" I demanded, leaning on the booth's high back. "Didn't you get paid today? That should cheer you up."

Carla eyed me with disdain. "What's money compared to love?" She looked at Ginny. "It's totally nothing. Right, Gin?"

Ginny gave a dispirited nod. Rick Erlandson's glum face was fresh in my memory. He and Ginny had been dating for several months, though I didn't think they were very serious. Maybe I was wrong.

"Carla's going to the bank for me," Ginny said in a listless voice. "I refuse to go there. Under the circumstances."

"Which are?" I sighed, impatient with the vagaries of youth. Having an office manager who wouldn't set foot in the local financial institution was going to be a problem.

Ginny turned away; Carla was aghast. "I can't believe you don't know! Rick dumped Ginny! For Denise

Petersen! Emma, where have you *been* the last two days?"

"At home," I answered truthfully. I'd spent the weekend getting both house and yard ready for winter. Awkwardly I patted Ginny's thin shoulder. "I'm sorry. Maybe Rick's going through a phase."

"He's going through it with Denise." Ginny's voice was bitter and her cheeks were pink. "She got tired of waiting tables at the Icicle Creek Tavern, and came to work at the bank a month ago when Alyssa Carlson quit to have a baby. Denise thinks she's hot because she's a teller! Easy for her, with Dad and Granddad running the place. Now she thinks she can get the hook up with Rick. I hate her—she was such a bitch in high school, especially junior year!"

Never had I heard Ginny make such an impassioned speech. Nor had I ever seen her so angry. Mentally I kicked myself for butting in on my miserable female staffers. Out loud, I apologized. Carla and Ginny seemed indifferent. I was trying to make a gracious exit when I felt a big hand on my shoulder.

"Lasagna special's damned good," said Sheriff Milo Dodge. He spun a toothpick out of the corner of his wide mouth.

"It's left over from yesterday's Sunday dinner special," I retorted. "I saw it on the sign outside."

"I know," Milo said. "I had it last night, too. Bob Lambrecht and I ate here after we got back from fishing."

Carla and Ginny were again absorbed in their misery. Casually I stepped across the aisle to a booth that had just been vacated. I asked Milo if he'd finished his lunch. He had, but was waiting for Honoria Whitman, his ladylove from Startup, a few miles west on Highway 2.

"I took the day off," Milo said, arranging his lanky frame across from me in the booth. "I've still got vacation time coming. If I don't use it, I lose it. Honoria and I are going to Lake Wenatchee to have dinner at the Cougar Inn."

I nodded, approving both the choice of restaurant and Honoria. She and Milo had been seeing each other for over a year. I, however, hadn't seen Honoria for several months.

"How's she doing?" I inquired, glancing at the menu I knew by heart.

"Great." Milo's face didn't match his words. His hazel eyes were fixed somewhere to the right of my shoulder as he ground away at the toothpick. "She got her wheelchair fixed."

I hadn't known it was broken. The wheelchair was necessitated by Honoria's late husband, who had pushed her down a flight of stairs in one of his more macho moods. Honoria's brother had moods of his own, and in the course of one, had fatally shot his sister's husband. The Whitman family saga wasn't pretty, but somehow Honoria had emerged with soul, if not body, intact.

"Anything new with Honoria's pottery?" I asked, wishing Milo would stop twirling his toothpick. It was a new habit, and not very edifying. "Didn't she have a big show in Everett last month?"

"Huh?" He ran a hand through his graying sandy hair. "Oh, right. Good deal for her. She sold a bunch of brown stuff."

Milo's interest in Honoria's pottery was limited. I often wondered what they talked about. Fishing, maybe. It was always a safe topic with the sheriff. I returned to it, for reasons of my own.

"You and Bob Lambrecht have any luck?" I posed

the question after my waitress had poured coffee for both of us and allowed me to order a crab omelette.

Milo's long face grew longer. He'd finally dumped the toothpick and was fidgeting with the salt and pepper shakers. "No, just a couple of bumps. I felt sorry for Bob. He doesn't get a chance to go fishing much. Price of success, I guess. And city living." Milo shook his head, as if he couldn't believe anyone would choose to live anywhere other than Alpine.

"Bob's still in town," I remarked. "Are you going to hit the river again tomorrow?"

Milo sipped his coffee. He had put the salt and pepper shakers aside, and now that we weren't talking about Honoria, he seemed more relaxed. "No, Bob's due back at work. He'll drive home this afternoon, I guess."

"Really?" I widened my brown eyes, hoping to look guileless. "I would have thought he'd have gone home yesterday. Did he stay over on business?"

The sheriff and I have no history of intimacy, yet we know each other well. Next to Vida, Milo is my best friend in Alpine. Thus, my efforts at subtlety are not always successful. Milo may seem obtuse— sometimes he is—but under that laconic exterior lurks the lawman's keen perception of the human race. At least when he is on the job. Occasionally I get the impression that he removes his insight along with his uniform.

Milo was in civvies, but my subterfuge failed anyway. "Jeez, Emma, why don't you flat out ask me about Bob? He went to see Marv Petersen this morning. You've heard rumors about a Seattle bank coming in here."

"I have," I admitted. "But they don't make sense. Alpine isn't that big, the economy's down, and if the locals want to take their money elsewhere, they can go to four different banks between Sultan and Snohomish. I smell buyout, Milo. Am I right?"

But Milo merely shrugged. "Don't ask me. Bob and I didn't talk business. He came up here to get away from all that corporate bullshit."

I tried to believe Milo. He seemed to have convinced himself. But Bob Lambrecht's financial worries would intrigue Milo about as much as Honoria Whitman's brown stuff. Both topics were beyond Milo's usual range.

Yet his square jaw had dropped a trifle. "A buyout? Hell, that would turn this town upside down!" Obviously the enormity of my suggestion was a little late sinking in.

I hadn't noticed Carla and Ginny leave. Their table was now occupied by Scooter Hutchins of Hutchins Interiors and Decor. The overeager young man who joined Scooter was fondling a smart attaché case. A salesman, I figured, as Milo and I nodded at Scooter.

"Hey! It's after twelve-thirty!" Milo put a big hand over his watch as if hiding the time could change it. "Honoria should be out front. See you, Emma." Clumsily he unfolded himself from the booth and loped away.

I leaned to one side, trying to glimpse Honoria in her specially rigged car. But a pair of wide-bottomed Alpiners I knew only by sight were waddling down the aisle. My lunch arrived a minute later, and I turned my attention to food.

But not all of my thoughts. A potential buyout of Alpine's only bank was a much bigger story than Halloween vandalism or curtailed highway construction. Vida had set the stage with her "Scene Around Town" item. Could I follow through with a page-one lead for

Wednesday? A call to Marvin Petersen was in order as soon as I got back to *The Advocate*.

Marv wasn't in. The polite but cool voice of Linda Lindahl delivered the message. I said I'd settle for Larry. If not the father, then the son. I doubted that they had secrets from each other, at least about the business.

But Larry was unavailable, too. I began to suspect a conspiracy. In a last-ditch effort, I asked for Andy Cederberg. According to Linda, Andy was at the dentist. He had a root canal scheduled with Dr. Starr.

I was dogged. Maybe Linda knew something. Marv Petersen probably shared bank secrets with his daughter as well as his son. Despite Linda's aloof tone, I asked if she knew why Bob Lambrecht had stopped to see her father.

"I didn't talk with Mr. Lambrecht," Linda said crisply. "Excuse me, Emma. I have a call on line two."

Thwarted, I hung up. It was one-thirty, and I had the rest of the afternoon and most of Tuesday to run down the story. Meanwhile, I studied Carla's vandalism photos. Broken jack-o'-lanterns and splattered paint aren't very dramatic, especially if similar shots have appeared the last three years in a row.

Suffering from pique, I called Carla into the office. "Look, can you get a couple of crying kids looking at broken jack-o'-lanterns?" I shoved the contact sheet across my cluttered desk. "Nobody feels sorry for pumpkin pieces."

Carla was sullen. "They threw the broken parts into the garbage after I took these. Collection's today." A glint of satisfaction showed in my reporter's eyes.

"Then stage it. I can't use these." I made a sweeping gesture at the contact sheet. "The Alpine Mall spray-paint stuff isn't any better. It's just blobs on a building. Whoever did it missed the stores. That section is where the rest rooms and the offices are located. Couldn't you find an overturned outhouse?"

"What's an outhouse?" Carla looked blank, not an uncommon expression.

I sighed. "Never mind." Picking up the pumpkin prints, I shook them at her. "Look, I'm sorry you and Dr. Flake broke up. I'm sorry Ginny's mad at Rick. I'm sorry we all aren't madly in love with Mr. Perfect. But that doesn't excuse us from putting out a good newspaper. Go find some pathetic-looking kids and bust up another pumpkin. Get me something we can run at least on page three."

Still sullen, Carla rose from the chair on the opposite side of my desk. "I thought you told me that contrived news is no news."

I had. Long ago, in the dark ages of my novice publishing career and Carla's apprenticeship, I had given her hell for staging the reactions of a couple whose eight-year-old son had driven their Ford Escort into a ditch. Maybe it was the silly grins on the parents' faces or the beer cans they were clutching that had blown their credibility. The only thing the picture lacked was their insurance agent, producing a large check resembling a pro golf tour prize. The out-of-work family had made enough from the accident to move to Everett.

"This isn't the same," I argued. "This is real—the effect of vandalism on the victims. Kids, in this case, who love their pumpkins." I had trouble keeping a straight face.

Carla didn't. "Okay." With slumped shoulders, she began her retreat to the newsroom.

I called her back. Carla didn't need more rejection

in her life right now, and basically, she's a good photographer. Her visual talents far exceed her verbal skills.

"Look," I said, hoping to sound encouraging, "you take great pictures as a rule. Much better than I do, even better than Vida. The problem we have this time of year is that so many of the photo opportunities are clichés. Pumpkins, turkeys, Santa Claus. Why don't you take some extra rolls of film and just start shooting whatever looks interesting? Concentrate on angles and composition and lighting. You like to play around with that sort of thing. Don't worry about whether your subjects seem to be newsworthy."

Carla didn't appear soothed, but at least a spark of interest showed in her eyes. "Are you saying I need the practice?"

"No, not in that sense. Let's face it, Alpine doesn't offer much drama from a pictorial point of view. Like most weeklies, we tend to run the obvious shots. But," I went on, buttering up Carla in my most ingratiating manner, "with your eye, we can build a photo file to fall back on when there isn't much else out there."

Carla actually preened a bit. "You mean artistic stuff, like photographers show in exhibitions?"

"Well . . ." I wasn't willing to push myself over the edge. "Let's say imaginative, fresh, eye-catching. In terms of *The Advocate*, a shot of somebody pushing a grocery cart through Safeway is news, as long as we identify the shopper. It's a visual version of Vida's 'Scene Around Town.' "

Carla had definitely perked up, though I sensed her change of mood was fragile. "I'll start with the mall," she said. "With feet. Tired feet. Hurrying feet. Kids' feet."

Pig's feet, I thought, as Carla rushed off. I held my

head, and was questioning my managerial skills when Leo Walsh hopped into the office.

I cringed. "I thought Dr. Flake gave you crutches."

Leo collapsed into the chair Carla had vacated. "He did. I hate them. Hell, Emma, have you ever used crutches?"

I had, after a bad sprain the previous year. It was an excruciating experience, but I'd managed to avoid missing work. I said as much. Leo was frankly admiring.

"You must be better coordinated," he remarked. It wasn't true, of course. "You're kind of small. That helps."

He was right about my size. At five foot four and a hundred and twenty-five pounds, I was in the featherweight division. Leo was just under six feet tall and probably weighed close to one eighty. I gave him a quirky smile. "I didn't much like the crutches, either. My armpits were bruised for a week."

Leo nodded. "There's a knack. I don't have it." He extracted a cigarette from a pack in his shirt pocket and, as usual, made me wish I hadn't given up smoking. "Say, babe, can you give me a ride home tonight?"

I could. I would. I didn't bother telling Leo to stop calling me *babe*. Or any other cutesy nickname. I couldn't break him of the habit any more than I could get him to stop smoking. It seemed to me that Leo was lost somewhere in the 1940s.

So was his apartment. The building was old, the manager was a drunk, the rent was bearable. Somehow, it all suited Leo. I wished it didn't.

"You know," I began, feeling a bit embarrassed, "you ought to save for a house. Real estate is relatively cheap in Alpine. It's because of the downturn in the timber industry."

Leo flicked imaginary tobacco off of his tongue. He was, after all, smoking filters. "Is that a hint that you're keeping me on?"

In agitation, I ran my fingers through the gamine cut that had grown shaggy over time and neglect. "You've brought in new revenue, Leo. I'm pleased. But you've got some personal problems that could affect your job performance." I'd already had this talk with another staffer. Summoning courage, I eyed Leo head-on.

He was unmoved. "Such as?"

"Money." I felt on safe ground there. "The Bank of Alpine is unhappy with your overdrafts. How do you feel about proxy banking?"

Leo seemed relieved. "It sounds fine. What is it?"

I explained as best I could. After some consideration, the concept seemed to please Leo. He said he could live with it. The faintly sly gleam in his eyes alarmed me, but his conclusion was gratifying. I hate conflict, and Leo had had plenty of it in recent years. I knew we were avoiding potential controversy, but that was all right. We'd bought time, and it suited us both.

"I'll take you to the bank before five," I said. Maybe I could catch one of the Petersens in person.

"Great." Leo struggled to his feet—or foot, in this case. "Automatic everything? Like my rent and car payments and utilities?" I nodded; Leo let out a long sigh. "One less worry."

I noted, however, that Leo didn't look particularly carefree as he hopped out of my office. I felt uneasy. I often did. The optimists say that when a door closes, another always opens. Maybe, but the corollary is that while sweeping out old troubles, another batch blows in. There were definite trade-offs in the Ed-Leo exchange. And then there was the lovelorn pair on the distaff side. I tried to bury myself in *The Advocate* for the rest of the afternoon. Work is always my best solace.

At a quarter to five, I ushered Leo into my car. The ice had long since melted, but heavy dark clouds hung low over the mountains. The temperature hovered just above freezing. There was still snow in the area weather forecast.

Leo had wanted to hop the half block to the bank, but I insisted he ride. I pulled the Jag into a loading zone by the entrance and left a note on the windshield for Milo's deputies.

Larry Petersen was standing by the mahogany rail, chatting with Cal Vickers, owner of the local Texaco station. As might be predicted, Cal had had a banner day, between his garage and his towing service. I made a mental note to call him in the morning to get a quote about winterizing vehicles. Maybe Cal would take out a bigger ad.

Larry seemed delighted to see Leo. After commiserating about the sprain, the two men retreated to Larry's desk. I fixated on the frosted-glass door to Marv Petersen's office. Andy Cederberg told me that the boss had gone home.

"He's sniffing retirement," Andy said with a lopsided grin. I remembered that he'd endured a root canal earlier in the afternoon. Apparently the novocaine hadn't yet worn off. "It's too cold for golf. Maybe he went fishing. Marv's got a hole he likes to hit on Icicle Creek."

In summer, Icicle Creek didn't have enough water for guppies. The stream ran off the face of Mount Sawyer, tumbled past abandoned silver mines, zigzagged through the campground, then bisected the housing de-

velopment of the same name before losing its identity in
the north fork of the Skykomish River. Depending upon
the amount of rainfall and the snowpack, the creek
could swell in autumn, winter, and fall. It had even been
known to flood, scattering early campers and alarming
residents in the development. But I doubted very much
if there were any fish in Icicle Creek. I said so to Andy
Cederberg.

He was still grinning. "You may be right. But as I
mentioned, old Marv smells retirement. He's only got a
little over a year to go before he turns sixty-five."

I flashed a smile, though I was growing impatient.
"How's the tooth?" I asked. I might as well make conversation. I had to kill time while Leo got his financial
affairs in order.

Andy's grin disappeared. He put a thin hand to his
thin face and scowled. "Gosh, I don't know yet. But it
took Dr. Starr almost an hour to drill the thing. I've got
a temporary in now."

I made sympathetic noises. Andy, who was still under
forty, looked older. Because he was so thin, he also
looked taller than what I judged to be just over six feet.
His father, Kermit, was known as Stilts, being the same
height as his son and never having weighed more than
a hundred and forty pounds. However, the Cederberg
women were all heavy, including Andy's wife, Reba,
who taught at Alpine Middle School and was dubbed
Miz Cederbutt by most of her students.

Andy basked in my sympathy. He had taken off his
wire-rimmed spectacles and had opened his mouth to
show me his temporary tooth. I admired it and clucked
some more. Leo was still engaged in earnest conversation with Larry Petersen. I decided to take the plunge
and ask Andy about Bob Lambrecht. After all, Andy
was the bank's manager; he should be in the know.

But he claimed he wasn't. "Gee, I think it was just a courtesy call, Emma." Andy put his glasses back on, carefully adjusting them on the bridge of his thin, almost delicate nose. "Bob grew up here. He's an old chum of Milo's. He probably stopped in to see how we were doing. Nostalgia, you know. Hometown stuff."

I felt like a dunce. For the first time, I realized I should have interviewed Bob Lambrecht. He was an outstanding example of Local Boy Makes Good. In fact, I didn't know of anyone else from Alpine who had risen as high in the world of commerce. I would call him at his Seattle office in the morning. A phone interview would have to suffice. We didn't have a current mug shot, but maybe Vida could dig something out of our disorganized photo morgue.

Christie Johnston was at the double doors, allowing the last customer, Betsy O'Toole, into the bank. Then the shades were drawn and the CLOSED sign was hung out. Betsy, whose husband, Jake, owns the Grocery Basket, waved to me.

"See you in church?" she called.

I nodded. November first wasn't only payday; in the liturgical calendar, it was also All Saints' Day. I hadn't taken time to attend the morning Mass, so I planned on going to the seven P.M. service.

Andy Cederberg was looking at his watch. "Gosh, it's later than I thought! I'd better clear my desk so we can close out the books for the day. See you, Emma."

I was left to stare at the walls. A discreet glance told me that Leo was signing papers, no doubt committing his money to the bank's clutches. My wandering gaze took in the pilasters, which, upon closer inspection, could have used a fresh coat of paint. The marble floor was worn in a path from the front entrance to the tellers' cages. There were scars on the mahogany and cracks in the ceiling. Earthquakes, maybe, or merely the ground settling over sixty years.

My eye sought the medallions with their noble, if possibly enhanced, profiles: Carl Clemans, who was reputed to be kind, intelligent, benevolent—and as it was then called, a lady-killer; John Engstrom, the original mill's longtime superintendent, who was beloved by all, criticized by none; Rufus Runkel, Vida's father-in-law, and a man of many parts, who helped salvage Alpine's future by joining several Norwegians in building a ski lodge; and Frank Petersen, the mill's treasurer at the time of closure, and thus, by extension, a logical choice as the bank's original chief financial officer.

For the first time in the almost four years that I'd visited the Bank of Alpine, I noticed that there was a fifth medallion. It was smooth—and blank. I moved closer, craning my neck, trying to see if, like the others, there was a name carved in the border.

There was not. Yet the decoration must have been intended to commemorate someone. Perhaps it was dedicated to a group of investors who had pooled their resources to help start the bank. I would ask Vida. She would know.

Leo was on his foot, leaning against Larry's desk. I made as if to open the grilled gate, but Larry gestured at me.

"Thanks for everything, Emma." He picked up the phone. "Thanks, Leo. This is effective as of right now. Give your mind a rest." Larry stabbed in a number and became absorbed in his call.

Resignedly, I helped Leo to the door and into my car. Then I removed the note from my windshield. Something had been added: *Hi, Ms. Lord!* It was signed by Bill Blatt, one of Milo's deputies and Vida's nephew.

With a small smile, I slipped behind the wheel and started the car.

"Was it relatively painless?" I asked Leo.

He shrugged. "It'll feel better after a slug of Scotch. Care to join me, babe? Unfortunately, I'm on the second floor and there's no elevator."

I hadn't been in Leo's apartment, but I knew the building. It dated from the Forties and was managed by Dolph Terrill, whose wits had long been addled by booze. From the outside, the unimaginative brick exterior looked bleak and neglected. Maybe the inside was better, depending upon the individual renters. I didn't intend to find out, at least not this evening.

"Sorry, Leo. I've got to get gas, go home, check the mail, my answering machine, and head for church at seven." Inspiration struck. I'd never seen Leo at St. Mildred's, but I knew from information he'd leaked over the past three months that he had been raised Catholic. The church and school were across the street from Leo's apartment. "You want to come?"

Leo looked at me as if I'd asked him to eat a cyanide sandwich. "Are you kidding? I don't go to Mass on two good legs, let alone one. I left all that crap behind me thirty years ago."

"Oh." I shrugged. My brother, Ben, is a priest. He's heard it all. I've heard enough. Thus, I didn't pry into Leo's reasons.

I braked at Fourth and Cedar, rounded the corner, and pulled up in front of Leo's apartment building. "I'll help you with the stairs," I offered.

But Leo declined. "Thanks, but no thanks, babe. If I can't repay you with a drink, I'll take a rain check. I'm going to have to get used to the stairs. I'll go up on my butt."

I let him, figuring that Dolph Terrill probably had

come down the same way many times. It was almost dark as I watched Leo struggle to get into the apartment house. The Jag was chilly from the burst of cold air.

It took less than two minutes to reach my log house on Fir Street. The mail was predictably dull; there were no calls on my answering machine. On Sunday, I'd talked to Adam, though he had ruffled what peace of mind I possessed. His transfer from the University of Alaska to Arizona State wasn't a complete success. He had qualms, and wasn't sure that he wanted to be an anthropology major after all.

"You need math and science and that stuff," Adam had whined into the phone. "What's the point? I've worked on a dig."

He had, during the summer, with his uncle Ben. My brother's current parish was in Tuba City, Arizona. Ben likes to dabble in the Anasazi ruins, too. His enthusiasm had rubbed off on Adam, who promptly decided to switch both colleges and majors. If my son's interest in the academics of anthropology had waned since starting school in Tempe, his fondness for the Southwest had remained. Hawaii had been too tropical; Alaska was too wet. But Adam thought Arizona was just right. He was some two thousand miles from me, but only two hundred from Ben. The thought was reassuring. Both my son and my brother had been in Alpine during August. Adam planned to come home for Thanksgiving. Maybe. It all depended on a girl named Jade.

By the time I left for Mass, the temperature had dropped below freezing. I drove cautiously, and though we'd had no rain during the day, there was fog drifting among the evergreens. Still, I didn't feel any hint of snow.

Neither did Francine Wells, apparel-shop owner and

local fashion plate. As we congregated after Mass in the vestibule with Father Kelly, the weather was the big topic of conversation.

"You can *feel* snow in the air," Francine assured our pastor. "I don't feel it—yet. I don't care what the weather forecast says."

Betsy O'Toole didn't agree. "Jake said the store was really busy today," she declared, referring to the Grocery Basket. "People were stocking up in case it's a real blizzard."

Father Kelly's dark eyes regarded both Francine and Betsy with interest. He had a rare knack of actually listening to what other people had to say. "It's been a long time since I've been in a blizzard," he remarked. "The only time I saw snow while I was teaching in the seminary was when I went skiing over at Lake Tahoe."

Francine set her perfectly coiffed blonde head at a knowing angle. "You'll see it here, Father. Lots of it. From about now until the spring thaw."

Father Kelly didn't seem displeased at the prospect. His round face with the high forehead and snub nose broke into an ingratiating grin. "I'd better go wax my skis. Is it true that people ski right through town?"

"It sure is," Betsy exclaimed. She and Francine edged closer to the priest. Neither had been enthusiastic when they'd heard our new pastor was African-American. Alpine's racial mix is overwhelmingly Caucasian. Indeed, anyone without Scandinavian blood is considered a trifle odd. But now that Dennis Kelly had been at St. Mildred's for almost four months, Francine, Betsy, and several other middle-aged women acted like schoolgirls vying for the teacher's attention. I figured Father Kelly could handle the situation—he'd had dinner with Ben and Adam and me in August, and while my brother and the new pastor hadn't met before, it didn't take long for them to get down and dirty on the topic of serving in small-town parishes. Den, like Ben, had his head screwed on straight.

I drifted off, remembering to leave my All Souls' Day offering for the morning Mass. I was exiting the church when I felt a poke in the ribs.

"Emma! Say, what's up?"

The hearty voice belonged to Ed Bronsky. No wonder I was startled. His manner was so changed from the galley-slave days of his employment with *The Advocate* that I didn't recognize him at first.

But upon turning around, it was the same old Ed. Except that he was better dressed, as was his chubby wife, Shirley. She was pirouetting on the small front porch of the church, showing off her new mink coat.

"I know, fur's politically something-or-other, but I don't care. This is Alpine, and it gets cold." She patted the lush dark fur collar. "Besides, I always wanted a mink coat more than anything."

I was trying not to think how many minks had given their lives to cover Shirley Bronsky when Ed poked me again. "Say, we've got to talk. Now that I'm a member of the chamber of commerce, I want to go over some of my ideas with you for zapping up business around here." He lowered his voice and grew very serious. "You know, it's up to the local newspaper to set the tone for the economy. Advertising is the voice of commerce. You really ought to consider more promotional opportunities, Emma."

Since in his previous life Ed had rebelled at the concept of any ad bigger than a bedbug, I all but reeled. "Sure, that's fine. We'll talk. Call me." I nodded rapidly, aware that at least two of the five Bronsky offspring were sitting on the hood of my car. I wasn't sure why, since the much-used Jag must be old hat to them now that the family had acquired a Range Rover as well as a Mercedes-Benz 300E.

I escaped, fleeing up Third Street. I had reached the intersection at Spruce when I realized I'd forgotten to get gas. It was after eight o'clock, but Cal's Texaco might still be open. Like many Alpine businesses, his hours tended to be erratic. Local merchants have an independent, damn-all attitude, even in hard times.

Apparently Cal was in one of those moods. The station was closed, despite the fact that the adjacent Alpine Mall was open on Monday nights. Admittedly, Cal and his employees had put in a long, hard day. I debated whether to go home or drive all the way across town to the only other local gas dispenser since Buzzy's BP closed in September. I might as well. I was already out and about, and morning could bring more ice.

Front Street was virtually deserted. While the mall was open, the downtown stores were not. A month from now, they would extend their hours for Christmas shoppers. Meanwhile, the few lighted display windows still featured a mixture of Halloween and Thanksgiving decor. The chamber of commerce has a long-standing moratorium on Christmas decoration until the last weekend of November.

As I waited for one of Alpine's five traffic lights, I glanced at the bank. Somewhat to my surprise, Marvin Petersen was walking toward his not-so-new Cadillac. It was parked in the bank's loading zone that I'd used earlier. Marv was no more than four feet from my Jag. I lifted a hand in greeting, but he got into his car so quickly—and, it seemed, furtively—that I was ignored. The light changed to green and I moved slowly down the street. Marv revved his engine and took the corner on two wheels. He didn't drive like a banker, I thought. Indeed, he drove like a man in a panic.

I couldn't imagine why.

Unfortunately, I'd find out.

Chapter Three

THE ICICLE CREEK Tavern is definitely not a tourist attraction. It's old, it's run-down, it has traditionally catered to brawling loggers. In better days—depending upon your point of view—the tavern went for years without replacing its broken windows. On Saturday nights, customers would pitch each other through the glass with such regularity that the owner couldn't keep up with the repairs. Apparently plywood wasn't as tempting as glass. But if layoffs in the woods hadn't improved dispositions, they had curbed the clientele's belligerence. Maybe they were bonding together in their common misery. In any event, the tavern's windows were now intact. And the customers were in place, judging from the number of pickup trucks and beaters in the parking lot.

Across the dirt track stands Icicle Gas 'n Go, which is also a minimart. The enterprise isn't as old as the tavern, but the blight seems contagious. The gas pumps are outmoded, the stock could use dusting, and the whole place smells stale. A high school kid with braces on his teeth took my money after I pumped my own gas. They don't believe in credit cards at Icicle Creek.

My hands were numb with cold when I got back in the Jag. I rarely wear gloves because I can seldom find a pair that match. I was about to drive away when I saw

Linda Lindahl get out of a metallic blue compact. In the Big City, I would have thought it odd to run into two people from the same family within ten minutes; in Alpine, such coincidences are commonplace.

Still, I was curious. Opening the car door, I called to Linda. "Did you try Cal's Texaco first, too?"

Linda jumped. "What?" She peered at me, then at the Jag. I was used to being recognized second to my car. "Oh, hello, Emma. No. I figured Cal would be closed." She turned her back and tended to the pump in her methodical manner.

I waited. But apparently Linda had dismissed me from her mind. I wasn't surprised. Linda Petersen Lindahl has none of her father's affability nor her brother's eagerness to please. Indeed, Vida had described Linda as *prickly*. The description was apt.

My perverse streak surfaced. Linda was a Petersen, and the bank's bookkeeper. She had fobbed me off on the phone, but I couldn't believe she didn't know why Bob Lambrecht had dropped in at the bank. Despite the cold, I got out of the car and waited patiently for Linda to look up. She was watching the nozzle, occasionally checking the rolling numbers on the pump. Ever the bookkeeper, I thought, ever precise, ever watchful. I always felt I was lucky if I got the nozzle into my car on the first try. I'd been known to miss and end up with inflammable shoes.

My breath was visible on the night air. Fog drifted close to the roof of the Icicle Creek Tavern, and dipped above the faded metal sign in the parking lot. I could barely make out the lights of the newer homes across the creek. Most of their inhabitants didn't approve of the ramshackle tavern. An exception was Milo Dodge, who lived in one of the more modest houses and didn't give a damn unless he or his deputies got called in to stop a fight.

Linda had filled the tank and was finishing her task in a maddeningly orderly fashion. At forty-plus, she was a bit shopworn despite the short highlighted blonde coiffure, the artful cosmetics, and the effort at keeping her weight within ten pounds of what it should be. Briefly I made a mental comparison: I was a year or so older, but my brown hair was my own, round faces don't seem to wrinkle as quickly, and I'd never had to worry about dieting. I felt smug, though the truth is, I'm shamefully neglectful of keeping in shape. Luck and good genes get all the credit.

Linda managed to avoid looking at me until she'd gone inside and paid the bill. When she came back to her car, she deigned to give me a tight smile.

"You're still here," she said, one hand poised on the fleecy white muffler she wore with her double-breasted gray wool coat. In a town that considers Eddie Bauer a designer label, Linda seemed overdressed. "Are you having car trouble?"

I shook my head. "I still haven't talked to your father and your brother about Bob Lambrecht." I kept my smile fixed in place as I pulled the hood of my duffle coat over my bangs. "I hate to be a pest, but why was Bob Lambrecht at the bank this morning?"

For a moment, I thought Linda looked frightened. Or wary. But when she spoke, she was her usual composed self. "He felt obligated to call on Dad."

I waited for her to go on, but she didn't. Linda Lindahl wasn't one to elaborate. My dealings with her had been limited to an occasional question about *The Advocate*'s account.

"I suppose," I said in a musing and, I hoped, confidential tone, "Bob was curious about how the bank gets along in times of economic duress."

Linda was opening the door of her car. "Maybe." Her smile was arch. "Good night, Emma." She ducked her head and disappeared inside the compact.

Earlier, Larry had cut me off by hiding behind his telephone; now Linda was making a getaway in her car. I was beginning to feel as if the Petersen family was avoiding me. Defeated, I got into the Jag and drove onto Railroad Avenue.

Linda had just pulled away from the arterial at Highway 187. I knew she lived in a relatively new condo at Parc Pines. The dozen dwellings look nice from the outside, but Carla says they're cramped. She also says she has no problem with spelling Parc with a *C*. She is wrong—Carla has problems with spelling in general.

Parc Pines is on Alpine Way, just off my own street. I didn't want Linda to think I was following her, so I turned off at Front Street. Linda continued up Highway 187, the in-town stretch already having been paved and widened. I cut up Eighth Street, past the 7-Eleven and Alpine Appliance, then turned onto Pine, zigzagging my way up the mountainside. It hadn't iced up yet, but the route was safer, if slower. I was in no hurry; no one waited for me at home. The thought made me feel a trifle bleak.

My recovery was quick: Linda Lindahl was right in front of me again, if not for long. Her car turned off at the Lumberjack Motel. I put my foot on the brake and crawled along past the twenty units that took up a half block.

All the rooms faced the parking lot in the two-story structure. I felt like a voyeur as the Jag crept to the corner of Pine and Seventh Streets. But snooping is my job. And I wanted to know why Linda was wearing her good wool coat to get gas at Icicle Creek.

She had parked at the far end of the lot, under cover of a tall Douglas fir. There were only five or six other vehicles in front of the Lumberjack. In early November before ski season starts, tourists are scarce in Alpine.

There was no arterial at the corner. I couldn't come to a dead halt. My last sighting in the rearview mirror caught Linda walking purposefully toward a unit on the bottom level. She disappeared as the Jag drifted across the intersection.

Somewhat guiltily, I headed home. Except for leaving her car in the shadow of the tree, Linda hadn't seemed to fear discovery at the Lumberjack Motel. I knew she was divorced, with an ex-husband living in Everett. I recalled a child, a daughter maybe. I realized I knew very little about her.

Vida would know, of course. On a whim, I rounded the corner of Sixth and Tyee. The lights from Vida's small, neat bungalow glowed through the gathering fog like a beacon.

"Well!" My House & Home editor expressed surprise, curiosity, and pleasure all at once. So did I, since Vida had her gray curls covered with a ragged bandana tied in the middle of her forehead and was wearing a tattered flannel bathrobe and rubber gloves. "Whatever are you doing out at nine o'clock?" she inquired. "There are no meetings tonight."

Vida, Carla, and I all cover our share of civic and social gatherings. We each usually get stuck for at least one a week. But not on this first Monday in November.

I explained about going to church and getting gas. Vida listened as she put on the teakettle. Her usually cozy kitchen was covered with old newspapers, including *The Advocate*. The house smelled strongly of Comet cleanser.

"I'm cleaning," she announced, waving a rubber glove at various appliances. "I'm having Thanksgiving. I like to get a head start for the holidays. I'm also having Roger this weekend. Amy and Ted are going to spend the weekend in Seattle. They have tickets to the Repertory Theatre."

Personally, I would have waited until after Roger had left to clean house. Then I would have called in the Bomb Squad first. Roger is Vida's ten-year-old grandson, and the apple of her eye. Amy is the only one of Vida's three daughters who lives in Alpine. Never mind that Roger is a horror. While Vida is highly critical of other people's children, Roger can do no wrong.

I tried to conceal my dismay. As far as I'm concerned, a weekend with Roger would be like a month in the clutches of the Spanish Inquisition. I didn't ask how Vida would amuse him, but she told me anyway.

"Friday, we're getting videos, all his favorites. Saturday, I'll take him to the mall and he can buy something special. In the evening, we'll get a big pizza. Sunday, we'll go to church and then practice shooting his new BB gun in the woods."

I blinked. Roger with a BB gun sent off danger signals. He should run up the Jolly Roger on his bike. "What if it snows?" That was the only nonpejorative comment I could manage.

Vida shrugged, then removed two bone-china teacups and saucers from her cupboard. "We could drive down the pass to Sultan. Everyone practices shooting at the gravel pit there."

Everyone would soon stop if Roger came along. But I let Vida run her course before I got to the purpose of my visit. She was steeping the tea by the time I was able to tell her about my latest encounters with the Petersens.

"So I still don't know why Bob Lambrecht met with Marv Petersen, and now I wonder who Linda was meeting at the Lumberjack Motel," I concluded as Vida poured tea.

"I can't use *that* in 'Scene Around,' " Vida remarked with some asperity. "If I mentioned everyone having an extramarital affair in this town, we'd run out of room."

"I know that, Vida." I allowed myself a teaspoon of sugar. Vida is a diligent housekeeper and a fine gardener, but her culinary skills are limited. Even her tea lacks flavor. "I'm not really prying. If there's a bank buyout in the works, this is big news." I ignored Vida's scowl. "I need background on the family."

Vida refused to address the issue. Instead, she asked if Leo had gotten his financial life straightened out at the bank. I assured her he had, then steered the conversation back to Linda.

Vida removed her glasses and vigorously rubbed her eyes, always a gesture of annoyance or distress. "Ooooh . . . This is all very silly. The Petersens would never sell out. It would be tantamount to admitting that the town itself is going under."

I didn't say anything. My arrival in Alpine had coincided with the downturn in the timber industry. Since then, Front Street had become dotted with FOR RENT signs. Some of the vacancies were caused by businesses that had moved to the mall, but others had simply failed. Not only had Buzzy's BP gone belly-up, but so had the Chinese-American restaurant in the same block, a gift shop, a feed merchant, a pet store, and a building contractor. I waited for Vida to face reality.

"After high school, Linda went to Everett Junior College." Vida put her glasses back on and gave me a look of resignation. "During the summers, she worked for her father as a teller. She had a very unhappy romance with a boy from Gold Bar. They called off the wedding less than a month before they were to be married. Linda has always been difficult. She married Howard Lindahl on the rebound and moved to Everett. She was— what?—twenty-three, I think. They had a daughter who must be about twelve. Howard worked for one of the mills over there, but later he started his own cabinetry business. That was before the divorce, which was three years ago, just after you moved to Alpine. Linda came back here and went to work for her father again, first as a teller, then as his bookkeeper when Alma Olson retired. Howard has custody of young Alison." Daintily Vida sipped her tea.

"Interesting. Why?"

"I can only guess." Vida set the cup down with great care. "Howard's remarried, for one thing. Linda never struck me as very maternal. I've always suspected that Alison was a mistake. When Linda and Howard broke up, I think she wanted to be free of responsibility."

"Men?"

Vida frowned, then poured more tea for both of us. "Possibly. Though Linda was never what we used to call boy-crazy. Still, she's fond of men. Unfortunately, they haven't always been fond of her—not after they get to know the real Linda."

"Prickly," I murmured. Unlucky, maybe. That's how I preferred to describe myself. "Maybe I shouldn't assume the worst about Linda being at the motel."

"Why not? I always do. I'm rarely wrong." Vida's tone was matter-of-fact.

We were silent for a moment. My mind's eye traveled back to the bank. "Say, Vida, why is there an empty medallion on the bank wall?"

Vida looked puzzled. I elaborated. "Ah." She dabbed at her lips with a paper napkin. "The Silent Partner. I'd forgotten about that. The medallion, I mean. Someone—I never knew who—invested money in the original bank but wouldn't allow his name—I assume it was a man, being 1930 and all—to be made public. Possibly it was a former Alpiner who had moved away and done well." She shrugged. "It was, of course, before my time."

Things that happened before Vida's time really didn't count for much. "What about the rest of the family?" I inquired.

Vida was eyeing her stove. Judging from what looked like a faint streak of spaghetti sauce, she hadn't yet cleaned it. I got the impression that having disposed of Linda's background, Vida was now anxious to resume her chores.

"You know Larry and his wife, JoAnne. She's a Bergstrom. Their two boys are away at college. Denise just started at the bank a short time ago. Her only experience has been waiting tables at the Burger Barn and the Icicle Creek Tavern. At least she knows how to make change." Vida was speaking very fast, one slippered foot swinging under the table. "Marv is the youngest of Frank's three children. There's a story—anecdotal, perhaps—that Frank was made the original president because my father-in-law, Rufus Runkel, wanted to call it Frank's Bank. I think not. In any event, Frank's elder son, Elmer, had absolutely no interest in banking. He still lives with his wife, Thelma, on their farm near Icicle Creek. Thelma was a Dodge. Milo's aunt."

I knew of the farm, which consisted mostly of chickens, ducks, a dozen cows, two horses, and a large vegetable garden in the summer. I didn't realize that Milo was somehow connected with the Petersens. But this was Alpine, and the fact wasn't amazing.

"Frank's daughter, the middle child, is DeAnne," Vida continued, still with one eye on the stove. "She married an Iverson first, then a Sigurdson, and has lived in Seattle ever since. As for Marv, the youngest of Frank and Irmgaard's children, he went into the business because he liked it. So did his son, Larry. Marv's wife isn't from around here. Cathleen Petersen was born and raised somewhere near Puyallup. I don't recall how she and Marv met. He served in Korea."

My mental processes were awhirl. I should have taken notes. As usual, Vida's biographical account had been thorough. "There was Frank originally," I said slowly, "then along came Marv, with Larry waiting in the wings. Linda, too, maybe. Denise is the fourth generation."

"Oh, Denise!" Vida waved a hand in dismissal. "She's a feather-wit! One of her brothers will follow in their father's footsteps. It won't be Denise. But Larry has to have his turn first."

I remarked that Andy Cederberg had said Marv Petersen would retire when he turned sixty-five. "If the Bank of Washington takes over," I speculated, "they might keep everyone in place."

Vida finally stopped staring at her stove. "They won't take over the Bank of Alpine. They can't. They mustn't." She seemed to be talking to herself, or possibly communing with the banking spirits in Seattle. "Frank would roll over in his grave."

"He died—when?" I asked, getting to my feet.

Vida seemed relieved that I was leaving. She tried to cover by picking up the teapot and tapping it. I shook my head. She put the pot back on the table.

"Frank died in 1976, the Bicentennial year. His wife,

Irmgaard, went in 'seventy-nine. She outlived him, but not by much." Vida made it sound as if mortality were a competitive event.

I made it to my car. The fog was now thick, swirling above the ground and forcing me to drive at a snail's pace. Again I ticked off the Petersens, generation by generation: Frank, the founder, now deceased; farmer Elmer, daughter DeAnne, banker Marv; Larry and Linda, both working for their father; Denise, dim, and eventually to be supplanted by one of her brothers.

I had the family lined up. I knew the players. But I didn't know the facts. Tomorrow I'd try to pry the truth out of the bank personnel. I'd also call Bob Lambrecht in Seattle. I hoped to be out of my mental fog by deadline.

My hope was unrealistic. Bob Lambrecht was an intelligent, courteous man who was perfectly willing to give me a concise rundown of his banking career. He spoke affectionately of his wife, Miriam, and their four children. He even gave me a quote about his impression of Alpine after a thirty-year absence. But he only chuckled when I asked if he'd come to the bank on business.

Nor were the Petersens more forthcoming. I went over to the bank around eleven, after I finished writing the feature on Bob Lambrecht. Larry was engaged in an earnest conversation with Garth Wesley, the current owner of Parker's Pharmacy. Linda, according to Andy Cederberg, was tied up in her office. Marv, however, could spare me a few minutes.

Marvin Petersen's usual geniality seemed strained on this cold, overcast November morning. His blue eyes were wary and his handshake was tentative. Marv was taller than his son by an inch and heavier by at least twenty pounds. He grunted as he sat down in his leather-covered swivel chair.

"Emma, let's be frank. I hate rumors. This town is always full of them." He picked up a gold ballpoint pen and twirled it in his stubby fingers. "If I say anything for public print, everybody will interpret it six different ways. When—and if—I've got something to tell you, you'll be the first to know."

Briefly I considered baiting Marv by telling him that I was now forced to write ". . . that when asked if the Bank of Alpine was for sale, President and CEO Marvin Petersen had no comment." But I wanted to keep Marv on my side.

"If you change your mind, will you call me before five o'clock today?" I asked. "We have to send the paper off to the printer in Monroe first thing tomorrow."

Marv nodded his big, balding head. "You bet. But chances are I won't call. Honestly, Emma. I don't have a damned thing to tell you."

I had to be satisfied with that statement. Frustrated, I left the bank. Christie Johnston was on my heels.

"Late coffee break," the teller explained as we stopped to wait for a US West service van to pass. "I liked your editorial on litter last week."

The piece hadn't exactly been my proudest moment. Usually I limit antilitter editorials to once a year in early June, just before the summer visitors start arriving. But the Rotary and Kiwanis Clubs had each voted to adopt a mile of cleanup along Highway 187 when the resurfacing was finished. I had used them as an example of public-spirited organizations, and urged others to join in the cleanup crusade.

I smiled at Christie, who is in her mid-thirties and has worked at the bank for a couple of years. She is about my size, and pretty, if sharp-featured. Her masses of curly brown hair were now hidden by the hood of her navy ski parka. "Thanks, Christie. Are you encouraging your fellow employees to take on the project?"

Christie grimaced as we crossed the street. "I don't think so. Mr. Petersen—Marv—is kind of sensitive about the bank's image. I don't think he'd go for it."

I envisioned the Petersens and their employees rooting around the side of the road that led up to the campground and the ranger station. "It might do them good. The Petersens project a folksy family image."

Christie was poised to turn left; no doubt she was headed down the block to the Upper Crust. "Compared to bigger banks, they do," she acknowledged. "I've worked for some real stuffed shirts in Seattle and Everett. But Marv still likes to keep his dignity."

Editorial or not, I wasn't going to knock myself out to get recruits for the litter project. I knew that Christie's husband, Troy, worked for UPS. He'd been transferred from an Everett route to Highway 2. I made one last stab at putting my words to work.

"What about Troy and his fellow drivers?" It was almost eleven-thirty; I was hungry. If I bought something at the Upper Crust, I could work through my lunch hour. I started along Front Street with Christie at my side.

Christie hunkered down against the wind that had blown the fog away. Her teeth seemed to be chattering, though the temperature had risen into the mid-thirties. "Troy doesn't like to be bugged in his spare time." Her voice was almost lost inside the high collar of her parka.

I gave up. We entered the bakery, where a half dozen customers were drinking from steaming paper cups and eating fresh goodies. Christie selected a cinnamon roll and hot coffee. She paid for her purchase, then said goodbye and left.

I had thought she'd linger. By the time I departed with my maple bar and hot chocolate, Christie was nowhere in sight. Or so I thought until I dropped my handbag while trying to juggle the hot cup and my white bakery sack. When I straightened up, I glimpsed Christie far down Front Street, crossing over by the Clemans Building. Running errands, I thought, and dismissed Christie from my mind.

I shouldn't have done that.

By five o'clock, I hadn't heard from Marv Petersen. By five-thirty, the paper was almost ready to go to Monroe in the morning. I'd saved a four-inch hole on page one for the Tuesday night City Council meeting that I would cover and report. Carla had performed adequately on the jack-o'-lantern reshoot, Vida had found a high school head shot of Bob Lambrecht, and we had all contributed to filling up the "Scene" column.

Carla and Ginny had gone home. Vida was sorting through the mail that had piled up while she worked on her section of this week's paper. Leo was getting a head start on the Thanksgiving special edition to be published November eighteenth. With our Wednesday publication date, we actually have to put out two Thanksgiving papers, with the first carrying all the grocery and other celebration-related ads. The paper that's delivered the afternoon before the holiday is stuffed with Thanksgiving-related copy and art, but most of the ads are looking ahead to Christmas.

Leo was laying out an ad for Delphine Corson's Posies Unlimited. "Is that a co-op with FTE?" I inquired, stopping at Leo's desk.

"Not this time," Leo replied with the crooked grin

that matched his broken nose. "I talked her into going full-bore for Thanksgiving. A quarter page, with a drawing by one of the kids in the high school art class. Look—it's not bad, it's different, and it's free. The kid just wants his name in print."

I admired an ikebana arrangement of chrysanthemums in a wooden bowl. The sketch was signed by one of the Olson kids. His mother was half-Japanese, the daughter of a Seattle soldier and his war bride. Nancy Olson didn't sound Asian, nor did she look particularly Japanese. Still, she was definitely considered different in Alpine, or, at best, exotic. So was her son, Matt, the artist.

"Can Delphine do ikebana?" I asked. "It's a real art form."

Leo shrugged and lighted a cigarette. "Who knows? Who cares? How many locals can tell ikebana from a ripe banana? I told Delphine if anybody asked for an arrangement like this one, to charge a hundred and fifty bucks. That ought to get them to switch to a nice potted plant."

Vida's voice erupted from the corner desk. "Delphine's lost weight. I almost put it in 'Scene,' but you never know how people will react these days. They might consider it sexist, or else they're dying of cancer." Vida's expression displayed disapproval of both rationales.

Leo, who had his foot propped up on a new box of copy paper, turned to Vida. "Hey, Duchess," he said, using the nickname he'd coined and which Vida detested, "you ought to live in L.A. if you think people around here are touchy. You wouldn't believe the kind of shit I got myself into down there."

"Which," Vida replied archly, "is no doubt why you

are now here." With a withering look, she ripped open another envelope.

Leo laughed, blew out a cloud of smoke, and addressed me again. "Hey, babe, guess what? I was going to pay bills today. But I didn't have to—one of those goddamned little gnomes at the bank is doing it for me. Thanks for hauling my ass over there yesterday."

I nodded and smiled, albeit thinly. Ed Bronsky was hardly an upper-class kind of guy, but he'd almost never used crude language. I was no prude, certainly not after twenty years of working on a met daily, but in my tenure on *The Advocate*, we'd set a certain tone. Or maybe Vida had. It might be a good idea to ask Leo to watch his mouth. He wouldn't bother Carla, who probably didn't notice, but I was certain that he was, as Vida herself would put it, "getting her goat." And Ginny's, too.

This wasn't the proper time, however. Vida was present, Leo was in a good mood, and I still had to face the City Council meeting at seven-thirty.

"I'm glad it's all worked out for you, Leo," I remarked, starting toward my office. Out of the corner of my eye, I saw his grin fade and an almost wistful look pass across his face. I turned slightly, throwing him a verbal bone: "You're saving on postage, too. Every little bit helps." I felt like a colossal nerd.

"Speaking of which," he called after me, "I'll buy dinner if you'll give me a ride home."

It occurred to me that I hadn't asked how Leo had gotten to work in the morning. I suppose I'd assumed that he'd managed to drive his Toyota. But I was wrong.

I didn't want Leo treating me to dinner. When he started working at the paper, I had put on my most reserved manner to show Leo that there would be no fraternization. Reserve isn't my style, however, and I wasn't sure he'd gotten the point. We'd had lunch twice, done drinks a couple of times, too, but I did as much in various ways with the other staffers. I couldn't completely freeze out Leo just because he was a single man and I was a single woman.

Besides, I'd planned to eat downtown before the City Council meeting anyway. "Dutch," I insisted. "You're on."

"Good." Leo was grinning again. "In that case, let's go to King Olav's at the ski lodge. I've only been in the bar."

I nixed King Olav's. It's fairly expensive and dining there is an event, at least by Alpine standards. I didn't have time to linger. As usual, we were stuck with the Venison Inn.

Somehow, Leo had managed to maneuver the crutches. He griped every inch of the way, which fortunately was not far, since the inn is in the same block as *The Advocate*. We were passing Cascade Dry Cleaners, which is nestled in between, when I recognized the lanky figure of Andy Cederberg walking down the street, briefcase in hand. I was about to call to him when a carload of teenagers passed, radio blaring and bass throbbing. Andy moved much faster than we could, and was now turning up Fifth Street. I seemed to recall that he lived only a few blocks from the bank, by John Engstrom Park.

I wasn't going to order a drink, but when Leo asked for Scotch, I caved in and requested bourbon. Mayor Baugh and the rest of the City Council would no doubt start a rumor that Emma Lord had shown up for their meeting drunk as a skunk.

Leo lighted another cigarette, and regarded me through a haze of smoke. "So what's up with the bank? Were you going to grill whazzisname out there?"

"I've grilled all of them," I answered with a sigh. "They either won't say or they don't know."

"Buyout," Leo declared, leaning back in the booth as our drinks arrived. "I'd bet on it, babe. Larry said as much."

I stared at Leo. "He did? To you? What did he say?"

Leo took a big gulp of Scotch. "He didn't intend to say anything, of course. But when he was telling me about how this proxy deal works, I asked if the fee was guaranteed to stay at what I signed up for. Larry hedged, and said as far as he could tell." Leo lifted his thick eyebrows.

"Hmmm." I rested my chin on my hands. "In other words, there may be changes made."

Leo made no comment. He was very involved with drinking and smoking. When he finally spoke again, it was of Linda Lindahl: "What's with the blonde? Is she single?"

Recalling Vida's recital of Linda's ill-starred love life, I wrinkled my nose. "Yes, but she's not your type. Prickly. Difficult."

"Hey," Leo said, stubbing out his cigarette in a small glass ashtray, "don't be too sure! You're kind of prickly, and you could put your fuzzy slippers under my bed any time!"

I tried to look prim. "I'm not prickly. And I don't have fuzzy slippers. Get over it, Leo."

I expected him to come back with some half-assed compliment, but he didn't. "Bookkeepers usually look like they should be sitting around in a jar of formaldehyde. But Linda seems kind of hot. She was giving me the eye when I was in the bank last week covering one of my overdrafts."

I feigned indifference. "Go for it. Maybe she knows

what's going on with the bank. You can wheedle it out
of her during pillow talk."

The ensuing silence wasn't awkward, which I found
reassuring. Having finished his drink, Leo was drumming his fingers on the table and studying the menu. I
already knew what I was going to order. Our waitress
returned, and we put in our requests. Leo asked for another Scotch. I tried not to notice.

"She's backed off," he said suddenly.

Puzzled, I took a sip of bourbon. "Who? Linda? The
waitress?"

Leo shook his head. "Liza, my ex. I think she's going
to marry that guidance counselor SOB. His divorce is
final about now."

"Oh." I made an effort not to know too much about
Leo's California past. He and I had met the previous
summer while I was vacationing in Port Angeles. His
car had broken down while he was there. He had broken down, too, passing out drunk in the local library.
Somehow, I had been sufficiently foolish—and good-
hearted to give him a lift into Seattle. I'd never ex
pected to see him again. Then I had received the letter
from Tom Cavanaugh, recommending Leo for Ed
Bronsky's vacant job. I hadn't told Leo much about my
private life and nothing about my profession. He had returned the favor, but had expanded somewhat on his immediate background, which included the defection of
his wife and getting fired from his job. It shouldn't have
surprised me that he had ordered a second Scotch.

"How do your kids feel about Liza remarrying?" I
asked, feeling obligated to show a minimum of interest.

"Damned if I know," Leo answered, lighting up
again. "They don't call or write. They still hate me for
causing their mother to walk out after twenty-seven
years. Demolition Dad, they call me. Or something like

that." Leo's brown eyes had a faraway look, and he held his head with the hand that didn't hold the cigarette.

"You and Liza should have tried a marriage counselor," I said, and immediately wished I'd kept my mouth shut. "I mean, if she felt you didn't pay enough attention to her, she shouldn't have let it get to a point where her only option was to leave." Inwardly I berated myself. I sounded as if I were sticking up for Leo. I'd never intended to get that involved in his private life.

Leo's eyes had narrowed and he was giving me a knowing smile. Ed Bronsky not only couldn't read a rate schedule, he definitely wasn't capable of reading my mind. "Bingo!" Leo exclaimed, though he kept his voice down. "That occurred to me, too, but unfortunately it was six months later. Liza was already cozied up with Pete the Greek Geek Guidance Counselor."

Desperately I wanted to change the subject. We were sitting by the window that faced Front Street, because it had been the closest vacant booth to the door. Ordinarily I preferred a more private table, but I hadn't wanted Leo hobbling to the rear of the restaurant. Now I was grateful for our proximity to the street: Through the window, I saw Andy Cederberg, still carrying his briefcase, and heading for the Venison Inn.

I leaned across the table and hissed at Leo. "Hey, let's collar Andy. Trip him with your crutch."

The door swung open, but the lanky man with the briefcase was not Andy Cederberg. Indeed, I had never seen the new arrival before in my life. He was built like Andy, he had a long dark overcoat like Andy's, and his snap-brim cap was the same style as Andy wore. But up close, he was ten years older, much swarthier, and smacked of the Big City.

Leo and I gawked as the hostess showed the man to a table on the other side of the room.

"Stop the presses?" Leo murmured.

I gave a little shake of my head. "I don't know. He may be passing through from Eastern Washington."

Leo waited for the waitress to deliver our salads. "Do people driving the pass usually go a mile off the highway to have dinner this time of year?"

They didn't, especially not with snow in the forecast. Cross-state travelers were anxious to get as far below the summit as possible, lest they get caught in a storm.

When the waitress returned with Leo's second drink, he handed her a five-dollar bill. She started to protest, no doubt to tell Leo it was on the dinner tab, but he gave her hand a quick squeeze.

"This is a bribe, honey," Leo said in a low voice. "You know Ms. Lord here?"

The waitress, whose name was Dina and who was a recent graduate of Alpine High, nodded. I smiled encouragement at Dina. Leo gave her his most conspiratorial look.

"We want you to do some newspaper sleuthing for us, honey." He inclined his head in the direction that the unknown man had just gone. "Go roll those big blue eyes at the guy with the briefcase and pretend you're with the chamber of commerce. Ask where he's from, why he's here. You know, all the guff you do so well with the tourist trade."

Dina's big blue eyes got even bigger. I suspected that she was too shy and too new at the job to ask for more than food orders. But she was game. Gulping and nodding, she hurried off to the other side of the dining room.

Leo complacently savored his fresh drink. "I like giving women a thrill. She probably feels like a spy from World War Two."

"She's probably never heard of World War Two," I

remarked. "My son thinks the War in Nam is a rock group."

Leo seemed amused. But then I'm his employer. "What about Pop? Did he fight in Nam?"

This was the first time that Leo had ever asked about Adam's father. He knew Tom Cavanaugh; he had worked for one of Tom's weeklies in California. He also knew that I knew Tom, since that was where the recommendation had originated. But Leo didn't know how well I knew Tom. Eventually he would have to find out. But not just yet.

"No," I answered, trying to sound natural. "Pop was too old." And married.

I was spared further disclosures by Dina's return. Her fair face was flushed and she was tugging nervously at her blonde pigtail. "He's from Seattle," she whispered. "He's on *business*." Her breath came in little gasps.

"Well done." Leo's smile didn't ring quite true. "What kind of business?"

Dina's face fell. "I don't know, sir. He didn't say."

"Where's he staying?" Leo was clearly making an effort to keep his voice casual.

Now Dina looked close to tears. "I don't know that either. And I *did* ask."

Leo patted Dina's arm. "That's okay. You got the goods, honey. Thanks. How about that T-bone?"

Finding comfort either in Leo's manner or the request for something she knew how to do, Dina scurried off to the kitchen. Leo pushed his empty salad plate aside and lighted yet another cigarette.

"What do you think?" he asked in a musing tone.

I considered. "He could be a salesman. But he didn't look like it."

"That's a six-hundred-dollar overcoat," Leo said. "The briefcase is real leather."

"Somebody from the state? A lobbyist, maybe?"

"That's possible," Leo conceded. "But why not say so?"

I rubbed my chin. "BOW?" Leo wasn't familiar with the acronym. "The Bank of Washington," I explained.

Leo's eyes glinted. "Let's say you could bank on it." He gave me a quick wink. His T-bone and my trout arrived, courtesy of Dina, who was now all shy smiles.

I didn't feel like smiling. If the lanky man in the expensive overcoat really was from the Bank of Washington, it looked to me as if this was the end of the Bank of Alpine.

Chapter Four

THE LATEST EDITION of *The Advocate* had made no more than the usual waves. Clancy Barton of Barton's Bootery and Ione Erdahl of kIds cOrNEr weren't happy with the City Council's decision to ban overnight parking at the Alpine Mall. An unidentified woman railed against the Halloween antivandalism editorial, insisting that kids will be kids. I assumed one of hers had been caught vandalizing. Joe Igryskzsty, local tax consultant, called to inform us that we had misspelled his name—for the fifth time. I apologized, refraining from telling him that he was lucky Carla hadn't misspelled *Joe*. Only my alert proofreading had prevented the Episcopal rector's last name of Bartleby from being spelled with an *F*.

The snowstorm had never materialized. By Thursday, it had disappeared from the forecast, and temperatures were close to forty with a ninety percent chance of rain. That suited me fine, since I had to attend the monthly county commissioners meeting at seven P.M. Two of Skykomish's three commissioners had held their elective positions for over twenty years. George Engebretsen owns the local saw shop, and Alfred Cobb is retired from Blackwell Timber. The third member, Leonard Hollenberg, was elected six years ago. He's also retired, a former railroad man, and lives on the river about four miles west of town.

For reasons that elude me, county commissioners meetings usually draw a fair-sized crowd. The meetings are held in the main courtroom, with the three commissioners sitting behind the judge's bench like a troika. This month's agenda was mundane, dealing mainly with road improvements, participation in a proposed Highway 2 Greenway, and somebody's herd of cows that had wandered across the Snohomish-Skykomish County line. The last item might prove to be the most controversial. I scanned the audience of fifty-plus to see if I could spot any unfamiliar faces. The Snohomish County farmer might have shown up with a phalanx of supporters.

One face did stand out: Big Mike Brockelman was in the fourth row, his burly arms folded on his barrel chest. I leaned across the elderly couple sitting next to Mike at the end of the aisle.

"Hi—you scouting more jobs?"

Mike didn't recognize me at first. Then his rugged, weathered face broke into a grin. "Oh! Ms. Lord. You bet! I like to know what's coming up, especially this time of year when the weather cuts back so many projects. A lot of county roads around here are maintained in conjunction with the state."

I nodded. "Because of the timberlands," I said, then smiled and moved away. The couple I'd been blocking had started muttering to each other.

The meeting began, with the commissioners droning on about whether or not an offshoot of the Martin Creek Road should be maintained at county expense. If anyone in journalism school had ever warned me that much of a reporter's life would be spent sitting on hard chairs listening to tedious talk, I might have gone into veteri-

nary medicine. Or medieval history. Or ceramic
engineering . . . My attention dribbled off until Averill
Fairbanks asked for the floor.

Averill always asks for the floor. He is Alpine's resident sighter of UFOs and other space aliens. Now he
was asking the county commissioners if they were making any progress building a landing pad on Mount
Baldy. Figuring this was as good a time as any to take
my mediocre pictures, I knelt on the hardwood floor
and snapped away.

The commissioners did their usual stall on Averill,
then did the same with somebody's legitimate query
about a county bond issue to fund the sheriff's department. My brain returned to outer space, along with
Averill Fairbanks's UFOs. Unless the meeting grew
more lively, I'd rely on the minutes for the bare bones
of my story.

It was nine thirty-five when we were finally ad-
journed. The wandering cows had been tabled until December. Some of the audience had already left,
including Big Mike Brockelman, who had made his exit
after the commissioners finished blundering their way
through the back roads of Skykomish County.

With my handbag slung over one shoulder and my
camera on the other, I headed for the door. At the back
of the room, I saw Larry Petersen standing under a portrait of George Washington and chatting with Henry
Bardeen from the ski lodge.

Larry looked as if he wanted to avoid me, but he
smiled anyway. Since it was getting late, and I was
tired, I decided to let him off the hook. Any official
questions about the bank could wait. I'd already been
talked to death by the county commissioners and their
commentators in the crowd. Or maybe I was getting too

old for fourteen-hour days. Either way, I was anxious to go home.

On Friday, the Petersens still weren't talking. I tried not to press Marv or Larry, but I'd dropped by the bank in the morning to send a money order to Adam, and I couldn't resist asking if there was any news. Marv had given me a baleful look; Larry had laughingly thrown up his hands. But Rick Erlandson, who had actually waited on me, seemed even more glum than he had on Monday. I tried to banter with him, but found every jolly remark falling flat.

As usual, I was not sorry to see the workweek end. Vida went home early, to begin her revels with Roger. Ginny and Carla left like a pair of funeral mourners. Except for Carla's brief spurt of enthusiasm over her new photography assignment, neither had regained her emotional equilibrium. My only hope was that on their announced trip to Seattle over the weekend, they would find happiness and romance. If not, maybe they'd stay there. I was getting sick of their doleful faces.

Leo, however, was cheerful. He was abandoning his crutches, and felt sufficiently healed to walk to the clinic.

"I can drive again," he announced, preparing to leave. "How about those Sonics?"

Leo and I could bond over sports. I didn't, however, share his enthusiasm for Seattle's current NBA team. "Five bucks says they don't get past round one in the playoffs," I responded. "They're too erratic."

"You're on," said Leo with a grin. "Come April, don't forget. I hate welshers."

I was putting on my duffle coat, wondering about dinner. I had to grocery-shop. The thought turned my mind to restaurants. "Instead of money," I said on a sudden whim, "let's make it dinner at King Olav's. Or do you still want to go there?"

Leo glanced up from the drawer he was closing. "I've been there." His brown eyes avoided me. "Besides, we're talking springtime. If you want to make a serious bet, let's say fifty."

Somehow, I felt foolish. "Oh—well, okay." I did a small jig at the door. "How'd you like King Olav's?"

Leo seemed intrigued by something under his desk. "It was okay. Mostly Scandinavian stuff. Kind of heavy." He'd all but disappeared.

"That's because Alpine is mostly Scandinavian." I paused, waiting for Leo to come up for air. He did, barely.

"Have a good one, babe," he said.

I shrugged. "You, too." I left.

By the time I restocked at the Grocery Basket and got into my car, the revised weather forecast was calling for snow, at least above the two-thousand-foot level. Since Alpine is well within that range, I took notice. But if weathermen are sneered at in other parts of the country, their task in dealing with the Cascade Range is even more onerous. The Pacific Ocean sends the warming Japanese Current inland until it hits the mountains. Winds blow down from Canada and air floats up from the Columbia River. All sorts of strange currents buffet the coast of Washington. It's a meteorologist's nightmare, and advanced technology hasn't helped long-range forecasting.

Still, I wanted to be prepared. I had rock salt for my walk and enough food to last through Wednesday. In case of a power failure—which could happen in any kind of weather in Alpine—there was a Coleman lantern left over from Adam's camping days and a battery-run radio. My woodpile was well stocked, and during the most recent earthquake alarm, I'd purchased several gallons of well water. I should have felt secure as I unloaded the groceries in my pine-paneled kitchen.

And maybe I did. But I also felt lonely. There was one message on my answering machine, from City Librarian Edna Mae Dalrymple, asking if I'd host a bridge date the week after Thanksgiving. That, I realized, was the extent of my current social life. I finished putting away the groceries and poured myself an unusually large bourbon and water. Halfway into it, I called Milo Dodge.

"I've got enough salmon for two," I said, which wasn't true when taking Milo's prodigious appetite into account. "Are you hungry?"

But Milo already had his TV dinner in the microwave. My only consolation was that he sounded genuinely sorry. I suspected, however, that his regrets were more for the fish than my company.

Briefly, almost nervously, I considered calling Leo. But that would be reckless. Then I wondered who had been Leo's companion at King Olav's. Perhaps he'd dined there alone. It didn't seem likely; the restaurant wasn't the sort of place where people ate solo.

Carla and Ginny had gone to Seattle; Vida had Roger. There were plenty of single people in Alpine who were probably as lonely as I was.

But I wasn't unhappy. Being alone was quite different from being lonely. I was merely going through a bad patch, probably triggered by Ginny and Carla's long faces. I marched out to the kitchen and put the salmon under the broiler. All of it.

And I ate it, along with a potato and some green beans.

I still felt lonely. Maybe I was unhappy, too.

* * *

Saturday morning didn't exactly dawn, it hovered over Alpine like a pall. The clouds were low and gray, with the rain coming down in buckets. I did laundry and vacuuming and dusting. By noon, the rain had stopped, but the clouds were still there, so heavy that I could almost feel them.

In the afternoon, I decided to drive to Monroe. I had no reason, I simply wanted to get out of Alpine. Once I hit Highway 2, my mood began to lighten. So did the sky. As I descended the pass, the clouds lifted and brightened. My mouth twisted into a wry smile. Like most native Pacific Northwesterners, I wasn't bothered by gray, rainy days. In fact, I like them. I didn't blame my emotional slide on the weather. It was caused by something else, and I felt at a loss to figure out what it was.

The strip malls in Monroe helped. My only purchases were a couple of paperbacks and a shirt for Adam's Christmas. I stayed long enough to eat an early dinner at a Japanese take-out restaurant, and arrived home shortly after six.

There were two messages on the machine, a fact that somehow cheered me. At least it did initially. Edna Mae wanted to know why I hadn't called her back. The truth was, I hadn't felt like it. I would ring her as soon as I listened to the second message.

The voice belonged to Vida, though it took me a few seconds to recognize her. She was squawking. I listened with half an ear as I took the price tags off Adam's shirt. I started to smile, until I realized what she was trying to tell me:

"So awful . . . especially for Roger . . . young and sensitive . . . scarred for life, poor dear . . . dead as a dodo . . . that beat all?"

Startled, I rewound the machine and turned up the

volume. Now my entire attention was fixed on Vida's voice:

"It was so awful, finding Linda Lindahl dead. Especially for Roger. He's so young and sensitive. No doubt he'll be scarred for life, poor dear. Linda was dead as a dodo, and probably had been for several hours. Doesn't that beat all?"

My hand fell away from the answering machine as if I had been burned. Edna Mae was forgotten. I punched in Vida's number so fast that I misdialed and reached the Whistling Marmot Movie Theatre. Like a coward, I hung up without apologizing and dialed again. This time Vida answered.

"Where *were* you?" Vida's voice practically shattered my ear. Nor did she give me a chance to reply. "Why aren't you *here?*"

Because Roger is, I wanted to say but didn't. Vida wasn't being her usual rational self. "What happened to Linda?" I asked. "Is she really dead?"

"Of course she's dead. Didn't I say so?" Vida had lowered her voice, no doubt to spare Roger's delicate ears. "Really, Emma, you must get right over to my house. I can't tell you everything on the phone."

Obediently I put on my coat and drove to Vida's. The first few flakes of snow began to fall as I pulled up to the curb.

Roger was sitting in front of the TV, watching somebody shoot the bejesus out of somebody else. He seemed unmoved by the program and my arrival. Roger was stuffing his face with Fritos.

Vida was too preoccupied to bother forcing Roger to greet me. She ushered me into the kitchen where the teakettle was already heating on the stove.

"I want to be organized about this," she declared, sitting across from me at the table. Vida still wore her hat, a furry toque that was about the same color as her hair. It was almost impossible to tell where one left off and the other began.

But Vida was indifferent to everything but the matter at hand. If I hadn't already been alarmed by her news, Vida's grim manner would have sobered me in a hurry.

"Roger and I were going to the mall today," she began, speaking almost in her normal manner. "But he was so eager to shoot his BB gun, and I was certain it would snow tonight." She glanced out the window, as if to give herself credibility. "So we drove up 187, as far as we could before hitting the new construction. As of now, that's about a mile this side of the road to the ranger station."

Silently I noted that Big Mike Brockelman and his crew had made considerable progress since Monday's layoff. Vida kept talking as the kettle whistled and she rose to tend the tea.

"There's nothing in those woods just off the south side of the road. In a fifty-foot area, it's rather flat before the mountain starts to climb again. It was a landing stage for felled trees back in the Twenties. I thought that would be a good place for Roger to practice, as long as he didn't aim across the highway. The golf course isn't far from there, you know."

I pictured the setting in my mind. No doubt I'd often passed that section of the forest. On the north side of the road was a Cyclone fence, marking the boundary of the golf course. The fairways were shrouded by evergreens, and beyond the east end of the course was a large gouge left by the most recent logging operation. Across the road, just past the Icicle Creek Bridge, stood Elmer Petersen's farm. The rest of the road's south side was covered with second-growth timber, planted seventy years ago by Carl Clemans's men.

Vida paused to pour our tea, which was even weaker than what she'd fixed Monday night. I winced as I picked up the cup, remembering how I'd rushed to this same house to squeal on Linda Lindahl. I felt like a ghoul.

"Roger was doing beautifully," Vida went on. "He almost hit a crow. Naturally, all the small animals have gone down the mountain to a lower elevation. That's why I knew it would snow."

I was getting impatient. "When was all this?" I asked, hoping to spur Vida along.

"We arrived shortly before one. Roger wanted to eat lunch at the Burger Barn. He adores their cheeseburgers. You should see him sink his little teeth into—"

"Vida!" I'd turned snappish. "Tell me about Linda or I'll call Milo!"

The threat worked, though Vida gave me a sour look. "Roger thought he'd hit a pigeon. I didn't agree, but allowed as how Grams could be wrong, being older and of failing eyesight. I humored him"—Vida caught herself—"by starting to search the ground under a big hemlock when Roger called out that there was somebody in a stump." She paused, rolling her eyes. "Naturally, I thought he meant someone had come along who was stumped—about directions or such. I looked, but didn't see anything except Roger, standing by an old fallen log. He wouldn't move, which is odd for Roger. So lively, you know. I walked over to where he was standing and realized he'd grown quite pale. Then I saw her." Vida took a deep breath, squeezed her eyes shut, and then flared her nostrils. "It was Linda Petersen Lindahl, and even at a glance, I could tell she was dead."

* * *

Vida had hustled Roger back to the car, despite his protests. He had never seen a dead body before, and who could blame the little fellow for natural curiosity? Or so Vida put it.

Vida's first thought was to call from the Petersen farm, which would have the nearest phone. But upon realizing that Elmer and Thelma Petersen were the uncle and aunt of the dead woman, she decided to go another half mile into the Icicle Creek development and hope that Milo Dodge was home on a Saturday afternoon.

He was cleaning out his gutters. Vida's shouted announcement almost caused him to fall off the ladder. Within minutes, he had asked two of his deputies to join him off Highway 187. Vida had at first refused to return to show Milo where Roger had found Linda.

"So gruesome—I didn't want Roger to come with us, but the brave little man insisted on staying with Grams." As it turned out, Milo had called Sam Heppner and Bill Blatt, Vida's nephew. "Roger worships Billy, so it took a while for me to pry them apart. Milo and Sam were photographing the body when we finally left. That was about three o'clock. I took Roger out for a hot fudge sundae to distract him. Milo is coming by at any moment to take my formal statement. The sheriff's office is no place for Roger."

Maybe not, but the county jail suited the little ghoul just fine as far as I was concerned. Even now, Roger's chunky little body was wedged in the kitchen doorway.

"Hey, Grams, I'm out of Fritos and pop. There's nothing on TV. Can I watch *Robocop* again?"

Vida dashed to the cupboard, where she produced a bag of Cheetos, then removed a can of cola from the refrigerator. "Here, darling, frosty cold just the way you like it. You know how to run the VCR; go ahead and watch your little show."

With a hostile glance for me, Roger left the kitchen. I felt distracted and disturbed. Vida's ramblings about Roger had taken the edge off Linda's death. That was wrong. It was also uncharacteristic of my House & Home editor. Under ordinary circumstances, Vida was the most down-to-earth of creatures. But Roger turned her mind to mush. He seemed to be doing the same to mine.

"Vida," I began, giving up on my tea and wishing my hostess kept something stronger than cooking sherry on hand, "Linda didn't crawl inside a hollow log and die. What did Milo say? Is it . . . murder?" The last word came out hushed, though with Roger immersed in bloody mayhem, I didn't know why.

Vida, who drinks hot water almost exclusively at work, now dispensed with the tea bag, too. She sipped slowly from her cup and narrowed her eyes. "Of course it's murder. Didn't I say so?"

I gave a faint shake of my head. The sukiyaki I'd eaten in Monroe turned over in my stomach. I'd known all along that Linda had been murdered. But having Vida validate the fact out loud made me feel ill. I put my head in my hands, silently sending up a muddled prayer for Linda's soul. "How?" The lonely syllable was a gasp.

"It would appear," Vida replied, now sounding like her usual brisk self, "she was strangled with her own muffler. Her face was quite an unbecoming shade of puce."

The sukiyaki declared war on Vida's weak tea. I was about to head for her bathroom when the front doorbell rang. Naturally, Roger didn't bother to get off his fat duff to answer it. By the time Vida brought Milo Dodge into the kitchen, I had my stomach under control.

Oddly enough, Milo didn't look much better than I

felt. His color was off and his long face looked drawn. There were snowflakes on his down jacket, and his usual long-legged lope faltered as he approached the table.

"I've just spent the last hour with the Petersens," he said, dropping into a vacant chair. "You got any beer, Vida?"

"I don't keep liquor in the house, Milo," Vida sniffed. "You know that. I'm Presbyterian."

Milo's expression was wry. "I also know you'll take a cocktail now and then. Where's the beer?"

With an exasperated air, Vida reached into her highest cupboard, rummaging behind some empty fruit jars. She produced an unopened bottle of vodka. "I drink only on festive occasions. I was saving this for Thanksgiving. My sons-in-law enjoy a vodka martini."

Milo preferred beer or Scotch. But he didn't balk. Neither did I. We allowed Vida to mix drinks for both of us. She turned out to be a better bartender than she was a cook.

"Don't let Roger see you," she urged, handing us each a highball glass, which I suspected was the extent of her cocktail vessels. "Now give me that statement to sign, Milo. I'd like to be done with it."

Milo looked chagrined. "I forgot the forms. We'll do it tomorrow. Or Monday." He made a face. "It's going to take at least that long for the M.E. in Everett to have his report. Damn, I wish we had our own facilities in Skykomish County. This jerk-assed business of sending everything to Snohomish County hampers us too much."

"Mind your language," Vida said primly. "There's a child in the other room."

Milo shared my opinion of Roger. His skeptical gaze was ignored by Vida. "It was definitely foul play," he said, perhaps for my benefit. Milo knew I needed some facts by Tuesday to meet our deadline. "That's about all we can say until we hear from Everett. I'm not even going to try to guess how long she's been dead. Linda left work around six-thirty Friday. As far as we know, she was never seen again."

Vida gave a nod. "Yes, the bank stays open until six on Fridays. How are the Petersens taking it?"

A desolate expression passed over Milo's face. "As you'd expect. Hard. Real hard, especially Marv and his wife. Sam Heppner and Bill Blatt went to Everett with the body. They'll notify the daughter and Linda's ex-husband while they're there. I don't envy them that one. The kid's only twelve."

Vida was shaking her head. I fingered the bridge of my nose, feeling waves of sympathy for Linda's little girl. And the rest of the Petersens, of course.

"I hope," Vida said at last, "that—Alison, isn't it?—gets along with her stepmother. That will help."

Milo seemed distracted. Indeed, he was now looking troubled. "Huh? Oh, right, the daughter. Kids adapt. God knows mine seem to think that creep Old Mulehide married is big stuff."

Old Mulehide was Milo's former wife. Upon her remarriage several years ago, she and their children had moved to Bellevue, across Lake Washington from Seattle. Maybe Milo's distracted air was caused by thoughts of his fragmented family.

Vida, however, felt otherwise. "Well? What is it, Milo? What's bothering you, besides the obvious?"

Milo let out a big sigh. "Probably nothing. But when I told Larry Petersen about his sister's death, he acted more scared than shocked. Denise was there, too, and she damned near got hysterical."

I regarded Milo curiously. "I don't blame her. Linda was her aunt."

But Milo wasn't buying my argument. "Linda and Denise weren't close, even though they worked together. What upset Larry and his daughter was fear. Nobody reported it to us, but Wednesday night, somebody tried to run down Andy Cederberg on his way home from work. The Petersens think there's a plot to get rid of everybody who works for the Bank of Alpine."

I started to scoff, but Vida was gazing at Milo with unblinking eyes. "Maybe," she said in a firm yet chilling voice, "there is."

Chapter Five

THE POLICE LOG is always fair game for the media. Andy Cederberg had now reported the alleged attempt at running him down. A near miss, however, is not news even in Alpine. But it could be an item for Vida's "Scene Around Town." Given her outspoken fear for the Bank of Alpine's employees, eventually it could be much more. Since the Cederbergs lived only two blocks from Vida's house, I drove down to Pine Street after finishing my drink. Milo was officially off-duty, but he felt an obligation to call on Elmer and Thelma Petersen at their farm. Thelma, after all, was Milo's aunt.

My studded tires coped nicely with the fresh layer of snow. A few kids were outside, trying to make snowballs. They seemed entranced by the falling flakes. The novelty would wear off long before the first thaw.

I'd never been inside the Cederbergs' house before. It was old, but well maintained. Reba Cederberg had an eye for decorating. Heavy Victorian furniture was offset by beige carpets and pastel drapes. Bright silk floral arrangements stood on the spinet piano, an oak credenza, and an end table. Still, a melancholy pall hung over the room.

Upon my arrival, Andy shooed his two children upstairs. A girl of twelve and a boy about nine seemed to obey, but later I noticed their feet planted on the landing. Obviously they didn't want to miss any of the excitement that had so recently touched their family.

"Marv called us about Linda," Andy said after we were seated in the living room and Reba had gone off to make coffee. "I still can't believe it. Some nut passing through, I suppose. I wish those people would stay in the city where they belong."

Reba returned, wringing her hands. While she was definitely overweight, especially through the hips, her golden hair was artfully styled to frame surprisingly delicate features.

"I can't think when I've been so upset," Reba said, sitting next to her husband on the floral print–covered sofa. "It's not safe to go out alone anywhere these days. Not even in Alpine."

It occurred to me that Linda might not have gone out alone. Her killer could have been her companion. But I didn't want to say so. The idea raised too many ugly questions.

A tremor seemed to pass over Andy's thin frame. "Linda, of all people!" There was awe in his voice. "Now, there was a woman I would have thought could take care of herself. Savvy, cautious, did everything by the numbers. Boy, it sure goes to show you never can tell about people."

I agreed, casting about for a way to discuss Andy's near miss with the errant driver. But both Cederbergs were wound up in Linda's death. I couldn't blame them.

"Andy asked Marv if she'd been robbed," Reba said, nervously entwining her fingers. "Or . . . assaulted. I guess he didn't know." She gave her husband a questioning look.

Andy nodded. "That's right. Sheriff Dodge didn't have all the facts yet. It's just a darned shame that everything has to be sent over to Snohomish County. We're like a bunch of stepchildren here in Alpine."

It wasn't the first time I'd been motivated to start an editorial campaign to put a law-enforcement bond issue on the ballot. The problem was the economy: Skykomish County residents were more concerned with putting food on the table. It would be a tough sell to convince them that there was a corollary between poverty and crime.

"I don't suppose Linda told anybody at work Friday what her plans were for the weekend," I remarked.

Andy looked blank. "She didn't tell me. But Linda was always closemouthed. She kept her private life private."

Reba had gotten to her feet, presumably to fetch the coffee. "Oh, how true! When she moved back here after her divorce from Howie, I made a real effort to be friendly. We belong to Gut-Busters, the gourmet dinner group Vida writes up sometimes, and I asked Linda to join us. I tried to get her involved in the Lutheran church—the rest of her family is quite active, you know. Then I asked her to go with me and a couple of other women into Seattle for the annual garden show at the convention center. She always had some excuse, so I finally gave up." With an air of lingering resentment, Reba headed for the kitchen.

I decided her absence would provide an opportunity to ask Andy about the attempted rundown. "This hasn't been a very good week for the bank," I said in my most sympathetic manner. "I heard you almost got hit by a car Wednesday night."

Andy removed his wire-rimmed glasses and let his head loll on the back of the sofa. "Golly, that was something! It scared the heck out of me! I wasn't going to tell Reba about it, but I was still shaking by the time I got home. She guessed something was up."

"Where did it happen?" I inquired, wishing I had the nerve to take notes. Unlike Vida, my memory is not infallible.

Another tremor passed through Andy's body. "Right by John Engstrom Park, just after I passed Driggers Funeral Home." Andy's expression was ironic as well as anxious. "I'd left the bank a little later than usual—around six-thirty—except Fridays, of course, when we're open late." His Adam's apple bobbed as he swallowed hard. "It was foggy again, even though it had started to warm up. There I was, just walking along, minding my own business, and . . . whaaang!" He smacked a fist into his palm. "This car comes up over the curb and sends me flying. I landed right at the base of old John's memorial plaque."

"You were actually hit?" I asked, aghast.

Andy shook his head and put his glasses back on. "Gosh, no. I mean, I heard the guy coming and I jumped out of the way. I suppose he lost control, or else he couldn't see in the fog."

The explanation was logical. Having had the luxury of publication day when there is seldom any pressure at work, I'd gone home around four-thirty on Wednesday. The fog hadn't yet settled in and there was still considerable daylight. About the same time that Andy Cederberg was being chased by a car, I was settling in with my laptop to write some letters. As usual, I'd included a weather report. It had definitely been foggy. And dark.

"Maybe it was Durwood Parker," I suggested. When it comes to vehicular assault, Durwood is always the usual suspect. He supposedly has had his driver's license revoked, but that hasn't stopped him from taking to the road—and the sidewalk and an occasional store-front.

"Oh, no, it wasn't Durwood. I know his car." Andy's certainty wasn't questionable. Everyone in Alpine knew Durwood's car; they had to. It was a matter of life and death.

"Then you don't think it was deliberate," I said, trying to sound casual.

Andy sighed. "I don't know, Emma. It could have been kids. You know how crazy they can be."

I did. Cruising Front Street, especially on weekends, was a favorite hobby of Alpine teenagers. Milo and his deputies tried to curb the activity, but it wasn't easy. The town didn't offer much for young people. Besides, Milo admitted that he, too, had been a world-class Alpine cruiser in his day.

"The main thing is that you didn't get hurt. Badly, I mean." The amendment was caused by Andy's wince. Apparently he'd suffered some bumps and bruises.

"It took me ten minutes to find my briefcase," Andy said, rubbing his left forearm. "It landed next to the pond."

Reba returned, carrying a tray with a coffee carafe, three mugs, sugar, cream, and napkins. "You're talking about Andy's accident? My goodness, it scared me out of my wits! I wish he'd gotten the license number." She gave Andy a glance of mild reproach.

"Heck, hon, I couldn't eyeball it. As I told Emma, I *heard* the blasted thing first. By the time I looked around, it had taken off like a shot. All I know is that it was a car, not a truck or a van or a bus."

Reba handed me a mug of hot coffee. "He tore his overcoat and ruined his pants. I took the coat over to Everett to be mended properly, but it won't be back until next week. And now it's snowing!" She grimaced as she looked out through the bay window. The snow was coming down much harder.

"Hon, I've got my down jacket," Andy reminded her. "I'd probably wear it anyway if this stuff gets really bad."

Reba had sat down again on the sofa. "Kids," she said in a disgruntled voice. "Every year they get worse. All these broken homes. I see it every day at school. Divorce, remarriage, more divorce, live-ins, liquor, dope, and no jobs. I wonder what's going to become of this generation. It's pathetic."

Andy put a skinny arm around his wife's plump shoulders. "Now, hon, don't get started on all that." He gave me an amused look. "Just about this time of year when the first report cards are due, Reba gets really down on the kids. And their parents."

Reba's green eyes flashed. "Why shouldn't I? Everybody blames the teachers for students being so poorly educated. They have no discipline because they aren't being raised properly at home. It's not easy being a parent, I know that, but Andy and I've tried to raise our children the old-fashioned way, with rules. Too many others are ruined before they ever get to kindergarten. Maybe it's a good thing Linda didn't get custody of her daughter. Look at what a mess the poor girl would be in now!"

I didn't try to suppress my surprise. "Linda was in a custody battle?"

Andy appeared to give Reba a warning nudge, but she wasn't about to be intimidated. I suspected she never was. "Linda would never confide in anyone, of course. But Marisa Foxx let it slip that she knew Linda." Reba leaned forward on the sofa, regarding me in a conspiratorial manner. "You must know Marisa—she's one of the new lawyers in the Doukas firm, and I believe she goes to your church. I got her to join Gut-Busters. She's marvelous with pasta."

I recognized Marisa only by sight. She was in her early thirties, and because of her short-cropped hair, long-legged stride, and interest in softball, was rumored to be a lesbian. The only thing I knew about Marisa for certain was that she was very bright and, along with another young lawyer, Jonathan Sibley, had brought in some new clients from along the Highway 2 corridor.

"So what else?" Reba was saying.

Distracted by conjuring up Marisa Foxx, I hadn't been paying close attention. "What? Ah—you mean the custody fight?"

Reba nodded, both chins waggling. "The divorce was final a long time ago, there was no haggling over money because they didn't have any, and Howie has remarried. What could Linda have wanted but custody? And why didn't she get it in the first place?" She turned to Andy, chins jutting. Reba looked as if she'd scored a tic-breaking point.

"Don't ask me, hon." Andy was perfectly amiable. "Linda wasn't the type to blab all her personal stuff around the bank. I'm not complaining. Over the years, we've had some personnel who didn't know when to shut up. Mostly women, and especially the younger ones, like Denise Petersen. No offense," he added hastily, lest Reba and I gang up and snap him in two like a twig.

Being neither young nor a Petersen, I wasn't offended. I'd been exposed to Carla and Ginny all week. Ginny had moped around the office in comparative silence, but Carla had voiced her sufferings to anyone who would listen, including the Federal Express driver, the Audit Bureau of Circulation representative, and any poor soul who brought in a news release. I understood

Andy's gripe. I also knew it was time to take my leave. The only news value in the near-miss incident was for Vida's "Scene." I asked Andy if he would mind being included in next week's column. Usually we don't request permission, but I try not to hurt anyone's dignity. And Andy, after all, was an extension of Marv Petersen's dignified image.

"Heck no," Andy replied as he and Reba accompanied me to the door. "Maybe somebody else saw what happened. I doubt it, though. I couldn't see a foot in front of me in that blasted fog."

I, however, could still see four feet up on the staircase landing. Maybe the Cederberg kids were breaking some of their parents' rules. Maybe that wasn't such a bad thing. I've never been one to squash natural curiosity. It was, after all, one of the reasons I'd gone into journalism.

But as I left the Cederberg house, I knew I didn't have any answers.

I drove by John Engstrom Park on my way home. Under the pristine white blanket of snow, the half block of trees and shrubs took on a magical aura. Unlike Old Mill Park on the other side of town with its picnic tables and bandstand and tennis court and life-sized statue of Carl Clemans, this small oasis is not just a monument to the Alpine Mill's beloved superintendent, but a microcosm of local flora. The park was built among existing evergreens, and the other plantings are native growth, from trilliums to wild ginger. Only the pond and the plaque are artificial, but they are artfully integrated. There is no purpose to the place, except to provide a memorial to John Engstrom and a haven in the middle of commercial and residential structures. City dwellers might scoff at the need for such a refuge when the town itself is surrounded by nature's grandeur. But I find the park quaint, charming, and a reminder that sometimes our vision is limited. We cannot see the forest for the trees. And often, we cannot see the mountains for the rooftops.

It was after nine o'clock by the time I got home. At least an inch of snow had fallen. I called Vida. She was watching TV with Roger.

"Giraffes," she said, "on PBS. I thought Roger needed something educational. He's all tuckered out from our Big Day."

I recounted my so-called interview with the Cederbergs, including Reba's claim that Linda was in a custody battle. Vida pounced on that tasty tidbit.

"My niece, Stacey, works for the Doukas firm," she said. "I'll see what she knows. She's been very lax lately about keeping me informed."

I had forgotten about Stacey. Indeed, I required a family tree to keep track of Vida's relatives. "The Cederbergs think some outsider killed Linda," I noted. "It's possible, I suppose."

There was a brief silence at the other end of the line. "Anything is possible," Vida allowed. "I would like to believe that, naturally. Do you?"

I gave a truncated laugh. "How would I know, Vida? My experience with murder in Alpine is somewhat limited, but the victim usually knows the killer."

Vida refused to comment. Instead, she returned to Andy's close call at John Engstrom Park. "I don't like that. If it wasn't Durwood Parker, who could it be?"

I repeated the earlier theory of teenagers, lost in the fog. "They don't take weather factors into account," I said, recalling some of Adam's vehicular disasters. Fortunately, they had all occurred before I bought the Jag.

"Perhaps." Vida sounded noncommittal. I suspected

she was still considering the possibility that the Bank of
Alpine's employees were all potential victims. "I'm not
going to use it in 'Scene.' It's too morbid. I'm also cutting out Darla Puckett's tidbit on JoAnne Petersen scurrying around Safeway to buy crackers and cheese
spread. I certainly wouldn't embarrass Ginny by running Heather Bardeen's report of Rick Erlandson and
Denise Petersen necking at the Whistling Marmot. Besides, we shouldn't have anything frivolous in this issue
that involves the Petersens or the bank. Just because
Leo has a filthy mouth doesn't mean we should lower
the rest of our standards."

I quite agreed with Vida, though it always amused
me when she delivered a lecture as if I were the green
reporter and she the veteran publisher. "Andy thought a
mention of the careless driver might elicit a witness," I
said.

Vida snorted. "In that fog? If anyone had been there,
Andy would have noticed. It's best to leave it out. I
have more than enough this week, what with all the
items from the Baptist church's Fall Follies." She
paused, then spoke away from the phone, presumably to
Roger. It sounded as if she were cautioning him not to
pull the pin on a hand grenade, but I probably didn't
hear her correctly. "There are several things bothering
me," Vida said, the worry coming through in her voice.
"It's odd that Marv Petersen never called back. I don't
like that, either."

I, too, had found the lack of communication peculiar.
"Don't tell me you're beginning to think that there's a
buyout in the wind after all?"

Vida's sigh was eloquent. "I'd hate to think it. But
it's happening everywhere. Hardly a month goes by
without some big bank taking over a smaller one somewhere in the state. I suppose it's unrealistic to believe

that ... Eeeek!" Vida's screech startled me. "Roger is throwing up! All this violence! I must run!" The phone clicked in my ear.

Attributing Roger's stomach troubles to gluttony rather than gore, I wasn't alarmed. I was, however, disturbed. I hardly knew Linda Lindahl, but her death had shaken me. As if suffering from an aftershock, I found myself suddenly unnerved. I checked both doors to make sure they were locked. I left the light on in the carport. I spent five minutes staring out the front window. The snow was coming down so hard that I couldn't see beyond my split-rail fence. Surely no homicidal maniac would be out in this kind of weather.

Or so I told myself as I prepared for bed an hour later. When the phone rang just before midnight, I was still awake. Anxiously I picked up the receiver and said hello. There was a slight pause before the caller hung up.

A wrong number, a coward like me. I hadn't had the courage to tell the Whistling Marmot that I'd made a mistake in dialing. A few minutes later, I drifted off to sleep. I'd expected grisly dreams, of bodies stuffed in rotting logs, of murderers lurking in the shadows, of Roger eating Fritos.

Instead, I dreamed of Tom Cavanaugh. It was a familiar, frustrating dream I'd had for over twenty years. We were working together on *The Seattle Times*, and trying to conduct our affair with the utmost discretion. In the dream, as in real life, we were always trying to find an opportunity to be together. Unlike real life, we never did. The city editor, my ex-fiancé, Tom's wife— someone would intrude to keep us apart. Every time, the dream ended on the same note, with me sitting alone, watching Tom walk away. Never once had I ever dreamed of making love with Tom, not even after our ecstatic reunion at Lake Chelan the previous June.

It had been twenty years since we'd been together. We hadn't even seen each other for almost that long. When Tom's mentally unstable wife, Sandra, had gotten pregnant about the same time I had, all hope of marriage had evaporated. Stubbornly, I refused Tom's help.

I'd headed for Mississippi where Ben had his first parish in the home missions. When I returned with little Adam, I put Seattle behind me and finished my schooling in Eugene, at the University of Oregon. After graduation, I'd gone to work for *The Oregonian* in Portland. There Adam and I remained until I got the opportunity to buy *The Advocate*.

It was then that Tom reentered my life, having heard about my purchase through his weekly newspaper grapevine. He had been based in Sandra's hometown of San Francisco for years, using her inherited money to fund his entrepreneurial activities. Or what was left over from that money after paying for bail bondsmen, lawyers, court costs, fines, hospitals, and custodial care. Sandra may have been rich, but she didn't come cheap—not in terms of upkeep or emotional erosion. It was a testament to Tom's character that after twenty-five years, he wasn't as crazy as she was.

I was still thinking about Tom the next day after returning from Mass. I'd had to put chains on the car because Alpine was now under five inches of snow. Had it been a Monday, the city might have roused itself to plow the streets. But it was Sunday, and Mayor Fuzzy Baugh could walk to the Baptist church. If he felt like it. Besides, the latest forecast called for a warming trend, with the snow turning to rain by afternoon. If that happened, come the March elections, Fuzzy could boast that he'd saved the taxpayers money.

The Sunday paper had nothing on our local murder. The edition delivered to Alpine was printed earlier than the one received by Seattle subscribers. Perhaps tomorrow *The Post-Intelligencer* or *The Times* would carry an inch or two in their Northwest sections.

Indeed, for all its pages, I found little of interest in the current edition. Or maybe I was still in the clutches of my dream. I hadn't seen Tom since Lake Chelan, though I had spoken with him on the phone as recently as mid-October. He had called to ask if I thought Adam had finally found his niche in anthropology. Tom knew I wouldn't know, so I presumed he'd also called to hear my voice. Having finally relented and let him meet Adam, I was still adjusting to Tom's active interest in our son's well-being. Adam was adjusting, too, and seemed to like Tom. Or maybe Adam merely liked the money that Tom gave him for plane tickets. I had the feeling that Tom's belated arrival in Adam's world conveyed an aura of impermanence. Fathers who suddenly show up after the first twenty years must seem ephemeral, like a wizard materializing out of a puff of smoke.

Meanwhile, I was customarily taken for granted, and often for a ride. It being Sunday, I half expected Adam to call, asking for money, clothes, or various audiovisual components. When the phone hadn't rung by four o'clock, I was tempted to pick it up and make sure the thing was in working order.

It was, for it rang even as I stared at it. But it wasn't Adam. Instead, Milo Dodge's laconic voice droned in my ear.

"It's raining," he said. "You want to go eat someplace?"

It had been raining for a couple of hours, and the snow was melting quickly. "Where?" I asked, almost certain I knew the answer: the Venison Inn.

But Milo surprised me. "I can get anywhere with my

Cherokee Chief's four-wheel drive. You want to try that French place down the highway?"

I was stunned. Milo has about as much interest in foreign food as he has in petit point embroidery. "Café de Flore?" I said incredulously. "With words on the menu you don't understand? What next, Mozart at the Seattle opera house?"

"I need to broaden my outlook." The words came out in a mumble. I could hear Honoria Whitman's voice echoing in Milo's ears.

I smiled. "Don't we all. It sounds fine. I haven't been there since last spring."

An hour later, as I was putting on my good green wool dress, I wondered why Milo hadn't asked Honoria to go to dinner. Maybe she wasn't willing to drive up the pass from Startup. Her car didn't have four-wheel drive, and, like Leo, she was from California. On the other hand, Milo could have driven down to get her.

Most of all, I wondered why Milo had asked *me*.

Chapter Six

IT'S PAINFUL TO watch Milo Dodge read a menu that doesn't feature cheeseburgers. At best, he was baffled; at worst, he was alarmed.

"What's this *marmite de poisson* stuff?" he demanded, mangling the French pronunciation. "It sounds like something I should send to the lab in Everett."

"It's fish soup. Let's make this simple. What do you feel like eating? Tell me, and I'll order whatever comes closest."

Naturally, Milo wanted a steak. I pointed out the *bifteck au poivre*, which made some sort of sense to him, particularly when I added that he could get fries and a salad as well.

"Maybe these French people really do know how to cook," he remarked after the waiter had taken our order. "This place seems busy, but I don't recognize most of the customers."

Milo was right: Café de Flore catered to a wide-ranging clientele, from Seattle to Wenatchee. On a Sunday night, it was usually jammed, with reservations required. But because of the snow, the restaurant wasn't quite full.

"The prices are pretty stiff," Milo went on, hoisting his Scotch glass. "I remember that from the last time you and I were here."

I couldn't resist the question: "You haven't eaten here with Honoria?"

Milo shifted awkwardly in his chair. "I've been meaning to bring her. Somehow, we always end up someplace else. Like Monroe or Snohomish or even Everett." Milo was now blushing.

Over my bourbon, I gave Milo my most kindly smile. "Hey, don't tie yourself in knots because you didn't major in French. Half the people here probably mispronounce the entrées."

The high color began to fade from Milo's cheeks. "It's not just that, Emma." He pulled his chair closer and hunched over the linen-covered table. "Honoria speaks French like a native. Spanish, too. She knows everything about art and music and all that stuff. She reads books by writers I never heard of and she honest-to-God really does watch PBS. I feel like the village idiot when I'm with her."

"Nonsense," I retorted. "Crazy Eights Neffel has that title wrapped up." Noting Milo blanch at my flippancy, I patted his arm. "Stop beating yourself up, Milo. You're a successful law enforcement officer, one of the best in the state. You're well liked, you've helped raise decent kids, and you're anything but dumb. So what if you don't know Puccini from Pushkin?"

"Huh?" Milo was scowling at me.

"Never mind. Honoria likes and admires you for what you are, not for what you know. She wouldn't still be around if that weren't true."

Almost a full minute passed before Milo spoke. He removed his elbows from the table, took a swig of Scotch, and gazed forlornly over my shoulder. "Maybe she won't be around much longer. We don't have much in common."

While that was true, I suspected that the crux of the

problem lay elsewhere. Milo has been reluctant to make a commitment. Honoria has been growing impatient. I broached the dreaded subject.

"Have you talked about the future?"

Milo glared. "Hell, yes. Over at the Cougar Inn, I asked her to marry me. She said no." He finished his Scotch in one defiant gulp.

"Oh." I was at a loss for words. The waiter returned, inquiring if we'd like another drink. Milo nodded curtly; I decided I might as well join him. He was driving, and chances were that he wouldn't arrest himself for being under the influence.

"Did she give you a reason?" I asked after the waiter had parted.

Milo was toying with the salt and pepper shakers. At least he hadn't brought along a toothpick. Slowly, painfully, he nodded. "She says I don't love her."

I blinked several times. "Don't you?" The words tumbled out.

"I don't know." Milo's expression was miserable. "I thought I did. But Honoria asked me how I envisioned us ten years from now. Hell, I can't envision tomorrow. I said so. She told me that we'd grow apart, because our . . . how did she put it? . . . our emotional ties weren't strong enough, and we didn't have much else to keep us going. Or something like that." Milo practically snatched the fresh drink out of the waiter's hand.

Having known Milo longer than I'd known Leo, I was more inclined to offer advice as well as sympathy. I had plenty of the latter, but not much of the former.

"So what are you trying to prove?" I asked as the party of four at the next table gasped over the dessert cart. "That you can expand your horizons? Or that you really do love her?"

Milo's long face was puzzled. "I'm not sure. Maybe

I figure that if I get interested in cultural stuff, it'll prove I . . . ah . . . love her."

"You shouldn't have to prove it." I spoke with surprising fervor, and regretted it immediately. "I mean, either you do or you don't. If you don't know, Milo, maybe Honoria is right." Now he was completely crestfallen. My sympathy overflowed. Men can't help their inability to face up to genuine emotions. Intuitively Milo would know when to call for the hit-and-run instead of a bunt. But he's dense as a Douglas fir when it comes to personal relationships. "Have you thought about what your life would be like in ten years *without* Honoria?"

Milo's hazel eyes roamed the room, from the wall that was covered with wine racks to the copper pots suspended from the ceiling and back again. "That depends on whether I'm still sheriff."

I tried not to look aghast. Maybe Honoria was right. I may have known Milo longer, but she knew him better. I'd run out of advice, and my sympathy was beginning to dry up. Fortunately, our salads arrived, and with them, Milo drifted off our main conversational course.

"I don't have a lock on this job," he said. "Take this Linda Lindahl thing. The voters aren't going to be happy with the fact that I can't even get a coroner's verdict until about Tuesday."

"That's because the county hasn't the funds to provide you with proper equipment and manpower." My tone was reasonable.

Milo gave a jerky nod. "Sure, you and I know that. But the voters aren't logical. If we put a bond issue on the ballot in March, they'll veto it, big time. But they'll still blame me because I can't solve crimes like some hokey sheriff on TV. Hell, Emma, I've got one hand tied behind my back, and the other one feels a little crippled. Once Marv Peterson gets over the shock, he's going to be breathing down my neck to find his daughter's killer."

"You must know something," I said, trying to sound less like a journalist and more like a friend. "Crime-scene stuff. Tire tracks? A struggle? Time of death?"

For the first time since we'd sat down, Milo grinned. "You're fishing, Emma. You're going to get skunked." The grin disappeared. "So am I, at least until we hear from Snohomish County."

I was wide-eyed. "You mean there was nothing of interest at the murder site?"

Milo pushed his empty salad plate to one side. "I didn't say that. There were tire tracks, all right. Plenty of them, including Vida's. The road crew has cleared a ten-foot strip on each side of the existing highway. That's where Vida parked. So did a lot of people— hunters, lovers, fishermen, even hikers who don't mind freezing their butts off. Footprints are another matter. The ground's covered with all kinds of growth, from berry vines to fallen branches to moss. We did our best trying to find a good print, but then it started to snow. If there was a struggle, we didn't see much sign of it."

I shuddered. "Why would anybody do that? Put her in that old rotten log, I mean. It's ghoulish."

"Murder is ghoulish," Milo muttered. He shrugged, and finished his second Scotch. "I figure the killer wanted to hide the body, and the log was handy. Whoever did it probably counted on the snowstorm and hoped Linda wouldn't be found until spring." He paused and gave me a sharp look. "That's a guess, Emma. You're not taking mental notes, I hope."

I was, of course. I always do. But I wasn't foolish enough to print the sheriff's speculations. Milo should know as much.

"It sounds as if the killer is a man," I remarked, the grisly statement contradicting my sunny smile for a departing couple I recognized as fellow shoppers at the Grocery Basket.

Milo must have known them, too, though he merely nodded. "Probably. Linda wasn't tiny. But we can't rule out a woman, unless she's feeble. Hell, you could have done the job, Emma. Strangling people when they don't expect it isn't as hard as you'd think. And the log was pretty big. It'd take some tugging and hauling, but it could be done by just about anybody."

"It would take some time," I noted. "But as I recall, that little clearing is shielded from the road. Or did the highway crew cut down the trees? I haven't been up that far on 187 since Big Mike Brockelman started working on it."

They had cut no trees, Milo assured me, only vine maples and underbrush. Linda and her killer would not have been visible from the road.

"But . . . you didn't find any . . . uh, clues?" I hated to use the word because I knew how much Milo and other law enforcement people despised it as amateurish.

"I already told you, no. It's a love nest, especially for teenagers in good weather. Also a drinking hangout. You can imagine what they leave behind." Milo looked disgusted.

"Any guesses about how long she'd been dead?" The question had barely escaped my lips when the waiter presented Milo's steak and my *coquilles Saint Jacques*. Fortunately, it takes a lot to make me lose my appetite.

Milo eyed his steak appreciatively. He, too, was made of sterner stuff. "It's hard to tell with the weather we've been having. That's another one for the forensics folks. If you really want a guess, I'd say twelve hours."

Vida and Roger had discovered the body around two

o'clock Saturday. Since the bank was open until six on Fridays, Linda had probably left work no earlier than six-thirty. In all probability, she had been killed somewhere between seven P.M. Friday and two A.M. Saturday. I hadn't yet dropped my little bombshell on Milo. But Vida might have beaten me to it.

"What was she wearing?" I asked, forking up a tender scallop.

"Clothes." Milo's eyes glinted. "You want a fashion description, go ask Francine Wells. Linda had on slacks, a sweater, a fuzzy hat, a long coat, boots—and that damned muffler. Oh, and underwear, I suppose." Once again, Milo was looking faintly embarrassed.

It was then that I told Milo about seeing Linda go into the Lumberjack Motel on Monday night. The sheriff was mildly surprised. I was amazed that Vida hadn't already relayed the news. But of course Roger had been her priority.

"It might not mean a thing," Milo allowed, "but we'll check the register."

I also informed Milo about the alleged custody fight. He confirmed that Reba's rumor was true: Larry or his wife had mentioned it when he called on them Saturday.

"Howard Lindahl will be questioned," Milo assured me. "Spouses and ex-spouses are always the primary suspects."

I studied Milo's face as he devoured three french fries at once. It certainly wasn't handsome, but it had character. It also had bread crumbs on the chin. Reaching across the table, I gave Milo a swipe with my napkin.

He looked chagrined. "See? Honoria would think I'm a clod."

"No, she wouldn't. Besides, I've probably got lettuce stuck between my teeth." I bared them for Milo's inspection, but he shook his head. For several moments, we ate in silence. I didn't know what Milo was thinking, but my mind was on the Petersens. "How are they taking it?" I finally asked.

"Depends," Milo replied, buttering more crusty bread. "Marv and Cathleen are a mess. Larry and Jo-Anne seem to be in shock. Denise is hard to figure. Kind of an airhead. Uncle Elmer and Aunt Thelma are a pair of stoics. Marv and Elmer's sister in Seattle is in New Zealand with her husband. The family—well, Marv, actually—decided to wait to tell them when they get back next week."

We were silent again, finishing our entreés. The waiter took our plates and inquired about dessert. We declined, but ordered Bailey's Irish Cream.

"You don't think a stranger killed Linda, do you, Milo?" I posed the question after our liqueur glasses had been delivered.

Slowly, Milo shook his head. "From what I know of Linda, she's not the type to go off with somebody she didn't know. And she did go off with whoever it was. Her car is still in the Parc Pines condo garage. I'd bet my badge that Linda knew her killer."

I wouldn't take that bet. The fact that Milo's reasoning ruled out a homicidal maniac should have been comforting.

But it wasn't. There was a killer among us, and the odds were excellent that the face was familiar.

Midway through Monday morning, I called Bob Lambrecht again in Seattle. My pretext was to ask if he'd received the courtesy copies of *The Advocate* that we'd sent him last week. The real reason, of course, was to try to wheedle more information out of him about his visit to the Bank of Alpine.

Bob was in a meeting. Since I'd identified myself as the editor and publisher of a newspaper, his secretary insisted on turning me over to the public-relations department. A brisk female voice came on the line and informed me that not only had Mr. Lambrecht received *The Advocate*, he had sent off a thank-you note. The PR staff had kept a copy for file.

"That's great," I said, trying to sound enthusiastic. Then, on a sudden whim, I tried an old newspaper ploy: "Is it true that the Bank of Washington plans to buy out the Bank of Alpine?"

The silence at the other end of the line lasted so long that I thought we'd been disconnected. Finally the voice lost some of its briskness:

"Just a moment, please."

Chewing my lower lip, I waited with a sense of excitement. I could hear nothing; the PR staffer must have hit the mute button. I was still waiting when Leo rapped once on my open door. I gestured for him to come in. He was still limping, and looked tired.

"The Bank of Washington has absolutely no plans to buy the Bank of Alpine," the brisk voice said suddenly in my ear. "Thank you for your interest."

I thanked her for the information. Or lack of it. My face must have registered surprise. Leo gave me a ghost of his cockeyed grin.

"Another stiff?" he asked, balancing precariously on the back legs of my visitor's chair.

"No." I frowned at the phone. "No bank buyout. That's odd."

"Why? It was never more than a rumor. Didn't you start it yourself?" Leo's brown eyes were amused.

I felt silly. "In a way. But it made sense."

Leo was ready to dismiss the bank, even if I wasn't.

"That's a hell of a thing about the Lindahl broad. You hear anything from the sheriff?"

I hadn't, and didn't expect to for at least another twenty-four hours. Upon arriving at work, I'd briefed my staff on what little I'd learned over the weekend. Leo was fascinated; Carla was indifferent; Ginny was distracted; Vida was annoyed. Having been pried loose from Roger, my House & Home editor felt left out. She had harrumphed into her typewriter and shortly thereafter had stomped out of the office. I suspected that her nephew, Deputy Bill Blatt, was about to get the third degree.

"What do you think?" Leo's dry voice cut into my thoughts.

"About ... what?" I was feeling as distracted as Ginny.

"Linda Lindahl. You've been here quite a while," Leo said, taking the last cigarette out of his pack. "You must know this cast of characters. Come on, babe, who-dunit?"

"I've no idea." It was true. "As I told you this morn-ing, ex-husbands are always good suspects. But so are spurned lovers and jealous rivals."

For a split second, I thought Leo flinched. Maybe I imagined it, or his ankle was hurting. Instead of making a further comment about Linda's death, he changed the subject. He was trying to get all the merchants at the mall to sponsor a special insert each Wednesday be-tween Thanksgiving and Christmas.

"You've always got a few who hang back, especially those fast-food restaurants," Leo explained. "The video arcade, too. But we'll offer a co-op deal they can't re-fuse."

I was impressed. Leo was limping out just as his predecessor bustled in. Ed Bronsky greeted Leo with a hearty slap on the back. He shook my hand so hard that I thought he'd dislocate my shoulder.

"Just the folks I want to see," Ed exclaimed. "Here, sit down, Leo, old buddy. I've got something really great for you and Emma."

I cringed. Leo looked wary, but resumed his seat. Ed wedged himself into the other visitor's chair. His right pinky sported a gold ring with a flashing ruby. The next thing I knew, Ed would be wearing spats.

"It's like this," Ed said, planting his pudgy fists on the edge of my desk. "We need to zap up the economy, right? At this week's chamber of commerce meeting I'm going to propose that the stores start decorating a week before Thanksgiving. Let's get this Christmas thing rolling. The longer the haul, the more we haul in. Get it?"

Leo and I exchanged dazed glances. "Uh . . ." I began, "the local merchants have a long-standing agreement not to decorate until after Thanksgiving. I think we should honor that. Many Seattle stores do."

Ed's laugh was derisive. "Seattle! What do *they* know? We don't have anything in common. Alpine's got big economic problems. You know it, I know it. Now we're going to act. Extended credit, that's the ticket. I intend to propose that any item costing over a hundred dollars requires only ten percent down and ninety days to pay without interest. How do you like them apples?" Sitting back in his chair, Ed folded his hands over his paunch and looked well pleased with himself.

Leo reached for a cigarette and came up empty. "I think it stinks," he replied, though his tone was affable. "The local merchants need cash flow. How do they ensure collecting? It sounds like Deadbeat City to me."

Ed wagged a finger at Leo. "Aha! That's where

you're wrong, Mr. Southern California. People in Alpine can be trusted. We're not like L.A. or even Seattle. A man's handshake is still good enough for us."

It was too soon in the day, too early in the week, for me to get a headache. But I felt one coming on. I saw Leo's skepticism, written as large on his face as his desire for a cigarette.

"Ed," I sighed, rubbing at my temples, "if you can talk the merchants into advertising for Christmas early, that's fine. But I honestly don't think they should start decorating until after Thanksgiving. It's just not right."

Ed shook his head in a manner that suggested I was a willful, stupid child. "That's sentiment talking, Emma. You're harking back to when you were a kid and those fancy-pants department stores in Seattle didn't unveil their Christmas stuff until Thanksgiving night. I know, I've heard you talk about stuffing yourself with turkey and then driving downtown to see the windows at the Bon Marché or Frederick & Nelson or one of those other ritzy places."

Ed was right. Alas, the once-fabled Frederick & Nelson was gone, but the Bon still held off until Thanksgiving to light its big star, and Nordstrom also waited to sparkle with Yuletide delights. But Ed was also wrong. Part of the merchandising mystique lay in anticipation. I stated my case for Ed.

"You're still talking Seattle," Ed responded, heaving himself out of the chair. "God only knows what they did in Portland while you lived there. But wait and see—the chamber will have a group pants-wetting by the time I'm through with them tomorrow."

With that sally, Ed departed.

Leo was looking bemused. "Was he always such a dumb fuck?"

"No. Yes." I couldn't explain Ed to Leo. I couldn't explain Ed to myself.

Apparently Vida had forgiven me. Upon her return, she insisted that we eat lunch at the Burger Barn. She also insisted that we go early, at eleven-thirty. I acquiesced, and at precisely eleven thirty-one, we were seated in the booth nearest the door.

"What's up?" I asked, noting that Vida had sat on the opposite side of the table where she could watch the entrance.

"Linda's funeral is Thursday, if the body has been released by Snohomish County by then," Vida replied, her eyes fixed on the door. "I called Al Driggers at the funeral home. The services will be held at the Lutheran church. The bank will be closed anyway on Thursday because of Veterans Day."

"And?" I knew Vida had much more to tell me. Usually she didn't need prodding.

Her gaze didn't waver. Two furtive teenagers who were undoubtedly skipping school entered the restaurant. "Milo went over to Everett this morning to talk to Howard Lindahl. He's not back yet." Vida barely blinked as Tara Wesley, co-owner of Parker's Pharmacy, and Nancy Dewey, Doc Dewey's wife, made their way to a booth at the other side of the small dining room. "Sam Heppner is at the Lumberjack Motel, checking out their guest list for last week. Jack Mullins is interrogating the other bank employees. The non-Petersens, that is. Dwight Gould has today off, though I can't think why, since there's a homicide investigation under way. Billy is holding down the fort."

Having accounted for all of Milo's deputies, Vida was ready to order. Our pudgy, middle-aged waitress, Jessie Lott, was as harried and efficient as ever. She trudged off to the kitchen while Vida announced that she was temporarily giving up her diet.

"So difficult, all these carbohydrates and proteins and grams of fat and such. You have to be a mathematician to keep track. What harm can an occasional fishwich do?"

Vida's diets never last long, though there are days when she sticks to her regimen of hot water, carrot and celery sticks, cottage cheese, and sometimes a hard-boiled egg. She never seems to lose weight, nor does she gain. Having ordered a french dip, I had no right to comment.

Vida had started telling me how she had nursed Roger back to a semblance of health when she suddenly interrupted herself. Springing halfway to her feet, she waved and called out to someone I couldn't see without turning to stare.

"Christie! Yoo-hoo!" Christie Johnston hesitated before approaching our booth. Vida was all smiles. "Do join us and I'll finish telling you how to protect your shrubs during cold weather."

Like most people, Christie couldn't refuse an invitation from Vida. As the bank teller sat down next to me, I realized why Vida had insisted on posting us by the door. Christie had been set up. No doubt Vida had learned earlier in the day when and where our new arrival was going to lunch.

"Isn't this cozy?" Vida was still beaming even as her brown fedora slipped to the rim of her glasses. While Christie mulled the menu, Vida recited a litany of floral precautions. I suspected that Christie wasn't paying close attention. I also figured that Vida had more than plantings on her mind.

And so she did. "What *will* you do?" Vida asked, from out of nowhere. She rarely worries about tactful transitions. Noting Christie's puzzled expression, Vida tipped the fedora back on her gray curls and inclined her head in a sympathetic manner. "Without Linda, I mean. You have no bookkeeper. How will the bank manage until Marv can find someone else?"

Christie looked relieved. Perhaps she was expecting a gardening quiz from Vida. "Andy Cederberg can handle the books for the time being. I could, as far as that goes. I've got quite a bit of experience working for banks."

Vida gave a quick nod. "Good, good. But you'll have to find somebody soon. The bank's busiest time of year is right around the corner."

"That's true." Christie had resumed studying the menu. She didn't seem particularly concerned about her employer's personnel problems. When Jessie Lott arrived with our orders, Christie put in hers, which was complicated by various substitutions and requests for "on the side." Jessie kept her patience, barely.

Vida nibbled her fishwich. "So sad," she remarked with a deep sigh. "Linda, I mean. You must be terribly upset."

Christie, who had been rearranging her thick brown curls with her fingers, gave a little start. "Upset? Oh, of course! It's terrible!" Her sharp features assumed a sorrowful air.

"You weren't close." It wasn't a question from Vida, but a statement of fact.

"Not really." Christie seemed to be eyeing my french dip with longing. "Troy and I had her over for a barbecue last summer. She never asked us back. I think Linda was antisocial."

"Did she bring a beau?" Vida was so matter-of-fact that I wondered if Christie realized she was being pumped.

Christie shook her head, but waited to speak until

Jessie Lott had delivered the baconburger basket with its extensive variations. "Linda was going with some guy from Sultan, I think. The only reason I know about him is that one day she had to leave early because his car broke down this side of Index and she had to go rescue him."

Having played Vida's stooge since Christie sat down, I felt it was time to speak up: "Do you know who he was?"

Christie didn't. "I don't think she'd been seeing him for quite a while now. Linda didn't bring anybody to the Petersens' Labor Day picnic."

Nor did Christie know where Linda had gone after work on Friday. In fact, Linda had still been at the bank when Christie left at six-twenty. "She and Andy Cederberg were usually the last to leave," Christie added. "Linda closed the books for the day, and Andy locked up."

I saw the glint in Vida's eyes and knew what she was thinking. Linda and Andy as a couple didn't seem likely, but anything was possible. Vida did not, however, press the point with Christie.

"You must be tired of so many questions," Vida said, polishing off her coleslaw. "I understand Jack Mullins interrogated everyone at the bank this morning."

Christie seemed to have lost interest in Linda's murder. Her gaze was wandering about the dining room, apparently taking in the cutouts of turkeys, Pilgrims, Indians, cornucopias, and *The Mayflower* that were suspended from the ceiling.

"Oh—yes, he talked to Andy and Rick and me. There wasn't much we could tell him. You don't want to guess." Christie's brown eyes finally came back to our level.

Vida pounced. "Guess? At what?" She tried to hide

her eagerness by casually tipping her hat back on her head.

Christie shrugged. "The obvious. Linda picked up some guy in a bar and he killed her. What else could have happened?"

Since Vida had now managed to knock her hat onto the floor, I intervened. "Was that a habit with Linda?"

Christie looked troubled by the question. "I don't know if you'd call it a habit, but Troy and I saw her one night last spring at Mugs Ahoy. She came in alone and left with some guy from the bowling alley. It looked to us like she came on to him. But maybe we were wrong," she added hastily.

Jessie Lott had presented all three of us with separate checks. Christie, who had eaten very fast, announced that she had to run. She could only take half an hour for lunch because Denise Petersen was home with her grieving family. Vida and I lingered over my coffee and her tea.

"Christie didn't like Linda much," Vida remarked. "Nobody did, it seems. How sad."

It was very sad. Now I, too, stared up at the cheerful Thanksgiving cutouts. It was the bright-eyed turkey that caught my eye. Plump and unsuspecting, the big bird reminded me of Linda Lindahl. Neither knew what fate held in store for them.

I must have had a wry expression on my face, for Vida asked what I was thinking.

"About neck-wringing," I said. "Gruesome, huh?"

Vida glanced at the turkey as she got out of the booth. "But apt. Let's go see the Petersens."

"We can't," I protested. "They're mourning. Milo said Marv and Cathleen were a mess, and Larry and JoAnne are in shock."

Vida made exact change at the register. "I don't mean

those Petersens," she said as we left the Burger Barn. "I'm talking about Elmer and Thelma. Thelma and I went through school together. I'd feel terrible if I *didn't* call on her. You might as well come along."

I had qualms. I'd never met the Elmer Petersens. My desk was piled with work for the Wednesday edition. But, like Christie Johnson, I couldn't turn down Vida's offer. In less than ten minutes, we had pulled onto the dirt road that led off Highway 187 to the Petersen farm.

The house was shielded from the road by two huge holly bushes that must have been planted when the foundation was laid forty years ago. Unlike the well-maintained homes in town that belonged to the Marvin and the Larry Petersens, Elmer and Thelma lived in genteel squalor. The house was large, and its white paint had faded to gray. The roof was tin, as are many in Alpine, to better ward off the winter snows. The ramshackle barn looked as if a strong wind might topple it, and the chicken coop definitely listed to starboard. Two scruffy Morgan horses grazed behind barbed wire. Except for some withered cornstalks, the vegetable garden was plowed under. And everywhere there were stumps, remnants of trees that had been cut not to create a view, but for firewood.

"Thelma's no housekeeper," Vida murmured as we waded through mud to the wide verandah. "Be careful where you sit."

Thelma Petersen embraced Vida with a reserved show of affection. Tall and gaunt, she bore a familial resemblance to her nephew, Milo Dodge. Elmer greeted us in what sounded like a series of grunts. He was a heavier, older version of his brother, Marv, and his face was weathered and weary.

We were led into what Thelma quaintly called the

parlor. Vida's advice was well taken. On the first try, I almost sat on a chicken.

After the introductions and condolences, Thelma offered coffee. Vida declined, and gave me her gimlet eye. Judging from the amount of feathers, animal hair, and just plain dust, I surmised that sanitation might be a problem.

"Damnedbastardsoutthere." Elmer was muttering into his bib overalls. He was almost impossible to understand.

Thelma gave her husband a flinty look. "Time will tell," she said cryptically.

Vida was perched stiffly on the edge of a rail-back chair with a worn leather seat. "What will it tell, Thelma?"

Our hostess gave her husband a scornful look. "Elmer is convinced that Linda was killed by the Republicans. He blames everything on the Republicans. Elmer's still mad at Herbert Hoover." Thelma discussed her husband as if he weren't in the same room.

Vida sniffed. "Elmer had better get over it. Besides, there's a Democrat in the White House now. Don't blame me—I didn't vote for him. Arkansas! Imagine!" Vida all but spat on the floor, which probably wouldn't have mattered, given the accumulation of dirt and other filth.

"DamnedfoolGOP. MoviestarsandCIAspooks." Elmer muttered away on the tattered mohair sofa. Next to me, the chicken flapped its wings and took off for the kitchen.

Vida seemed equally capable of ignoring Elmer. "I take it you must have a different theory of what happened to poor Linda." Her comment was directed at Thelma Petersen.

Thelma, however, shook her head with its topknot of silver hair. "As I told Milo, she never showed up."

Vida gave a slight start and I swiveled in the faded faux velvet armchair. "Never showed up where?" Vida inquired.

Thelma looked as if Vida ought to know. But of course everyone in Alpine assumed that Vida always knew everything. Usually she did. "Here," Thelma replied. "Linda called around seven to say she was coming by. She never showed up." For a fleeting moment, Thelma's long chin quivered.

"FederalReserveBoard. CIA. Country'srunbybothof'em. Bankexaminers—huntedLindadown." The chicken had returned, and was now squatting on Elmer's lap.

"Why," Vida asked, her forehead furrowed, "was Linda calling on you?"

Thelma's steel spine was back in place. "She didn't tell me. She said Larry was coming, too. But when they hadn't showed up after over an hour, I called Larry and he didn't know anything about it."

"Were you worried?" I felt duty-bound to ask questions of my own.

"Not really." Thelma's face showed regret, however. "It wasn't the first time that Linda had promised to visit and then backed out at the last minute. She never spent much time with us. Or with her own parents, for that matter. Linda was what you'd call a loner."

Vida nodded sagely. "She and Larry never got along when they were children. Typical sibling rivalry."

Thelma shot Elmer another contemptuous look. "Typical Petersens. Cat and dog, black and white. No sense of family ties between brothers and sisters. Elmer and Marv have always wrangled. They couldn't agree that the sun will come up tomorrow."

"Itwon't," Elmer retorted. "Toodamnedcloudy. MarvvotedforIke. Nixontoo."

Vida could hardly keep from sneering at Elmer's political views. But her question was for Thelma. "Did Linda and Larry often come together to visit?"

"Never," Thelma replied. "I wondered if there was some family ruckus. A row with their father, maybe. But after . . . afterwards, I asked Larry, and he said no. He couldn't imagine what Linda was talking about or why she thought he was coming here with her. Larry and JoAnne were having a card party that night."

Vida was looking thoughtful, until a goat wandered into the parlor. I tensed, and clutched my handbag. Thelma paid no more attention to the animal than she did to her husband.

"Ornerycuss," Elmer remarked, giving the goat a dirty look. "Larrylethimlooselastweek. Name'sGoldwater."

"A handsome beast," Vida said, standing up and sidestepping Goldwater. "Intelligent eyes, too." She patted Thelma's bony shoulder, but ignored Elmer as we began our progress to the door. When Vida's back was turned, I smiled at our host, who was petting the chicken.

"Who's that?" I asked.

Elmer's small blue eyes regarded me with suspicion. "ClareBoothLuce," he replied. "She'sagoodlay . . . er." Elmer winked. I could have sworn that the chicken did, too.

Chapter Seven

BY FOUR-THIRTY on Tuesday afternoon, I was a nervous wreck. We were up against deadline, and Milo Dodge still hadn't heard from the Snohomish County medical examiner. To be fair, Milo's emotional state wasn't much better than mine.

"It's a big county over there," he allowed, grumbling into the phone. "They had their share of homicides over the weekend. For every one we get in Skykomish County, they get a dozen. How do you think I feel? The voters will want my hide if I don't make some progress. Not to mention that the longer they wait in Everett to examine the body, the harder it's going to be to fix the time of death. But then it's not their body—or their sheriff."

So far, I had only the bare bones of the homicide story, which was all over town anyway. *The Advocate* was about to go to press with stale news. My county commissioners coverage was as dull as warmed-over mush, and the photographs I'd taken weren't worth running. The focal point of the front page would be Carla's two-column picture of the murder site, which conveyed no drama, since the log had been removed by the sheriff. Linda Lindahl's head shot looked as if it had come off of her driver's license. Frustrated, I lashed out at Milo.

"Can't you guys do *anything* on your own? What about alibis? The motel register? Strangers sighted in town, anything that might pump up our front page?"

Milo retaliated. "Since when did you start printing rumors? Come off it, Emma. You always brag about how you deal only in facts. What's with you, midlife crisis?"

Milo's rebuke stung. But it was fair. I simmered down. "Okay," I sighed. "Buy me a drink after work. Then I'll buy you one. Then we'll be even."

I'd barely hung up when Leo limped into the office. The chamber of commerce had voted down Ed Bronsky's plan to put up Christmas decorations before Thanksgiving. It had been close, however, and would be reconsidered next year. The main problem, according to Ed, had been that most merchants couldn't dismantle their Thanksgiving displays and get out their Christmas trimmings in time.

Ed had, however, prevailed with his plan to extend credit. I agreed with Leo that it was a bad idea. Still, it probably would spur more advertising in the newspaper.

"The problem will be collecting in February," Leo noted as he showed me his layouts for the next edition. "What do you think of the Veterans Day insert?"

I thought it was just fine. Leo's idea to have various merchants take out individual ads thanking Alpine's living war veterans had elicited an enthusiastic response. He had managed to talk Al Driggers of Driggers Funeral Home into buying a half page, listing deceased servicemen who were buried in the local cemetery. I congratulated Leo on his ingenuity and powers of persuasion.

"No big deal, babe," he replied, taking back the layouts. "Driggers can pay for the ad with the money he makes just standing around looking like a stiff himself at Linda's funeral. I hear the Petersens are going all out for the poor broad."

I tried not to wince at Leo's crassness. But before I could think of a proper rejoinder, Leo continued: "Speaking of money, that bank deal isn't working out so great. I took my Toyota into the dealership at lunchtime to check out a problem with the tape deck and they told me they hadn't gotten my payment this month. Do you think I should ask Larry Petersen about it? I hate to bother him right now."

I was glad I hadn't winced. Basically, Leo has a good heart. His cynicism is caused by many things, including the typical newspaperman's—and woman's—need to put up barriers between the job and the heart.

But I couldn't answer his question. "Well . . . you could wait until after the funeral. If Alpine Toyota isn't getting nasty, of course."

Leo lighted a cigarette. "I told them about this proxy deal. They thought maybe Linda getting murdered had screwed things up. If the payment doesn't come through in a day or so, maybe their bookkeeper will call the bank."

"What about your rent?" I asked, sniffing wistfully at Leo's smoke.

Leo shrugged. "My landlord was last seen trying to teach his cocker spaniel how to play a guitar. Dolph Terrill's a real rummy. That was one of my problems with those overdrafts. The old asshole sat on my checks forever. That's what threw my accounting out of whack."

I nodded. Dolph Terrill only needed enough money to keep himself in booze. I was about to say as much when the phone rang.

It was Milo, and he sounded slightly more cheerful. "Okay, Lois Lane, here's something for your stop-the-presses. We—we being those dumbbells from the Skykomish County sheriff's office—did a check on Linda's car. The dirt in the tires showed a match with the new verge off Highway 187. She had her car up there, all right. You can print that."

I squeezed the receiver as if it could divulge more information. "Linda drove to the murder site?"

"Somebody did," Milo replied. "The only thing we know for sure is that she didn't drive back."

Oren Rhodes, the bartender at the Venison Inn, personally served Milo and me. Like everyone else in town, he was full of questions about Linda's murder. As usual, Milo fended them off with vague, noncommittal answers.

"Well?" Milo said to me after Oren had gone back behind the bar. "You got enough to perk up your front page?"

"The dirt bit helps," I admitted. That Linda's car had been driven to the murder site opened up much speculation. But in terms of actual news value, it only qualified for paragraph three. "At least it's fresh information."

Sipping his Scotch, Milo seemed satisfied. "I saw Howard Lindahl this afternoon."

I had forgotten that Milo was calling on Linda's ex-husband. I didn't know whether to kick Milo—or myself. "Now, *that's* news," I exclaimed, choking on my bourbon. I sputtered briefly, then gave Milo my sternest look. "Why didn't you say so earlier?"

Milo was unmoved. "What's to say? He's shocked, he's sorry, he's upset for their daughter. I didn't get much out of him to help either of us. His alibi's a little shaky, but you can't print that."

I had to agree. "What's shaky about it?"

Milo pulled a toothpick out of his shirt pocket and began to munch. "For one thing, we still don't have a real handle on the time of death, and won't, until we hear from the M.E. Even then, I don't expect to come within more than two–three hours of the exact time. But if we assume—take in that word, Emma; it's like your 'alleged'—if we assume that Linda was killed sometime after seven P.M. on Friday and before sunup Saturday, then we've got alibi problems with every suspect. The killer could have gone to bed with whoever, and sneaked out during the night. That's one scenario."

"Great." Discouraged, I took a slow pull on my bourbon.

"As for Howie Lindahl, he says he had an appointment with some guy at the cabinet shop around eight. The guy never showed." Milo's hazel eyes waited for my reaction.

"Who was the guy?" I asked.

"His name was Dick Johnson, from Seattle." Again Milo eyed me expectantly.

I knew, along with everybody else raised in the Puget Sound basin, that Johnson was the most common name in the area. Not Smith, not Jones, not Brown—the Scandinavian influence was so great that the listings for Johnson, and its various spellings, took up eight pages in the Seattle phone directory. Forty listings could qualify as Dick Johnson.

"Do you believe Howie?" I asked.

Obviously Milo had considered the problem. "I kind of lean that way. For one thing, his wife took the call. Or says she did."

We both knew that one spouse will lie for the sake of the other. That might be especially true with the murder investigation of an ex-wife.

"If the call was long distance from Seattle, can't the phone company trace it?" I asked.

Milo squinted at his Scotch. "We're working on it," he said vaguely, nodding at a couple of millworkers who apparently were still employed. "Howie and Susan—that's the new wife—seem like decent folks. I didn't see the kid. She was in school. Howie and Susan thought it would be best for her to stay in the routine. She's at a real bad age for this to happen."

There's never a good age to lose a parent, as I well knew. Both of mine had been killed in an automobile accident when I was twenty. I doubted that I would have been more bereft if I'd been twelve or even forty-two.

"Besides," Milo continued, definitely in one of his more loquacious moods, "this is their second brush with the law in a week. They're beginning to feel jinxed."

"Really? What else happened to them?" I smiled at Big Mike Brockelman and his five-man crew as they headed for the bar.

Milo was frowning at Big Mike's broad back, which was covered with a plaid work shirt and wide black suspenders. "Huh? Oh, the Lindahls had a break-in last Thursday night while they were at an open house for Alison's school. Nothing was taken, but it upset the hell out of the family. It always does; I can vouch for that." Milo was still observing Big Mike.

"That's natural," I said, then leaned across the tiny table to hiss in his ear: "What's with you? Are you keeping Brockelman and his men under surveillance?"

Milo turned back to me with a sheepish grin. "I was

wondering how I'd look in suspenders. They're kind of in these days, aren't they?"

If Milo thought suspenders would improve his chances with Honoria Whitman, he was wrong. "Leave the suspenders to bankers like Marv Petersen. And big burly guys like Mike. You look just fine the way you are, Milo. Stop fussing."

My compliment made no dent on Milo. He was frowning as he finished his Scotch. "Oh," he said suddenly, his voice dropping a notch, "I forgot to tell you about the Lumberjack Motel register. Nothing for print, right?"

"Probably not." I was giving up on Milo as a source of hot new information. But he'd paid for our first drinks, so I felt obligated to string him along and pick up the tab for a second round.

Catching Oren Rhodes's eye, I waited to ask Milo about the motel until after the bartender had brought our reorders. "So who's sleeping with whom?" I inquired as Oren returned to his bantering with the highway crew.

"Business wasn't booming at the Lumberjack last week," Milo said, lowering his voice. "Not the Tall Timber Inn or the ski lodge, either. We checked all of them, at least for Friday night. As far as your sighting of Linda on Monday is concerned, there were six registrations at the Lumberjack. An older couple traveling from Montana, a salesman for some countertop outfit in Seattle, a detail man who calls on Parker's Pharmacy and the medical clinic regularly, a pair of honeymooners from Yakima, a kid from Wenatchee Junior College whose car wouldn't start after he pulled off to eat at the Burger Barn, and Big Mike Brockelman." Milo's eyes slid in the direction of the bar.

I felt a rush of excitement. "Have you talked to Mike?"

Milo shook his head. "It's kind of tricky."

"Why?" My excitement was replaced by exasperation.

"For one thing, Brockelman's been out working on the highway yesterday and today. They've got a deadline to meet, especially if we get more snow. I'll admit, he's the most likely of the motel guests to have been banging Linda Lindahl, but we can't rule out the countertop guy or even the college kid. Doc Dewey and Marje Blatt swear the pharmaceutical rep is a real straight arrow."

I recalled the eager young man I'd seen lunching with Scooter Hutchins the previous Monday. Mr. Countertop, probably. He looked like the type that Linda Lindahl would have eaten alive. Mentally I crossed him off my list of possible lovers. I was inclined to do the same with the college student from Wenatchee JC.

Then, as if to prove that a second bourbon hadn't dulled my wits, I remembered my phone call to Mike Brockelman. "Mike was at home in Monroe when I talked to him Monday. Why would he drive up to Alpine in the evening *unless* he had a tryst with Linda?"

Milo gave a shrug. "To get an early start the next day? He had to catch up because they couldn't work Monday."

It seemed to me that Milo was going too far in rationalizing Mike Brockelman's behavior. "Can it, Milo. Mike's your man. And don't look at me like that. I know that just because he was sleeping with Linda doesn't mean he killed her. What about Friday's motel guests?"

"A washout." Milo gnawed on his toothpick. "Mostly couples, either visiting friends and family here, or older folks who were afraid of the weather and decided to pull off the pass for the night. The only two singles were both at the ski lodge. They're a couple of California developers cruising the area for exploitation purposes. Those guys are too busy putting together deals to take time out for murder."

There was a grain of truth in Milo's statement. Traditionally, Pacific Northwesterners have despised Californians who move north to make a fast buck. But recently I've sensed that not everybody wants to yank the welcome mat from under outsiders who can help our sagging economy. Thus, I offered no criticism of the men from California.

"In other words," I said, getting back to the more pressing matter of murder, "there were no strangers that you know of romping through Alpine last Friday night."

Milo nodded and discarded his toothpick. "But strangers who kill don't necessarily check into motels and hotels. We can't eliminate the possibility of an outsider, or someone from down the pass."

I had to agree. I wanted to, in fact, since it suggested that Linda might not have been killed by an Alpiner. But several facets of the case nagged at me. "How do you explain the dirt on her tires? Are you saying she drove to the clearing off 187, but the killer returned the car and parked it in her condo garage?"

"Somebody did, and it probably wasn't Linda." Milo pulled out another toothpick and began to make marks with it on his cocktail napkin. "First of all, it *could* have been Linda. Let's say she met somebody—maybe her killer, maybe not—out at the clearing. Or she was heading for Aunt Thelma and Uncle Elmer's, changed her mind about seeing them, drove on up the road, and turned around on the verge to come home. She parked the car in the garage, and left with her killer." Milo leaned far back in his chair; I worried that he might tip over.

"That all makes sense—I think. I suppose you checked the car keys for fingerprints?"

"Sure. We got zip. They're all smudged."

I remembered Linda's gloves. Just about everybody in Alpine wears gloves this time of year, except me. "Where were the keys?"

"On an end table, next to the sofa. Sam Heppner found them when he and Dwight Gould went to the condo." Milo crumpled up the cocktail napkin, then let it fall onto the tabletop.

Mulling over motives, I asked an obvious question. "Did Linda have any money?"

Milo wrinkled his long nose. "Not big bucks. After the divorce, Linda and Howard sold their property in Everett. They split the profits, which were just enough for each of them to use as down payments on Howie's house and Linda's condo. Marv had given her some good advice about investments, but they were mostly long-term. I don't suppose her estate is worth more than a hundred grand, including life insurance."

"Did she have a will?"

Milo nodded. "A simple one, drawn up after the split. Everything goes to the daughter. It's in trust, until she's eighteen."

In other words, Howard Lindahl would have control of Linda's money. A vague sense of unease settled over me. "What about those alibis?" I asked.

"What about those suspects?" Milo sounded wry. "Sure, I'll talk to Big Mike, maybe this evening, if he sticks around. We've questioned Linda's family and her coworkers. Howie and Susan Lindahl. That's it. If they're suspects, then everybody has some kind of alibi for Friday evening. Howie was home or waiting for Dick Johnson. Larry and JoAnne were giving a card party. Marv and Cathleen entertained those two new attorneys in the Doukas firm. The Cederbergs were home—together, with their kids. Rick Erlandson went to the movies with Denise Petersen. Christie Johnston and her husband rented a video. Uncle Elmer and Aunt Thelma went to bed with the chickens."

Literally, I assumed. "You don't seriously consider Uncle Elmer and Aunt Thelma, do you, Milo?"

Milo's face drooped. "I have to consider everybody."

Milo was right. Unfortunately, at this point, everybody in Alpine was a suspect.

Vida didn't think much of Milo's investigation so far. She particularly didn't like the idea of her fellow Alpiners being under suspicion.

"Is Milo a bigger fool than I thought?" she demanded over the phone. "Does he seriously think Marv and Cathleen would kill their own daughter? Or Thelma and Elmer? Or . . . ooooh!" I could practically hear Vida rub her eyes. "It's got to be an outsider. Big Mike Brockelman is from Monroe. He qualifies. I'd like to see that motel register for myself. What if Mike and Linda signed in as man and wife?"

"They'd have been recognized," I pointed out. "Mike stayed there Monday night. His picture has been in *The Advocate*."

"People don't notice things. Are you in your bathrobe, Emma?"

I wasn't, having just finished the meager meal I'd prepared after getting home from the Venison Inn's bar.

"It's only seven-fifteen," Vida said. "I'll pick you up

as soon as I put Cupcake to bed. He's been very frac-
tious today. I think having Roger here upset Cupcake's
routine." Cupcake was Vida's canary. I wondered if
Roger had slipped the bird a mind-altering drug. I
wouldn't put it past the kid.

The plan to peruse the motel registers had a certain
appeal. I trust Milo, but as a journalist, I firmly believe
in verification. Besides, I had nothing better to do.

The phone rang again just as I was putting on my
boots. Perhaps Vida had changed her mind. But when I
picked up the receiver, there was no response. There
was also no click. I said hello about four times, then
banged down the phone. Another wrong number, I supposed, or mischievous kids. The imperious sound of a
car horn put the call out of my mind.

It was raining as Vida steered her big Buick into the
Lumberjack Motel's parking lot. On this Monday night,
there were only four other cars, two with Washington
plates, one from Oregon, and the other from Idaho.

The motel office was small, but tidy and pleasant.
Mel and Minnie Harris had bought the property from
one of the Gustavsons several years ago. The Harrises
were from Seattle, and Mel had taken early retirement
from the phone company. He and his wife had fled the
city's turmoil for the rustic peace of Alpine. They probably wouldn't appreciate being connected to a homicide
investigation.

Minnie was on duty, or at least it was she who came
into the office from the Harrises' living quarters. A
chunky, sharp-eyed woman in her late fifties, Minnie
recognized Vida at once.

"Mrs. Runkel." She put out a pudgy hand. "You were
at the Burl Creek Thimble Club a while back."

"So I was." Vida tossed off the rejoinder as if she'd

been spotted at the Oscars. "Your annual board election. Have you met Emma Lord?"

We had met, though neither of us were sure when or where. Perhaps, Minnie suggested, it had been at *The Advocate*. She had brought in an ad at the beginning of tourist season, back in the days when Ed Bronsky wouldn't get off his fat rear to personally solicit the local merchants.

Vida explained why we had come to the Lumberjack. Actually, she phrased the words in a vague sort of way, suggesting that we were actually interested in a story on off-season tourism.

"You're checking for homicide suspects," Minnie said flatly. "Don't try to fool me; the sheriff's deputy was here already today." Minnie shoved the guest register in front of us. "Here, take a look. You won't find much, I'm afraid. The deputy didn't."

Minnie Harris was right. The guests who had signed in Friday, November fifth, definitely sounded innocuous. The names and addresses had a ring of authenticity. And Minnie Harris vouched for them.

"I was on duty that night, too. Not a weirdo in the lot," she declared, adjusting the clip that held her long gray hair in place.

Vida was still studying the register. "Thursday—this Priestly person. Who was that?"

Minnie broke into a big smile. "Chuck Priestly. He's an old friend of Mel's. They started out in the commercial department at the phone company together. Chuck retired when Mel did. He stayed with us before heading on to hunt in Eastern Washington Friday."

Vida hid her disappointment well. But she wasn't giving up. "On Wednesday, there's a name I can't make out. Very cramped penmanship. Tsk, tsk." She turned the register around so that Minnie could have a look.

Putting on the glasses that had been hanging on a chain around her neck, Minnie frowned at the page. Then she brightened and removed her glasses.

"Ruggiero, that's the name. D. M. He spent two nights." She tapped the page with a fingernail that looked as if it had been well chewed. "See, he was here Tuesday *and* Wednesday."

Vida had fixed Minnie with her formidable gaze. "Who is he?"

Minnie didn't waver under Vida's scrutiny. "A businessman. He asked for the corporate rate." She pointed again to the registration. "See? His address is downtown, on Third Avenue."

I was trying to place the location. "Did he use a corporate credit card?"

Minnie looked as if she were going to balk, but sighed instead, and went over to an old steel filing cabinet. "You know," she began, her back turned to us, "Mel and I left Seattle to get away from all that corporate claptrap. You wouldn't believe what he went through with the phone company the last few years while divestiture was going on. We wouldn't care if the Mayor and the whole damned City Council showed up in Alpine. But," she added, waving a charge slip at us, "we'd take their money."

I looked around Vida's shoulder while she examined the merchant's copy of the motel charge. The only information on the imprint was the card number, the name of Daniel M. Ruggiero, and the expiration date.

"That's not much help," Vida said. She sounded as if she were chiding Minnie. "Exactly what is that address on Third Avenue?"

Minnie was beginning to lose patience. "Twelve-oh-one. I think. You're right, the handwriting's hard to read." She picked up the charge slip and firmly closed the register. "I'm sorry, that's all I know about Mr. Ruggiero. He wasn't a talker."

Vida turned to me. "Twelve-oh-one Third—what is it? You ought to know, Emma. You're from Seattle." She swung around to look at Minnie. "So are you. Well? Don't either of you know your own hometown?"

For the life of me, I couldn't recall what stood on the twelve-hundred block of Third Avenue. "I haven't actually lived in Seattle for over twenty years, Vida. It's changed beyond recognition."

"She's right," Minnie chimed in. "It's even changed since we moved in 1988. They've built one skyscraper after the other downtown. You might as well be in New York."

Vida was not appeased by our excuses. "As I mentioned earlier, people don't notice things." Though Vida seemed to be speaking to herself, the rebuke was clearly intended for Minnie and me.

Minnie's sharp eyes had narrowed. "I told you the sheriff's deputy didn't get anywhere. What did you expect?"

Vida squared her shoulders. "I expected women to do better than men. That's often the case."

To my surprise, Minnie took the challenge. "Would it be any help to tell you that Mr. Ruggiero didn't use a credit card?"

Puzzled, I stared at Minnie. "But . . . you just showed us the charge slip."

Minnie nodded. "It was what they call a debit card. I think it comes directly out of your checking account or a line of credit. They're not common, but certain banks issue them."

That was when I suddenly remembered what stood at

Twelve-oh-one Third Avenue. It was relatively new, it was architecturally splendid—and it was the Bank of Washington Tower.

Chapter Eight

CARLA WAS THREATENING suicide. Again. I tried to ignore her, but it wasn't easy, especially when she began to make a noose.

"I thought you were going to jump off the bridge over the Sky," I said, trying not to sound caustic. It was Wednesday, and another edition would hit the mailboxes by midafternoon. Between issues, my work attitude tends to be cavalier until I start getting irate phone calls and threatening letters.

"It's too cold." Carla seemed to be having trouble with her knot. "I'm going to climb onto the bandstand at Old Mill Park and hang myself from that big hemlock."

"It's a western cedar," I pointed out. "Where did you get the rope?"

Fumbling away, Carla swore under her breath. "I found it out by my car the other morning. I put it under the seat so I could throw it away later. You know how I feel about litter. Drat!" Frustrated, she threw the rope across the room, narrowly missing Leo, who was on the phone. Propping up her chin with her hands, Carla uttered an exaggerated sigh. "Are you sure that's not a hemlock in Old Mill Park? I could drink from it and die that way."

"I'm sure," I replied cheerfully. "There are lots of

hemlock trees around, though. But wouldn't it be easier to meet a new man?"

"No." Carla sounded definite, and it was hard to disagree with her. I certainly hadn't found a new man in Alpine, or anywhere else.

"How are those pictures coming?" I inquired, hoping to divert Carla from morbid thoughts.

"I've taken three rolls so far. Indoors, outdoors, morning, noon, and night shots. I didn't drop them off at Buddy Bayard's studio until this morning. He's taking tomorrow off for the holiday, so he won't have the contact sheets until Monday. I told them there was no hurry." A defensive note chimed in Carla's voice. "Isn't that what you said?"

I nodded and smiled encouragement. "That's right. Go ahead and shoot a couple more rolls if you feel like it."

Carla looked as if she felt more like retrieving the noose. At that moment, Ginny entered the news office, carrying the morning mail. Her previously glum face was set with determination. She looked like a woman on a mission.

"I've got an idea," she declared, dropping a three-inch stack of envelopes on the top of Vida's crowded in-basket. Vida wasn't at her desk, having gone off to interview Grace Grundle about a recent trip to Topeka. "Why don't we run classified ads for singles? Not just for Alpine, but Skykomish, Snohomish, and Chelan Counties."

Leo glanced up from his phone call, one eyebrow raised. Carla was unresponsive. My initial reaction was negative, but then I began to see possibilities, including new revenue for *The Advocate*.

"We'd have to set certain standards," I said, taking my mail from Ginny. "We'd also have to do some advertising of our own in the other two counties to let them know about the ads."

"Creeps," Carla said. "Perverts. Ax murderers. That's what we'll get, Gin. Did you ever know of anybody who met a decent guy through a singles ad?"

"Yes, I do." Ginny all but stamped her foot. "My cousin Beverly in Redmond met her husband through an ad in *The Weekly*. He works for Microsoft and he's really nice. Don't you remember when I went to their wedding a year or so ago?"

If Carla recalled the event, she pretended otherwise. "I'll bet he looks like Mr. Porkery. Or is a complete dweeb."

"Dwayne's both, but he treats Beverly like a queen. Looks aren't everything, Carla. Neither is personality." Ginny's face was slightly flushed.

"It's nice to have one or the other," Carla retorted.

"I'd settle for a decent guy with a job about now," Ginny replied. She dumped Leo's mail on his desk and tromped out of the news office.

The rain was drumming on the roof. Withdrawing to my office, I found Leo right behind me. He sat down, and from across the desk I noted that his eyes were slightly bloodshot. It was probably best not to ask any questions. I kept telling myself that what Leo did in his private life was none of my business. Certainly he seemed stone-cold sober this morning.

"It's not a bad idea," he said without preamble. "It's lucrative. Hell, singles have more money than married people. Not that you won't get a few of those, looking for some action on the side."

I scowled at Leo. "That's one of the reasons I don't like it. We're not a dating service, we're a newspaper."

Leo snorted. "Shit, just about everybody runs personals these days. What makes this rag so high-and-mighty? Besides the fact that you're running it?"

I narrowed my eyes at Leo. "That's the bottom line."

Leo shrugged. "Fine. So how's your love life, babe? You got the guys standing in line taking a number?" Before I could utter a stinging rebuke, Leo grinned and held up a hand. "Hold it, I'm not insulting you. That's my point. You're single, you're smart, you're damned attractive, you're a lot of fun when you're not trying to take my head off. But look at this place." He swept an arm around my little office. "No pictures of handsome hunks, no phones ringing off the hook, no flowers with discreet little notes tucked amid the greenery. If you can't get a date, who can? Without help, I mean."

As far as I was concerned, the only thing that made a dent was the remark about flowers. Primly I wrote myself a note to stop by Posies Unlimited and get something for Linda's funeral. It was the least I could do.

"I'll think about it," I said through prissy lips. "I'm always interested in new sources of revenue."

"Ginny's sharp," Leo noted, his bloodshot eyes regarding me with more amusement than I liked. "Don't discourage her when she comes up with new ideas."

In truth, Ginny's imagination wasn't her strong suit. She had had her last idea the previous spring when she'd suggested that Alpine perk up its economy and its image by holding a Summer Solstice Festival, rather than the somewhat arcane Loggerama. To my credit, I had supported her, and presented the proposal to the chamber of commerce. They were still mulling.

Leo mistook my silence for disagreement. "Look, how many single guys move to Alpine? Not counting yours truly, of course. The newcomers are all families, mostly commuters to Everett and Monroe. When was the last time you saw a strange man in Alpine?"

"About five minutes ago when you came into my office," I retorted, then had a sudden flashback. My attitude changed swiftly. I leaned toward Leo, unfortunately knocking over the stack of mail with my bosom. "Leo—remember the man we saw at the Venison Inn last week? The one you had the waitress check out?"

Leo was eyeing my bosom. He seemed to approve. I ignored him. "Sure, why?" He didn't raise his eyes.

Somewhat awkwardly, I crossed my arms over my chest. "Didn't you say he looked like a banker?"

Leo's expression was droll. "That I did. He looked like a stuffed shirt, which could translate as a banker. So?" His forehead creased as he finally stared at my face.

The phone rang before I could respond. If I have someone in my office, I usually let the call trunk over to Ginny. But I was anxious to hear from Milo Dodge. I grimaced at Leo in apology, and picked up the receiver.

It was Milo, all right, and he had news. I was elated, despite the fact that we had already gone to press. By next week's edition, we might have wrapped up the homicide investigation. Then again, we might not. Ever.

"Linda was killed between seven P.M. and midnight Friday," Milo said in his driest tones. I guessed that he was reading from the medical examiner's report. "There's no indication of sexual assault or of intercourse in the last twenty-four hours. There's no sign of a violent struggle, which indicates she was taken by surprise and possibly wasn't afraid of her killer." At this point, Milo paused, not unlike a puppy expecting to be praised for performing a cute trick.

I, also like a puppy, responded. "In other words, she knew him. Or her."

"*Possibly.*" Milo was being the noncommittal lawman. With an astute look, Leo made his exit. "Time of death is difficult to pinpoint in this case because of weather conditions. The cold slows down rigor. That's why there's a five-hour window. The murder probably occurred near the site where the victim was found, since the only external evidence on the clothing was dirt, underbrush, and other matter indigenous to the locale."

I was silent for a few moments after Milo finished. "So either Linda's car was driven back to the condo by her killer or she went there with him—or her—of her own free will."

"Right." I could hear Milo slurping coffee.

"In the M.E.'s opinion, could a woman have done it?"

"He won't commit himself."

"Which means?"

"Anything's possible."

"What about crime-scene evidence? Or from the car?"

"What we've got is being examined by the lab technician in Everett."

"Such as?"

"Nothing spectacular." Milo sounded vexed. "Let's face it: We haven't made much progress. In fact, we're damned lucky to have gotten this far. Snohomish County is barely keeping afloat with their own forensics reports. I've had to push, kick, and shove to get this out of them. At least the Petersens can hold the funeral tomorrow."

I remembered to tell Milo about Dan Ruggiero. The sheriff was not impressed. "So you and Vida went to the Lumberjack Motel to bug Minnie Harris? And you and Louie saw this guy at the Venison Inn? So what?"

"*Leo,*" I said, glad that my advertising manager had left the office. "Not *Louie.* Jeez, Milo, pay attention."

"Ruggiero checked out Thursday morning. Make your point." Milo was definitely annoyed.

Maybe he had a reason. Dan Ruggiero couldn't have murdered Linda Lindahl. "Vida's checking on him," I muttered. "When she gets back from ... wherever she is. Say, could Andy be a news story in the next paper?"

"Andy?" Milo now sounded puzzled. "Cederberg? You mean the lousy driver at John Engstrom Park?"

"Andy finally reported it, right? Anyway, he told me about it, so it's a matter of record. How should we use it?"

Milo snickered. "Put it on the sports page. 'Andy seven, Car zero.' Andy didn't get hit, did he?"

Milo's attitude was starting to irk me. The sheriff prefers to deal only in facts. He seldom allows himself the luxury of letting his imagination roam free. I gather it's an occupational hazard. "Andy was lucky. The point is, was it an accident or deliberate? Could Andy's near-miss tie in with Linda's murder?"

"That's stretching a point," Milo replied. "It was dark, it was foggy, Andy was wearing a black overcoat. We've got newcomers who don't know how to drive in local weather conditions. Or how to walk. Look at Louie."

"*Leo.*" I was gritting my teeth. But I knew when to run up the white flag. "Okay, so we'll drop it for now. Are you going to check the closets of suspects for dirt particles that match Linda's clothes?"

Milo's tone turned grim. "Have you ever heard of *probable cause*? We'd need a search warrant, and we have no legal grounds to get one."

I knew Milo was right. "What about Big Mike Brockelman? Did you interview him last night?"

"After you left, I bought him a beer." The sound of Milo whacking his coffee mug against something solid resonated in my ear. "He was home in Monroe Friday night. He says his wife backs him up. Or will, when she gets home from visiting her mother in Walla Walla."

I brightened. "You mean he admitted he was seeing Linda?"

"I didn't say that." Milo's voice held a warning note.

I knew better than to push Milo too far. He wasn't obligated to tell the press everything, and we both knew that in certain types of investigations, discretion was necessary. "Are you going to ask Mrs. Brockelman about her husband's whereabouts?"

"If we have to. We aren't that far along yet. Anyway, she won't be back until next week. Hey, I've got to run. There's snow up at the summit and three cars just landed in the ditch. No serious injuries. You want Carla to take a picture?"

By the next edition, thirty cars might have gone off the road. I decided against sending Carla. Besides, I didn't want to give her any ideas about plunging off Stevens Pass in a dramatic bid for tragic fame.

Vida had returned by the time I'd gone through the mail and caught up with phone calls. Leo and Carla were both out, and Ginny was pouting in the front office.

"Two months in Topeka is too long," Vida declared, slipping a fresh sheet of paper into her typewriter. "If Grace Grundle wasn't a twittering ninny before she went to visit her sister in Kansas, she certainly is now. All she could talk about was the state fair at Hutchinson. Huge dahlias. Enormous squash. The largest sunflower on record. The world's biggest ball of twine. Aaaaargh!" Vida plunged her hands into the typewriter keys.

"Any pictures?" I asked hopefully.

Vida glared at me from under the brim of her blue derby. "Of what? Twine?"

"Squash is nice. So are dahlias." I tried to sound reasonable.

Vida set her fists on her hips. "Grace takes Polaroids. They're all dark and fuzzy. Just like her brain. No wonder she's lost all her money! It's a marvel she could find her house when she got back from Kansas. Grace probably thought she was in Oz."

Listening to Vida rail, I thought Oz sounded promising. "How'd she lose her money? You mean she spent it on the trip?"

Vida was flipping through her notes. I was surprised that she had taken any. Usually she trusted to her faultless memory. Noting my gaze, Vida felt compelled to explain: " 'The grandnephews and great-nieces and whatever other gaggle of Grundles or whoever they are. Grace spewed them out like peach pits. I couldn't keep up."

I nodded in sympathy. "So she's broke?" That didn't seem likely. Grace Grundle was a retired schoolteacher with a less-than-flamboyant lifestyle. She had been widowed long before I came to Alpine, and there were no children. As I recalled, this was the first trip Grace had taken in years.

"She's not *broke*, as you put it," Vida replied, typing away. "But after she got home last week, she went to cash in a CD she thought had come due, and they couldn't find it. I suspect it was never there in the first place. Grace has always been a bit vague."

Before leaving Vida to her travel story, I filled her in on Milo's report from the M.E. Vida wasn't impressed. "He has nothing to go on," she remarked, then reached for her Seattle directory. "I should know Bobby Lambrecht's number, but I don't." Vida flipped through the yellow pages, then picked up the phone. After a brief exchange, she put the receiver down with a clunk. "Rats! He's in an all-day meeting. Tomorrow he'll be off for Armistice Day."

I concealed a smile at Vida's somewhat arcane reference to the holiday. "Are you calling Bob about Dan Ruggiero?" I asked.

She nodded. "I don't suppose I should bother Bobby at home. It can wait. I suppose." But the glint in Vida's eyes indicated that she wanted some answers, and she wanted them now. She returned, however, to Grace Grundle's adventures in Topeka and the Kansas State Fair.

Because this was publication day, I had the luxury of researching next week's editorial. Various possibilities presented themselves, including the sheriff's need for funding. But I chose to congratulate the chamber of commerce on refraining from putting up Christmas decorations before Thanksgiving, and to urge them to do the same next year and forever after. While on the subject of the chamber, I gave them a nudge regarding Ginny's proposal for the Summer Solstice Festival. Several other logging communities in the Pacific Northwest were inaugurating civic celebrations aimed at boosting tourism and giving the local economies a shot in the arm. Alpine should be among them, I pointed out.

It was midafternoon when I finished my draft. When I wrote an editorial so far in advance, there was always the chance that a more pressing matter might come along before deadline. The chamber piece wasn't time-sensitive: I could use it at a later date.

But the part about new ideas caused me to remember the two Californians who had been guests of the ski lodge. I put in a call to Henry Bardeen, the manager. He was gone for the afternoon, according to his daughter,

Heather. Her father would return my call in the morning.

"When was the last time you had dinner in Everett?" It was Vida, standing in the doorway of my office.

I didn't recall. "Why do you ask?"

"We-ll . . ." Vida was trying to look ingenuous. She never manages it. "If we eat in Everett, we could pay a call on Howard Lindahl and his family. It would be awfully good-hearted of us, don't you think?"

I was aghast. "Vida, do you *know* Howard Lindahl? I sure don't."

"I met him a few times," she replied vaguely. "I attended his wedding to Linda. He came here with her upon occasion. Once. I think." Vida's gaze no longer met mine.

"Then it'd be presumptuous of us to visit. We don't even have the excuse of researching a story."

"Yes, we do." Vida had regained her aplomb. " 'Victim's Survivors Cope with Violent Death.' Well? We ran the homicide story, we ran the obit, we ran a sidebar on Linda's life and times. Now we go for the human interest. We'll do all the Petersens, too, and Andy and Christie and Rick."

"That's pushing it."

"We've already talked to Thelma and Elmer. Not that you can talk to Elmer, but he's *there*. In his way."

I was weakening. "It's an hour's drive to Everett. The weather forecast is calling for snow again."

"It won't snow in Everett." Vida glanced at her watch. "It's ten after three. It's Wednesday, you can leave early. Four, shall we say?"

"I should change," I protested. My old gray slacks and baggy green sweater were adequate for work, but not for dinner.

"Four-fifteen then," said Vida. "My car or yours?"

We decided on Vida's Buick. In case of snow, it was the heavier vehicle. As I headed back into my office, I noticed that Vida was much more relaxed. She had settled on a course of action. Vida couldn't stand sitting idly by. Some might call it meddling; I wouldn't have dared. There were few who would, to Vida's face.

The Dithers sisters were pitching a fit. Judy and Connie Dithers sometimes played bridge with my group when they weren't home watching TV with their horses. At the moment, they were doing neither, nor were they speaking in the fragmented fashion they often adopt for social occasions. Larry Petersen was on the end of their ire, and both women were up in arms.

"You ought to be reported to . . . somebody," Connie was screeching at Larry. "This is dishonest! What's going on?"

Larry was looking both embarrassed and flabbergasted. "Judy . . . Connie . . . It's just a simple mistake. The computer, probably. Give me a few minutes, and I'll figure it out."

Just after the paper was delivered around three, I'd gone into the Bank of Alpine to get some cash for dinner in Everett. Because of the Veterans Day break coming up, the bank was busier than usual. I was at the end of a seven-person line, and thus almost backed up to the mahogany rail that separated Larry from the inner lobby. It was impossible not to hear the Dithers sisters, especially Connie, who couldn't bid one club without screaming.

"Then do it," Connie demanded with a swish of her graying brown ponytail. "We've got four grand tied up in that CD. Winter's coming. We need feed for the horses."

Mercifully, I moved up two places in the teller line.

Christie, Rick, and Denise appeared to be working as fast as they could. A couple of minutes later, I was number three. Judy Dithers had abandoned her sister to wander around the lobby. She saw me standing in line and clutched at my arm.

"They've lost one of our money-market accounts. Can you imagine?" Judy whispered, flipping her own chestnut ponytail off her pudgy shoulder. "What's going on around here? Linda Lindahl is murdered. Now the bank is in a mess. Why don't they hire a new book-keeper?"

"I heard they were getting somebody from the CPA's office," I said, which was a bald-faced lie. It seemed logical, since I'd never figured out how the local ac-countant could afford to keep two people besides him-self on staff.

"We've always banked here," Judy said, her wide, freckled face looking worried. "There's never been a problem. I told Connie we shouldn't have waited so long to order feed. She never listens to me."

Connie was the elder of the sisters by a year and a half. There had been a brother, according to Vida, who was born a cripple. His wheelchair had gone out of con-trol one fine summer morning twenty years ago and a logging truck had mowed him down. Connie and Judy had inherited the horse farm, a considerable amount of life insurance, and the settlement from their brother's wrongful-death suit. If local lore could be believed, the Dithers sisters hadn't left Alpine since they were teen-agers.

"Computers get blamed for a lot of things," I said, trying to remain neutral. "It's probably a numerical mis-take. You know, the wrong account number."

"It's Linda," Judy said in her flat voice. "She was a wonderful bookkeeper. Connie got everything out of balance last year. We asked Linda for help. In two days, she had it all straightened out. It was worth every penny we paid her."

Moving up another notch, I gazed at Judy Dithers with interest. "You liked Linda?"

Judy arched her scraggly eyebrows. "Liked? That's not the point. She was competent. Connie had to admit it. Hiring Linda was my idea."

At that point, Connie stormed across the lobby. She grabbed her sister by the arm. "Larry can't find the mistake. I had to tell him to take the money out of our regular savings account. Maybe we ought to move everything to SeaFirst in Sultan." She paused, apparently noting my presence for the first time. "Hello, Emma. Are you having any problems?"

Before I could answer, Judy broke in: "Most people can manage their money, Connie dear. They aren't financially challenged. Like us." Judy gave Connie a scathing look.

"Oh, so it's *my* fault you can't balance a checkbook! You never entered the amounts you spent! Judy, you have no money sense! I admit, I was never good at math. That's why we have a proxy account, you dummy!"

Ponytails a-flying and still wrangling, the Dithers sisters joined the queue behind me. I was now next in line. My brain was doing calisthenics. Like Leo, the Dithers sisters let the bank handle their financial affairs. Maybe Grace Grundle was in the same boat. If so, it appeared that the bank's customers were sinking fast. I was so caught up in my theorizing that Rick Erlandson had to call to me twice before I snapped to and approached his teller's cage.

"What's going on around here, Rick?" I asked in

what I hoped was a pleasant voice. "Are you folks having some problems?"

The color seemed to drain from Rick's earnest face. "I don't know, Ms. Lord. The last few days have been just . . . weird. Everything was fine until . . . well, Linda got killed, to really ruin everything. I'm thinking about quitting." He keyed in my transfer of funds and ran an agitated hand through his short, natural brown hair. "Do you know of any job openings around town?"

I didn't. "Have you thought about Monroe? Or Everett?"

Rick handed me my receipt and gloomily shook his head. "I don't want to move. I've got . . . obligations." He glanced guiltily at Denise Petersen, who was counting out cash for Dixie Ridley, wife of the high school football coach. Rick's voice suddenly cracked as he posed a reluctant question: "Is Ginny really mad?"

"Oh, dear." I didn't like getting caught up in my employees' personal lives. "Well—she's upset. It appears that you're . . . involved with . . . someone else." The Someone Else was now waiting on the Dithers sisters. "You've got to decide, Rick. Is it Ginny—or Denise?"

Rick seemed miserable. "I really like Ginny. She's so . . . *nice*. But sometimes a guy likes . . . to play the field." He gave me a helpless look.

In translation, that meant that Denise was putting out and Ginny wasn't. Rick was human. He was a young, virile male who needed a warm, willing body in the sack. I gave Rick a feeble smile.

"Why don't you ask Ginny out and see what happens? Take her someplace nice, maybe out of town." Inspiration struck, in the form of restaurant menus, flashing before my eyes like a gourmet fan. "Try Café de Flore down the highway. It's French, very romantic. Ginny will love it."

Ginny might hate it, but it was the best I could do with six people waiting in line behind me. I gave Rick another smile and hurried out of the bank. There was an air of frenzy about the place that had nothing to do with the bustle of customers. Worse, I sensed the pall caused by Linda's death. The marble pillars no longer seemed so sturdy, nor did the polished mahogany exude prosperity. The lobby seemed tarnished. So did the Petersens and the rest of the bank's employees. Driving up the hill under the darkening skies, I felt bleak.

Which, I reminded myself, was fitting. Linda's funeral would be held in less than twenty-four hours. I was in the proper mood for it. As I turned in to my driveway, I chastised myself: My spirits might be low, but I was still alive. Linda Lindahl wasn't as lucky.

As if luck had anything to do with it.

By five-thirty, Vida and I were at Confetti's in Everett, overlooking the marina. It was still raining, but the change of scenery perked me up. So did the Rob Roy I ordered on a whim.

Vida was checking Howard Lindahl's address in the Everett directory. I was halfway through my drink before she reached the table.

"Did you call him?" I inquired, wondering what had taken her so long.

Vida was admiring the multicolored streamers that hung from the ceiling. "Lovely," she murmured. "Are you having a cocktail?"

I tapped my glass. "So it appears. How about you?"

Vida hemmed and hawed, looked around to see if she recognized anyone from her church, and summoned our server. "A Tom Collins is practically nothing in terms of liquor," she said blithely. "Do you realize that many people live on their boats here in the marina?"

Judging from the number of lights and the activity along the docks, I could believe it. "The marina's really big," I noted. "Did you call Howard?"

"The second largest on the West Coast, behind Long Beach, California. Or is it San Diego?" Vida appeared mystified.

I wasn't giving up. "Did you call Howard?" I repeated.

Vida was studying the menu. Her eyes grew enormous. "Oh, look! We got here in time for the Early Bird Special! How nice! We'll save several dollars."

"Vida . . ."

"No." Vida was very prim. "I'll call after we eat. I have the home and the business addresses. The Lindahls live off Grand Avenue. It shouldn't be hard to find. I'm familiar with the neighborhood. The cabinet shop is by the railroad tracks, above the Snohomish River."

Vida's cocktail appeared. I allowed her to savor it before I pressed her again. "What took you so long at the pay phone?"

She sipped, then sighed. "If you must know, I called Bobby Lambrecht. It's after five, the rates are down, and I thought this would be a good time to reach him, just before dinner."

I tried not to smile. "And?"

Vida gnawed on her lower lip. "Daniel M. Ruggiero is the Bank of Washington's chief auditor. Bobby couldn't—wouldn't—say why he had come to Alpine." Vida's expression was rueful.

The only reason I could think of for a bank's chief auditor to show up in town was to check the books of another financial institution. Since we had but one, Dan Ruggiero must have been sent to look into the Bank of Alpine. My initial guess about a buyout had to be on target. But if I could believe the PR woman in Seattle, somewhere along the line, the Bank of Washington had chickened out. I verbalized my thoughts to Vida.

She grimaced. "Yes, yes, it would appear that the Petersens were willing to permit a takeover or a merger or whatever. I was wrong about a possible sale. I hate to admit it, but there it is. Now the question becomes, why did BOW back away?"

I gave a faint shake of my head. "Actually, there are two questions. Yours—and mine, which is, what does a potential buyout have to do with Linda's murder?"

Vida frowned. "Maybe nothing."

"Maybe." But I didn't really believe it. Nor, I sensed, did Vida. Even in a small town, there are some circumstances in which coincidence is not credible.

After we finished our entrées of spit-roasted chicken, Vida used the pay phone in the lobby to call Howard Lindahl. She laid on her sympathy with a trowel, then grew even more solemn about our professional obligations and the public's need to know. If Howard Lindahl swallowed all of this, he was too dumb to have killed his ex-wife.

Indeed, I could tell from Vida's pursed lips that he was trying to rebuff our visit. That was when she asked to talk to Susan Lindahl.

The second wife couldn't resist Vida's wheedling. Five minutes later, we were in the Buick, headed for Grand Avenue.

The neighborhood was old, and in the process of being gentrified. The Lindahl home, which overlooked Puget Sound, had obviously undergone considerable renovation. I suspected that Howard's craftsmanship had allowed him to do most of the work himself.

Susan Lindahl welcomed us in a brisk, no-nonsense manner. I was surprised. Her surrender to Vida had suggested a cream puff. But Susan had her own agenda:

"We could use some fresh faces around this house," she declared, leading us into the living room, which was filled with almost-antiques as well as a few new pieces that had probably been built by Howard. "It's been gloom and doom around here for the last week. First, the break-in, then Linda gets killed, and last night, Alison's kangaroo gerbil died. Would you like a glass of wine?"

"How nice," Vida said, taking her place on a depression-era davenport that had been re-covered in bright red poppies and green leaves. "Your home is charming. Wherever did you get the old Victrola?"

Before Susan could answer, Howard entered the living room. His round face was sulky, but he shook our hands. "We don't read the tabloids here," Howard announced. "Just because my ex-wife went out and got herself killed, that doesn't mean we want our names smeared all over the place."

Vida's shock was genuine, and mirrored my own. "*The Alpine Advocate* is scarcely a sensational tabloid," she retorted. "It's a most respectable weekly. You must have seen it."

Howard shrugged his broad shoulders. He was a beefy man in his mid-forties, not-quite-average height, and his light brown hair was thinning. Standing side by side, Susan was taller than her husband by an inch, spare of figure and plain of face. I suspected that Howard had learned from experience that character was more important than looks.

"I'm lucky if I get *The Everett Herald* read every day," he said. "I'll be damned if I didn't end up with my name in the Monday edition. They carried the story about Linda. Thank God it wasn't on the front page."

The Herald is one of several area newspapers we receive at *The Advocate*. Because it's a daily, and sometimes includes Skykomish County along with its home base of Snohomish County, quite a few people in Alpine subscribe. I'd noted the article about Linda's death, which had stated that the body of a former Everett woman had been found near Alpine, that she was a possible homicide victim, and that the Skykomish sheriff was conducting an investigation with the cooperation of Snohomish County law enforcement personnel. The last sentence of the story noted that while living in Everett, Linda had been married to a local resident, Howard Lindahl.

"I didn't like it," Howard said, looking pugnacious as he sat down in a deep blue recliner. "It sounded as if I were the prime suspect."

"Oh, stick it, Howie," said Susan. "The paper only used your name to let people know who Linda was when she lived here. You overreact." With a long-legged stride, Susan headed for the kitchen.

Howie was regarding Vida and me as if we were card-carrying members of the KGB. "I'm not telling you about any sex stuff. Or why we split. It's disgusting how everybody wants to spill their guts these days."

I hastened to agree, then remembered to pick up my cue from Vida. "We're more interested in what you can tell our readers about handling grief in this kind of situation."

"Grief?" Howard seemed surprised. "At the risk of sounding like I *am* the prime suspect, I can't say I'm crying in my beer." The words motivated Howard to call to Susan: "Suze—make that a beer for me."

"Were you surprised?" Vida's hands were folded neatly in her lap. The derby had slipped down on her forehead, almost concealing her eyes and glasses.

"Of course I was surprised." Howard looked at Vida as if she were a mutant. "Weren't you? I mean, do people go around expecting somebody they know to get killed?"

Vida pushed the derby high on her forehead. "I was extremely surprised. I found the body." The statement was only a small fib.

Howard was obviously shaken. "No shit!" He glanced anxiously toward the kitchen, as if he needed the beer to bolster his fortitude. "That's terrible! For you, I mean."

"Indeed it was." Vida's voice had turned wispy. I was afraid she was going to launch into Roger's sensitivity, but she was forestalled when Susan entered the room, carrying a tray laden with glasses of wine and a bottle of beer.

"Let's not mislead anybody," Susan said after she'd handed out the drinks. "Linda was a world-class pain in the butt. Even after the divorce, she gave Howie a bad time. She always would. That's why we can't honestly say we're in mourning."

Howard registered mixed emotions. "It sounds hardhearted, doesn't it?" His round face asked for understanding.

Vida inclined her head. "It sounds like good sense. Who really wants to get involved in a custody fight? It's so hard on the child."

Susan, who had sat down on an ottoman next to Howard, sprang to her feet. "Stop!" The wine in her glass sloshed over the rim. "Where's Alison?" The whispered question was for her husband.

"In her room?" Howard didn't sound certain.

Next to me on the davenport, I felt Vida's elbow in my ribs. "Emma, you should talk to Alison. You have such a way with youngsters. Your Adam is so close to Alison's age."

Vida knew she was off by ten years, but that didn't

matter. I knew she wanted me to interrogate Alison. I gave the Lindahls a self-deprecating look. "Do you mind?"

Howard and Susan exchanged leery glances. "She's pretty upset," Susan finally said. "I'd better introduce you."

We went upstairs, following a pattern of bright spring-garden wallpaper and serviceable gray carpet. I could hear the bass from Alison's boom box as soon as we reached the second landing.

Alison's dormer room wasn't any messier than that of most twelve-year-olds, which is to say that it could be mistaken for Hiroshima after the A-bomb was dropped. I had frequently told Adam that if he wanted to live in a demolition zone, I would oblige by practicing a scorched-earth policy, and torch the place. Naturally, I never carried out my threats, and just as naturally, he had only recently begun to take pride in maintaining order. In natural law, that always occurs after the child has moved out from under the parent's roof.

Consequently, I stumbled over a pile of clothes, various CDs, magazines, books, cowboy boots, and a poster of Keanu Reeves. Alison reluctantly turned off her boom box and stared at me with hostile blue eyes. She was at that awkward age, when her genes hadn't yet made up their mind if they were going to favor her mother's statuesque good looks or her father's short, stocky stature.

"Talk to Ms. Lord," Susan urged, her arms around the girl. "She wants to hear how you feel. About your . . . mother." With a faintly guilty air, Susan danced over the obstacles on the floor and left the room.

"Was that Soundgarden?" I inquired, having a nodding acquaintance via Adam with rock groups, especially the Seattle scene.

"Yeah." Alison wasn't impressed by my effort to be cool. She had found a bare spot on her unmade bed and was sitting on her feet.

I was forced to stand on mine. Resting my handbag on a six-inch stack of teen magazines, I tried to find some wall space that wasn't covered with three-dimensional objects. Among the skills that a single parent acquires is the need for candor. When a child is raised by a mother and a father, one can tell white lies and let the other dish out the brutal truth. But raising a child alone puts the burden for everything on Mom. Or Dad, as the case may be. Long ago, I had found it simpler, if not always easier, to be frank with my son.

"My friend from the newspaper in Alpine and your dad and stepmother are talking about your birth mother," I said, leaning against a calendar that featured thoroughbred horses. "They don't want to upset you. I'm the designated adult to keep you out of hearing range. How do you feel, Alison?"

"Okay." Her voice was as listless as her dark blonde hair. She seemed absorbed in what I guessed to be a hangnail on her right thumb.

"Did you see your mother much?" I asked, deciding to sit on Keanu Reeves.

"Not really." Allison continued to avoid my eyes. I waited for her to elaborate. It's another trick I learned from raising Adam. Children are so self-centered by nature that they *must* talk, especially about themselves. It's just a matter of being patient.

"She moved." Alison finally made eye contact, if briefly. "You know that. She lived in Alpine."

"That's right. She went to work for her father—your grandfather—at the bank. That kept her pretty busy." I wasn't making excuses for Linda Lindahl; I was trying to elicit an opinion from her daughter.

"I guess." Alison traced the hole in the knee of her blue jeans. Again I waited. "She took me school shopping at the Everett Mall."

"Oh?" I put warmth into my voice. "When was that? Just before school started in September?"

"We started the last week of August." She paused, then gave a toss of her long, lackluster hair. "That's dumb. It's still summer."

"It *is* dumb." I was serious. "But summer really doesn't end until the third week of September."

Alison made no comment. Then, with an unwinding of pudgy arms and legs, she hopped off the bed. "Do you want to see my kilt skirt? Mom bought it for me at The Gap."

I assured her I'd be delighted. Alison rummaged in her closet, and to my amazement, the wine-colored skirt was actually on a hanger.

"There's a mock turtleneck and a white shirt that go with it," she said, a note of vitality finally emerging in her voice. "I think the shirt's in the wash."

"Nice," I said, fingering the fabric. Female appreciation of clothes cuts across almost any barrier, including age. "You could go dark green with this."

Alison studied the kilt. "Yeah—I guess. But I'm saving my money for a rabbit."

I nodded. "They make good pets. I'm sorry about your gerbil."

Surprise showed in Alison's blue eyes. "Luke Perry? You heard about him?"

It took me a moment to realize that Alison apparently had named her pet for a prime-time TV hunk. It figured. My brother and I had owned a lizard named Elvis.

"He got a tumor," Alison said, tossing the kilted skirt on the floor with the rest of the clothes. "We gave him medicine, but he died anyway. My folks didn't want to spend two hundred dollars on chemotherapy."

"It might not have worked." It was a guess. My interest wasn't piqued by Luke Perry the Gerbil, but by Alison's reference to "my folks." I assumed she didn't mean Linda.

"The vet said he'd only live another year anyway," Alison remarked in a doleful voice. She twisted a strand of hair and fell back onto the bed. "I'd really like my own horse. But my folks say we can't afford it."

"It's an expense," I allowed, and before I could elaborate, Alison burst into tears.

I staggered across the piles to put a hand on her arm. "What's wrong, honey?" The obvious answer made me feel foolish.

"My mom wasn't bad!" The words were thick and muddled, but they hit me like a whip. "She had needs! She wanted a life of her own! Why did she leave me?"

My shoulders slumped. I wasn't sure what Alison meant by the question. "You mean . . . after the divorce?"

But Alison was crying convulsively, her face buried in her hands. Kneeling next to the bed, I patted her and waited. Over the years, I've covered many stories involving parents and children. No matter how indifferent, how selfish, how cruel the mother, there is a bond that no amount of evil can break. Children love their mothers in a way that defies reason. It's both reassuring and terrifying.

Alison was saying something, but the words were incoherent. She was bordering on hysterics. I gave her arm a sharp little shake. At last, she pushed the long hair off her face and looked at me.

"He didn't do it," she declared, the tears still streaming down her face. "I don't care about the map. He didn't *do* it."

My fingers pressed into Alison's arm. I was mystified. "*Who* didn't do *what*?" I asked, afraid that she was about to go off the deep end.

The bedroom door was flung open. Susan Lindahl wore a frightened expression. "What's going on here?" she asked, her tone sharpened by fear.

In what seemed like one blurred motion, Alison jumped off the bed, flew across the room, and shut herself in the closet.

Chapter Nine

ALL THE WAY downstairs and into the living room, Susan Lindahl was apologetic. "Alison is suffering from a lot of conflicting emotions. I work in Human Resources for the City of Everett, so I get my share of lives in chaos. We can't expect much else from Alison right now. Linda is going to become a saint before Alison resolves her feelings about her birth mother."

We had reached the open archway that led to the living room. I could hear Vida commiserating with Howard. The snatches of conversation indicated that they were talking about Linda's maternal inadequacies.

"It's understandable," I remarked. "It must be hard on you in particular. By definition, stepmothers have a lousy image."

Susan's smile was wry. "You bet. But I knew what I was getting into. The bad part—no, it's the good part, really—is that I can't have children of my own. That's let me throw myself full bore into the role of mother. At least Alison doesn't have to worry about competing with my, quote, *real* children." Susan made quotation marks with her fingers.

Vida was on her feet. "We really shouldn't bother these nice people any longer," she declared, sounding reproachful. "Besides, if it snows in the pass, we ought to be heading home. It's going on nine."

Clearly Howie wasn't going to coax us into lingering. He had scrambled to his feet and was handing Vida her purse.

"Now, don't go printing something personal," he warned. "I kept out of Linda's private life after the divorce. Alison is my only concern."

Vida nodded. "I understand completely. Very difficult, these custody battles. And so disturbing to the children. Your stance is admirable, Howie. I'm glad you won't end up in court."

As Vida turned toward the front door, I realized that Howie hadn't handed me my purse. Next, I realized that he couldn't: It was still upstairs in Alison's room.

Making apologies, I hurried up the stairs and knocked on Alison's door. It seemed to take forever before she peeked out into the hall. I asked her to fetch my purse. She disappeared for about fifteen seconds, then opened the door wide.

"Here," she said, with red-rimmed eyes and puffy cheeks. "I'm sorry I was such a butt."

I gave her an encouraging smile. "Being a butt is being human. Don't worry about it."

Turning away, I was startled by the tug on my raincoat. Alison was fixing me with helpless, hopeless blue eyes. "Look," she said in less than a whisper.

The piece of paper had been torn from a small spiral notebook. At first, it made no sense. Then, as I studied the squiggles and lines and numbers, I realized what it meant: The felt-pen markings were a map of sorts, showing Highway 187 from the bridge over the Skykomish River to the ranger station cutoff. And there, just past the Petersen farm, was an X. It didn't take a Michelin guidebook genius to figure out that it marked the clearing where Linda Lindahl was killed.

"Where'd you get this?" I demanded in a voice almost as inaudible as Alison's.

The girl swallowed hard. "In the magazine rack. One of my chores for this week was to clean it out. It was stuck in between some *Sports Illustrated*s and *Home-Crafter*s." The blue eyes were pleading. "It's not important, is it? I mean, you're a reporter; you'd know, wouldn't you?"

"Sure." I prayed that my smile was reassuring. But even as I pocketed the piece of paper, I had a sinking feeling. And if I was dismayed, I could only imagine how sick at heart Alison must be.

". . . wanted joint custody just to be perverse." Vida made the turn onto the highway that crossed Ebey Slough and eventually led to the Stevens Pass corridor.

I hadn't been paying strict attention. Alison's piece of paper was burning a hole in the pocket of my raincoat. "Joint custody?" I said, somewhat vaguely.

Vida gunned the big Buick. "Isn't that what I said? Linda got the bee in her bonnet last summer. She took Alison school shopping and let her buy all sorts of things at The Gap and Nordstrom's Brass Plum. Until then, she had only visitational rights, once a month. That was part of the divorce decree, which, according to Howie, was agreeable to both of them. But last August, Linda changed her mind. She wanted Alison every other weekend and for the summers. Howie and Susan fought it. A hearing was scheduled in Everett for the Tuesday before Thanksgiving."

The little map seemed to burn my hip. "Did Alison know?"

Vida headed up the hill that led to Snohomish. "No. They didn't intend to tell her until after the hearing. If the judge ruled in their favor, they'd decided to leave well enough alone. Why tell the poor child? If not, then Alison would have to know. But they planned to wait until after Thanksgiving anyway."

We had bypassed Snohomish on the Highway 2 cut-off before I told Vida about the piece of paper. She almost lost control of the car.

"What? In the magazine rack? Oh, Emma, that's peculiar! I don't like it. I don't like it at all."

Neither did I. "Did you ferret out any information about Howard's alibi?"

Vida was gripping the wheel with tightly clenched hands. "Only in a vague sort of way. Howard and Susan both stuck by their story about Dick Johnson. Howard said he'd never heard of the man, but that meant nothing—he often got calls from people who'd been referred to him by a second or even a third party."

We drove in silence from Monroe to Sultan. Somewhere beyond Gold Bar, I mused aloud that Milo Dodge should see the hand-drawn map.

"I don't like it," Vida said again, clicking her windshield wipers to a higher setting. As we climbed in altitude, there was snow mixed in with the rain.

"We can't conceal evidence," I pointed out.

"Define evidence." Vida's tone was terse. "How long was that piece of paper in the magazine rack? Is it in Howard's handwriting? Or Susan's? How did Alison know it was where her mother was killed?"

The last question made my spine tingle. "You aren't suggesting that Alison . . . ?" I let the query die. "The girl would know. It would be important to her. Children are like that."

"Yes, yes, I suppose." Having raised three daughters, Vida understood female adolescents as well as anybody. Which isn't saying much.

"Maybe it was for a hike or a fishing trip or camping

out." I, too, found myself making excuses for the Howard Lindahls.

"It could be any of those things," Vida agreed as big wet flakes of snow splattered the windshield. "We mustn't jump to conclusions."

"The custody fight provides a motive," I said as we crossed the county line.

"Only if Howard and Susan lost." Vida slowed the car to forty miles an hour, keeping a lengthy space between the Buick and the van in front of us.

"I think they would have lost," I said after a long pause. Now, as we made one of several crossings over the Skykomish River, the rain had turned completely to snow. "It sounds as if Linda voluntarily surrendered custody at the time of the divorce. That being the case, there wouldn't be much reason to deny her request."

"I'm not the judge." Despite her words, Vida looked as if she could handle the part, along with that of an entire jury.

The problem was that we had no idea who played the role of executioner.

The phone was ringing when I walked into my log house. By the time I picked up the receiver, no one was there. And, as will happen, the caller didn't wait to leave a message. I was hanging up my raincoat when I heard the phone ring again. I dashed over to the desk.

"Mom, what do you do about typhoid fever?" Adam's voice sounded unnaturally plaintive.

"Adam!" I fell onto the bleached pine chair that matches the desk. "Are you sick?"

"The word is *virulent*," my son continued. "How do you stop it?"

My heart was racing. "You get to a doctor. A hospital emergency room. Call 911 if you have to." My brain was rampaging along with my heart. I fumbled for the phone book. How soon could I get a flight to Tempe? Or Phoenix?

"The thing is," Adam was saying in what I construed as his dying voice, "there aren't any doctors or hospitals or 911s. What happens then?"

I had never been farther south than Flagstaff in Arizona. Somehow, I imagined that Tempe was relatively civilized. Adam was making no sense. Maybe he was delirious. From fever. I was shaking like a leaf.

"There's got to be *something*," I said in a panic. "Look in the yellow pages."

"There aren't any yellow pages either, Mom." Adam was beginning to sound impatient. "I guess I'll have to use the medicine man. You're no help."

I absorbed the reproach with true maternal martyrdom. "I can't help it—I'm here, not there, with you, where I belong. Oh, Adam, how did it happen?"

"The white man. He brought all these diseases that the natives couldn't fight off because they had no resistance. You know—smallpox and measles and all that stuff. I got references for most of them, but not typhoid. How do you spell it? It's with an *f*, right?"

Slumping in the chair, I dropped the phone directory. "This is for a *paper*?" I didn't know whether to be relieved or furious.

"Right, Anthro 101. You know, it's really grim how the Europeans screwed up the native cultures. I'm thinking maybe I should be a social worker, and help them regain their self-esteem."

"T-Y-P-H-O-I-D." I paused. "D-O-P-E. That spells Adam. Don't you ever scare me like that again. I thought you were dying."

"I am," Adam replied. "If I don't hand this paper in

tomorrow, I'll lose a whole grade point. How do you spell typhoid? I didn't hear you."

The rest of the conversation ran its customary gamut, with me giving Adam advice on how to complete his assignment, and Adam giving me a want list that should be overnighted the following day.

"You're going to be home for Thanksgiving, right? You can wait. Christmas is coming, too. I'm not sending you another thing." I meant it: The time had come for Adam to distinguish wants from needs.

"Okay, that's cool." Adam now sounded more distant than plaintive. "It gets cold here at night, even in Arizona. Let everybody stare and point at Emma Lord's son shivering next to a cactus. I like having my teeth chatter because I'm down to one tattered jacket. My shoes are pretty pitiful, too. I was thinking of cutting out pieces of cardboard and lacing them up with string for the Roman look. It's no problem as long as I don't step on an iguana."

I wasn't sure if I preferred Adam's more mature sarcasm to his youthful cajolery. "You can buy shoes when you come home," I said. "As I recall, you headed for Tempe with six pair."

"That was three months ago. They all wore out while I was walking up and down the street with my sign that read 'Will Screw for Food.' "

"Adam!" I didn't know whether to laugh or cry. Ultimately we agreed that the purchase of one pullover sweater and one pair of shoes at Thanksgiving would suffice until Christmas. We were about to sign off when I thought to ask a question:

"Say, did you dial my number and hang up for some reason? Or have you tried to reach me in the last couple of days?"

Adam hadn't. He'd meant to, over the weekend, but

he'd been studying for a history test. Or so he claimed. I explained about the hang-ups.

"Wrong numbers," Adam said in consolation. "It's all these old people. You'd be amazed how many of them live here in Arizona. The average age must be about a hundred. They can't use a push-button phone."

I accepted Adam's explanation. It was rational, it was easy to understand, it was undoubtedly right.

I would learn later that it was none of the above.

The snow of the previous night hadn't amounted to much. It had turned to rain by morning, though the steady downpour felt close to freezing. Newspapers, even weeklies, can't afford the luxury of taking every holiday that comes along. Thus, *The Advocate,* along with several other Alpine businesses, remained open on Veterans Day. I compensated my staff for the inconvenience by paying them time and a half.

As expected, the coverage of Linda's murder elicited a great hue and cry from readers. The news itself was old, but seeing it in print roused our subscribers to respond. Some wanted more coverage; others wanted less. There were those who were certain a serial killer was on the loose, and one insisted it must have been suicide. After fielding phone calls for most of the morning, I started for the sheriff's office. I was crossing Third Street when I felt the heel on my left boot come off. Silently I cursed Adam and his six pairs of shoes. I'd bought only one in the past year. I could really use a new pair of boots. Alpine's weather is very hard on footgear.

The cobbler shop is tucked in between the Upper Crust Bakery and Alpine Ski. Amer and DeeDee Wasco have worked—and lived—in tandem for almost fifty years. Amer's father wasn't a Wasco, but bore an unpronounceable Finnish surname that he had legally changed upon becoming a United States citizen. About that same time, his son was born, and the newly created Mr. Wasco had named him Amer, in honor of America.

Amer speaks in monosyllables, probably because DeeDee never stops talking. Luckily, he was behind the counter when I hobbled into the shop.

"Fifteen minutes," he said. "You'll wait?"

I had the flats I wore around the office in my capacious handbag. I told Amer I'd run an errand, but it wouldn't take long. He nodded, and I left.

Milo's office is just across the street from the Clemans Building, which houses not only the cobbler shop, the bakery, the ski store, and various offices, but also Sky Travel. My eye was caught by a colorful display of the Southwest. Adam had attended college in three different states. The only one I'd visited so far was the University of Hawaii. When he was an eighteen-year-old freshman, I was sure that he couldn't possibly find the campus without my help. I was right, of course. He would have had trouble finding Honolulu, since he thought it was located on the island of Hawaii.

Janet Driggers is married to Al, the local funeral director. Janet's exuberant and somewhat ribald personality isn't suited to the pale, hushed interiors of the family business. She sometimes works behind the scenes, but her husband has convinced her that greeting mourners is not her forte. Thus, Janet spends a few hours a week helping out at Sky Travel, where high spirits are considered an asset.

"Emma!" Janet all but sprang out of her chair as I came through the door. "Hey, didn't you about fall on your ass the other night when Edna Mae Dalrymple bid game in diamonds and only had four of them to the ten? I practically wet my pants!"

Fortunately, I had been Edna Mae's adversary at our October bridge-club meeting. It had been an ugly moment, particularly for her partner, Mary Lou Blatt, who also happens to be Vida's sister-in-law.

We discussed the card party for several minutes. I began to realize that I was stalling for time. Never held hostage to tact, Janet finally asked if I'd come in to talk about a trip.

"You could use one, honey. You hardly ever leave this dump." Her pert face studied me closely. "You need a change. You're looking all dragged out. What's wrong? Empty-sack syndrome?"

Even after four years, Janet's bold tongue can still jar me. I gave her a pallid smile. "I'm used to that. I don't mind the weather, either. I'm a native Pacific Northwesterner. But I wouldn't balk at some new scenery. January, maybe. Arizona."

Janet shook her head. "They're all too old, especially in January. That's snowbird season. If you want action, try Vail. You don't have to ski. Just get Francine Wells to fix you up in some sexy snow togs and lie around the lodge with a powerful drink in your hand. Go for a young one. How long has it been since you've had sex with a teenager?"

I tried not to look appalled. Janet was serious. Not for the first time did I wonder about her conjugal relations with Al Driggers, through whose veins embalming fluid seemed to run.

"Look, Janet," I said, hoping to sound confidential, "the reason I was thinking about Arizona is because my son is going to school at Tempe this year and—"

"Aha!" Janet's sea-green eyes widened. "College

studs! Great! When and how long? The trip," she added
with a mischievous grin. "Not . . . you know what."

Mercifully, the phone rang. I had already recovered
from my sudden urge to visit Arizona. Making hand
motions, I tried to signal to Janet that I had to run. But
she had turned away and was punching the keys of her
computer.

"You can pick them up tomorrow morning. No, it's
the same price. Because of the funeral. We're all heart
here at Sky Travel. Sure, that's great. See you." Janet
hung up and regarded me with a knowing smile. "Impulse travelers. They want a cut rate when they're lucky
just to get booked. Thanksgiving is coming. We're into
peak travel time. Is Christie Johnston nuts?"

I stared at Janet. "Christie? Where's she going?"
Vaguely I recalled seeing Christie Johnston heading in
the direction of Sky Travel the previous week.

Janet glanced at her screen. "Michigan. Final destina-
tion, Grandville. *Bor*-ing. But I guess she's got relatives
there."

"A Thanksgiving visit?" I was slowly backpedaling
toward the door.

"I guess." Janet suddenly shook her head. "No,
maybe not. She and Troy were originally scheduled to
fly out of Sea-Tac last night. This morning, actually.
Then Linda got killed and Christie asked to change the
date to next Sunday. No problem, since there was a
death involved. She got the same fare via Northwest
into Grand Rapids, with a change in Minneapolis. Of
course, she missed out on a really good deal because
she waited too long. Then she starts asking about one-
way fares, and figures it's cheaper to do it that way."
Janet ran a hand through her frizzled auburn hair. "Bullshit, it actually costs less to get a round-trip than it does

a one-way. What's wrong with people, Emma? You ever tried a three-way?"

"What?" I sounded shaken.

Janet waved a hand. "You know—you, your guy, and—"

"I've got to run," I squeaked, all but falling through the travel agency door. The rain pelted my head as I hurried back to the cobbler shop. Five minutes later I was in Milo's office, feeling safe but unnerved. I resisted the impulse to ask the sheriff if he'd ever arrested Janet Driggers for lewd behavior.

"You caught me just in time," Milo said, tossing a form he'd just completed into his out-basket. "The funeral is at one, and I've got to go home and change into a serious suit."

"You don't own a suit," I remarked, suddenly feeling panicky. "Oh my God, Milo, I forgot to order flowers! I must run over to Delphine's shop before it's too late!"

Milo glanced at the big clock with the Roman numerals that hung askew on the opposite wall. It was almost eleven-thirty and the funeral was scheduled for one P.M. "Send a memorial somewhere. You can do that anytime. That's what I'm going to do. The Lutheran Scholarship Fund for the Lutefisk-Impaired or whatever the hell they call it."

I shook my head. "I send memorials to Ben. But I don't think the Petersens, being so staunchly Lutheran, would approve. Ergo, it's flowers. See you."

"Whoa!" Milo was on his feet, astonishing me as he always does when he moves swiftly. He grabbed my wrist and gave me a goofy grin. "What's with you today? You never come to see me unless you want something. What does your brother do with the money? Buy booze?"

"Of course not!" I was huffy. "He uses it for the mission. Ben can buy his own booze."

Milo chuckled. "I don't understand Catholic priests. They drink, they smoke, they do everything but screw, and from what I read, they do that, too, on the sly. What's the point?"

"Skip it, Milo. You're a Protestant." Trying to teach the sheriff about Catholicism was probably right up there with getting him interested in Wagner's *Ring* cycle. "Let go; I've got to hurry over to Posies Unlimited and then go home to change. This holiday threw me off. I keep thinking the funeral's tomorrow!"

Obediently Milo released my wrist. Four minutes later I'd galloped through the rain to Delphine Corson's flower shop. Fortunately, she hadn't closed for the holiday. Delphine welcomed me with a broad smile and a lot of cleavage. That was her style. She was also an excellent florist.

"You're up against it," she said, her manicured hand sweeping over at least three dozen arrangements clustered next to the front door. "I got behind with orders because I've been sick as a dog. Don't catch this lousy bug, Emma, unless you want to lose weight. Which I do, but you don't need to." She pinched off a wilted azalea blossom from a huge bright pink plant, then waved a hand at the array of flowers. "This is the third load to go off to the service. You waited so long that you're going to get stuck with an orchid spray."

I asked for a price quote. Delphine's response wasn't as horrendous as I'd feared. "I'll take it," I said.

"It's a good decision," she replied, her bleached blonde head bent over an order form. "We won't send them to the church, but we'll strew the orchids around the grave site. It makes a nice touch. Linda would have liked it."

Vaguely, I nodded. A lavish arrangement of at least four dozen white and yellow roses caught my eye. Unlike some of the memorial bouquets, there was no ribbon with the deceased's name etched in gold.

"Lovely," I remarked. "Is that family?"

Delphine patted her blonde coiffure. "You'd think so, wouldn't you?" She simpered at me, her generous bosom jiggling. "You must pay handsome salaries, Emma. Those roses for Linda are from Leo Walsh."

Chapter Ten

IF CHRISTIANS CARVED totem poles, the Lutherans would sit at the top in Alpine. The predominance of Scandinavians has persisted since the beginning, and most of them have remained loyal to their national religion. Faith Lutheran Church is the most handsome house of worship in Alpine. It stands in conservative modern brick splendor on the corner of Seventh and Cedar Streets. The Lutherans were the first denomination to erect a church in Alpine, but this is their third building. The cornerstone was laid in 1979, at the same time that the synod started construction on the adjacent retirement home.

The church was packed, as was the parking lot. I arrived two minutes before the hour and ended up leaving the Jag across Cedar Street. Nodding at Al Driggers in the vestibule, I scanned the polished pine pews for an empty seat. Up near the front, I saw Vida on the aisle, waving her arms like a windmill. Apparently she had saved me a place.

"Where were you?" she demanded in a whisper that could have been heard by deaf residents in the retirement home next door.

"I couldn't find my shoes." Feebly I smiled at Christie Johnston and a husky, crew-cut man I assumed was her husband, Troy. They were sitting next to Vida, while Reba Cederberg and her in-laws were on their immediate left. I assumed that all of the Petersens were in the curtained mourning room just off the sanctuary.

The organ was playing a hymn I didn't recognize, a doleful number that announced the entrance of the pallbearers and the closed casket. As we rose, I noticed Howard, Susan, and Alison Lindahl on the other side of the church. They were jammed in between Cal and Charlene Vickers and the Dithers sisters. Alison's young face was very pale, and it seemed to me that Howard had shrunk into himself. Maybe he was trying to look inconspicuous.

Rick Erlandson and Andy Cederberg were two of the pallbearers. I vaguely recognized the other four—a Gustavson, a Bergstrom, an Erdahl, and an Everson. Or an Iverson—I wasn't sure.

Then, from the back of the church, came a terrible cry, a keening noise that seemed to be ripped from not one, but several throats. Startled, I turned around. Even in my black suede three-inch pumps, I couldn't see beyond the second row behind me. The sound stopped as abruptly as it had started. To my amazement, several people seemed to be staring at *me*.

"The Wailers," Vida murmured. "They come to all the funerals. Except the Catholics and the Episcopalians. Pay no attention. They like to show off."

Pastor Donald Nielsen ascended the pulpit, looking suitably grave. Vida nudged me.

"He'll talk forever. He won't say a thing. Lutherans are like that." Fortunately, this time her whisper couldn't be heard by more than a dozen others. Vida set her face in a prim line, tucked a stray gray curl under her black velvet cloche, and folded her hands in her lap. After the opening prayers and readings and a few more wails from the rear, Pastor Nielsen began his eulogy, praising Linda Petersen Lindahl for a life of service to her fellow human beings. "Piffle," muttered Vida.

She had worked her way through "hogwash," "twaddle," and "oh, for heaven's sakes!" by the time Pastor Nielsen concluded. I had to admit that his tribute to Linda lacked credibility.

The Wailers outdid themselves during "Just a Closer Walk with Thee." They moaned and blubbered through all three verses, but the rest of the congregation paid no heed. "Who are they?" I asked Vida in an almost inaudible voice.

Vida scowled at me. "I told you—the Wailers." She made a pointed gesture of directing her attention toward the sanctuary where Pastor Nielsen was about to offer the closing prayer.

At last, the casket was wheeled back down the aisle. There were some genuine tears mingled with the back-row wailing. Throwing discretion to the wind, I stood on tiptoes. By craning my neck, I identified two of the three woeful women as Gerta Runkel and Nell Blatt, Vida's sisters-in-law. The third could have been one of the Carlsons, a member of the family that owned Blue Sky Dairy. I decided not to mention the Wailers again to Vida. As Linda's casket rolled out of the church, the trio let out one last ghastly burst, then went dumb. Despite a convulsive giggle from Christie Johnston, I pretended as if I'd been hearing the Wailers weep through funerals all my life. Just like Vida. Perhaps the most amazing thing about the distraction was that after four years, I was still experiencing new small-town eccentricities.

The cemetery is only a block away from the church, but ironically the main entrance is on Highway 187. We processed in a long line of cars, vans, and trucks through the rain to the grave site, which was in the Petersen family plot. I saw Frank and Irmgaard's headstone, with an open Bible engraved in the weathered granite. Like the rest of the town, the cemetery is built on a steep hillside, which made footing treacherous. We stood at angles, like mountain goats, many clustered under umbrellas, some holding their programs from the service over their heads, and others, like me, braving it out bareheaded because we're used to the rain. The black clouds seemed appropriate for Linda's burial. Sunshine would have evoked her bright blonde head and happier days. If she'd had any. I didn't know Linda Lindahl well enough to be sure.

The Lutheran ladies put on an excellent spread in the capacious church hall. There were finger sandwiches and vegetable plates and cookies and coffee and tea and nonalcoholic punch. Early on, I got separated from Vida, and found myself face-to-face with Denise Petersen. I resisted the urge to start the conversation by asking, "So how about those Wailers?"

"Funerals are so sad," Denise declared, nibbling on a smoked salmon sandwich. Figuring that the statement was about as profound as Denise could get, I merely nodded. But she had more to say, so I listened politely. "Aunt Linda would have hated it. She never went to church. She said God was an idea."

"Really." I smiled, still being polite. "You must have been close to Linda. To discuss religion and such," I added, noting the blank response on Denise's pretty, vapid face.

Denise considered. "We were eating egg rolls. You know, at the mall. She said Buddha was fully illuminated. I said so was my new TV. So what? Then we talked about God and religion and stuff. That's about the only time we really discussed anything serious. I ran into her at Barton's Bootery. They were having a sale. I think it was last month."

It had been in mid-September. I remembered the half-page ad. Trying to put aside thoughts of how anyone as dopey as Denise could handle a teller's job, I kept on smiling. "You worked together, though. You must have had lots of opportunities to talk to your aunt."

The suggestion seemed to puzzle Denise. "Not really. I only started at the bank this fall. And she was always at her desk, doing ... whatever she did."

"She did it well, I imagine." I spoke lightly, not expecting a serious response.

"I guess. Grandpa told me once—he was sort of mad at me because I'd screwed up somebody's deposit and put it in the wrong account—that even though Aunt Linda was family, she wouldn't keep her job unless she paid attention to what she was doing. Grandpa told me I'd better do the same. I'm trying, but there's so much to remember." Denise sighed, a painful sound, as if she'd been asked to sacrifice herself to ravenous wolves. "It isn't just waiting on customers, which is totally awful, but balancing out at the end of the day and keeping track of all those different accounts and signing off on Rick and Christie's stuff and making sure to know the interest rates for ..." She stopped, looking stumped. "It was a lot easier waiting tables at the Icicle Creek Tavern. You don't get tips at the bank."

My head was beginning to spin. The Lutheran church hall is large and well ventilated, but the noise level had risen and I seemed to be hemmed in on every side. Mercifully, Rick Erlandson had edged his way toward Denise. After we exchanged greetings, I made excuses for securing some smoked salmon sandwiches of my own.

Directly above the buffet table was a well-known picture of Jesus, knocking at a door. As a child, I wondered why. It always struck me that He looked like a

Fuller Brush salesman making a late-night call. Having skipped lunch, I grabbed three finger sandwiches and was chewing lustily when Milo Dodge approached, looking uncomfortable in his brown sport coat and not-quite-matching slacks. The orange-and-yellow-striped tie didn't help.

"Well?" Milo's expression was sardonic. "Are you picking out a killer?"

"That's your job," I responded, trying to sound flippant but feeling something heavy in the pit of my stomach that had nothing to do with the salmon sandwiches. Milo was right: Linda's murderer might be among us, mourning along with the other four hundred people who had gathered to commemorate her life. And death.

"I've heard how I should be making an arrest from about a hundred people already today," Milo grumbled. "Marv Petersen is getting pretty damned impatient. Now that the funeral is over, I'm going to feel some real heat. All three county commissioners are his cronies. The next thing I know, they'll want to impeach me."

"Don't be silly, Milo. You're doing the best you can. The murder happened less than a week ago." I hoped my attitude would bolster the sheriff's self-confidence.

Milo's grumpy expression didn't change a jot. "Six days is a long time in a homicide investigation. If we had a prosecutor in this county who wasn't senile, he'd be on my butt, too." The sheriff's reference to Emmett Swecker was apt; Emmett was well into his eighties and had held the job since the Eisenhower era. He'd had his successes in the recent past, but only because Milo had presented him with airtight cases. Emmett's last solo attempt to get a conviction had involved a tourist who had been arrested for playing a trombone in the nude at Old Mill Park. For some reason, Emmett had tried the case on the grounds that the town's antinoise ordinance had been violated. In covering the story, I'd been forced to ask Emmett why he hadn't resorted to the indecent-exposure law. Emmett, who claimed to have seen the trombonist, insisted the man wasn't naked. His eyes were as defective as his mind. The case was dismissed, but somewhere along the line, Deputy Jack Mullins had managed to lose the trombone. A lawsuit was said to be pending.

"Your staff isn't very well represented," Milo observed, his melancholy hazel eyes fixed on Vida, who, as usual, was the center of attention in front of a portrait of Martin Luther.

I acknowledged that Carla and Ginny were holding down the fort at the office. I didn't mention Leo's roses. The thought of his bouquet made me realize that I hadn't spotted him among the mourners. Maybe he'd decided that a floral bouquet was sufficient. I couldn't help but wonder why he'd bothered to make any sign of recognition. He couldn't have known Linda that well. Perhaps he'd seen the occasion as a public-relations gesture. Or so I hoped.

Milo must have noted the confusion on my face. "What's wrong?" he asked. "You look sort of strange."

I decided not to mention Leo's roses. "This whole thing is strange," I said. "I don't see Mike Brockelman."

Milo raised his sandy eyebrows. "I wouldn't expect to. Married lover attends girlfriend's funeral? I don't think the state would approve the time off. Besides, the highway crew has a deadline. I'm betting on snow over the weekend."

It was a safe bet. After the first of November, it always is in Alpine. The murderer, however, had miscalculated. I mentioned the fact to Milo.

He agreed. "It makes you think the murder was premeditated. So does the part about Linda's car. Somebody set her up, including the supposed meeting with Larry at Aunt Thelma and Uncle Elmer's."

Across the room, I could see Larry and JoAnne Petersen accepting condolences from a group that included Harvey and Darlene Adcock. Marv Petersen was there, too. The short, stout woman at his side was no doubt his wife, Cathleen. She looked vaguely familiar from various sightings at the Grocery Basket, Safeway, and Parker's Pharmacy.

"I wonder how Linda was contacted," I said, seeing Howard Lindahl approaching out of the corner of my eye. "A phone call? A note?"

Milo shrugged, then made an attempt to loosen his tie. "It could have been in person. Somebody came by the bank. Anybody. Who doesn't go into the Bank of Alpine?"

I was about to mention the complaints of various customers concerning discrepancies in their accounts when Howard Lindahl cleared his throat in a deferential manner.

"How's that story coming?" he inquired after a brief greeting. "I'm still not happy about it."

With a guilty glance at Milo, I shifted from one foot to the other. "Well ... it's what we call an in-depth piece. It'll take some time. We're thinking about interviewing other survivors. You know, from logging accidents, car crashes, that sort of thing. We don't want to be ... superficial."

A wave of relief swept over Howard's face. "Then it won't be in the next edition?"

I shook my head emphatically. "Definitely not. Grief is timeless. We might even wait until after the first of the year. So many people get killed on the road during the holidays." Inwardly I winced. *Superficial* had become my middle name. I felt as shallow as Denise Petersen.

In an uncharacteristic show of affection or something that might have been taken for it, Milo draped an arm around my shoulders. "So you're doing an article on Howard here? Interesting. I didn't know you knew the Lindahls."

I felt like stepping on Milo's foot. "Journalists get around," I mumbled. "It's part of the job."

Howard's expression was very serious. "Ms. Lord and Ms. Runkel convinced us they're doing a public service. Frankly, I was against it. But Susan believes in reaching out." Even as he spoke, Susan Lindahl was at an exit, waving to her husband. She had a very miserable Alison in tow. "Excuse me, I think my wife wants to leave. This has been really hard on my daughter. Maybe we shouldn't have brought her along." With a morose air, Howard Lindahl made his way through the chattering mourners.

Milo dropped his arm. "So you and Vida hightailed it over to Everett. Why didn't you say so?"

"What should I say?" I tried to act both indignant and innocent. I still had the hand-drawn map in my purse. There were too many people around to overhear me mention Christie Johnston's proposed trip to Michigan. The customer complaints about the bank could wait. "You'd already talked to Howard. Vida and I were looking for a story angle."

"Right." Milo's skepticism blazed as brightly as his orange-and-yellow tie. "Look, Emma, I sure as hell could use some extra hands. But I want them working for the county, not *The Advocate*. Back off. One of these days you and Vida are going to get yourselves into real trouble."

Gobbling up my last finger sandwich, I scoffed at the sheriff's warning. His long mouth was set in a grim line. It didn't scare me.

But it should have.

Leo Walsh was in a good mood. When I returned from the funeral shortly after four, he all but danced into my office.

"You seem to have recovered from your spill," I noted.

"Hell, it was only a sprain. That was ten days ago." He dropped onto one of my spare chairs. "Say, I thought this was payday. Not that I have to worry, what with the proxy banking deal."

I explained to Leo that when the fifteenth of the month fell on a Sunday, we moved payday to Monday. "If the fifteenth's a Saturday, then the checks are delivered on Friday. It all works out in the end." My smile was benign.

"It makes sense." Leo extinguished his cigarette in the ashtray I'd resurrected just for him from a cupboard shelf. "They finally got the payment at the Toyota place, by the way. I guess it takes a while to set these things in motion."

"Good." I tried to keep my smile in place. "That was a beautiful arrangement you sent for Linda." Feigning interest in my accumulated phone messages, I watched Leo from under my lashes.

His color deepened and he shifted nervously in the chair. "Yeah . . . right . . . well, I feel like I should try to fit into this place. If I'm going to stick around. It doesn't hurt to show I'm part of the community. I mean, Alpine isn't freaking L.A."

"No, it's not." My eyes had traveled to the cigarette butt in the ashtray. To my horror, I found it enticing.

My smile evaporated. "You're right, Leo. It's good of you to participate. But you can't put out for every funeral, wedding, and anniversary in town. You'll go broke."

"I've been broke before." Leo had regained his aplomb. "Hey, babe, you look great in that black dress. But you're a little washed-out. Too much time with those Lutherans. How about a drink after work? It's almost quitting time."

It occurred to me that Leo had already had a drink. Or two or three, before quitting time. Maybe he'd been in a bar instead of at the funeral.

"Sorry," I said, hoping to sound sincere. "I've got a date tonight."

Leo stared, then broke into a grin. "No kidding? Who's the lucky stiff?"

Leo's choice of words was unfortunate. My plan was to visit the murder site off Highway 187. Maybe Vida would go with me. There was no man involved, of course. I hadn't had a real date since I moved to Alpine. The tryst with Tom Cavanaugh had been a matter of circumstances, and evenings with Milo Dodge didn't count.

"I didn't say it was romantic," I hedged, caressing a phone message from Averill Fairbanks as if it were a request to meet Mel Gibson at the ski lodge instead of the usual sighting of aliens crash-landing at the fish hatchery. To soothe Leo's feelings, I came up with a brainstorm: "Why don't you come to my house for Thanksgiving? My son will be there, and I'm asking Carla and her roommate, Marilynn Lewis, too." Vida was going to her daughter's in Bellingham, and Ginny would be with her own family. Marilynn, who was a nurse at the Alpine Medical Clinic, had moved in with Carla the previous June.

Somewhat to my surprise, Leo hesitated. "Well—we'll see. Can I let you know next week?"

"Sure." It crossed my mind that Leo might intend to fly to L.A. over the long weekend. Considering that he seemed estranged from his entire family, it was a long shot. I kept my mouth shut.

Leo wandered out of the office, and five minutes later, Vida stomped in. Her velvet cloche was drooping sadly, a victim of the rain. "There's definitely something fishy going on at the bank," she declared. "I talked to several people at the funeral reception who have had problems, particularly cashing in CDs. They're not all as addled as Grace Grundle."

If Vida was right, *The Advocate* had a responsibility to get the story. "Do you think that's why the Bank of Washington bowed out?"

Having finally conceded that the Petersens could be sufficiently traitorous to sell their establishment to a big-city blockbuster, Vida was ready to consider other possibilities. "It could be so. Let's say that Bobby Lambrecht came to Alpine to talk business with Marv Petersen. Marv agreed to a buyout, or a merger. Then Bobby went back to Seattle where he sent Dan Ruggiero up here to check the books. But things didn't look right. So this Ruggiero fellow goes back to Seattle and alerts Bobby. The proposal is scrapped. That's what the woman in their PR department told you, isn't it?"

I nodded. "If it was still pending, but unofficial, she could have said, 'No comment,' or some such ambiguous statement."

Vida was also nodding, but slowly, ponderously. "I know so little about financial institutions. I've banked here all my life. I was eleven years old when I had my first account. Savings-bond stamps, twenty-five cents apiece, every week, through the school. We had what they called Bank Day, and everybody brought at least one quarter. When we filled up the little books, we had eighteen dollars and seventy-five cents—enough to buy a twenty-five-dollar war bond. By the time the Allies defeated the Germans and the Japanese, I had five bonds. I didn't cash them until I was twenty-six." Vida grimaced. "My, but life is full of ironies. I suppose we should consider it a blessing that a bank from Japan isn't trying to buy us out. Yet."

It didn't matter to me whether the potential buyer was from Tacoma or Tokyo. The point was that there was no buyer. What we needed to find out was the reason.

"I'm going to call Milo," I said, punching in the sheriff's number. "He ought to know what happens when one financial institution discovers that there's a serious problem with another financial institution."

"Bank examiners," Vida murmured. "I'm sure they call them in. But who are they?" Her face was an uncustomary mask of puzzlement.

Jack Mullins answered the phone. Sheriff Dodge was out. Assuming that Milo might have taken the rest of the day off after attending the funeral, I asked if he'd be back before five.

"Oh, sure, he'll be here," Jack replied in his dry, droll manner. "Our favorite law enforcement officer wants to keep a high profile with the electorate while this Lindahl thing is still perking."

"What'd he do, go home to burn his ugly tie?" I asked.

Jack chuckled. "I missed that. He'd taken it off when he came back here. No, he's actually working. He went up to Linda's condo to have a look-see for himself. I guess he doesn't trust Sam and me to do the job."

As it turned out, I didn't make contact with Milo that

afternoon. There were too many phone messages that had accumulated in my absence, and the AP wire had provided us with yet another in-depth overview of the timber controversy. I would let Carla do the usual checking for local comments, but the issue was becoming so complicated that I needed to understand the latest developments in order to provide direction for my scatterbrained reporter.

I actually forgot to tell Vida about Milo's visit to Parc Pines until the next morning. In my defense, Vida had been caught up in writing the funeral story, which we'd feature prominently in the next edition. When I mentioned the condos, Vida turned thoughtful.

"We should go over there. We should have done it sooner. It might be well to study the layout of the complex." Vida looked at her watch. "It's almost eleven. Are you free?"

I had never been inside Parc Pines, but I was certain that Vida had. There was nowhere in Alpine that she hadn't been. I hesitated, then caved in. The Jag was parked a few places closer to the front door than Vida's Buick. It took less than five minutes to get down Front Street and climb Alpine Way to the Parc Pines complex. The condos are off my own Fir Street, but five blocks west, facing the entrance to the expensive homes in the Pines development. Pines Villa, the apartment building' where Carla lives with Marilynn Lewis, is separated from the condos by a high cedar fence and some decent landscaping.

Unlike most condos in the city, the security at Parc Pines is minimal. There are only twelve units on three stories built around a courtyard that, Vida informed me, contains a swimming pool and sauna. We parked on the street and made our way up a winding walk lined with

Oregon grape and butterfly bush. Vida buzzed for Ella Hinshaw, who was somehow related to her by marriage.

Ella let us in after the second buzz. She was close to seventy, with a startling blue rinse, and wing-shaped glasses that contained hearing aids. I vaguely recognized her from sightings around town.

"Vida!" she exclaimed, offering a hug. "I haven't seen you since Labor Day weekend! I missed the last Cat Club because I had the flu."

Vida's Cat Club was a collection of women who got together once a month to trash the rest of the town, and then, according to Vida, spent the following day exchanging phone calls trashing each other.

Ella's condo was tidy but jammed. I guessed she was a widow who'd moved from a big house that had been able to accommodate her many possessions. I could scarcely find room to swing my legs as I sat in a high-backed chair covered with a fabric that looked like damask.

"You've had a terrible tragedy," Vida said, getting straight to the point. "Emma and I are covering the murder story. Did you know Linda well?"

Ella assumed a shocked expression. "I was so stunned when I heard the news that I almost fainted! Imagine! In Alpine! What's this world coming to? You're not safe in your own bed!"

Vida let Ella run down. "Did you know Linda well?" she repeated.

"Luckily, no." Ella squirmed a bit on one of a pair of matching love seats. "I mean, if I had, I *would* have fainted. From grief."

"But," I put in, "you must have been acquainted. You have condo-owner meetings and such, I believe."

Ella looked as if she'd like to disavow any knowledge of Linda. "Well, yes. But Linda worked all day and she wasn't what I'd call the outgoing type. Very businesslike at the meetings, always trying to hurry people along and get to the point."

I had a twinge of sympathy for Linda. "You didn't visit with her on the weekends or in the evenings?"

"Not really." Ella sighed deeply, as if she suddenly regretted her failure to make friends with Linda. "I don't go out much at night. A good thing. It's not safe." Under her heavy pullover with its crewelwork at the neck, Ella shuddered. "It's not as if I'd see her coming and going. On the ground floor, we each have our separate entrances. The people who live on the second and third floors go in the back way, off Maple Lane. There's an elevator next to the courtyard."

Surreptitiously Vida checked her watch. "Which was Linda's unit?"

"One C," Ella replied. "I'm One A. Maybe you noticed."

Vida nodded. "I've been here before."

"Of course you have!" Ella exclaimed. "How silly of me! I had Cat Club in May."

"April," Vida corrected, but Ella didn't seem to hear her. "Were you home the night Linda was murdered?"

Ella put a hand to her flat bosom. "I was! Watching TV and crocheting. To think that poor girl went off and got herself killed while I enjoyed *Jeopardy*! Isn't life cruel?"

"Beastly," Vida retorted. "You and the other residents were questioned by the sheriff's men, I presume."

"Oh, yes! Just like on TV. Well," Ella amended, "not quite. Sam Heppner isn't exactly Andy Griffith, is he?"

Vida was starting to look grim. "Didn't anyone see or hear anybody that night?" Her tone implied that not all of the Parc Pines residents could be as dim as Ella Hinshaw.

But Ella shook her head. "These condos are built very sound. Arnold Nyquist put them up, and he never skimped. Quality, that's what, through and through. I must say I paid a pretty penny to buy in here. But I never hear a thing. Of course, I *am* a wee bit deaf."

"As a post," Vida muttered. In a louder voice, she pressed her earlier point: "You're certain no one saw Linda come or go that night? Or anyone visiting her?"

Ella now regarded Vida with a smirk. "Come, dear, if anyone would have heard about it, it would be you. Isn't Billy Blatt our nephew?"

Briefly I tried to make the family connection between Bill Blatt and Ella Hinshaw. I recalled that Bill's mother, Mary Lou, had been born a Hinshaw. If Ella had married Mary Lou's brother—or uncle—then . . . I gave up. Vida's family tree had too many branches for me to climb.

". . . unlikely, with the ground-floor entrances all on different sides of the complex." Apparently Ella was explaining why no one at Parc Pines had seen Linda or her visitor on that fateful Friday night.

Seemingly satisfied, Vida stood up. "One small favor, Ella," she said, managing to resurrect her peculiar brand of charm. "Can you show us the outside entrance and the garage? Oh, and Linda's condo, of course."

Ella turned a trifle pale. "But we can't go in! It would be . . . ghoulish!"

"It would probably also be illegal without approval from the sheriff," Vida responded, heading for the door. "You'd better get your coat, Ella. It's down to thirty-five."

But Ella demurred. "All I need is another sweater. Come along, Vida, dear. We'll go out the back way. It won't be so cold."

Vida glanced at me in surprise. "I didn't know there

was a back way," she whispered as Ella went to fetch her extra sweater. "Interesting. Perhaps."

Ella's kitchen had sliding glass doors that opened up onto the courtyard. There was a small lanai that led to a walkway that went around the inner walls of the complex. Standing at the bright blue iron railing, I saw that the pool was covered to protect it from the weather, but some hearty Scandinavian type in bathing trunks was heading for the sauna.

"That's Mr. Bjornsen from Two B," Ella said. "He'd swim all winter, if we'd let him."

Ella led us around the corner past another condo. "One B," she remarked. "Marisa Foxx. The lady lawyer. Very mannish."

Vida sighed and rolled her eyes. But when we were about to turn the next corner, we saw the elevator. It was built into a pillar of concrete that ran up to the third deck. Directly across the walkway was an open corridor. And next to it was One C, Linda Lindahl's condo. Vida moved swiftly to peer in the floor-length windows, but all of the drapes were closed.

"Drat," she groaned, turning back to face Ella and me. "Very well, let's see that outer door."

Ella led the way again. The narrow hallway was the length of Linda's unit. It took a moment for Ella to get the door open. When it finally swung wide, there wasn't much to see: another short walkway, small shrubs, frost-bitten flowers, and Maple Lane, a cul-de-sac off Fir Street that ended where the Pines Villa Apartments began.

Vida went outside to check the security arrangement, such as it was. There was a list of names and condo numbers, each with a buzzer and a tiny speaker.

"If you come in this way, you simply ring the occupant, correct?"

Ella nodded. "Whoever you're visiting pushes a button to let you in. The entrance itself is primarily for the residents on the second and third floors."

"But your name is here. So is Linda and Ms. Foxx and"—Vida squinted at the fourth listing—"the Hansons. Goodness, I don't know these Hansons." Momentarily Vida seemed bewildered.

"They're new," Ella said, coming to Vida's rescue. "All our names are listed here because of deliveries. If we're not home, the post office and UPS and all those other carriers will leave parcels in this box." She indicated a large chest beside the door, then pointed to Vida's left. "There's the entrance to the garage. I don't drive anymore, so I don't use it. I think it's one of those automatic things, though."

"Probably." Vida was surveying the steel mesh grid. "All right, take us down there on the elevator. Please."

Ella complied. It appeared that the L-shaped parking area was built around the base of the pool. The other half of the L was used for storage and utilities and equipment, Ella explained.

I counted the parking places, which were numbered for each condo. There were an extra half dozen for guests. Linda's One C slot was the fourth space down from the elevator. Vida stared at that empty parking place for a long time.

"It *is* cold down here," Ella said suddenly, hugging herself and her two sweaters.

Vida, however, didn't move. It was only when I began strolling back to the elevator that she wrenched herself away. She put a hand on Ella's shoulder.

"You're right. It's very cold. You shouldn't be here, Ella. You've had the flu."

We got in the elevator. It rose slowly to the first floor. When we emerged onto the walkway, with the rain falling steadily into the open courtyard, I felt as if I'd come up out of a cave.

Or a tomb.

Chapter Eleven

THAT FRIDAY WAS one of those days when Vida stuck to her diet. "I forgot to mention that Ella has the brains of a bee," she said, waving a celery stick at me. "But she's nosy. I thought that might help."

"She's also deaf," I said, wondering why I'd bothered to pick up a taco from our local ersatz Mexican eatery at the mall. It looked utterly unappetizing in its sea of salsa and pale sour cream.

"The problem is," Vida went on, munching away at the celery, "Ella couldn't see anyone come in or out of Linda's condo. Nobody could, because her ground-floor entrance is at the back."

After returning to the Jag, I'd drawn a quick floor plan of the condos. Sitting at Ed's desk, I studied it with a critical eye. "That's not entirely true," I noted. "Marisa Foxx has a window that looks out back onto Maple Lane."

Vida frowned in an effort of concentration. "You're right, she would. All the condos are at right angles to each other. You know her, don't you? Doesn't she go to your church?"

"I've seen her at Mass, but I don't actually know her." I hesitated, aware that if there is one professional in the world who doesn't believe in candor, it's a lawyer. "Should I go see her?"

Apparently Vida was operating on my wavelength. "No," she sighed. "If Marisa Foxx saw anything suspicious, she would have told the deputies. Attorneys usually feel compelled to be forthcoming with law enforcement officials. Unless their clients are involved, of course."

Our tour of Parc Pines seemed to have been in vain. Vida finished her fodder, then headed off to cover the monthly group birthday celebration at the Lutheran retirement home. Ginny and Carla were still out at lunch, and Leo was working on an ad at Barton's Bootery. I was choking down the last of my so-called taco when Denise Petersen drifted in.

"This is for Mr. Walsh," she said, handing me an ad mock-up that commemorated Linda Petersen Lindahl. "Dad said I was supposed to bring it over here Tuesday, but I forgot. Does it matter? I mean, Aunt Linda's still dead, right?"

"As far as I know." I tried to keep any inflection out of my voice. I could imagine the scene that had ensued at the bank when Larry discovered that his daughter had neglected to deliver his sister's memorial. There was a slip of notebook paper attached with a handwritten message: *Denise—For Leo Walsh. ASAP. Thanks.* I wondered if Denise knew what ASAP stood for, or if she thought it was a description of Mr. Walsh.

Uninvited, Denise dropped down into the vacant chair next to Leo's desk. "It's too busy at the bank today. It's nice to have a holiday, but then there's such a rush afterwards. Before, too. Maybe I should quit and get a job at Safeway. I heard they needed extra checkers for the holidays."

The mock-up that Larry—or Marv, or both—had put together for Linda was in simple, good taste. Judging from the long pageboy hairstyle, her photograph probably dated from at least five years ago, but she looked softer as well as younger. The wording was brief: IN MEMORIAM. LINDA PETERSEN LINDAHL. THE BANK OF ALPINE. Except for the dates of her birth and death, there was nothing else in the black-bordered layout.

I hardly caught what Denise had just said. "Safeway?" I looked up. "But the bank's going to be shorthanded. Christie is going on vacation and Linda's ... dead. Wouldn't you be leaving your dad and granddad in the lurch?"

Denise shrugged. "They'll find somebody. Lots of people are out of work in Alpine. Besides, I hate the bank. Let my stupid brothers work there. It would serve them both right. They're such jerks."

I didn't know Denise's older brothers. They'd been away at college most of the time I'd been in Alpine. If they hadn't been expelled by now, maybe they were smarter than their sister.

With an exaggerated air, Denise hoisted herself to her feet. "I should head back to work. The line was pretty long when I left." Suddenly she stopped, giving me a puzzled look. "What did you say about Christie? She's not going on vacation. She already went, last August, to Cabo San Lucas. It's all she talked about when I first came to work at the bank."

It was too much to expect that Denise Petersen would be aware of anyone's plans but her own. There was no point in arguing. "Thanks for the mock-up, Denise. I'll see that Leo gets it."

"Leo?" Denise was looking blank. "Oh, Mr. Walsh. Right. Thanks. 'Bye." She drifted out of the office, as aimlessly as she had entered. I almost wished that Ginny had shown up so that she could pounce on Denise and claw her into reality.

Vida returned around three, looking smug. I asked if

she'd unearthed a hot item at the retirement home birthday party. To my surprise, she had—at least by her
standards.

"Leona Hanson was celebrating her eighty-first,"
Vida said, unloading her camera. "Her great-nephew
and his wife have moved to Alpine. They're the Hansons I didn't know in One D at Parc Pines. His name's
Walt, and he works for the State Fisheries Department.
She's Amanda, and is going to work for the post office
when the holiday rush starts. I don't think Leona ap-
proves."

"Of what? The post office?"

Vida ignored my flippancy. "Leona says Amanda
wears very short skirts. Tight, too. She foresees Trouble, capital *T*. Walt still has to finish up duties from his
previous assignment in Eastern Washington, so he's often away from home. Now, how can I work the Hansons into 'Scene Around Town'?"

Offhand, I couldn't think of any way that wouldn't
invite a libel suit. "Wait until Amanda starts at the post
office," I suggested. "Then you can do one of your bits
about '. . . a new face at the blah-blah.' "

Vida gave a nod. "I suppose. I do miss the Welcome
Wagon. Before Durwood Parker drove it into the river,
we always found out about newcomers right away. I de-
test not knowing who's who."

I left Vida to her group birthday story and returned to
my cubbyhole. It was late afternoon when I got around
to calling Milo Dodge to see if he had any new information. This time Dwight Gould answered.

"If you want to catch him, look out your window,"
Dwight said. "The sheriff's just across the street, at the
Bank of Alpine."

"Maybe," Vida allowed after I'd passed on Dwight's
information, "Milo is . . . banking." Standing by my

desk, she caught sight of a cigarette butt Leo had left in
the ashtray. With a repugnant gesture, she emptied it
into my wastebasket. "Really, Emma, how can you let
that man smoke in the office? It's such a disgusting
habit!"

I offered Vida a lame little shrug. "It's no more disgusting than Ed's eating habits. Smoking just smells
worse. Sometimes."

Vida shuddered. "Advertising people are very odd.
When I first came to work here, Marius Vandeventer
had a young man from—"

The phone rang, and on the hope that it was Milo, I
answered. But the sheriff wasn't on the other end. To
my surprise, it was his light-o'-love, Honoria Whitman.

We exchanged somewhat effusive, though genuine,
greetings. Then Honoria, in her charming, well-bred
way, came to the point:

"I'm worried about Milo. We had dinner in Sultan
last night and he seemed terribly upset about the lack of
progress in this murder case. Do you suppose we could
get together and talk about it? I'll treat you to a meal at
the Dutch Cup. Tonight, unless that's short notice. I realize that you must be awfully busy. . . ."

"You're making my sides ache." The words sprang
out of my mouth. "I mean, my social life isn't exactly
putting me in an airplane spin. Sure, that sounds fine."
Noting Vida's frankly curious expression, I felt a twinge
of guilt. "Shall I pick you up?" My voice dropped a
couple of notches, as if I could spare Vida's feelings.

"You don't need to." Honoria was proud of her independence with her specially rigged car and high-tech
wheelchair.

"But your place is right on the way into Sultan. Why
take two cars?" It was true; I would have made the

same offer to someone who wasn't physically handicapped.

"All right," Honoria agreed. "You know the turnoff. Be careful, the road is rather muddy and some potholes have developed since you were here a year ago last summer."

I pictured Honoria's cedar-shake cottage nestled among evergreens and vine maples. She had invested it with charm, and her own personality, which were probably the same thing.

"What time?" I asked, awkwardly aware of Vida's splay-footed exit from my office.

"Six-thirty?" Honoria's suggestion was made easily, as if time were of no importance. Maybe it isn't, when wherever you're going can't be reached on your own two feet.

"Fine," I agreed, mentally scratching my plan to visit the murder site. "I'll see you then."

"Ah . . ." The familiar husky laugh was self-conscious. "Do you think . . . would you mind . . . that is, I was wondering if your . . . what do you call her? Vida, isn't it? Do you think she might be coaxed into joining us? I don't really know her that well, and Milo makes her sound so formidable."

Through the doorway, I could see Vida at the window above her desk. She had put on her tweed coat and was holding a black, broad-brimmed pointed rain hat in her hand. Her broad shoulders were oddly hunched as she stared out into the gathering darkness that enveloped Front Street. For just one fleeting moment, there was something touching about her stance.

"I'll do my best," I promised Honoria. Then I whispered into the phone: "Vida's really a dear. She scares Milo because he's . . . a man."

The husky laugh grew deeper. "Don't we all? By the

way, don't mention our little get-together to Milo."
Honoria rang off.

I was on my feet, hurrying out to tell Vida about the
dinner invitation. She brushed me off, racing for the
door. "Never mind just now. Milo's coming out of
the bank." Vida jammed the black rain hat on her head
and left the news office.

Throwing on my jacket, I chased after her. Vaguely I
noted that Leo had left. So, apparently, had Carla and
Ginny. A quick check of the old-fashioned clock that
stood on a tall pedestal by the bank told me it was 5:01.
My staff was entitled to be gone.

Vida had already corralled Milo and was dragging
him back to the office. Milo wasn't exactly kicking and
screaming, but he wasn't pleased.

"Damn it, Vida, I've got work to do," he protested.
"Why don't you people go home?"

"Journalists never sleep," Vida asserted, all but shov-
ing Milo into her visitor's chair. "What's going on at
the bank?"

Briefly Milo looked rattled. "The bank? What about
the bank? Why are you asking?"

Vida was slowly pacing the news-office floor, one
hand fingering her chin. She looked like an inquisitor
working for Torquemada. "There's trouble over there,"
she said. "Emma and I already know that. There've
been a number of complaints. Grace Grundle. The Dithers sisters. Leo." She glanced at our ad manager's
empty chair. "One of the Gustavsons. Two Bergstroms.
Henry Bardeen from the ski lodge." Vida whirled, a ma-
jestic figure with her coat wrapped around her and the
pointed black rain hat atilt. It would have made a great
picture for Halloween. If only we'd thought of it at the
time.

"Screw off, Vida." Milo was at his most phlegmatic.

He extracted a toothpick from the pocket of his regulation jacket and began to munch.

"Now, listen here, young man." Vida was wagging a finger in Milo's face. "Don't speak to me like that! We're conducting an investigation of our own at *The Advocate*. We have reason to believe that there have been some serious—possibly criminal—irregularities at the Bank of Alpine. It grieves me to say as much, but there it is. The public has a right to know. Are you going to fly in the face of the United States Constitution?"

Milo broke his toothpick. But he didn't lose his nerve. "I'm not going to fly anywhere. I don't know what the hell is going on yet, and I don't intend to say one damned word until I find out. Give me a break." Wistfully he looked in my direction. "You got any coffee left, Emma?"

I shook my head. Ginny's last official duty of the day was to make sure that the coffeemaker was unplugged and cleaned. Despite her broken heart, she had lived up to her responsibilities.

Milo unwound his big frame from Vida's extra chair. "Then I'm going back to work." Resolutely he walked past Vida. "When I know something for sure, I'll let you know. Meanwhile, don't call me. I'll call you." The sheriff slammed the door behind him.

Ten minutes later, I was home, renewing my makeup and changing clothes. It was not quite six when the phone rang. Warily I picked up the receiver, half expecting another hang-up. Instead, I heard the voice of Tom Cavanaugh. My heart turned over and my knees went weak. How silly can a woman of forty-plus be? I had the emotional range of a teenager.

"It's happened," Tom said, his voice not so mellow as usual.

The two words and their delivery forced me to sit down. "What's happened?" I asked stupidly.

There was a pause at the other end. Tom was sitting in the handsomely decorated study of an expensive San Francisco mansion, or so I always imagined. Adam had never been to the Cavanaugh house. Tom had not yet had the nerve to introduce his illegitimate son to the two children born in wedlock.

"Sandra wants a divorce." Tom's voice was oddly flat. It stayed that way as he asked what I realized was the inevitable question: "Will you marry me?"

The words were the ones I'd longed to hear for over twenty years. I'd given away my youth to that proposal, I'd sacrificed a half dozen eligible men at the altar of Tom's married state. Now I actually heard the question, reverberating off my left ear, while I struggled with a pair of brown slacks that didn't seem to fit either of my legs.

"What?" It was all I could think to say. I wondered if I could reach the bottle of bourbon in my so-called liquor cabinet.

Tom was laughing. Sort of. "Sandra has met somebody else. A stand-up comic, in fact. He's twenty-six, and she's nuts about him. Emma, what did Sabatini say?"

The answer came by rote: " 'Born with the gift of laughter and the sense that the world was mad.' " Tom and I had often mouthed the quote when we were conducting our impassioned affair. There was more, something about that being the only patrimony of Sabatini's bastard hero. It had fit Adam only too well. But of course, our son had never read *Scaramouche.* "A stand-up comic?" I began to giggle; my laughter sounded akin to hysteria.

"That's right. Sandra saw him in some North Beach club she went to with her equally screwed-up girlfriends. They threw money at him. He joined them after his gig, and the next thing—so Sandra told me—they were holed up in some motel by Fisherman's Wharf. She's crazy about him and wants to bankroll a feature film for which he's written the script. But of course, she's just plain crazy anyway. You know that. He probably does, too."

A weary note had crept into Tom's voice. I was at a loss for words. "Tom . . . is it a phase?"

"Who knows? She's got an attorney—well, she's always had an army of them, what with her various legal problems, such as shoplifting sable coats from I. Magnin and punching out hot-dog vendors on Market Street. But she actually filed yesterday. No, it was Wednesday—Thursday was a holiday." Tom's voice dropped, and I could picture him holding the phone in one hand and his head in the other. His noble Roman profile was probably nuzzling the receiver.

"Well." I was still dazed. "What about your kids?"

"Sandra called them today. I haven't spoken with them yet." He sighed, the long heavy breath traveling the nine hundred miles between San Francisco and Alpine. "It's a mess, Emma. But she seems to have made up her mind. Maybe it's for the best."

"Come up to see me," I said, throwing caution to the wind. "Adam will be here for Thanksgiving. We'll try to sort it out. You need to take a break."

"I can't." Tom sounded pained. "The kids are coming home from college for the holiday. Sandra insists that we spend Thanksgiving together, as a family. Christmas, too. But she's going to be with Zorro for New Year's."

"Zorro?"

"That's his name. At least, his stage name. Zorro Black. Emma—am *I* crazy? All along, has it been me, and not Sandra?"

Tom sounded so bleak that I was moved to tears. That takes a lot, considering that I haven't cried since my parents were killed over twenty years ago.

"Of course not," I said staunchly. "Sandra is wacked out of her mind, and always has been. You're just suffering from the fallout."

"I've got to see you." Tom seemed to have gained momentum. "New Year's. I'll fly up after Christmas. It's only a little over a month. Or could you come down here for a couple of days? I'll pay for it."

The old, familiar streak of independence reared its head. "No!" It was bad enough that I'd allowed Tom to pay for some of Adam's transportation. He sure as hell wasn't going to foot my bills as well. Yet I hadn't meant to distress him. "It's a bad time," I went on hastily. "We've got a big story brewing. Two, maybe. Either one may break before the Wednesday pub date, or maybe not until just before Thanksgiving."

If there was one excuse Tom could accept without an argument, it was breaking news. "Alpine sounds like a hotbed," he remarked. I couldn't tell if he was serious.

Now that his situation was becoming real to me, I tried to think logically. "New Year's is fine. Adam and Ben will both be here."

"Do you need backup?" The irony had returned to Tom's voice.

"Maybe I do." I chewed on my lower lip. "You've got to admit, this is a shock. I can't help but wonder if Sandra will change her mind. Or that Zorro will."

"It's been going on since September. I didn't find out until about two weeks ago. Having Sandra disappear isn't exactly unusual." Tom's tone had again turned flat.

"I know." I was well versed in Sandra Cavanaugh's escapades. Not too long ago, she had flown to Bombay without any notice. Tom had only found out where she was when the local police had notified him that his wife had threatened a sacred cow with a meat fork.

"He won't stay with her," Tom said. "Zorro, I mean. But that doesn't guarantee she'll come back to me."

I took a deep breath. "Do you want her back?"

The laugh I loved so much sounded shaky. "I don't know. For twenty-five years, I've considered Sandra my responsibility in life. I made a commitment, not just when we were married, but later." His voice lowered. "You know about that. I had a choice to make when you got pregnant. By then, I knew Sandra wasn't well. I had to give you up, which was penance enough, but I never was one to do things by half—I also vowed to take care of her for as long as she needed me. Marrying Zorro doesn't necessarily mean she won't need me again."

Naturally, Tom was making perfect sense. Naturally, that didn't matter. "Then why the hell are you asking me to marry you?"

Tom made an exasperated noise. "Because I want to. And because even if Zorro dumps Sandra, I could still take care of her. I could be appointed her legal guardian or something. She wouldn't be left on her own."

I bit back the words that rose to my lips: How wonderful to be married to Tom, and have Sandra living out in the carport, stabbing sacred cows and scurrying off to shoplift at Harvey's Hardware.

"We need some time," I said gently. "Let's see what happens with Sandra and Zorro over the next few weeks. Plan on coming to Alpine after Christmas. Don't try to push things. We've waited all these years—will a month or two make much difference?"

"I wish I knew." Tom's voice actually broke. I might not have cried in twenty years, but maybe he had. Often. "If only I could see what was going to happen between now and . . . Emma?"

"Yes?"

"Do you still love me?"

"Of course I do! Why do you ask?"

There was a pause. "Well . . . if you were as bright as I think you are, you wouldn't. Not after all this time. People are supposed to fall out of love."

People are supposed to do a lot of things, smart things, wise things, things that make life easier. But they don't. Instead, they act foolishly, sometimes self-destructively. Nobody knew that better than I did.

"Don't be a jackass," I said, wishing away the catch in my own voice. "Call me, if you need to. Any time. Let Sandra run with whatever it is she thinks she wants. You couldn't stop her if you tried."

"I never could." Tom's sigh was heavy with hopelessness. I could all but feel his warm breath on my ear. Five months ago, we'd stood at the edge of Lake Chelan, pretending we belonged together. Maybe we really did. Maybe. "I'll look forward to seeing you," Tom said briskly. "My calendar's clear for the end of December."

The sudden formality in his voice indicated that someone had entered the room. Sandra, perhaps. Tom said goodbye in a detached manner. I held on to the phone for almost a full minute after we were disconnected.

I hadn't heard Vida honk her horn. After only the most halfhearted of demurs, she had agreed to join Honoria and me for dinner. Again she had insisted on driving her big Buick.

The loud knock at my door snapped me out of my

love-struck daze. Finally managing to get one each of my own legs into one each of the brown slacks', I let Vida in.

"Well! I thought you must be in the shower. Are you ready?" Vida was wearing a winter-white turban with her brown tweed coat. Before I could respond, she leaned forward and stared into my face. "Mercy, what's wrong? You look like a sheet! Are you sick?"

"Let's save it for the ride to Startup." Grabbing my jacket and handbag, I turned off all the lights except for the desk lamp and the ship's lantern on the front porch. Three minutes later, we had crossed the bridge over the Skykomish River and were heading for Highway 2.

Vida was the only person in Alpine in whom I would confide my sorry love life. She listened to my recital without comment. We were zipping past the turnoff to the town of Skykomish when I finally finished.

"Typical," Vida said, tromping on the accelerator to pass a swaying RV. "Sandra isn't merely unstable, she's ungrateful. Poor Tommy."

Nobody but Vida called Tom *Tommy*. She got away with it. Indeed, when Tom had visited Alpine two years earlier, he and Vida had formed the basis for a friendship. The relationship pleased me, almost as much as if my own mother had approved.

"It's too soon to tell what will happen," I said, my voice sounding forlorn in my ears.

"Definitely. Sandra's unpredictability is so predictable." With that cryptic comment, Vida said no more and concentrated on her driving. The farther west we drove, the harder the rain seemed to fall. It was very dark, and if Vida hadn't known the road by heart, I would have worried. Despite the weather, traffic on Highway 2 was heavy. It usually was on a Friday night, with cross-state travelers going between Seattle and

Spokane, along with various smaller cities along the route, including some college towns.

Honoria had been right about the mud and the pot-holes. Vida's left front tire hit a big one right after we left the main road. She negotiated the rest of the short drive very carefully.

"Milo should fix those for Honoria," she said as we pulled up outside of the cottage. "If nothing else, he's handy."

Obviously Honoria had been watching for our arrival. We exchanged hugs, and I formally introduced her to Vida. Then we began the task of getting Honoria and her wheelchair into the backseat of the Buick.

"I'm sorry to be such a bother," she said after we were heading back to Highway 2.

"Nonsense," Vida replied crisply. "If you have to have a handicap, it's better to be physically crippled than mentally deranged." Vida shot me a knowing look.

Honoria laughed at Vida's candor. "It would be better to be neither."

"That's rare," Vida said, pointing the Buick toward Sultan. "Most people have some sort of handicap. The difficulty for others is when it doesn't show."

The drive to the Dutch Cup was brief, covering less than five miles. It was six-forty when we sat down in a comfortable booth and were presented with big three-fold plastic menus. The waitress announced the specials, which included prime rib and prawns Madeira. When she asked if we'd like something first from the bar, Vida said no; Honoria and I chorused in the affirmative.

"It's my treat, remember." Honoria widened her gray eyes at Vida.

But Vida seemed resolute. "Not tonight. I rarely imbibe." She gave the waitress a guileless smile. "Unless, of course, your bartender can make a sidecar."

The bartender could. Vida feigned surprise. "My, my, so often these days restaurant employees don't know the old-fashioned drinks. I'm quite flabbergasted."

Honoria appeared to be stifling a smile. "Sultan is sort of an old-fashioned place. I believe the present owners have been here for years."

"Seventeen," Vida answered promptly. "The Eslicks. Or something like that. I take it you're adjusting to rural life?"

Honoria's oval face registered uncertainty. "I get homesick for Carmel. It isn't exactly a metropolis, but it does possess a great deal of sophistication. Startup is . . . different. I enjoy the tranquillity. But I miss California, especially going into the Bay Area."

Vida's nose wrinkled. "I haven't been to Frisco in years," she admitted. "But the last time I visited, it was so *noisy*. And crowded. However do people put up with all that bustle?"

"Well . . ." Honoria gave me a quick, bemused glance. If she thought it was lost on Vida, she was wrong. Next to me, I could feel Vida bristle. "It's a matter of adjusting to tempo. And of personal interests. I miss the opera and the ballet and the theatre. I try to get into Seattle once in a while, but I'm hampered." Lest we mistake her meaning for a reference to her handicap, she waved a strong, yet graceful hand at us. "It's not because of the wheelchair. It's that Milo isn't much interested in culture."

"Surprise." Vida let the word fall like lead. "If it doesn't swim, Milo is oblivious. Now tell us if you're worried about Milo and this murder investigation or if you're worried about him, period. Perhaps Emma and I can help."

Among other things, I had always admired Honoria's poise. But in the face of Vida's blunt speech, even Honoria seemed a trifle shaken. She bowed her head, then smiled in a self-deprecating manner.

"Both, actually. I wasted a lot more than time on my first husband." Her lovely face turned grim. "I'm not prepared to throw away any more years on a man. I honestly don't think Milo wants to get married again. He seems quite content with his job and his fishing and an occasional hunting trip. But more importantly, the heart of him *is* the job—and he's very depressed over this recent homicide. It may be pointless—from a personal point of view—to get him through this crisis. Still, I owe it to him to try. You two know him very well. Is there anything I can do to help?"

Honoria had certainly laid her case on the line. I slumped back in the booth, feeling inadequate. But as usual, Vida rose to the occasion.

"Yes, there is. You can start by opening an account at the Bank of Alpine. You're handicapped, and you have a reason to request proxy banking. Go in there Monday morning and ask for it. Then we'll see what happens next." Vida folded her arms across her bosom and waited for Honoria's reaction.

Thoughtfully Honoria ran a hand through her short ash-blonde hair. "How will that help Milo?"

Keeping her voice down, Vida explained our misgivings about the bank. "I'm not saying that Linda's murder is tied into these apparent discrepancies. On the other hand, it's almost too much to be a coincidence. And Milo was at the bank late this afternoon. He wouldn't tell us why."

Honoria was still looking pensive. "If Milo is conducting an investigation of the bank—along with Linda's murder—he'll find out that I'm a customer."

"That doesn't matter," Vida replied promptly. "You have an excuse—the proxy banking arrangement. Let's say Emma told you about Leo Walsh. You thought it was a good idea."

Honoria lifted her fine eyebrows. "Leo . . . who?"

It was my turn to offer an explanation. By the time I finished, Honoria had made her decision: "I'll do it. Actually, it might come in handy, though I suppose my present bank in Sultan could offer the same service. Is there any way I can be sure that I won't lose money?"

Vida might not claim to be an expert on financial institutions, but as usual, she was well versed in practical information: "As long as you keep receipts and records, the bank will have to reimburse you. It's the law. But addlepates like Grace Grundle lose things or throw them away. That's when the trouble starts."

Honoria seemed satisfied. After we put in our orders, she extracted the latest copy of *The Advocate* from her woven leather purse. "Milo brought me a copy of this week's edition. I really should subscribe." Honoria wore a sheepish expression as she pointed to the studio portrait we'd run of Linda Lindahl. "I didn't read the paper until this afternoon. But I recognize her. She was at this restaurant about ten days ago, having dinner with a man."

I scooted forward on my seat. "What did he look like?"

Honoria frowned. "That's the problem. I come here about once a week, with or without Milo. It's so tiresome to cook for one person. I was sitting over there"— she pointed to a booth across the aisle and down one place—"and Linda was at the next table. She was facing me, and the man's back was turned. All I recall is that he was about her age and rather average from my limited viewpoint. I think his hair was brown."

Vida's mouth twitched with curiosity. "Were they amiable? Romantic? At odds?"

There was nothing glib about Honoria. Perhaps she'd always been reflective. Certainly, spending months of recovery after her tragic accident must have made her introspective. I'd often wondered how much Honoria blamed herself for marrying her violent, abusive husband in the first place. The Honoria Whitman I knew wouldn't have made such a disastrous choice.

"Linda looked sour," Honoria finally said. "I remember thinking—in that fleeting way we all do when things don't seem important and yet catch our attention—that she was an unhappy woman. Rather hard, too. But her unhappiness struck me as a permanent condition, not just a temporary state." Honoria uttered her husky little laugh. "You probably think I'm embroidering my story in retrospect. But when you're eating alone, you get in a habit of studying people."

I understood. But my perceptions weren't as keen as Honoria's. "Were Linda and the man openly quarreling?" I asked.

Honoria shook her head. "No. They were talking very earnestly. I left before they did. Unfortunately, I didn't pass them on the way out."

Vida was mulling. "Fortyish, brown hair, average. Sitting down, so you couldn't judge height. It could be anybody."

Honoria didn't agree completely. "I don't think he was overly tall. He and Linda seemed to be close to eye level."

"Ah." Vida's face brightened. "When was this exactly?"

"A week ago Tuesday." Honoria seemed very certain. "I teach a class at the Monroe Reformatory on Tuesdays. I stopped here on my way home. It was around six-fifteen."

Tuesday, November second, seemed like a very long time ago. It was now the twelfth, but I felt as if weeks had passed since Linda Lindahl had been alive.

Vida was still contemplating. "If I had to guess, I'd say that the man with Linda was Howard, her ex-husband. Was his light brown hair thinning?"

But Vida's guess was off the mark. "No," Honoria replied. "He had a full head of hair. And it wasn't light—it was dark brown. Did I mention that he was wearing what looked like a suit? That's very odd for around here."

Vida blinked several times. "That's very odd for Alpine, too. In fact, that's very odd indeed."

Chapter Twelve

VIDA AGAIN HAD Roger for the day. His parents had gone over to Everett to do some early Christmas shopping. I secretly hoped they were buying him a cage. But his presence at Vida's house prevented me from asking her to drive up to the murder site. The thought of spending time with Roger was only slightly less horrifying than the murder itself.

Our capricious weather had changed again, with a sudden warming trend, westerly winds, and spasmodic rain showers. When I pulled off the road around eleven that Saturday morning, the rain had stopped. Still, I hesitated before getting out of the Jag. Another car was already parked off Highway 187. I immediately recognized Marv Petersen's Cadillac.

Cautiously, I moved into the clearing. Had Marv come to pay homage to the site where his daughter had been killed? But a few yards away, under a slim cedar, Marv appeared to be scouring the ground. He didn't look up until I accidentally stepped on a vine-maple twig.

"Emma!" Marv seemed more frightened than startled. "What are you doing here?"

I felt embarrassed. Marv's usually rubicund face was haggard, and his eyes darted nervously. "It's my job," I said simply. "I needed to see this for myself."

"So did I." He cleared his throat. "I wouldn't let Cathleen come. It would only upset her. Not that she isn't . . ." His voice trailed away as he bent his head.

Except for the wind moaning in the evergreens, it was very quiet in the clearing. The wet ground was covered with fallen leaves. Salmonberry vines, which had grown up after the second stand of timber was cut, were now bare and brown, twisted like snakes over fallen logs. All but a few of the ferns were withered; the trilliums had begun their winter rot; the wild bleeding heart had been trampled underfoot. The air smelled of decay, of damp, of death. And yet I knew that under the ground there was new life at work, slumbering, perhaps, but waiting for another season.

There were no more springtimes for Linda Lindahl, however. I searched for the hollow log where she had been hidden, but, of course, it wasn't there. Milo and his men had taken it away as part of the evidence. Marv followed my gaze and grunted.

"I'm glad it's gone," he said, reading my thoughts.

I gave a nod and wondered why I had come. I also wondered why Marv Petersen had come. Paying tribute, I had thought. But my first sighting of him had suggested something else. I could have sworn that he was searching the area. It was impossible to pose the question. Instead, I chose a more neutral topic.

"Marv, satisfy my curiosity." I thought he gave a little jump, but maybe he merely stepped on some uneven ground. There was plenty of it in the boglike clearing. "Why is there a blank medallion on the wall at the bank?"

Marv's shoulders seemed to slump under his heavy parka. "Oh, that!" The faintest smile played at his mouth. "That was for the silent partner who helped found the bank. According to my father, one of the early Alpiners was quite a gambling man. Lucky, too. Still, his wife didn't approve. One night he won over six thousand dollars in a poker game in Seattle. That was a lot of money in 1930. He didn't know what to do with it—he couldn't admit to the missus that he'd won it at cards—so he invested it to help start the bank."

"But you don't know who he was?" I found that unlikely in Alpine, where everybody knows everything about everybody else.

Marv shook his head. We were wandering around the clearing, retracing our steps. Milo was right about the trees along the highway. They definitely shielded any activity from the road or the golf course across the way. Besides, it had been dark when Linda was killed.

"For all I know, whoever it was didn't stay in Alpine," Marv said. "A lot of people left after the original mill was closed. Believe it or not, I was just a little kid at the time."

There were so many other questions I wanted to ask Marv, especially about the bank. But in that sad little clearing, with the west wind snapping off twigs and the rain pattering down once more, I couldn't bring myself to play the part of hard-bitten reporter. Monday, maybe, I could brace him in his office.

I stopped walking, my hands shoved into the pockets of my green jacket. "I'd better head back," I murmured. When Marv made no reply, I turned to face him. "Maybe you should, too."

He removed his plaid hunter's cap, then resettled it on his balding head. "I will. But not yet." Marv's attempt at a smile was valiant, almost desperate.

I smiled back. I didn't need to be valiant, but I wanted to be kind. It didn't seem right to leave him alone in the clearing with the wind and the rain and his grief.

But of course, he wasn't alone. Linda was with him.

The peace was broken by the rumble of road machinery, coursing down Highway 187. I recognized Mike Brockelman, driving something that I assumed was a paver. I waved; he stopped.

"We're done," he shouted from his perch in the cab. "We worked overtime today to make sure we finished before the snow really hits."

"Great," I congratulated him. "Where do you go next?"

"I won't know until Monday," he replied. "Wherever it is, it'll be below the snow line." An older sedan was coming from the other direction. Mike waited for it to pass. "Say, how's the sheriff doing with that murder? I don't get much chance to keep up with the news when I'm working a job like this."

Peering up from ground level, it was hard for me to read Mike Brockelman's expression. "He's making progress," I said, hoping it might be true. "It must be kind of creepy for you. I mean, the murder happened just about where you were working at the time."

Mike swiveled in his seat, looking behind him. "We were further up the road by then. But it was creepy, all right." Big Mike gave a shudder. "Damned terrible, if you ask me. Linda was a nice woman."

I tried not to show surprise at Mike's acknowledgment of acquaintanceship. "You were friends?"

"In a way. I met her at the Venison Inn one night a while back. We had a few drinks, a few laughs." He shrugged his broad shoulders. "Man, you sure never know, do you? One minute you're here, and the next—

zap!" He shook his head, then wiped his mouth with the back of his hand. "Say, has the sheriff talked to you much about this mess?"

I tried to look innocent. "There isn't much to talk about yet. Not officially, that is. Why?"

Mike's coworkers were coming up behind him in a convoy of state highway trucks and other road machinery, including a behemoth with a crane. "Just curious," he said, easing off on the brake. "I'd better move along before these yahoos rear-end me. So long."

Mike rolled off down the new smooth surface of Highway 187. His subordinates waved to me as they followed. My hair was now wet from the rain and I was beginning to shiver. Before I got into the Jag, I glanced at the entrance to the clearing. There was still no sign of Marv Petersen. The weather wouldn't bother him. It was the least of his problems. I sensed that Marv was already cold, all the way through to his soul.

Milo Dodge's coffee was weak as water, but at least it was hot. I cradled the Seahawks mug in my hands and listened to the sheriff rant.

"What did I tell you? Stop meddling, damn it!"

"I hardly call listening to Janet Driggers talk on the phone *meddling*." My tone was indignant. I didn't intend to tell Milo about Leo's roses or the map Alison Lindahl had given me. Not yet. And I certainly wasn't going to mention having dinner with Honoria. "As for driving up to the murder site, if I'm going to write about it, I have to know what it looks like. I hadn't been in the area for quite a while. It's not my fault I happened to run into Marv Petersen and Mike Brockelman."

The fluorescent lights in Milo's office blinked twice, a sure sign of a storm. "So what if Christie and her husband are going back to Michigan? What's that got to do with Linda getting killed?"

"But she asked Janet about a one-way ticket," I said. "Doesn't that strike you as odd?"

"She was probably trying to finagle a deal. Or maybe they're going on to someplace else." Milo was looking mulish. "What do you expect me to do? Tell her and Troy they can't leave town?"

I had to admit that Milo was in a bind when it came to handling potential suspects. There weren't any, except maybe Howard Lindahl.

"Mike Brockelman admitted to me that he was seeing Linda," I said, deciding to give up temporarily on Christie Johnston. "You might as well confess that he did the same to you."

Reaching into his pocket, Milo pulled out a roll of mints. He offered one to me, and I accepted. Maybe it would give the coffee some flavor. "I don't think it was anything serious. There wasn't time. Mike only got up here last month. I figure it was just a romp in the hay for both of them."

Milo's assessment made sense. Mike hadn't appeared overcome by grief when he'd talked to me about Linda. On the other hand, he wouldn't be in mourning if he'd killed her.

"I think Marv was looking for something," I said suddenly. "Does that make sense?"

Milo scoffed. "We combed that place pretty good. Of course, it started snowing, but we'd have found anything if it had been there. Maybe he was looking for Linda's car keys. They're right here." The sheriff opened a drawer and waved a plastic bag at me. "They've been checked out for fingerprints, so we might as well give them to Marv. He'll probably want to move Linda's car."

Milo's door opened and Bill Blatt poked his head inside. "Andy Cederberg's here. He's having second thoughts."

Milo frowned at his deputy. "About what?"

Bill's fair face colored slightly. "The car at John Engstrom Park. He thinks it wasn't an accident."

"Jeez." Milo tossed the bag containing the keys on his desk. "Okay, send him in. Just what we need—paranoia."

Andy Cederberg entered the office with a diffident air. I waited for Milo to dismiss me, but he didn't.

"If this is an official complaint, Andy, Emma might as well hear it. She'll get it from the log anyway."

Andy sat down next to me, his lanky frame tense. "I've been talking to Reba about what happened last week. I've dreamed about it, too, and it's so real that I wake up in a sweat. That car was going real slow, I remember that now, and then it suddenly speeded up and came right over the curb. You know, as if the driver saw me through the fog. In fact, I could almost swear that whoever it was had followed me from when I turned up Fourth Street and started down Pine." Andy now looked eager, awaiting Milo's response.

Milo found a toothpick on his desk. "This all came back to you now?" He began to chew in a speculative manner.

Andy nodded vigorously. "Yes, it did. I think I was in shock the first few days. Linda got killed, and everything at the bank's been such a mess—I hadn't really given myself a chance to concentrate. At first, it was just an impression. But then I started piecing it together."

Milo leaned back in his faux leather chair. "You can lodge your complaint, Andy. But you can't identify the car or the driver. We're up a stump."

"I know." Andy gave Milo a helpless look. "The

thing is, I don't know why anyone would want to run me down. As Reba says, I haven't got an enemy in the world."

It wasn't my place to point out that Linda probably didn't, either. Milo was nodding slowly, the toothpick twirling in his mouth.

"You go ahead and fill out the form," Milo said. "Bill Blatt can give you one. If you can bring up the car's make, license number, or what the driver looked like from your repressed memory, let us know."

Andy didn't miss the note of sarcasm. "Look, Sheriff, I'm not making this up! Think about it—why would anybody, driving in that fog at night, suddenly speed up and go over the curb? You could say he lost control, but on a residential street under those conditions? I don't buy it. If I were you, I'd have your deputies start looking for vehicles that may have some front-end damage."

Milo, who had apparently remembered that Andy Cederberg was a registered voter, removed the toothpick and sat up straight. "Okay, let's say you're right. But frankly, Andy, we've got too much on our plate right now with Linda's murder—and some other things—to check out every car in Skykomish County. If someone's really trying to kill you, they'll try again." Noting Andy quiver, Milo put up a big hand. "Relax. It's more likely that they were trying to scare you. But be careful, just in case. You might try walking home a different way. Or taking your car to work."

Andy was definitely unhinged. His voice shook as he replied: "But we only have one car. Reba needs it. And it's no trouble to walk."

"Work it out," Milo responded, exhibiting impatience. "Look, if it makes you feel better, we'll have somebody patrol your house for a few days. We'll check with the auto-body shop to see if anybody has brought in a car with suspicious damage. And speaking of cars," he added, picking up the plastic bag and shaking out the set of keys, "give these to Marv when you see him Monday. They belonged to Linda."

Timorously Andy took the keys in his bony fingers. "Shouldn't you give them to Marv?"

Milo shrugged. "You'll probably see him before I do. I don't think Marv is anxious to see me in the bank real soon," he added cryptically.

Andy didn't seem to hear Milo. He was staring at the keys, and for the first time, he smiled, albeit grimly. "That's weird," he remarked. "Boy, people are sure strange."

"Oh?" Milo sounded bored.

Andy was pointing to the keys. "See, Linda has all these marked with adhesive tape. She was so methodical. Her house key, her car keys, her key to the bank, even luggage keys. But she had a key to Howard's house, because she needed it when she went over to drop things off for Alison. This is really kind of . . . funny."

Milo looked as if he weren't amused, but I leaned closer to Andy. "Why is that?" I asked.

Andy's smile twitched along with the rest of his skinny frame. "I remember once when Linda's key chain broke. She had to get a new one, which was easy because we were giving them away with new accounts. You got a clock radio if you deposited over five hundred dollars. Anyway, I was with her when she was putting the keys on the new chain. She said she always put Howard's key as far away from her condo key as possible. It was symbolic, you see. But," he continued, waggling the keys at Milo and me, "they're right next to each other. Maybe she stopped hating him, huh?"

* * *

"You aren't supposed to drink on duty." My voice was stern as I spoke to Milo at the Venison Inn.

"One beer will not make me drunk," he replied in a surly tone. "After Andy Cederberg, I could use a stiff Scotch. In fact, if you'll excuse me, I'm going to get something." Milo rose from the booth and went off in the direction of the bar.

About the only time I ever drink beer is in the sheriff's company. Thus, I stared into my schooner and tried to make sense of Andy's visit to Milo Dodge. But my mind wasn't on murder or attempted murder. Rather, I saw Sandra Cavanaugh flitting around North Beach with a handsome, brainless hunk half her age.

I also saw Christie Johnston, but she was real, coming down the aisle with her husband, Troy. I smiled and waved.

"Thursday at the funeral was the first time I saw you out of your UPS uniform," I said to Troy. "I almost didn't recognize you."

Like Christie, Troy was not a native Alpiner. But wherever he went to high school, I was certain he'd played football. He was under six feet, but stocky, with a thick neck and broad shoulders. I'd seen him heft parcels that looked as if they could be handled only by a forklift.

"Yeah," he replied, looking ill at ease. "Most people don't know me in my civvies. Christie and I haven't been here long enough to make a big impression."

"Small towns are like that," I said lightly. "You two are taking a trip, I hear. We should mention it in Vida's 'Scene Around Town.' "

Christie seemed to be leaning on Troy, edging him toward the door. "Go ahead. It'd be as interesting as most of the stuff she writes about."

"Michigan, right?" I feigned fascination. "You have relatives there, Troy?"

Troy looked surprised at my knowledge. "My brother. I grew up in Royal Oak, outside of Detroit."

Christie's gaze narrowed. I could have sworn there was malice in her eyes. "You people sure snoop around a lot at the newspaper. I suppose you want to know the rest of our itinerary."

I played the stooge to the hilt. "That would be wonderful. Then, when you get back, Vida can do a story about your trip."

"In that case, you can wait." Christie gave me a frosty smile. "Until we get back, that is. 'Bye." She propelled Troy out of the restaurant.

When Milo returned, I was still staring at the door that had closed behind the Johnstons. To my astonishment, he was carrying a pack of cigarettes.

"Whatever are you doing?" I demanded, the Johnstons momentarily forgotten.

Milo opened the pack, took out a cigarette, and produced a lighter I'd seen him use only on that rare occasion when he smoked a cigar. "I'm trying to kill myself. Any objections?"

"This isn't the smoking section," I protested. "And you're an idiot."

"You're right on both counts," Milo replied, puffing away. "But I'm the sheriff, remember? If they want to throw me out, they'll have to get my deputies to do it. Where the hell's the ashtray?"

"Use your beer glass," I snarled. "Here comes our lunch. What's gotten into you? How long has it been since you quit?"

Our waitress, who was yet another recent graduate of Alpine High School, gaped at Milo. Instead of repri-

manding him, however, she deposited our food and
raced off to fetch an ashtray.

"I quit the day my divorce was final. Six years ago.
Or is it seven? Who's counting?" Milo thanked the
waitress for the ashtray. She practically streaked away.
"I've tried gum, mints, toothpicks, everything but
chewing on utility cords. Oh, it wasn't too bad until this
damned Linda Lindahl case. But you should hear the
phone calls and read the letters I'm getting. You'd think
I'd killed Linda. I'll tell you one thing, Emma, that
woman's a lot better liked dead than she ever was
alive."

The point wasn't arguable. "It's her family, not
Linda," I remarked as the restaurant lights blinked.
"The Petersens are the essential Alpiners, going back to
Frank when he worked as treasurer at the mill."

"Right, right, right." Milo waved away my comment
with a swirl of smoke, then extinguished his cigarette
and tackled his cheeseburger. "When the locals aren't
raving about my incompetence, they're demanding we
haul Bob Lambrecht back to town and string him up.
Some of them are actually accusing me of shielding
Bob because we went to high school together."

I was aghast. "That's crazy! Bob couldn't have killed
Linda! He wasn't even in Alpine!"

"Hey, did I say any of this crap made sense?" Milo
was derisive. "These jerks are jumping on Bob because
he's an outsider. Worse than an outsider, because he
once was an insider. He defected, and went to the Big
City. He couldn't help it if he kept getting promoted."

Even Milo somehow managed to make Bob Lambrecht's success sound like a character flaw. "You need
a serious suspect," I said, falling back on the obvious.

"Jeez." Milo looked at me as if my head had come to
a point. "Big news from *The Advocate*'s editor in chief.

What do I do? Arrest the Petersens and charge them with conspiracy? They're as good an example of Alpine as you can find. Frank and Irmgaard were involved in every civic enterprise and charity that came along. Marv and Cathleen have kept up the tradition. Larry and JoAnne do their share, too. Linda wasn't made in the same mold, and Denise was lucky she didn't get kicked out of Camp Fire Girls. But by and large, the Petersens are a big noise around here."

"You left out Uncle Elmer. And the sister. Was she at the funeral?" I asked, dipping my deep-fried cod into a small dish of tarter sauce.

Milo nodded. "DeAnne and her husband came up from Seattle. I talked to them for a few minutes. They'd just gotten back from New Zealand and were still in a state of shock."

"And Elmer?" I had glimpsed Elmer and Thelma at the services. Milo's aunt had been appropriately, if untidily, dressed in black. Uncle Elmer's attire had consisted of a denim jacket and rumpled brown trousers. He had kept his distance from the rest of the family, but given his lack of social skills, that was hardly surprising.

"What about Elmer?" Milo demanded through a mouthful of burger.

The lights flickered again. I could hear the distant rumble of thunder. "He and your aunt aren't exactly involved," I noted.

"They're farmers." Milo drank the last of his beer. "They used to be active in 4-H and the Grange when they were younger. At least Aunt Thelma did. Hell, they're lucky these days to keep that place going at all."

Milo was probably right. Elmer Petersen must be close to seventy. I was searching for a tactful way to tell the sheriff that I knew about Linda's dinner at the Dutch Cup when I remembered Christie and Troy Johnston.

"Christie was downright surly," I concluded. "They're leaving tomorrow. Are you sure you shouldn't talk to her first?"

Milo ate two french fries at once and cocked his head at me. "Who says I didn't?"

Milo would say no more about Christie Johnston. I was anxious to go home, clean house, and reflect on my love life, but the sheriff insisted on making the most of his lunch hour by having a piece of pumpkin pie for dessert. As long as we were lingering, I asked him what he thought about Andy Cederberg's remarks.

Milo shrugged. "He scared himself. Somebody—let's hope it wasn't Durwood Parker or I'll have to bust him again—lost it in the fog. But Linda was murdered, so now Andy sees a conspiracy or some damned thing." Milo lighted another cigarette.

"Vida was thinking along those same lines earlier," I said. "You're skeptical?"

"You bet. Look, Emma, there's some stuff going on with the bank that I can't talk about. You've guessed as much. I don't know all the details yet." Milo coughed once, then frowned at his cigarette. "I guess I'm not used to this stuff after so long. Anyway, if this bank inquiry develops into anything, we'll let you know so you can have your story. But don't go along with Andy and Vida and all the other characters who are looking under the bed for boogeymen." Milo coughed again.

"What about Linda's car keys?" I felt a bit like coughing, too. Milo was blowing smoke straight into my face.

"What about them?"

"Their placement on the ring. Milo," I went on, lowering my voice and leaning closer, "how was the Lindahl house broken into? A window? A crowbar? An underground tunnel?"

Behind the blue haze, Milo frowned. "Damned if I know. That's Snohomish County's responsibility. The City of Everett, actually. Why do you ask?"

There were times when Milo seemed as dense as the cloud of smoke that enveloped him. Yet I knew that he wasn't really dim, but methodical. And somewhat plodding. Thus, I often felt compelled to give him a boot. "What if somebody had a key to get in? What if it wasn't a real burglar? You said nothing was taken. How did the Lindahls know there'd been a break-in?"

"I didn't see the report." Milo evaded my gaze. His pie arrived, topped with ice cream. "Drugs, maybe. You'd be amazed at who's got them. You'd be even more amazed at where the dopers think they can find the stuff."

I was dubious. "It's too much of a coincidence that the Lindahls had a break-in the night before Linda was killed. Did you ever hear from the phone company about the call to Howard from Dick Johnson?"

Milo was still resisting eye contact. "Monday, probably. We're having them run a check on all the Petersens, too. That's why it's taking so long."

The sheriff's reply partially appeased me. "That's good work. I wish you'd take a look at that burglary complaint, though."

"Don't bug me, Emma." Milo forked up a hunk of pie. "How the hell could a break-in at the Lindahls have anything to do with Linda's murder?"

Involuntarily my hand touched my purse. A flash of lightning struck close enough that, for a fleeting moment, everything appeared as blue as Milo's smoke. The roll of thunder followed, resonating somewhere off the face of Tonga Ridge. I patted my purse. The little map still reposed in a zippered side pocket. I should mention it to Milo.

But what was the point? A hysterical adolescent whose mother had just been murdered had found it and jumped to conclusions. I was middle-aged and rational. Between my office and my home I had a dozen scraps of paper with notes and directions. They meant nothing, except that at some point in time, I'd needed to get someplace for some reason I'd already forgotten.

Milo offered to pay for lunch. I let him. It was small compensation for putting up with his cigarettes. It certainly wasn't sufficient to make up for the fact that I had a terrible urge to join him and puff my head off, too.

The knock on my door was so timorous that I didn't hear it over of the roar of the vacuum cleaner. It was only when I saw a face at my living-room window that I let out a squeak of surprise and turned off the vacuum.

"Rick!" I exclaimed, opening the front door. "What can I do for you?"

His manner was furtive as he slipped inside. "Hide me," he breathed. "The sheriff's on my trail."

It had been almost two hours since I'd parted from Milo Dodge at the Venison Inn. Glancing out into the street through the rain, I could see no sign of the sheriff's official car or his Cherokee Chief. The thunder-and-lightning storm had passed, happily without causing one of our frequent power failures.

"Are you sure?" I asked, winding up the vacuum cord and putting it in place.

Rick nodded, raindrops falling from his short hair. "He came to my folks' house just a few minutes ago. I saw him get out. I was coming back from the bowling alley. I kept going. You were the first person I could think of who'd let me in."

Rick and his parents lived two blocks away, on Tyee Street. It struck me as odd that there wouldn't be neighbors who would give Rick shelter. I mentioned the fact, even as I offered Rick a seat on the sofa.

"I wanted to get far enough away so Sheriff Dodge couldn't see me," he said, and for the first time, I realized that he looked not only wet and miserable, but scared, too. "He'd recognize my car."

"Oh." I sat down in my most comfortable armchair, across from Rick. "Yes, he probably would. Why don't you want to see him?"

Rick Erlandson's hands fumbled and twisted. "It's dumb, really dumb. Maybe I shouldn't be worried. But I think I made a mistake at the bank."

"What kind of mistake?"

Rick's earnest young face turned very pink. "This is such a mess. . . ." He scraped his fingers on the fabric of his faded blue jeans. "Everything's been all screwed up at the bank since Linda got killed. Well, no, it really started before that. I should have noticed then." He swallowed hard and gave me a helpless look.

"Noticed what?" My voice sounded sharp.

"Secrets." Rick brushed at his short damp hair. "Mr. Petersen—Marv, I mean—and Linda were behind closed doors a lot. He looked worried, and she looked mad. Somewhere along in there—I think it was Tuesday or Wednesday—Linda asked me if I was cosigning everything. I told her I thought so, but how would I know unless I was asked?"

Rick had me confused. "Cosigning what? Loans?"

Rick shook his head. "Every time a teller handles a big transaction—like a CD or a tax-exempt bond or something—somebody else has to sign, too. Christie and Denise and I do it for each other all the time. But Linda showed me a request for money market funds that somebody had asked for by phone. It had been made back in September, after Alyssa Carlson quit to have her baby and before Denise came to work at the bank. Christie had signed it, but I hadn't. Linda wanted to know why."

"Well?" Still bewildered, I tried to regain my patience.

Rick looked stricken, as if I were the one accusing him of wrongdoing. "I wasn't asked. Then Linda talked to Christie, and Christie just laughed and said she must have forgotten. We were short-handed, and it happened at a busy time. But the next day, Linda got on my case again. This time it was a payment for Mr. Walsh's car, and it only had one signature."

I arched my eyebrows. "Had Christie forgotten again?"

Rick shook his head in a despondent fashion. "No. I'd signed it. But the funny thing is, I don't remember. There's been all this stuff going on with Denise and Ginny, and I'm all mixed up. Women sure can make a man feel weird. Ms. Lord, do you think I'm losing it?"

Rick was a couple of years older than Adam, but I tried to think how I would answer my son. The hard part was imagining that Adam would ever own up to a personal flaw. Or harder yet, that Adam would ever have a real job.

"We all make mistakes," I said, resorting to a cliché. "Let's back up. Why is the sheriff after you?"

Rick's eyes darted to the front window. Maybe he expected to see Milo standing there with his King Cobra Magnum at the ready. "Sheriff Dodge was at the bank yesterday afternoon. He spent a long time talking to both Mr. Petersens, which was really strange because you'd think they wouldn't have come back after the funeral. Like I said, things haven't been right at work for a couple of weeks, even before Linda got killed. Maybe they think I've been ... skimming or something."

"You're not." My tone was emphatic, lest Rick think I suspected him of malfeasance.

"Gosh, no!" He looked horrified. "That's a crime!"

"Yes, it is." I was thinking hard, trying to put the pieces together. "Now, go over these procedures one more time—if you're dealing with certain kinds of transactions, the bank requires two signatures, right?"

Rick nodded. "It's like—well, checks and balances, to make sure that nobody can authorize certain debits or credits on their own. Mr. Petersen—Marv—used to be so fussy about that sort of thing that when I came to work for the bank two years ago, nobody who worked there could get in or out of their own account without having another employee sign for them. But that got to be a hassle. Since it's all practically family, he decided we could trust each other."

"But he didn't waive the requirement for customer accounts?"

"Oh, no. That's why I've got this problem. There's a code, too, on our computers. We have to enter that. It's supposed to be secret, but in a small bank like ours, it isn't."

I nodded as comprehension began to dawn. "So it's possible that any of you, from Marv on down, could authorize the liquidation of a customer's funds and put it into your own account?"

Rick blanched. "I'm afraid so. But nobody would do a thing like that! They'd go to jail!"

"If they got caught." Remembering my duties as a hostess, I offered Rick a drink of some kind. He refused at first, then surrendered to a soda.

In the kitchen, I poured us each a glass of Pepsi. Rick had followed me, and seemed inclined to linger. Perhaps he felt safer there than in the living room. Milo Dodge couldn't see through the log walls of my little house.

"You don't remember signing Leo Walsh's car payment authorization, right?" I indicated a kitchen chair to Rick. We both sat down.

"That's why I think I'm going mental," Rick said in a pitiful voice. "It was about then that Ginny wouldn't talk to me anymore. Otherwise, I would remember, because Mr. Walsh's proxy arrangement was new. And he works with Ginny. It would have . . . sunk in." Rick's eyes strayed to the far corner of the kitchen where I kept an old galvanized milk can filled with straw flowers.

For the moment, I wanted to avoid talking about Ginny. "Who handled Grace Grundle's CDs?"

Rick turned his blue eyes back to me. "Mrs. Grundle? Anybody. I mean, we can't offer personal banking in the way that a big branch can."

"But who waited on her when she came in recently to redeem one of her CDs?"

Rick's high forehead wrinkled. "Denise, I think. I was on break. But we all went looking for it when it didn't show up on the computer screen."

"No luck?"

"Not for the one she was asking about. Mrs. Grundle said it was good for a year and due in early November. But we went back through the records for all of last fall, and she hadn't been issued any CDs since 1990. Those had already been rolled over." Rick was squinting in a perplexed manner, as if he could visualize the computer monitor that listed Grace Grundle's assets.

"Mrs. Grundle is a bit . . . confused," I remarked. "That's why she has proxy banking, right?"

Now Rick turned very red. "I'm not supposed to talk about this stuff. It's confidential. Gosh, I feel like such a dork! But I'm so upset, I don't know what to do!" He wrenched himself around in the chair; I halfway expected him to burst into tears.

I was suffering from ineffectualness. Finance wasn't my strong suit. "Have you talked to Mr. Petersen? To either of them, Marv or Larry?"

"How can I? Not now, with Linda dead and whatever else is happening at the bank." Rick pushed aside his glass of Pepsi. Maybe he was denying himself any small pleasures as punishment for his imagined sins.

Getting up, I went over to the window above the sink. At an angle, I could see Fir Street. There were no cars parked there, except for the pickup that belonged to the family across the way. Rick had left his car in my driveway, presumably to mislead the sheriff.

"The coast is clear," I announced. "It seems to me you need a sympathetic listener. A sensible soul who understands you." I paused, waiting for Rick's reaction.

"Ginny?" Her name came out on a hush.

"Ginny. No woman can resist a man whose defenses are down. Trust me, Rick." I couldn't suppress a grin. "If Milo Dodge is really looking for you, her house is the last place he'd go. He must know you two have broken up."

Clumsily Rick got to his feet. "Everybody knows

that," he mumbled. "Everybody in Alpine always knows everything."

Escorting him to the door, I put a hand on his arm. "Then give them something new to talk about."

"But ..." He straddled the threshold, just inches out of the rain. "Maybe Ginny won't see me."

I gave him one last pat. With his forlorn, lost-puppy expression and the need for comfort brimming in his eyes, Ginny couldn't possibly throw him back out into the rain. "Take a chance," I said. "Go for it."

Rick went, at least across the soggy grass to his car. Through the front window, I watched him reverse onto Fir Street and drive away. There were a dozen questions I'd been burning to ask him, but, as he'd realized, the answers would violate customer confidentiality. Despite my ignorance of financial matters, the situation at the bank was coming into focus. If Rick could tear off his emotional blindfold, he'd be able to see what was happening, too. Maybe Ginny could help. After all, she kept the books for *The Advocate*. If any staff member could sort through Rick's work problems, it would be Ginny. And in the process, maybe she and Rick would resolve their personal problems.

I hoped so. It would be nice to think that there were people who could create happy endings for themselves. I wanted to do that, too. All the while that I was cleaning house, I'd tried to sift through my reaction to Tom's telephone call. I hadn't come to any conclusions, but at least I had a clean floor.

Maybe I'd sort through my desk drawers and find some answers. Then again, maybe I wouldn't. It was possible that there weren't any answers. It was probable that cleaning out the desk would only depress me. The drawers were stuffed with memories. It wasn't a good idea to look at them on a rainy Saturday afternoon with an empty Saturday night looming ahead.

Instead, I called Leo Walsh.

Chapter Thirteen

LEO WAS NOT only home, but he sounded sober. I was surprised, having expected my ad manager to spend his weekend in the bag. What I did not expect was that he wasn't particularly pleased to hear my voice.

"Oh, it's you, babe." Leo sounded disappointed. "I just got back from Snohomish. It's hell driving in this rain. How do you people put up with it?"

"We natives like it," I answered, trying to sound aloof. My ridiculous impulse to ask Leo to dinner died a-borning. "Say, have you any way of knowing who authorized the payments for your rent and whatever else you set up at the bank?"

"Hell, no. At least not yet. I haven't gotten a statement this month. I'm a *W*, remember? I'm at the end of the cycle. When the statement comes, it might show a teller code. Why do you ask?"

I opted for candor. "Something odd is going on at the bank—besides or maybe along with Linda's murder." The words sounded harsh; maybe I felt like trampling Leo's feelings. He'd already bruised mine.

"Oh, swell. I finally try to get my finances in order and then it turns out that my trusted bankers are a bunch of swindlers. That's typical of my luck. What next? My paycheck bounces on Monday?"

Annoyed, I snapped at Leo: "Don't be a jerk. *The*

Advocate is solvent. And don't go spreading around this stuff about the bank. I'm not absolutely—" There was a click on the line; I recognized it as Leo's Call Waiting. "Go ahead, I'll hang up—"

But Leo interrupted, asking me to hold. With an impatient sigh, I did. It took Leo at least a full minute to come back on the line.

"Sorry, babe. The flu bug has hit town. It seems to go away and then come on again. I suppose the germs hang around until April, like the rain and snow."

"That's about right. You have the flu?" I was more surprised than sympathetic. "Why did you go to Snohomish if you're sick?"

"No, it's not me. I'm too ornery to get the flu." Leo gave a little laugh. "Say, you want to put on your fishing boots and wade down to the Venison Inn for dinner?"

"I was there for lunch." And, I wanted to add, about six other meals since the previous weekend. "I'm housecleaning. I feel like staying in tonight and admiring my dust job."

"Oh." Leo was sounding disappointed again. "Now I'll have to go get some food at the store. I'll probably drown between here and Safeway. The only thing I've got in the fridge is a jar of horseradish and two kosher dill pickles."

If Leo expected me to feel sorry for him, he was right. I didn't want to, but in the wake of Milo's frustration and Rick's despair, my defenses were down.

"I've got some frozen prawns. How do you feel about yakisoba noodles?"

Leo felt very good about yakisoba stir-fry. In a chipper voice, he said he'd even bring the sake—to go with the yoba. I ignored the terrible pun and told him to show up around six-thirty. Then I put down the phone and wondered what hath Emma wrought.

Leo arrived, not with sake, but a bottle of California Chardonnay. "I ought to try some of the Washington wines," he said, putting his feet up on my coffee table, "but as a rule, I'm not much for wine of any kind."

"I know, you're a Scotch drinker. Like Milo." I handed Leo his beverage of choice. He'd get two drinks before dinner and one glass of wine while we ate. I wasn't going to send a hammered Leo driving down the hills of Alpine. He might end up with something worse than a sprained ankle.

The memory of his accident spurred me to ask a question that had been niggling at the back of my mind for almost two weeks. "Say, Leo, how did you get to work that Tuesday after you fell? Did you drive?"

Leo was in the process of lighting a cigarette. I was beginning to feel as if I were spending my life in a smoke-filled casino. "That Tuesday? Shit, I don't remember." He didn't look at me as he shook the match into oblivion and tossed it in what was usually an immaculate marble ashtray.

It was useless to press the point. If Leo had been involved with Linda, it was none of my business. Unless, of course, he'd killed her. I choked on my bourbon.

Jumping off the sofa, Leo circumvented the coffee table and slapped me on the back. "Hey, what's wrong, babe? Go down the wrong way?"

Spluttering, I nodded. "Ice," I gasped. Leo's hand lingered on my back. Shakily I pulled myself out of the chair. "Excuse me." Racing off to the kitchen, I poured a glass of water. I didn't really need it, but I had to escape Leo's hands.

He was standing in the doorway, watching me with a

worried expression. "I should have learned the Heimlich maneuver," he said. "Or is that only for chunks of beef?"

I gave him a quavery smile. "It's not for ice," I replied. "Ice melts. Beef doesn't."

We returned to the living room, decorously resuming our seats. "Tell me about the bank," he said. "I don't like the sound of it."

Leo had me on the spot. Though not a newsman, he was a staff member. If I'd shipped Rick Erlandson off to confide in Ginny Burmeister, I could hardly keep secrets from my ad manager.

"It's hard to explain because I don't know all the facts," I said, wrapping both hands around my bourbon glass. "It sounds as if Marv Petersen wanted to sell out to the Bank of Washington, or at least merge. BOW sent one of their auditors—Dan Ruggiero, the man we saw at the Venison Inn—to look over the books. He must have found something that queered the deal, because when I called BOW's headquarters in Seattle, it was off. Now Milo is conducting an investigation, and rumors are flying all over town about missing funds and lost accounts. They're not just picking on you, Leo. I could name half a dozen people who are having problems."

Leo brandished his empty glass at me. Dinner preparations had been made before his arrival. The work with the wok would take less than ten minutes. I got Leo another Scotch and freshened my own drink.

"An embezzler, huh?" he remarked, taking a big sip. "Who? The list of suspects is pretty short."

I agreed. "Denise is too dizzy, Rick is too honest, and Larry wouldn't steal from the bank he's about to take over. Marv, of course, wouldn't need to, unless he's a secret gambler or sniffing coke, neither of which sounds right."

"A woman," Leo said. "Marv's been married to that dumpy what's'ername for about a hundred years, right? Some flashy broad in Everett could have him by the short hairs."

My initial reaction was to disparage such an outlandish notion. But it wasn't entirely incredible. Solid citizens such as Marv Petersen often were undone by wily temptresses. The thought made me smile.

"Let's leave Marv out of it for now," I suggested. "It's more likely that Christie Johnston or Andy Cederberg is the culprit. Christie and her husband, Troy, are on their way out of town tomorrow. I have this feeling they may not be coming back."

Leo frowned. "Christie? The cute brunette? Okay, I'll buy her over that Cederberg guy. He wouldn't have the guts."

"Maybe not." I wasn't considering Andy too seriously myself. "You're forgetting someone, though." I watched Leo closely. "Linda Lindahl."

Instead of leaping to Linda's defense, Leo scratched his left ear. "Linda? She was the bookkeeper, right? Easy for her to juggle the figures." He shrugged. "If she did, and it came out, that could be a motive for murder."

"So it could." My spirits plummeted. Until Leo spoke, I hadn't made the connection between the supposed embezzlement and Linda's murder. "You mean that someone killed her because she'd loused up the buyout?"

Leo gnawed on a forefinger. "It's possible. The problem is that the person most likely to be furious is also Linda's father. Dads don't usually strangle their daughters—even if sometimes they feel like it."

A scenario in which Marv Petersen killed Linda was not only unlikely, it was repugnant. I preferred the picture of Marv himself as the embezzler, keeping his Everett mistress in jewels and furs and hot little sports cars.

"Or," Leo went on, following me into the kitchen, "Linda found out about the embezzlement. Maybe she blew the whistle and turned over whatever evidence she had to Dan Ruggiero. In which case, the crook had to shut her up."

Turning up the heat on the wok, I poured out a measure of tempura sauce. "But it was too late by then. The Bank of Washington already knew."

"Maybe they didn't know *who*." Leo passed his once-again empty glass under my nose.

Tossing green onions into the wok, I ignored his desire for a refill. Indeed, something Leo had said suddenly struck me: "That's it! Linda had dinner in Sultan with Dan Ruggiero!"

"Oh?" Leo sounded skeptical. "When was that?"

"The Tuesday before she died. Somebody saw them." I guarded my source from Leo. "This person recognized Linda later from her picture in the paper but didn't get a good look at the man she was with. But he was wearing a suit. Who else would do that in this part of the world except a banker?"

Leo stared into his empty glass. "You might be right. Are you sure Linda wasn't having dinner with Andy Cederberg? He dresses as conservatively as that Ruggiero guy."

The onions, water chestnuts, green pepper, mushrooms, and prawns were sizzling happily. I threw in the yakisoba noodles. "So do Marv and Larry, if it comes to that. But why would Linda and Andy go to Sultan to have dinner? They could speak privately any time at the bank."

"That's true." Wistfully, Leo set his glass down on the counter. "It makes you think, though."

Using a wooden paddle, I stirred the noodles in with the other ingredients. "About what?"

"About Andy. And Dan Ruggiero. They dress alike. From a distance, they look alike. Somebody tried to run Andy down by that park." Leo moved closer to me, and I stiffened. But instead of pinching my backside, he pinched a prawn from the wok. "Maybe it wasn't Andy they were trying to hit. Maybe it was Dan Ruggiero. Has your hotshot sheriff thought about that?"

The hotshot wasn't home when I called after Leo and I finished dinner. He wasn't at the office, either, according to Deputy Sam Heppner. Sam thought his boss was probably in Startup, paying a call on Honoria Whitman. I thought so, too. Maybe she was forcing him to listen to Gustav Mahler.

"I warned Milo not to let Christie Johnston leave town," I grumbled. "He said he had no grounds to detain her. I thought he was talking about the murder. Maybe he was, but it seems to me that if he's conducting an investigation of the bank, its employees shouldn't be allowed to go out-of-state."

From the sofa, Leo was giving me a cockeyed look. "You've zeroed in on Christie, huh, babe?"

Despite my resolutions, we were down to the dregs of the Chardonnay. Thus, my tongue was loosened. "Rick Erlandson mentioned Christie as the person who didn't get a cosignature on a phone request for money-market funds. How do we know anybody actually made the request? Why couldn't Christie sign for the transaction and make off with the money?"

Leo, who was looking as hazy as I felt, considered. "She could, I suppose. I'm the last one you should ask about banking crap. Half the time I never bothered to record the checks I wrote. Sometimes I didn't even sign the damned things. I'm glad to be free from all that. Or am I? Free, that is." He stubbed out his cigarette in the now full ashtray and leaned back on the sofa.

"It'll get straightened out," I murmured. "Eventually."

"Yeah, sure. 'Leo Loses Shirt in Bank Scam.' I can see the headlines now. What size type are you going to use?"

"Stop feeling sorry for yourself, Leo." I grabbed the ashtray, intending to empty it in the garbage. Leo grabbed my leg.

"I like to wallow around in self-pity. Want to wallow with me?" His tone was wry, but his brown eyes were oddly disconcerting.

Abruptly I pulled free, spilling some of the cigarette butts. I didn't dare bend over to retrieve them. "No, Leo, I don't. And frankly, I don't think you do, either. Let's have some coffee."

This time Leo didn't follow me into the kitchen. But his voice did. "You hear about how I worked my ass off for fifteen years on a paper in the San Fernando Valley and got canned for falling down drunk in my wastebasket? You hear how my wife ran off with a goddamned guidance counselor? You hear how my kids hate me for forcing my wife to commit adultery? You hear how I lost my house and my good car and the boat I almost had paid for?"

"Shut up, Leo," I called over the sound of water running into the coffeemaker. "I *have* heard all that. It's sad, it's true, but it's over." Returning to the living room, I gave Leo a wide berth. "You've got a chance for a fresh start. Don't blow it."

Leo shook his head. "There's no such animal. There's just plugging along. The only fresh start we get is the day we're born. After that, it's all crap. And it just keeps coming. Did I ever tell you about the novel I wrote?"

God preserve me from advertising people who write novels, I thought. But as I returned to the living room, I gave him a faint smile, which he took for encouragement.

"It was four years ago, before all the rest of the shit hit. I'd been fine-tuning the book for a long time, and it was a great idea. A housewife in North Dakota is bored to the eyeballs with farm life, and along comes this beatnik artist. They fall in love, and have a mad, passionate affair that lasts about three days. Then off he goes, and she's left with nothing but a portrait of herself in the buff, which she naturally can't show her old man and the kiddies, not to mention the three other couples in their square-dance club. She spends the rest of her life mooning about the artist, and he does ditto as he goes off to Italy to paint morose pictures. My smart-as-a-whip wife told me it'd never sell, so I sat on it. You fill in the blanks."

I tried not to smirk. "Dare I ask the title?"

"Cavalier." Leo was ironic. "It's a double meaning. Cavalier is a real county in North Dakota. No bridges, though. Not in *my* book."

Maybe Leo was fabricating his unpublished novel. If the story was true, I had to sympathize. "Bad timing," I finally said. "If you could write one novel, you could write another."

Leo curled his lip. "About what? A broken-down ad

man who moves to a small town and makes magic music with the beautiful but lonely publisher?"

"Try sci-fi," I snapped. "Maybe a Western. Or," I went on, less flippantly, "a logging saga. Four generations who lived off the woods."

Leo was still contemptuous. "Hasn't somebody already done that, too?"

"Maybe. But it's the kind of story that has plenty of latitude."

The coffee was done. I went to the kitchen, filled two mugs, and returned to the living room.

"I don't know shit about logging," Leo declared.

"This is the place to learn." Having set Leo's mug in front of him, I turned toward my armchair. But Leo had a firm grip on the hand that didn't hold my coffee.

"Relax, babe. I'm not going to ravish you. Sit down, loosen up. You're stiff as a two-by-four. How do you like that for timber talk?"

Maybe I should have been terrified. For all I knew, Leo Walsh had murdered Linda Lindahl. But Tom Cavanaugh had recommended Leo. Surely he wouldn't have done that if Leo's character were deeply flawed. On the other hand, Tom had married Sandra. So much for the love of my life's perceptions about people.

Still, I resisted the urge to pour hot coffee on Leo. He was my ad manager, and I needed the revenue he brought in. Otherwise, I couldn't brag about the paper's solvency.

"Don't complicate things, Leo," I warned, trying to free my hand. "You're nursing a grudge against your ex-wife. You don't need to get mixed up with your employer. Our staff's too small to handle an in-house romance."

In the lamplight, Leo's careworn face was a map of his tribulations: the furrows in the forehead, from beating his brains out making money for somebody else; the deep grooves around his eyes, evidence of worry and frustration; the lines in his face and the sag of the jaw were marks of erosion caused by a wife who didn't have enough love left to see her husband through the worst of times. Had the drinking come before or after? It didn't matter. The result was the same.

"I'm not proposing marriage," Leo said dryly. "I was thinking about a kiss and a cuddle. Hey, babe, do you like men or am I flushing out the wrong kind of bird?"

That did it. I threw the coffee, but not at Leo. The hot liquid splashed across the carpet, the coffee table, and the armchair. The mug bounced off the front door, just as a knock sounded on the other side.

I jumped. Leo let go. The mug rolled harmlessly toward the hall closet. Trying to compose myself, I went to the door.

"Well!" Vida was wearing a deerstalker and looking vexed. Her expression didn't improve when she saw Leo on the sofa, coffee spilled all over the living room, and a deep flush on my face. "Well, well!" she repeated. "I didn't realize you were entertaining."

Leo spoke up before I did. "She's not as entertaining as you'd think. But she's sure clumsy. Don't slip on the java, Duchess. Our boss had a little accident."

Bristling, Vida closed the door behind her. The shrewd gray eyes took in the empty Chardonnay bottle and the highball glasses. But it was my high color that seemed to interest her most.

"Perhaps I should have called first," Vida said stiffly. "But I had to drop Roger off at his parents' house, so I stopped here on my way home."

Roger's benighted mother and father lived off the

Burl Creek Road on the west side of town. My home is more or less on the route back to Vida's.

"It's no problem," I said hastily. "Leo and I were sorting out the bank situation."

Now Vida's expression grew hostile as well as curious. "You and *Leo*?" She glanced at him as if he were no more significant than your average earthworm. "Well! I suppose you've solved the case! Strong drink often induces brilliant ideas. Among other things." Again her gaze swept over the empty wine bottle and the equally empty cocktail glasses.

"Sit down, Vida," I urged, finally regaining my composure. "We haven't solved anything, but there are some gaps that may have been filled. I didn't bother you today because of Roger."

The hostility ebbed, replaced by incredulity. "Roger! What has my dear grandson got to do with it? You haven't found another corpse, have you?"

Wheedling and placating, I finally got Vida to remove her coat and deerstalker before sitting on the sofa. She scooted as far away as possible from Leo, as if he had a contagious disease. Then I began my recital, starting with Milo in the morning, Rick in the afternoon, and the evening with Leo. In spite of herself, Vida was impressed. More than that—she seemed shaken.

"Embezzlement! At the Bank of Alpine! It's unbelievable! Frank Petersen must be rolling in his grave!"

Since Vida already had suspected as much, I figured her performance was aimed at Leo, the latest newcomer. He must believe that, contrary to facts, Alpine was conceived without sin.

"We tried to call the sheriff," Leo explained, "but it seems he's gone a-wooing." The fuzziness had disappeared from Leo's voice. Or maybe my hearing wasn't as hazy.

Vida shot Leo a withering look. "We don't need Milo." She stood up and went over to the desk. A moment later, she had her nephew on the line. "Billy? . . . Yes, yes, I know you're not on duty tonight. . . . Yes, yes, I know Milo's off gallivanting in Startup. I trust you to use sense, Billy. Now, here's what I want you to do. . . ."

Leo and I exchanged bemused glances as Vida gave Bill Blatt his instructions. He was to keep Christie and Troy Johnston in town until Monday at least. He could use the murder investigation or the bank inquiry as an excuse. Vida wasn't interested in legalities; she brooked no constitutional arguments from her nephew.

"Just do it," she demanded, "and call me back at Emma's when you're sure the Johnstons are staying put." Vida returned to the sofa and dug in. I offered coffee; she requested hot water. "It shouldn't take long," she asserted. "Billy's going to go get Sam Heppner first."

It was already almost nine-thirty. The long day and the drinks had made me very tired. The coffee hadn't helped much. After heating Vida's water in the microwave, I slumped in the armchair.

"Do you agree that Andy wasn't the intended rundown victim?" I asked Vida, trying to keep my voice from sounding weary.

Vida blew on her mug. "That's possible. But does it mean that the driver and Linda's killer are one and the same? I suppose so, but once Dan Ruggiero discovered the embezzlement, or whatever it was, there was no need to kill Linda. The cat was out of the bag."

Leo had run out of cigarettes, which didn't improve his disposition or his deductive reasoning. "Spite. Revenge. The scam's blown, so why not whack somebody who was responsible for the discovery? People aren't logical."

Vida frowned at Leo. "That may be true in Los Angeles. This is Alpine. We aren't inclined to behave like maniacs. Even when we kill, we have our reasons." Vida's defense seemed bizarre, even by local standards, but the strangest part was that I had an inkling of what she meant: Alpiners didn't commit wanton crimes; their motives were always rational.

It was to Leo's credit that he didn't guffaw out loud. Instead, he shrugged. "I gather this Christie hadn't been around too long. Maybe she's still suffering from her out-of-town ways."

Vida took the comment seriously. "I believe she and her husband have lived in several different cities. The last was Everett. UPS keeps transplanting Troy, it seems."

I'd forgotten about the Everett connection. The Johnstons and the Lindahls—had they known each other? Had Linda been acquainted with Christie before the divorce? A new avenue of speculation opened, but I was too tired to read the road markers.

The phone rang. Vida and I both jumped up, but she reached it first. Her initial briskness plunged into irritation: "Can you be sure? Why would they do such a thing? Check back, say around midnight. Maybe they went to a movie. Call me at home."

Resuming her seat, Vida whipped off her glasses and rubbed furiously at her eyes. "Ooooooh! Billy says the Johnstons are gone. The house looks closed up. Why would they leave today if their flight wasn't until tomorrow?"

The answer could be innocent enough. "Maybe it's an early departure and they were afraid of snow," I suggested. "They may have driven down to spend the night in a motel at Sea-Tac."

Replacing her glasses, Vida wore her most owlish expression. "Maybe pigs will fly and Hitler has a hat shop in Cleveland. It sounds most peculiar. Dare we call Janet Driggers and ask her?"

Before Leo or I could reply, Vida was back at the phone. As with most Alpine numbers, she knew the Driggerses' by heart. But no one answered.

"They're out cavorting," she said with contempt.

I tried not to think of how Janet and Al Driggers might disport themselves on a Saturday night in Alpine. Somewhere, I hoped, in between Janet's lurid fantasies and Al's moribund demeanor.

Vida was still standing, her statuesque body twitching with frustration. Leo also got to his feet. "We're at a dead end. And I'm dead tired. Thanks, Emma, it was fun. Especially the part where we played coffee-toss. Sorry I didn't get to take my turn." He gave me an amused look and a chuck under the chin. I endured both, then showed him to the door. Leo went out into the rain, which was now sleet, then paused halfway down the walk.

"I know you're a girl," he said, keeping his voice down. "I just wish I knew what guy made you so scared of other men. I'd like to kick his ass. 'Night, babe. See you in the classifieds."

I wondered if I'd ever get the nerve to tell Leo the truth about Tom Cavanaugh. Certainly not until I had to. Turning back in to the living room, I saw Vida already in her coat and grappling with the deerstalker.

"I must head home, too, now that you're safe. Roger led me on a merry chase today. The video-game parlor, the hobby shop, the fish hatchery, and snacks all along the line."

I ignored Roger's adventures. "I was safe before you got here," I insisted. "Leo is harmless."

The deerstalker all but obliterated Vida's eyes. "Is he now? You can't be sure. You don't really know him. I'm surprised you didn't have Milo run him through the National Crime Information Center database." With a flip of her flaps, Vida departed.

She was right about Leo; she was wrong about Leo. I knew him, at least as a type. He'd take what was offered, making only a minimal effort to get it. If he was rejected, as he expected to be, he'd crawl away and nurse his wounds. Failure was his friend; he knew it well.

But it was Linda who preyed on my mind as the sleet punished the windows and splattered down the chimney. Had Linda dated Leo? She'd probably slept with Mike Brockelman. Who else had she taken into her empty bed? Had Linda died because she was a savvy bookkeeper or because she'd picked the wrong man as her playmate? Nobody deserved to end up with a log for a shroud in a deserted forest clearing. Linda wasn't likable, but she'd needed to be loved. We all did, and I was the last to criticize her for falling into a stranger's arms. She was prickly, she was difficult—but she'd given enough of herself to find comfort with another human being. Meanwhile, I hung back, not a wallflower who never gets asked to dance, but a vestal virgin, too detached, too aloof to say yes to a few turns around the floor. And too frightened.

The house was dark as I stared through my bedroom window. The sleet splashed against the glass like tears. Linda had been a pain, but she wasn't inhuman. I, however, was beginning to feel like a robot. Plug me in, I go to work. Switch me on, I communicate with my peers. Program me for the day, I try to meet everybody's needs.

Everybody's, except Emma's. My batteries were wearing down, and those funny little thuds in my breast signaled the need for recharging. I wasn't in the mood to admit that what kept me going was called my heart.

Chapter Fourteen

FATHER DENNIS KELLY was going to change the world. At least that was the impression some parishioners got when Father Den announced that the Social Causes Commission had created six new ongoing committees.

Unemployment, domestic abuse, youth activities, the elderly, single adults, and addiction were included. Not all were new areas of concern for St. Mildred's. Father Fitzgerald, in his autocratic, erratic manner, had addressed a number of these issues during his long pastoral tenure. But not only had Father Fitz operated out of a time warp, his efforts were often hit-and-miss. Thanks to a dedicated core of parishioners, the church had consistently helped stock the ecumenical food bank and, in a joint venture with the Episcopalians, had provided used clothing for the poor. The rest of the community's needs had gone unheeded except on an emergency basis, or left to the Lutherans.

Fearing that I might be corralled into joining one of the committees, and excusing myself on the grounds that publishers by definition exercise great public responsibility, I didn't linger in the vestibule. The rain had turned to snow during Mass, but it wasn't yet sticking. I was about to duck into my car when I heard Ed Bronsky's jarringly cheerful voice.

"Emma! Have I got a dynamite promotion for you or

what?" Ed barreled his way between cars, waving snowflakes out of his eyes. "This is *hot*! It's civic pride, it's anticrime, it's economic *hustle*! Now, listen up, here's the way it works. . . ."

Ed had me backed up against the Jag. The Bayards' Volvo sedan was parked close to my car. There was hardly room between the two vehicles for Ed's paunch and my bulky duffle coat. Buddy and Roseanna Bayard had to enter their car on the driver's side.

"Emma!" Roseanna called. "Why don't you head up the single-adult group? Otherwise, we'll get stuck with some old drip like Annie Jeanne Dupré."

Forcing a smile, I shook my head. "Annie Jeanne Dupré's fine with me." Better a sixtyish spinster who played the church organ as if she were wearing boxing gloves than Emma Lord. I waved the Bayards off.

"Okay." Ed's cheeriness had been chipped around the edges by the Bayards' interruption. "What we do is get everybody involved in this murder case. Linda was a Petersen, right? One of Alpine's first families. We owe it to her—to them—to bring the killer to justice. Milo's in over his head. He's understaffed, he's underequipped, and he can't rely on Snohomish County anymore. They've gotten too big, with too many problems of their own. So we get the local merchants to sponsor detective teams. Sort of like deputizing the whole town, the way they used to do it in the Old West. The chamber of commerce will offer a reward. Clues that are uncovered will be posted at the stores. That'll bring in customers. And you get yourself a special insert every week until the killer's behind bars."

Ed was bursting with enthusiasm. He was so caught up in his outrageous plan that he didn't notice the snow accumulating on his eyebrows. Nor did he take in my stupefied reaction.

"We're having a special chamber meeting tomorrow," Ed continued. "Noon, the banquet room at the ski lodge. You'd better come."

"Ed . . ." I didn't know where to begin in stemming the tide of bad taste. "Have you talked to Milo?"

Ed spurned the mention of Milo. "Why bother? Like I said, he's overwhelmed. Think how pleased he'll be when he finds out what we're doing for him."

I could envision Milo exploding like two tons of TNT. Ed's idea was dynamite, all right. It would make the sheriff blow sky-high. Maybe there was a way to circumvent Ed.

"Okay, I'll be there," I promised, my face stiff with cold. Giving Ed a stilted smile, I dove into the Jag. The getaway was easy enough, since the parking lot was paved. But instead of going home, I drove down to the sheriff's office. I had many things to discuss with Milo, including Ed's harebrained scheme.

The sheriff took everything in stride, except Ed. "What's that moron up to? I ought to bust his big butt for impeding justice! Jeez, Emma, why didn't you tell him to screw off?"

"Because I'd rather tell the chamber of commerce to back a bond issue," I replied, enduring yet another mug of Milo's weak coffee. "Harvey Adcock and Francine Wells and Henry Bardeen and the rest of them aren't stupid. They won't go along with Ed's dopey idea. But they won't want to offend him, either. Now that Ed's rich, he commands respect. It's silly, but it's true. My task is to rechannel Ed's proposal into something productive."

Milo was lighting a cigarette. He regarded me with frank appreciation, an infrequent reaction on his part. "If the chamber supports the bond issue, it might have a chance. Should I come, too?"

I considered the idea. "No. You stay out of it. Besides, you're too busy to spare the time."

"I am, for a fact. No day off tomorrow, none in sight." Milo puffed and sighed. "So you got Rick Erlandson to open up. I couldn't even find him yesterday. I had to settle for Denise Petersen, who couldn't remember who she waited on Friday, let alone a month ago."

"What about Christie? Did you talk to her?" I had already confided my suspicions of Christie Johnston to Milo.

The sheriff shook his head. "She and Troy took off around two o'clock yesterday afternoon, according to the neighbors. They had their luggage. The flight was a red-eye at one A.M. this morning."

Groaning, I leaned back in the chair. "Damn! Christie absconded; I'll bet my life savings on it. If I have any left," I added ruefully. Sitting up again, I eyed Milo with my most persuasive expression. "Can't you tell me now—since I've done my homework—if you don't suspect Christie of juggling the accounts?"

Milo held up his hands. "I can't say that officially. Because I don't know. Bob Lambrecht called Friday to say that after a complete review of the Bank of Alpine's books in Seattle, there was definitely evidence of serious discrepancies. That's how he put it. Bob didn't point any fingers; neither did Dan Ruggiero, or his local source, who may have been Linda. We were notified by the Bank of Washington because we're the local law enforcement agency. Obviously we haven't got a fraud division. All we can do is question the bank employees about possible irregularities. Then we call in the state bank examiners and, if necessary, the Feds. That may happen tomorrow. If it does, it's up for grabs. You'll

meet your deadline and everybody will be happy except
the entire population of Alpine."

I was so intent on Milo's recital that I only half noticed that while he spoke, his eyes had periodically
strayed behind me. When he concluded, I heard footsteps and swiveled in the direction of the door. Vida,
grim-faced and dusted with snow, plopped down next to
me in the other visitor's chair.

"We Presbyterians pray more and sing longer than
you Catholics," she said with only the most cursory of
glances. "I just got out of church. Milo, I'm appalled.
How could you let Christie get away?"

"How could I stop her?" Milo, however, looked
sheepish. "Besides, I didn't think the Johnstons were
leaving until today."

Vida wasn't assuaged. Indeed, she was glaring at
Milo's cigarette. "Oh, good grief! You're *smoking*! Why
don't you just shoot heroin into your veins and be done
with it?"

Milo chose not to defend himself. "This audit or
whatever they call it at the state level will take a while.
Christie may be back before it's over."

Slowly I shook my head. "Christie's not coming
back. Milo, do you think she killed Linda?"

Milo stubbed out his cigarette and sank back in his
chair. "I honestly don't know. She had a motive. But
why did she wait?"

At that point in time, it seemed the crucial question.
But we couldn't know how much Christie suspected.
Assuming she was indeed the embezzler, Christie might
not have realized until the fatal Friday that Linda had
blown the whistle.

Vida was wrinkling her nose. "Your office smells terrible," she declared. "Worse than usual. I must go
home. Cupcake is off his feed."

After two weekends with Roger, I didn't blame Vida's canary. I decided to leave, too. Our exit was well timed. Before we were out the door, Milo received a call about a two-car collision, due south of the Cascade railroad tunnel. Somehow, it was easy to forget that the sheriff had other demands on his time besides homicide and bank fraud.

The rest of the day passed uneventfully, except for the snow that began to cover the ground in the early afternoon. By six o'clock, we had three inches. I went out on the back porch to survey my little piece of wilderness. The land behind me is forest, second growth, but tall and sturdy. There was magic in the trees, with only the wind sighing down the mountainside and the pristine whiteness glistening in the November night.

My spirits lifted, though I didn't know why. Tom was still wrestling with his demons in San Francisco, Leo was probably drinking himself senseless, Milo was up to his badge in murder and mayhem, and Vida was at home, force-feeding birdseed to Cupcake. And somewhere, though maybe not in Alpine, a murderer was at large.

Despite all that, I went back into my little log house and let it wrap its arms around me. For now, it was sufficient. I was old enough, maybe wise enough, to take my comforts as I found them.

As long as they were of my own making.

Ginny hummed as she made the coffee Monday morning. She couldn't carry a tune, but I didn't mind. I took her change of mood as a good sign. Maybe she and Rick had made up. Later, when the first crush of business was over, I'd tactfully pose a few questions.

Carla, however, remained glum. But at least she

wasn't fashioning a noose. I inquired if the fresh snow-
fall had offered her any new photo opportunities.

She nodded in a disinterested manner. "I tried shadows. Contrasts, you know. And some blurry effects at
Old Mill Park with the snow almost obscuring the lens.
I'll drop the roll off at Buddy Bayard's this afternoon
when I pick up the other contact sheets."

There was no rush. We had photos Vida had taken of
Linda's funeral, both at the church and the cemetery.
Carla had managed to catch Mike Brockelman's parade
of machinery through town on Saturday. If the bank
story broke, we'd run pictures, either new or from
stock. We had no problem filling this week's front page.
There were also several auto accidents, the possibility
of a county bond issue, and Andy Cederberg's official
complaint about the errant driver.

It was precisely ten o'clock when Ginny delivered
the paychecks for my cosignature. I asked about her
weekend. She blushed.

"Rick came by. He was a mess. He's afraid of getting
fired." Ginny's smile was sly. "I hope he does. That'll
be the end of Denise."

It wasn't quite the reaction I'd expected. Still, I was
pleased that Ginny's spirits were on the rise. "I haven't
forgotten your personals ad idea," I assured her. "We'll
do some serious thinking after the holidays."

It suddenly occurred to me that we hadn't yet trotted
out our papier-mâché turkey and the plastic Pilgrims.
We'd deep-sixed the witch and the black cat, but re-
tained the plush pumpkin. I reached into my purse to
get my keys so Ginny could unlock the storage cupboard.

"Here," I said, pointing to one of two small, thin, un-
adorned keys. "Or is that for the filing cabinet we never
lock?"

"I'll try them both," Ginny said, heading for what was once the back shop and is now used for storing everything from obsolete printing equipment to new computer supplies.

"I should label my keys," I murmured aloud, thinking of Linda Lindahl's orderly methods. The thought also reminded me of the little map inside the zippered pocket. I'd forgotten about it in the chaos of the last two days. Maybe I wanted to push it out of my mind. But that was wrong. When Ginny returned with the decorations under her arm, I retrieved my keys, threw on my coat, and started for the sheriff's office. An idea that had been festering in my brain erupted like an abscess.

I got no farther than the corner when I saw Honoria Whitman pull into the disabled parking space by the bank. Cursing myself, I staggered across the street. The snowplows had already been on the job, but my mind had turned to slush. The map wasn't the only thing I'd forgotten: Honoria's trip to Alpine was no longer necessary.

"Honoria!" Trying to get traction on the six inches of snow that was piled up on the sidewalk, I leaned against the passenger window. Puzzled, Honoria used her power-lock switch to open the door. I was shivering as I slipped into the car.

"The bank job's off," I said, trying not to let my teeth chatter. "Milo's about to call in the state auditor and maybe the Feds. You don't have to go through the charade of opening a proxy account. I'm sorry, I should have called you yesterday after I talked to Milo in the morning."

Two pink swatches of color appeared on Honoria's porcelain cheeks. "Milo told you about this yesterday morning? He didn't mention the bank at all Saturday night. He talked about elk hunting."

I let my head fall back against the soft upholstered seat. "Damn! The conversation was strictly business, Honoria. I'd ferreted out some information Saturday from a bank employee. Milo wouldn't tell me anything until yesterday either."

Honoria was staring through the windshield, which was becoming covered with snow. "Milo almost never talks shop with me. Only in the abstract."

"I'm sorry." I was apologizing for Milo, as well as for myself.

"Elk are too handsome to shoot." The statement was curiously devoid of emotion. Maybe Honoria was thinking that the same couldn't be said for Milo.

Turning in the seat, I put a hand on Honoria's arm. "I owe you for all this inconvenience. How about me treating you to dinner next week at Café de Flore?"

The tiny lines at the corners of Honoria's eyes deepened. "We'll see. I may go down to Carmel for Thanksgiving."

"Oh." Feeling like a fool, I fumbled for words that would close the sudden chasm between us. But before I could say anything, Milo was pounding on my window. Honoria rolled it down, but made no effort to look in Milo's direction.

"Hey, what's up?" Milo asked, speaking past me to Honoria. "Why didn't you tell me you were driving up to Alpine today?"

Honoria's tone was as cold as the snow. "Because you didn't need to know. I came and now I'm leaving." She turned on the engine and the windshield wipers. "Excuse me, Emma, I'm heading back to Startup before the weather gets worse. Goodbye, Milo."

Practically falling out of the car, I was forced to let Milo steady me. Maybe Honoria didn't see him put his arm around my waist. Maybe she wasn't furious at both of us. Maybe she'd regain her usual equanimity by the time she got to Startup.

"What the hell was all that about?" Milo demanded, his fists now on his hips. "Are the women plotting against me?"

"We were," I admitted in a wretched voice. "If you split an elephant ear with me at the Upper Crust, I'll tell you about it." Among other things, I couldn't bear the thought of drinking another cup of Milo's puny coffee.

Milo glanced at the big clock that stood on the sidewalk in front of the bank. "Okay, I can spare you fifteen minutes. I was on my way to see you when I spotted Honoria's car."

At one of the bakery's four small round tables, I explained about our idea to turn Honoria into a mole. Milo's reaction was disgust.

"That's only slightly less asinine than Ed Bronsky's scheme. Don't any of you think I can conduct an investigation on my own?" He stuffed a big chunk of crisp cinnamon-and-sugar-covered elephant ear into his mouth.

My defense came out in a whine. "We know how shorthanded you are. We only wanted to help. It's because we like you, Milo, despite your sometimes annoying ways."

The sheriff looked askance. "You all treat me like a dim-witted child. I hate it. Sure, we've got problems in this county. Now our fax machine's screwed up. It has been, for a week, and we didn't even know it. We'll have to get somebody over from Everett to fix the damned thing. And I still don't know why Honoria is so pissed off at me. She should have been mad at *you*."

"She was. She was mad at the world. I've already explained all that." We were keeping our voices down, for the Upper Crust was doing a brisk business on this snowy November morning. Wanting to change the subject, I extracted the little map from my purse. "Alison Lindahl gave me this. What do you make of it?"

Milo scrutinized the map, then reached for a cigarette. I pointed to the NO SMOKING sign. Milo grimaced. "Where did Alison get this?"

"In the Lindahls' magazine rack." I waited for Milo's response.

It was fierce, though he tried to keep his voice lowered. "You got this—when? Almost a week ago? And you say you want to *help*? Bull!"

I tried to look both penitent and innocent. "I wasn't sure it meant anything. It could have been made a year ago."

Jabbing at the small piece of paper, Milo growled at me under his breath. "I'd like to kick your butt, Emma. Vida's, too. You should have turned this over to me right away."

"I told you, I wasn't sure. . . ."

"It pinpoints the murder site. It's the first real piece of evidence we've had. Along with the phone records, we can start building a case against Howard Lindahl."

I gave a start. "Phone records? You got them?"

Milo nodded abruptly. "First thing this morning. Howard Lindahl received no calls from Seattle during the first week of November. The only incoming long-distance numbers were from Sultan and Alpine, respectively. Both pay phones, by the way. But Howard had called Linda three times—Monday, Thursday, and Friday. Now do you see why this scrap of paper is so important?"

I hung my head. "I'm afraid so. Somehow, I didn't want the killer to be Howard. I don't particularly like the guy, but it seems too cruel for Alison to lose both parents."

"It happens," Milo replied shortly. "Here's the way it looks. . . ." He paused, acknowledging the arrival of Itsa Bitsa Pizza owner Pete Patricelli and one of the Carlsons from the dairy. "Howard and Linda had a court date coming up next week. Linda had voluntarily given up custody at the time of the divorce. But she changed her mind. She wanted joint custody. Howard and Susan didn't think it would be good for Alison. They've given her a stable home, the kid seems pretty well adjusted, and to suddenly chuck all that could cause some big problems. But Linda's got nothing on her slate to show she shouldn't have joint custody. She'd probably get it, especially since she's the mother. Never mind her earlier indifference, the court system tends to work that way. Besides, she could always argue that she was undergoing trauma from the divorce and felt it was better not to uproot Alison and bring her to Alpine." Milo stopped long enough to finish his share of the elephant ear. I waited for him to continue. "Howard, with Susan giving him a big push, makes up his mind not to let Linda get her way. He calls her to plead and beg and argue, but Linda is determined. She's not withdrawing her request. So there's only one thing he can do to stop her—and he does it. Howard comes over to Alpine Friday night when he's supposed to be meeting this Dick Johnson and strangles Linda. He gets rid of a meddling ex-wife and, as a bonus, he gets control of the money she leaves Alison." Milo dusted cinnamon and sugar off of his hands.

My eyes roamed around the bakery, with its enticing aromas and gleaming white tiles. Milo's theory made a certain amount of sense. But somehow it didn't ring quite true.

"How," I finally inquired, barely above a whisper,

"did Howard lure Linda out to the clearing off the Icicle Creek Road?"

Milo had carefully pocketed the little map and was standing up. "He didn't," the sheriff answered in what was almost a mumble. "Linda wasn't killed in the clearing. She was murdered at home, in her condo. Let's go, Emma. I've got work to do."

Chapter Fifteen

VIDA NEVER LOOKED at her paycheck when Ginny placed it on her desk. My House & Home editor's reaction to getting paid was always one of disdain. She would pick up the check as if it were a chore, and slip it inside her handbag. I often wondered if her attitude had arisen out of her need for employment after her husband's untimely death and her pride in accepting what she might have seen as charity from Marius Vandeventer.

Whatever it was, the habit endured. After Ginny went back to the front office, Vida snapped her bag shut and gave me a quizzical look.

"So Honoria's mad and Milo is gathering evidence against Howard," Vida remarked, resting her chin on one hand. "Tell me the rest of it. I'd like it all to make sense."

There was no one in the news office except Vida and me. Leo was at the Grocery Basket, finalizing the store's pre-Thanksgiving double-truck ad. Carla was covering a small fire that had broken out in a warehouse between the railroad tracks and the river. Reportedly, there was little damage, but fires of any kind make news in a town like Alpine.

Sitting down in Vida's visitor's chair, I dredged up the remainder of my conversation with the sheriff, which had taken place outside of the Upper Crust before we went our separate ways on Front Street.

"The call to Howard on Thursday was made from a pay phone at the Red Apple Market in Sultan at seven-fifteen in the evening. It went into the Lindahls' answering machine, but there was no message."

Vida nodded. "Of course. The Lindahls were out that night, at Alison's school."

"On Friday, the call came through at seven thirty-six in the evening. Howard claims to have answered it, but nobody was there. The phone-company records show it was made from the pay phone at the Icicle Creek Gas 'n Go."

"Hmmmm." Vida fingered her chin. "Maybe Howard *did* answer. But it could have been Susan or Alison."

"That's true. Howard admitted calling Linda several times that week, including Friday. He told Milo he placed the last call just before six-thirty in the evening. The records bear him out—it was actually six thirty-four. Howard said Linda couldn't talk—she had just gotten home from work and she'd call him back. Of course, she never did."

Vida was still looking very thoughtful. "It would take Howard less than an hour to get from his home in Everett to Alpine. Yes, it's possible that he could have murdered Linda. But what's this about Linda being murdered at her condo and not out in the clearing?"

I gave a little shake of my head. "It's sort of confusing. Milo finally got the analysis back from Snohomish County on the hollow log and Linda's clothes and whatever else that they'd gathered up where you and Roger found the body. But Jack Mullins and Sam Heppner had also gone over Linda's condo and, of course, her car. That evidence didn't go off to Everett until last Tuesday. There wasn't much there, either. But what was of

interest was that there were fibers on Linda's coat from
her carpet, as if she'd been dragged across the floor.
There was also the matter of her handbag. It was still
inside the condo."

"Ah!" Vida's eyes lighted up. And then they snapped
with annoyance. "You mean those stupid men—
including my nephew—at the sheriff's office hadn't figured that out right away?"

I gave Vida a wry look. "To be fair, they may have
thought that since Linda's car had been driven to the
clearing and back, the murderer had taken the handbag
along and then put it back."

"But the keys had been left on an end table at Linda's
condo," Vida quibbled. "Oh, dear." She ran a hand
through her already disordered gray curls. "The killer
was bold! In and out of the condo and its garage! And
hauling Linda's body to the car! So risky!"

"How risky?" I pictured the short walk from Linda's
back door to the elevator. It was dark. No one claimed
to have seen anyone, including Linda, come or go.

Vida, who was sitting on her stockinged feet, gave
me a quizzical look. "Did you save that diagram you
made of the condo complex?"

I had, though I couldn't find it at first on my messy
desk. I'd torn it out of my notebook and put it under
a pile of news releases. By the time I came back out
of my office, Leo had returned from the Grocery Basket.

"Money in the bank," Leo said, waggling the two-
page mock-up in my direction. "Or is that a bad joke
around here these days?"

I heaved a big sigh. "I've been putting off talking to
Marv Petersen. But it's got to be done. We'll have to
use the story for this week's edition. I'll talk to him
when I cash my paycheck."

Vida was admiring the Grocery Basket ad with its sketch of a snow-covered New England village that could have passed for Alpine if the ground hadn't been so flat and the buildings so tidy. "Very nice," she said. "It's such a relief not to see all that old clip art Ed used to run."

Leo seemed genuinely pleased by Vida's compliment. "There's clip art and there's clip art. These days, with all the computer technology, it's easy to come up with fresh ideas."

Vida gave a small snort. "Ed didn't think so." She checked her boots, which were drying by the radiator, then sat back down at her desk. I handed her the condo diagram. Vida studied it for a moment, and then nodded. "There was risk, yes. But not as much as you'd think. What if Linda left her car parked out in Maple Lane? It's well shielded by trees and shrubs. All the killer would have to do is strangle her, then carry or drag the body out the front door and down the walk to the car. What's the distance? Ten, fifteen feet?"

Leo's attention was captured by our discussion. "What's going on? Does Milo Drudge think Linda got whacked in her condo?"

I told him that was the case, adding a brief explanation as to why Milo had come to such a conclusion. Now Leo was also studying the diagram. "Parc Pines, right? They had a vacancy when I moved to town. I looked at the place, but decided to wait and see if Boss Woman here would keep me." Leo winked at Vida and jabbed me in the ribs.

I ignored Leo. "Across Fir Street is the veterinarian's office, which would be closed at night. Next door to Dr. Medved is the mobile-home park, but it has a high wall around it. I doubt that anyone could see into Maple Lane except maybe a couple of units in the apartment building. But going down the elevator and into the garage would be far more dangerous."

Leo pointed to the rough sketch I'd made of the condo basement. "But not impossible. As I recall, it's only a few feet from the lanai to the elevator. The garage isn't that big, so you wouldn't have far to go with the body."

Vida pursed her lips. "You might be seen by someone coming in."

"You can see the gate from the elevator," Leo pointed out. "I'm very particular about where I park my car. I'm from L.A., remember." He gave us both a puckish look.

I gazed innocently at Leo. "You certainly studied Linda's condo closely. To know about the elevator location and all."

Leo shrugged. "I was checking out the one next door. Somebody named Hanson bought it, I think." Leo's expression was bland.

Vida returned the diagram to me. "I'd like to think a woman couldn't have done this. But I suppose that's not necessarily true. Unless she were feeble, she could have managed Linda's body for such a short distance. The hard part would be getting her in and out of the car. Ugh!" Vida took off her glasses and rubbed her eyes in agitation.

"Adrenaline," Leo commented. "I've seen a hundred-pound broad deck a son of a bitch almost twice her size."

"Leo," Vida said, replacing her glasses, "please refrain from using such crude language. It's—"

Leo waved an unlighted cigarette in Vida's direction. "You didn't get to hear the good part. You'll like this, Duchess. The broad was my wife. The son of a bitch was me. Now don't you think I picked the right words?"

Vida gave Leo a haughty look. "Yes. But don't use them again. I'm quite a bit larger than your wife. Think what I could do to you. Adrenaline, you know." With a flip of her typewriter carriage, Vida began to hit the keys. For some reason, it sounded like a machine gun.

Francine Wells was telling Ed Bronsky he was out of order. She was right in more ways than one, but she did it nicely, with the same persuasive tact that was so effective in getting Alpine women to charge outlandish amounts of apparel on their bank cards.

Luckily for me, the emergency meeting was a working luncheon. There was no time wasted eating and making frivolous talk. With Thanksgiving only a little over a week away, the local merchants were as anxious as I was to get back on the job.

"Ed means well," Francine was saying in her capacity as this year's president of the chamber. "But the timing strikes me as off. It's the holiday season, and somehow a murder hunt doesn't fit in."

"We should have had it for Halloween," Janet Driggers declared, sitting in for the travel agency. "We could all have met at the cemetery. Hey, Ed, have you ever done the Humpty Dumpty on a tombstone?"

A couple of people laughed, but I wasn't one of them. Neither was Ed, who was shooting dark looks at both Francine and Janet. "We're talking civic pride here," he asserted. "What kind of a town do we want Alpine to turn into? Are we going to let cold-blooded killers get off scot-free?"

I took this as my cue to speak up. Francine saw my upraised hand and officially recognized me. That was

when I went into my spiel about the need for a county
bond issue. Judging from some of the expressions
around the table, particularly those of Cal Vickers
and Harvey Adcock, the idea had already occurred to
them.

A lively discussion followed. Not everyone agreed,
with Ed leading the pack of dissenters. But Francine finally called for a vote. A motion to take the bond issue
before the county commissioners was passed sixteen to
three, with one abstention. Savoring my moment of tri-
umph, I headed for the nearest exit. Ed was blocking
the door.

"That was a rotten thing to do, Emma," he growled.
"I thought you were on my side. Don't you know you
just shot yourself in the foot? Look at all the advertising
you lost!"

Grasping the lapels of Ed's cashmere overcoat, I led
him out into the lobby with its open beams and Native
American motif. "I *am* on your side, Ed. You want to
crack down on crime, right? The most effective way is
to beef up the sheriff's office. You focused everybody's
attention on the issue today. Now we're taking steps. By
March, we may have passed the bond issue and Milo
will have the facilities and the staff he needs."

Ed still looked angry. "So Milo gets to be a hero," he
grumbled. "What's he doing in the meantime? Busting
kids for speeding down Alpine Way?"

"Among other things." I tried not to smile too
broadly at Cal Vickers, who was giving me a congratu-
latory slap on the back. "Milo's making progress. You'll
read all about it Wednesday in *The Advocate*."

Ed snorted. "I used to read all that stuff *before*
Wednesday. I used to *be The Advocate*."

If Ed had been *The Advocate*, the Super Bowl MVP
was the water boy. Now I was irked. I gave Ed a flinty

smile and hurried across the flagstone floor. My afternoon would be busy. I hadn't written a word about the bank inquiry, and my homicide story was full of holes until Milo made an official pronouncement. There had been a certain amount of braggadocio in my words to Ed.

Back at the office, I was greeted by a full house. Vida was whipping her way through a wedding at the Baptist church, Leo was laying out the Safeway ad, Ginny was organizing the classifieds, and Carla was winding up her article on the highway construction. Sometimes a busy staff looks like a happy staff, even when they're not. Still, I enjoy the illusion.

Entering my office, I stopped dead. A huge golden chrysanthemum plant sat on my desk. It was wrapped in deep green foil, with an enclosure card. Hastily I opened the small envelope.

Emma—Coffee Toss II coming up. My place or yours? The note was signed *Leo the Lout.*

I couldn't help but laugh. Then I peeked into the news office. Leo was the only one who looked up. I beckoned to him.

"Pretty, huh?" he said, after I closed the door partway. "I wanted roses, orange ones, but Delphine's been sick and Linda's funeral wiped her out. I had to settle for a plant. This one just came in today. Delphine says you can put it outside in the spring."

"I can. I will." I gave Leo a rather fluttery smile. "You shouldn't spend your money buying me flowers. It's nice, and I love them, but it's not necessary."

Leo shrugged. "That's what makes it fun. The unnecessary part, I mean."

I considered giving Leo a kiss on the cheek, but settled for a handclasp. "Thanks again. I'll take it home and put it on the coffee table."

"Perfect," Leo said. "Let me know where you decide for our next venue." He winked as he went back into the newsroom.

I called Milo immediately to deliver the news about the proposed bond issue. He was pleased, but in a rush. "We're primitive, but we're perking," he said cryptically.

"If you're talking about Howard Lindahl, there's something you ought to know," I said. I'd withheld my theory in the morning because of Milo's hostile attitude toward amateurs. Now, however, I felt duty-bound to state my case.

"Later, Emma," Milo said. "The state auditors have just arrived. Go ahead, do your bank story. It's official."

My head was awhirl. I should talk to Marv Petersen, but I hated to face him. The inquiry must be humiliating. And he was still mourning his murdered daughter.

But I also needed to cash my paycheck. Resignedly I went over to the bank.

The tension in the lobby was palpable. With Christie gone, only two teller cages were open. Denise was her usual vague self, but Rick kept peering over his shoulder, as if he expected to be attacked from the rear. Larry Petersen was hiding behind *The Everett Herald*. Whispering into the phone, Andy Cederberg looked so somber that I expected to see the Four Horsemen of the Apocalypse gallop across the marble floor.

Marv was in his office, staring into space. He greeted me with a ghostly smile. "Isn't this a fine mess," he said, sounding disgusted and sick at the same time. "How can you ever be sure about the people you hire unless they're family?"

I assumed he referred to Christie Johnston. "She had references?"

Marv's nod was doleful. "Plenty of them. Larry said they were impeccable."

"You're certain it was her?"

He nodded again. "But we can't say so until the auditors have done their job. Oh," he went on, gazing up at the arched window set high in the wall, "I had a glimmer two weeks ago. Crazy Eights Neffel came in to ask why he couldn't buy pork chops. I thought he was off his noodle as usual, but he got all worked up. I finally pried the facts out of him. He buys on credit at the Grocery Basket, and they hadn't been paid in three months, so Jake O'Toole cut him off. I stayed here late and did some checking—sure enough, Christie had been handling Crazy Eights's proxy account. No disbursements had been made to his account with the Grocery Basket since the end of July. But similar amounts—say, a hundred and fifty to two hundred each month—had been withdrawn from Crazy Eights's savings. Where did they go? Under Christie's mattress, I'll bet."

I gave Marv my most sympathetic look. "I saw you tear out of here two weeks ago Monday night. Where were you going? The Grocery Basket?"

Marv had been nodding so much that he was beginning to wobble. "I couldn't let Crazy Eights starve. Poor nutty old coot, he's one of ours, and he deserves better treatment."

Allowing a moment of silence to observe Marv's compassion and Crazy Eights Neffel's nuttiness, I then put the bank president back on the right track. "Did you confront Christie the next day?"

"Oh, yes." Marv's expression was bitter. "She said she thought the funds were to be transferred directly into the Grocery Basket's account here at the bank. Which is what she claimed she'd done. She went off to get a printout to show me, but it took her too much time. I suspect she added in the numbers on the spot and made them retroactive. It would be easy enough."

I understood that much. But I still had a question. "Where did the money come from? I mean, she couldn't just type in numbers, could she?"

"She could and probably did. I wanted to believe Christie. To prove her a liar would have meant going through three months of Grocery Basket paperwork to see if everything balanced. Christie knew we wouldn't take the trouble to do it. We're talking about a total of under six hundred dollars on one of our biggest accounts. I wouldn't ask Linda to spend all that time on what might have been an honest mistake."

"But it wasn't," I pointed out.

"Oh, no, it definitely wasn't," Marv agreed. "Linda caught Christie in a couple of other foul-ups. Linda was getting suspicious. Then along came Dan Ruggiero from the Bank of Washington. I hate to admit it, but I tried to tell Linda to keep quiet. Maybe it wasn't as bad as we thought. Maybe Christie was rattled lately. It can happen—Denise has had some real problems settling in."

I didn't doubt it. But I kept a straight face and let Marv continue:

"I advised Linda to let Ruggiero check the books independently, with no input from us. But my daughter isn't—wasn't—made that way." His smile was rueful. And sad. "Linda was a stickler. Numbers were everything to her, the way some people love golf or chocolate. And honesty in finance—well, she should have been appointed to the Federal Reserve Board. Linda couldn't keep quiet about the irregularities. It wasn't in her. And," he added, with the glimmer of a tear in his eye, "I'm proud of her. Damned proud."

Fleetingly I thought that Pastor Nielsen should have

let Marv write Linda's eulogy. If nothing else, she had been a paradigm of integrity. In a shabby, careless world, that was an awe-inspiring virtue.

In my own world, I had to write a story. "Okay, Marv, let's discuss how the audit is conducted. All we'll mention at this point is that certain irregularities have been uncovered. You and Linda might as well take credit for that."

Marv bowed his balding head. "I'd like that. Linda would have, too."

For the next few minutes, Marv explained the nuts and bolts of a bank audit at the state level. I had to interrupt several times to make sure I understood. If a writer doesn't know his or her subject, it can't be conveyed to the public. It's incredible how many journalists seem to forget that basic rule.

When we finished, I had one last question for Marv. "Were you actually going to sell out to the Bank of Washington?"

Marv fidgeted with his gold ballpoint pen, then straightened his desk calendar. "It wasn't a buyout as such. It was a merger. And I would have insisted that we keep our name. Of course, the staff would have remained in place. Our customers would never have known the difference. Except that we could have expanded our services. It's getting to be a complicated world, Emma. There's not much room left for the little guy."

Marv spoke the truth. Down the road, there might not be any place for an independently owned weekly newspaper. I'd known that when I purchased *The Advocate* four years ago. But for now, it was still all mine.

And, until the state audit was over, the Bank of Alpine still belonged to Alpiners. I wasn't sure that was a good thing. It certainly hadn't worked out well for the Petersens.

I still had to cash my paycheck. Larry Petersen had finally emerged from behind *The Herald*. He saw me coming out of his father's office and a thin smile crossed his face.

"How bad is it?" he asked, leaving his desk and coming over to stand at the brass rail.

"Not too bad. I've got a strong quote from your dad about how customers don't need to worry about their money and that everything will be straightened out as quickly as possible. That's what the FDIC is for, right?"

Larry looked dazed. "More or less. But people panic. I keep thinking about those bank runs that my grandfather used to tell me about. You know, in the Thirties. I have visions of everybody in Alpine charging through the lobby and demanding to withdraw all their money at once."

"This isn't the depression," I reminded Larry.

He turned an anxious eye on me. "It's close enough, here in Alpine."

I tried to give Larry a reassuring smile. "The story I'm going to write won't be sensational. *The Advocate* isn't a grocery-store tabloid." A final query popped into my mind. "How much, do you think?" Noting Larry's sudden look of alarm, I waved a hand. "Not for publication, because you can only guess at this stage. But do you have a ballpark figure?"

Larry's face scrunched up as he gazed off over my head to the medallion of John Engstrom. "This has to be a really rough estimate ... but Christie made off with around twenty thousand. Maybe less."

Somehow, I was surprised. As I got in line behind

Ione Erdahl, I wondered if twenty grand was worth killing for. It wouldn't be for me.

But then I wasn't a killer.

Chapter Sixteen

"WE'RE GOING OUT for dessert," Vida announced at the exact moment I hit the printer key on my word processor. "We won't have dinner because we might die."

I had no idea what Vida was talking about. "I'm not going anywhere," I said. "I still have to find out what Milo's up to."

Vida leaned one hand on my visitor's chair. "Thelma and Elmer invited us to dinner. Elmer, it seems, took a fancy to you, which is very rare for him. It must be your peculiar politics. Anyway, only wild horses could drag me to eat an entire meal at their house. You wouldn't believe what that kitchen looks like. But dessert is safe. Thelma usually makes something out of a box."

I had no earthly desire to spend part of my evening with Elmer and Thelma Petersen. But Vida had made the commitment for me, and I knew I was stuck.

"What time?" I sighed.

"Six. They eat at five. That's because they go to bed so early."

It was now almost four-thirty. I must have been looking fretful because Vida shook a finger at me.

"You don't have to finish your homicide story until tomorrow. If Milo had anything new, he would have

called. I'll pick you up at ten to six." In her splay-
footed manner, Vida exited my office.

The printer was still spewing out copy when the
phone rang. I hoped it was Milo, if only to get me off
the hook with the Petersens.

But it was a woman, and she sounded upset. At first
I couldn't understand a word she said. Then she collected herself.

"Susan Lindahl? Remember, you and your friend
were here last week? In Everett?"

Susan must have thought I was a moron. "Oh, yes, of
course. What is it, Susan?"

Susan uttered a strange little squawk. "I . . . I'm so
upset. I've spent the last half hour trying to calm down
Alison. I really don't know anyone else in Alpine except you and Mrs. Runkel. . . ." A sob broke through in
her voice; I waited for her to go on. "Your sheriff was
here this afternoon with a search warrant. Howie wasn't
home. He's putting in some cabinets at an industrial
park near Marysville. What am I going to tell him when
he gets home?"

Distractedly I pushed my overlong bangs off my
forehead. "It's routine, I imagine," I said, lying through
my teeth. "If the sheriff wanted to talk to Howie, he'd
have tracked him down."

"He's coming back, around six. He'd still be here if
he hadn't taken some things to the police lab downtown." Susan's voice trembled, but she seemed to be
getting the upper hand on her self-control.

"What things?" I asked, ready to jot down information.

"Some of Howie's clothes. His shoes. A hairbrush."
She paused, and I could distinctly hear her swallow.
"And a piece of rope."

I bit my lower lip. "Milo Dodge is very thorough." It

was the only comforting thing I could think of to say to Susan Lindahl.

"But *why*? What's going on over there in Alpine? You own the newspaper; you must know what the sheriff's thinking." The quaver had gone out of Susan's voice, but she still sounded frantic.

I had scribbled Milo's haul in my little notebook. For a brief, electrifying second I stared at the page. "Don't get too upset about Sheriff Dodge," I said, hoping to convey confidence. "He's just doing his job. As I mentioned, he has to be thorough. Maybe it has something to do with your break-in."

"That?" Susan's attitude was scornful. "The Everett police handled it. It was probably kids, maybe even friends of Alison's. Nothing was taken."

"How did you know there *was* a break-in?" I asked in a casual voice.

Now that Susan was off of the subject of Milo Dodge, she sounded more like herself. "There were drawers pulled out, a glass in the kitchen was over-turned, one of the living-room lamps had gotten unplugged. As I told you, the police figured it was kids, looking for money or liquor or drugs."

"How did they get in?"

Susan hesitated before answering. "This is the silly part. Alison's hair clip broke after she got in the car, and she had to go back to get another one. She swears she locked the door on the way out, but you know how kids are. She was all excited about the open house and she probably forgot. We gave her a little lecture, but as long as nothing was stolen or vandalized, we couldn't complain too much. It's a good thing, since Linda was killed right after that."

"How's she doing?" I inquired, thinking of the pale-faced little girl at the Lutheran church.

"Oh—it's hard to say. At this age, kids tend to keep things inside, I think. She seemed to be doing all right until this afternoon when your sheriff showed up. That really threw her."

I allowed that Milo's search would certainly be upsetting. We chatted briefly, mostly about the trauma of adolescence. In the end, Susan thanked me and admitted that perhaps she'd overreacted.

She hadn't, of course. But there was no need for her to know that. Yet.

Thelma Petersen served dessert in the living room, which was probably just as well. Vida's warning about the kitchen had practically caused me to lose my appetite anyway. I tried not to cringe as I examined the watery chocolate pudding that was slipping and sliding in a slightly dingy cranberry glass dish.

We spent the first fifteen minutes with Thelma and Vida discussing Linda's funeral. Elmer sat in silence, slopping up pudding. Once or twice, I caught him watching me with a wary eye. If this was Elmer Petersen's way of extending friendship, I wondered how he showed hostility.

And then I found out. Somehow, after I drifted off course from the conversation, Vida and Thelma had started talking about the old days.

"You remember that dance, Vida," Thelma was saying. "You wore green tulle."

"It was my first grown-up dress. My mother made it." Vida looked oddly wistful.

"What a shame the big fight spoiled everything." Thelma glanced in her husband's direction. "Not that I blamed Elmer. After all, the dance was in his honor because he was going overseas. He looked ever so handsome in his Navy uniform, didn't he, Vida?"

"Very," Vida replied, while I tried to conjure up a picture of Elmer Petersen ever looking like anything but two hundred pounds of potatoes stuffed into overalls. "Marv was jealous, of course. He was too young to scrve."

"He was too young to drink," Thelma declared heatedly. A half century apparently hadn't cooled her ire at her brother-in-law. "Sneaking punch, that's what he did. And then he tried to kill Elmer!"

"Dutch courage," Vida remarked, chasing her pudding around the dish. "Marv wanted to be a hero, too. And I think he had a crush on you."

"Nonsense! I was way too old for Marv." Thelma simpered just a bit. "Those were the days, weren't they, Vida?"

Vida inclined her head. "Well . . . if you number putting Marv in traction among your most memorable moments, then I suppose we had a good time. Frankly, I thought Elmer would have killed Marv if their father and Stilts Cederberg hadn't broken up the fight."

"It *was* fierce." Thelma's seamed face softened at the memory. "But of course, Elmer and Marv never got along." She turned again to her husband. "Did you, Elmer?"

To my amazement, Elmer had been listening. Perhaps his wife's favorable attention had improved his diction. Or maybe I was getting used to the Petersen mumble. "I come back from the Pacific with a bum knee. Marv sits at home all safe and sound, then votes for Dewey. To hell with him."

I sensed that Vida was about to make a stinging retort. "Say, where's Goldwater?" I asked brightly.

Elmer's nostrils twitched as if he were testing the air to makc sure the goat wasn't still in the house. "Tied up again. Goldwater should stay outside. Otherwise, he steps on the chickens."

The chickens, however, were also absent. The only creature that strolled through the living room was a part-Persian cat with suspicious amber eyes and a shaggy brown coat. The cat brushed my legs, hissed at Vida, and settled down on a bare spot in front of the fireplace.

"That's Mamie Eisenhower," Elmer announced. "She's one dumb cat. Ornery, too. I had to put Ike to sleep."

Vida had stood up. "Really, Elmer, you're very disrespectful. It isn't funny to name animals after our presidents and their wives and famous statesmen."

Though Thelma and I had both risen, too, Elmer remained seated. "Aw, come on, Vida," Elmer said, and actually chuckled. "If you had a jackass, you'd call him Bill Clinton."

Vida was buttoning her coat. "I think not." She put on her knit stocking cap. "If I had a jackass," she said with a tight little smile, "I'd call him Elmer Petersen."

"Really, he does get my goat. So to speak." Vida was still irritated as we wound down the Icicle Creek Road's smooth new surface. It had been snowing off and on all day, but the plows had been busy.

"I think he's kind of . . . ah . . . unique." It seemed the only positive word that fit Elmer Petersen.

"It's a wonder Thelma hasn't killed him," Vida remarked, turning off by the high school. "But I do feel sorry for her and Elmer. And especially Marv and Cathleen. I'm going to make a casserole and take it over to them tomorrow night."

Like most of her cooking, Vida's casseroles are wretched. The Petersens probably would feel worse if they ate it. But the thought would be there. And they could always order a pizza.

"My clam casserole," Vida was saying to herself. "I have some frozen geoducks I could use."

Vida was lucky that I'd outgrown my car sickness when I was twelve. We were now on Fir Street, approaching my house. I hadn't yet mentioned the call from Susan Lindahl. I knew Vida would have a violent reaction to Milo's search warrant. It wouldn't have been a good idea to call on the Petersens while Vida was all worked up over Thelma's nephew.

As we pulled up in front of my house, I asked Vida to come in for a cup of tea. She protested, saying she should go home and eat.

"Just pickups," she said, using the terms she applied to almost anything that wasn't screwed into the frame of her refrigerator. "That pudding wasn't very filling."

But I persisted. "I've got something to tell you, Vida. I'm worried."

Curiosity overcame hunger. Vida sat down at my kitchen table while I related the phone call and its ominous portent. She listened in silence, making no comment until I was done.

"Milo was going back to the Lindahls'?" Vida finally gasped. "What for? To arrest Howie or merely to question him? Oh, Emma, I don't like this one bit!"

"Neither do I," I said, sinking tea bags into hot water. "Milo could be on the right track, but there are so many things—little things, I'll admit—that indicate he isn't. I don't want to see him make a fool of himself, especially now when the bond issue is going before the county commissioners."

The phone rang. I hurried into the living room to answer it. Carla's roommate, Marilynn Lewis, was on the line.

"Emma, I'm sorry to bother you, but Carla's come down with the flu. I've seen dozens of cases at the clinic this fall, and there's no way she can come to work tomorrow. I thought I'd give you some notice since you're close to your deadline."

Marilynn was a good nurse and a good friend. She had moved from Seattle to Alpine the previous spring. Her African-American heritage had created some nasty problems at first, but after six months, she seemed to be easing into small-town life.

"Thanks, Marilynn," I said. "Tell Carla to get well. I know you'll take good care of her."

"I'll try." She paused, and I heard a moaning voice in the background. Marilynn spoke again: "Carla says to tell you she brought some—what are they?—oh, contact sheets back from Buddy Bayard's studio. They're on her desk if you need them."

I thanked Marilynn, then hung up, and informed Vida of Carla's illness.

"That tears it," Vida said. She'd made the tea in my absence and now took a long sip. "We'll be shorthanded tomorrow, and heaven only knows how much of your time will be devoted to the homicide case. Let's go down to the office and get a head start."

"Tonight?" I was taken aback. Once again, I had to remind myself who was boss. But Vida was right. Either we could work for a couple of hours tonight, or face the possibility of a very long Tuesday.

We didn't linger over our tea. It was seven-thirty when we turned on the lights and the heat in the *Advocate* office. The next thing I did was call the sheriff's office. Bill Blatt informed me that Milo hadn't yet returned from Everett. He and Jack Mullins had been gone since before three o'clock.

"Are you in communication with Milo?" I asked, feeling the onset of a minor panic attack.

"Not since he was at the lab in Everett," Bill replied. "That was around four-thirty. He and Jack probably went somewhere to eat."

I was sitting at Carla's desk. Across the room, Vida watched me with narrowed eyes. "Is that my occasionally dim nephew, Billy?" Seeing me nod, she picked up her phone. "Now see here, Billy, the minute you hear from Sheriff Dodge, you let us know. We're at the office. This is very important." She slapped the phone back into place. "I trust it is," she said, eyeing me rather doubtfully.

I made a rueful face. "I'm still piecing my theory together. If I explained it to you, would you laugh?"

"Certainly not. We can talk as we work. Shall we start with layout? The copy's in good shape, except for the rest of your homicide piece and any late-breaking news." Vida had come over to Carla's desk. The House & Home section was the one part of the paper that was still laid out by hand. Vida refused to learn either the computer or the word processor.

I was tearing open the envelope from Buddy Bayard's studio. "Let's see if Carla has anything we can use," I said. There were dozens of contact prints, maybe eight rolls with thirty-six exposures each. "We could use a good snow scene. Something that says Thanksgiving, too. I don't imagine Carla got much out of that small fire." I handed half of the contact sheets to Vida.

Using a magnifying glass to study the prints, Vida wore a dubious expression. "Trees, trees, trees—the girl's obsessed with trees. She should have been an arborist. I'll admit, she's got some interesting composition in . . . Oh!" Vida dropped her magnifier. "Look, Emma, quick! What do you make of this?"

I usually don't need an enlarger to see contact prints, but this time I wanted to be sure. Squinting through the glass, I saw a truck parked behind a car. The truck belonged to the state highway department; the car had been owned by Linda Lindahl.

"It's Maple Lane," Vida said excitedly. "See—there's the walk to Linda's unit. There's the shrubbery between the condos and the apartments. It was dark, but Carla used some very fast film. She must have taken this from her deck."

I was transfixed. "There's no one in the car. But it looks as if someone might be sitting in the truck. We've got to get these blown up right away."

Vida, however, was trailing a finger down the contact sheet. "Look—here's the truck again, parked almost where we did, in front of Parc Pines on Alpine Way. The cab's empty." She paused, noting the exposure numbers on the sheet. "Number three is Maple Lane, number six is Alpine Way. The pictures taken in between are telephoto lens work. Carla was shooting down Alpine Way, to Old Mill Park. Then she switched over to the mall."

I had already punched in Carla's number. As I expected, Marilynn answered. "Ask your patient when she took the pictures from her deck," I requested, after first making sure that Carla was still alive.

Away from the phone, I could hear Marilynn's pleasant voice and Carla's croaking response. Then Marilynn relayed my reporter's message. I asked Marilynn if Carla was sure. A brief croak was in the affirmative.

Still clutching the receiver, I stared at Vida. "Carla says it was a week ago Friday. The night Linda Lindahl was killed."

Vida was holding her head. "Why didn't Carla tell us about these pictures?"

Naturally, I'd asked myself the same question. But Carla had shot so much film, in so many places, and been so indifferent to everything but her own little world, that I wasn't surprised. Besides, it hadn't been discovered until today that Linda was probably killed at her condo.

"Marilynn," I said, again speaking into the receiver, "do you think Carla could talk to me for just a minute?"

Marilynn was dubious. "She can hardly hold her head up. In fact, she's got it hanging over a basin."

Feeling like the ultimate callous employer, I asked if Marilynn could hold the phone to her roommate's ear.

"This must be some hot set of pictures," Marilynn remarked. "Is there something X-rated in Alpine that I don't know about?"

But Marilynn didn't expect a serious answer, and the next thing I knew, Carla's feeble voice was on the line. "What is it? Make it quick, I'm dying."

"Did you see Big Mike Brockelman drive his truck from Maple Drive around the block to Alpine Way?"

A violent retching noise assaulted my ear. I arched my eyebrows as Vida quietly picked up her phone to listen in. She made a face. Then Carla spoke in a series of gasps:

"Sort of . . . I know the truck . . . moved . . . because I didn't want . . . a blur of . . . headlights . . . so I changed angles and . . . took some . . . long-distance shots of . . . Old Mill Park." Carla paused and uttered a heartrending sigh. "Then I saw the truck in front of Parc Pines, so I took another shot."

"Did you see Mike Brockelman get out of the truck?" I tensed, waiting for Carla's answer.

"No." The single word was barely audible.

"But he must have," I countered. "In the second photo of the truck, he's not in the cab."

"I must have . . . been concentrating . . . on . . . Old Mill Park." The phone fell, and I heard more retching noises.

Marilynn came back on the line. "I'm sorry, Emma, Carla's really a mess. Shall I have her call you when she feels a little better?"

I assured Marilynn that wasn't necessary. Carla had told me all that she knew. I wished aloud to Vida that she had told me sooner. But of course, Carla really wasn't at fault.

Vida didn't look so forgiving. She was, however, ready to move on. "Roust Buddy. Get him to meet us at the studio so we can enlarge these."

"We'd better check the rest of the contact sheets," I said.

"I already did. The fire is a dud. Wet paper boxes do not a front page make." Vida was putting her coat back on.

As I dialed Buddy's home number, I flipped through the rest of the finished photos that I'd collected. There were more of Carla's, some of Vida's, and a couple of my own, including the static county commissioner meeting shots I'd taken over a week ago.

"Buddy doesn't answer," I said, putting the phone down. I snapped my fingers. "It's Monday—there's a parish council meeting tonight. Buddy's the chair and Roseanna's the secretary."

"Rats!" Vida worked her way out of her coat.

But at the moment, I was more intrigued by the courtroom where the county commissioners had held their meeting. With growing excitement, I pushed an eight-by-ten glossy under Vida's nose.

"Look. What do you see?" I sounded a bit breathless.

"Dunderheads. A roomful of them. The biggest dunderheads of all aren't in the photo because you shot the audience."

"I know that. But look in the fourth row. There's Big Mike Brockelman."

Vida still wasn't joining in my enthusiasm. "So? This was Thursday, not Friday. Why shouldn't he be there?"

I shuffled through the rest of the photographs I'd clicked off in about a two-minute time period. "Look at the back of the room."

"What?" Now Vida was getting testy. "I see Henry Bardeen and Norm Carlson and Darrell Pidduck and . . ."

I shook my head impatiently as I scrambled through Leo's wastebasket. "Damn!" I cried. "When's our trash pickup? Monday?"

"Of course it is. It always has been." Vida now stood in the middle of the news office, regarding me as if I'd joined ranks with Crazy Eights Neffel. "Settle down, young lady, and tell me what you're so wrought up about."

I gripped Leo's desk to pull myself up. "The rope. The one Carla was using for a noose. She threw it at Leo, and I suppose he tossed it in the wastebasket. That was last week. But Carla had found it earlier—out in the street by her apartment. Now, what do you think it was doing there?"

Vida put out a hand to feel my forehead. No doubt she thought that I, too, was coming down with the flu. "It probably fell off a logging truck. That would hardly be unusual around here."

"It wasn't that kind of rope," I said, dancing away from Vida's outstretched hand. "It was more like cording. Not so coarse or thick as what the loggers use on their trucks."

Vida's gray eyes had turned thoughtful. At last she

seemed to be taking me seriously. "But Linda wasn't strangled with a rope. The killer used her scarf."

"But maybe the killer didn't know Linda would be wearing her scarf. If this murder was premeditated, which I'm sure it was," I went on, speaking rapidly, "the killer brought the rope along, then didn't need to use it, but had to get rid of it. Why not simply toss it into the street?"

"Litter," murmured Vida. "So ordinary. So unnoticed."

"Especially since it was supposed to snow," I reminded Vida. And then I trotted out the theory that had been running in and out of my brain since morning. In the last fifteen minutes, several gaps had been filled. When I finished, I knew Vida wasn't going to scoff.

"It's quite simple, really," she said in a sad, tired voice. "But there's no proof. What do we do?"

As usual, Vida had driven straight to the heart of the matter. "I don't know," I replied, collapsing into Carla's chair. The wind had gone out of my sails.

"Call the Lindahls," Vida said suddenly. "See if Milo has shown up yet."

It was after eight, and as I recalled, Susan had said that the sheriff planned on returning around six. I got out Carla's Everett directory and looked up the Lindahls' number. A moment later, Susan answered in a tense voice.

"No," she said in response to my query about Milo. "He still hasn't come back. I don't understand it. And now Howie is working himself into ulcers."

"If you see Milo Dodge, have him call me at *The Advocate* before he does anything except walk into the house, okay?" I hung up, no doubt leaving Susan bewildered.

The phone on Vida's desk rang at that exact instant.

Vida answered, then nodded at me to pick up Carla's receiver. "Yes, Billy," Vida said. "Why did Jack Mullins go home?"

"Because," her nephew replied in a tone of uncharacteristic pique, "Sheriff Dodge didn't need him. After they went to the crime lab in Everett, the sheriff said he'd changed his mind about questioning Howard Lindahl tonight. It could wait until they got the report back from the lab tomorrow."

Vida fingered the contact sheet with the Parc Pines photos. "Very well. When you see Milo, tell him to get in touch with Big Mike Brockelman in Monroe. It's very urgent."

"The highway construction guy?" Bill Blatt sounded dubious. "What for?"

"Never mind, just have Milo do as he's told." Vida circled the third and sixth shots on the sheet with a grease pencil.

"I don't think I'll be seeing Sheriff Dodge tonight," Bill said, sounding a mite intimidated. "Jack Mullins dropped him off in Startup. I don't know how the sheriff's going to get back to Alpine."

"Oh, good grief!" Vida pulled at her hair, then composed herself and ordered Billy to have *someone* track down Big Mike. "Doesn't that beat all?" she demanded, jutting her jaw at me. "Milo's off playing kissy-face with Honoria Whitman! Oooooh!"

"At least he's not making a wrongful arrest," I noted. "We should have known he'd wait until he got the information on Howard's things back from the crime lab." I glanced at the little notebook in which I'd listed the items that Milo had removed from the Lindahl house. Inspiration struck. "Vida, maybe we *can* get some proof. It wouldn't be much, and it might not even be there. Do you think Ginny could talk Rick into letting us in the bank?"

"If she can't, I'll give her lessons." Vida dialed Ginny's number. Ginny balked. Vida talked. Ginny remained adamant. She and Rick were still in the process of making up. She refused to jeopardize their status by "using him," as she put it.

Admiration shone in Vida's eyes as she replaced the phone. "Very astute. Very obstinate. You have to respect Ginny."

I wasn't quite so charitable. "One stubborn woman around here ended up getting killed. You might have mentioned to Ginny that this is a matter of life and death."

Vida seemed unperturbed as she made yet another phone call. "You're exaggerating. Perhaps," she added, then spoke into the receiver. "Rick? How nice to find you home. Now, this may sound like an odd request, but Emma and I need to get into the bank. . . . Certainly, I know it's against the . . . Well, when else would we find it completely empty except when it's closed? . . . No, that's not the same thing. We want the effect of darkness, with the snow falling outside. Think how our readers—and your customers—will be touched. The Bank of Alpine, deserted on a cold November night, waiting to be warmed by the loving, loyal people it's served for over sixty years . . ."

Rick fell for it. Vida and I put on our coats, she grabbed a camera, I got a flashlight, and we trudged across Front Street. There was a fresh inch of snow on the plowed surface. Maintenance work would wait until early morning. I slipped slightly just before reaching the far curb.

Rick, who owned an old beater, drove slowly down

Fourth Street where he parked a good thirty feet from the corner.

"I don't want to be seen," he whispered after he'd all but skidded to a stop under the big clock. Hurriedly he inserted two keys into the double locks on the front doors. Vida rushed inside, but Rick held out an arm to bar my way.

"Sorry, Ms. Lord. I can only be responsible for one of you. Honest. You'll have to wait out here."

I started to protest, then decided not to make things any more difficult. "Okay." I shrugged and handed Rick the flashlight. "Give this to Vida."

Trying not to shiver, I huddled next to the clock standard. Only one car had passed by since we'd left the office. Now, half a block away, a young couple came out of the Burger Barn and walked in the opposite direction. They were laughing as they deliberately slid around in the new snow.

I was watching their figures grow smaller when a car quietly pulled into the disabled parking space a few yards from the clock. Anxiously I glanced at the bank. For one brief moment, I could see the flashlight waver.

"Emma?" called a voice from the car. I turned to see Larry Petersen, with one foot on the curb and his head and shoulders leaning in my direction. "What's going on?"

"Oh!" I brushed snow out of my eyes. "This sounds crazy, but we suddenly thought of a wonderful photo opportunity. Vida's in there now, taking a picture."

Larry frowned, or at least I thought he did. The snow was coming down harder by the second. "In the dark?" Larry asked incredulously.

A gust of wind from off Tonga Ridge threatened to topple me. I grabbed the clock pedestal for support.

"That's what makes it so dramatic. She's using very fast film."

Larry didn't move. He was looking up at the bank's arched windows. Again the flashlight wavered. "Who let her in?" Larry's tone had turned curt.

"Rick. He didn't want to, but you know Vida. . . . She could talk Noah into a leaky rubber boat." My attempt at a laugh sounded more like a sick chicken.

"I don't like this." Larry started to get out of the car, then beckoned to me. "Come here, Emma. I want to talk to you."

I hesitated, then took a few uncertain steps toward Larry. Except for the wind, Front Street was unnaturally quiet. Surely Vida had found what we wanted by now. If it was there. I took another couple of steps. I had reached the front fender of Larry's car.

Larry had moved across the front seat, resuming his position behind the wheel. "Get in, Emma. You must be freezing out there." His tone had changed again; he sounded almost jocular.

"No, that's all right," I replied, leaning against the car. "I have to wait for Vida. And Rick. They should be out any minute. Or should we go get them?"

"Get in, Emma." Larry's affability evaporated. "Just a word, that's all."

I wasn't getting into Larry Petersen's car. Never mind that I was shaking as well as shivering, and that my feet had gone numb. So had my hands, which were jammed into the pockets of my duffle coat.

"Why don't we go over to *The Advocate*?" I suggested in a cracked voice.

"Emma . . ." Larry was moving back across the seat. He could haul me into the car without much effort. I could scream, of course. If my voice still worked and it could be heard over the howling wind.

Larry's hand reached out to grab my arm. That was when I saw the dim glow of approaching headlights. I raised the arm that Larry wasn't holding in a viselike grip. But whoever was coming down Front Street probably couldn't see me through the snow. Certainly the driver would be concentrating on the street, not the sidewalk.

I let out one strangled yelp, fell against the open car door, and grappled with Larry as he tried to pull me inside. My handbag had fallen onto the slush at the curb. I tried to get traction with my boots, but they slipped on the new snow, and I slipped with them—right into the front seat.

Larry reached over me and slammed the door shut. I struggled to sit upright, but he kept a hand on my back. And then I became aware of a light shining into the car and a muffled, familiar voice.

"You're under arrest," said Milo Dodge to Larry Petersen. "Please step out of the vehicle with your hands on top of your head."

Chapter Seventeen

Milo and I have sworn each other to secrecy. I will never, ever tell anyone, including Vida, that he arrested a murderer for parking in a disabled space without a state handicapped decal if he won't reveal that I acted like a nincompoop by getting myself into such a mess in the first place.

Milo had meant well, of course. He had been returning from Startup with Honoria in her car, and seeing that someone had violated the disabled parking place, he'd aimed to show his newly reconciled ladylove that he could be sensitive, especially to her special needs.

"If Honoria hadn't been with me," Milo said the next evening at the bar in the Venison Inn, "I wouldn't have dreamed of busting Larry Petersen. *Larry*, for God's sake! In front of his own bank!" Milo's mouth was agape, as if he'd only just realized the enormity of his gaffe.

"*His own bank*," I repeated. "That was the key. Larry couldn't bear to think of not taking over from Marv. The bank was in his blood. I remember how he talked about it the very week that Linda was killed. It was like a mistress."

Milo leaned back in his chair, signaling Oren Rhodes for a second round. I didn't protest. The last twenty-four hours had been hectic. Horrible, too, with Larry

Petersen locked up on a homicide charge. It was now almost nine o'clock, the paper was ready to be sent off to Monroe, my aches and pains were subsiding, and the sheriff was basking in the glory of his arrest. Many considered it tarnished, however, if for the wrong reasons. A Petersen was not supposed to kill another Petersen. Alpiners would much prefer to see Dan Ruggiero or Bob Lambrecht or even me behind bars.

Instead, I was in one, and glad of it. "I can't believe Larry blurted out that he didn't kill Linda," I said with a shake of my head. "He started babbling like a madman, spouting alibis for things he hadn't been accused of."

"But should have been." Milo took a long drag on his cigarette. "Why the hell didn't you clue me in sooner?"

"I tried to," I protested as Oren brought our drinks and gave Milo another pat on the back. "At first it was only Linda's keys that made me wonder. Andy told us how fussy she was about keeping them in order, and how symbolic it was for her to put Howard's key as far away from her condo key as possible. Yet they were side by side on the ring when you gave it to Andy. I had to wonder if someone hadn't taken one of the keys when Linda wasn't looking. Someone at work, probably, where she'd be so caught up in her numbers that she wouldn't notice. It couldn't be her own key—she would have missed that. So it had to be Howard's. Then I racked my brain figuring out why. The break-in that wasn't a break-in explained it. Larry was setting Howard up, and he did it Thursday night while the Lindahls were at Alison's open house."

Milo allowed two more of his constituents to offer congratulations. "How did Larry know they wouldn't be home?" he asked after his fans had migrated to the bar.

"Larry, like so many Alpiners, gets *The Everett Her-*

ald. They run a calendar of community events, just like we do in *The Advocate*. Except, of course, they have a lot more of them. He must have seen the listing for Alison's school. She was his niece, remember, and he must have kept up with her to some extent. Still, he had to make sure they were gone, so he stopped in Sultan at the Red Apple Market and called the Lindahl house. Nobody answered. He knew the coast was clear. He continued to Everett, used Linda's key, made just enough of a mess to make it look like a break-in, and planted the extra rope and the little map. I'll bet that rope has goat hair on it. Larry took it off of Uncle Elmer's goat. That's why Goldwater was in the living room. Your aunt's husband hadn't gotten around to tethering him again."

A grin spread over Milo's face. "I'll be damned. The lab guys wanted to know how that goat hair got on the rope we took from Howard Lindahl's house. Goldwater, huh? That thing's always on the loose. I found him in their bathtub once." Still looking bemused, Milo rested his long chin on his hand. "Wouldn't it have been smarter for Larry just to stash his evidence against Howard and not leave any visible sign of an intruder?"

I cocked my head to one side, sniffing at Milo's trail of smoke. "Probably it would, but I think that Larry was looking for some other ways to frame Howard. Maybe he thought he could find something that belonged to Linda. Or some incriminating correspondence between the two. As far as we know, he didn't find anything, but he couldn't risk hanging around to tidy up. He had to be back in Alpine at the county commissioners meeting to give himself an alibi."

"Where you saw him," Milo remarked with a wry smile.

"I certainly did. But it was at the end of the meeting,

not at the beginning. You know how those county commissioner meetings go, Milo. They start out with a big crowd, and then, when the item that people are interested in has been covered, they often leave. But it's rare that anybody comes late. I always take my pictures within the first fifteen minutes, because that's when the audience is at its largest. When Vida and I looked at those pictures last night, I realized who *wasn't* there at the start of the meeting: Larry Petersen. I didn't notice him until it was over, after nine-thirty. He was at the back of the room. I suppose he'd slipped in after returning from the Lindahls' house in Everett."

Milo was nodding. "There'll be witnesses to that effect. How did you blow holes in Larry's alibi for Friday night? He was supposed to be at home with JoAnne hosting a card party."

"He was—later. I remembered that Vida had deep-sixed the 'Scene Around Town' item about Larry's wife, JoAnne, who had been spotted rushing around at the grocery store buying crackers and cheese Friday. Party food, obviously, and why the rush? Because she discovered at the last minute that she didn't have anything to serve their guests. So if JoAnne was gone for a while early Friday evening, she couldn't vouch for her husband being at home. How long would it take for Larry to go to Parc Pines, kill Linda, haul her body in her own car, and drive out to the clearing on the Icicle Creek Road? Fifteen minutes, maybe, and the same for the return. He had to stop at Icicle Creek Gas 'n Go to call Howard Lindahl and pretend to be Dick Johnson. Maybe he did that first, before he went to Linda's. If JoAnne got home before Larry did, he'd simply tell her he ducked out on some trumped-up errand. She'd be too busy playing hostess to care."

Milo scratched his graying temples. "I should have

checked further into Larry's alibi," he admitted. "Andy's seemed a little shaky, too, because I figured Reba would lie for him. Denise didn't remember the name of the movie she'd seen with Rick, let alone what time they got to the Whistling Marmot. As it turns out, Christie would have lied through her teeth to save her ass, and Troy would probably have gone right along with her."

"As indeed he did—all the way to Michigan."

Milo didn't want to think about Christie Johnston's flight from justice. Not yet, anyway. "What I couldn't quite get into my head was the part about the map," Milo confessed. No doubt he was as tired as I was, and his defenses were down. "How did you tie that in to Larry?"

I sipped my drink and took a deep breath. My brain hadn't yet turned as numb as my body. Adrenaline, Leo would say. "Denise brought us a memorial ad for Linda. Larry had attached a note. It appeared to be torn out of the same notebook that the map had come from. Same size, same paper, same dark pen—maybe the same printing. That's a guess, but the more I thought about it, the more it seemed likely. I keep a little spiral notebook with me. So do you. But neither of ours has the same kind of paper as the map and the memo. Both were better quality than what we get at the drugstore. I know my paper; it's my business. A banker would have a nice notebook with nice paper. But would he leave it behind at the bank or take it with him? That's what Vida and I were trying to find out last night."

"Larry had it with him in his briefcase. Your foray into the bank almost got you killed." Milo looked severe.

I, in turn, looked chastened. "Obstinacy. Righteousness. That's what killed Linda. Even before Dan Ruggiero was sent to Alpine, she wanted to call in the state auditors. Along about Tuesday, Marv must have let Larry know what was going on. Marv had to—Larry was second-in-command. Larry acted as fast as he could, given the circumstances. He didn't care what Dan Ruggiero found out—that could be kept under wraps, or so I think Larry figured. But Linda—she'd broadcast the news all over Alpine. Nailing Christie was her aim. And in doing so, Linda would bring Larry down with her."

Milo was now shaking his head. "No, no, Emma, you're pushing it. Sure, Larry worked himself into a homicidal fit because his sister was going to blow the whistle on a crook. But that didn't reflect on Larry himself."

"Yes, it did. Larry hired Christie. Either he never checked her references or he let her charm him into offering her the job. Whichever way it was, Marv would have had to sit back and reconsider his dynasty. Marv thought the world of Linda. I suspect he was already beginning to think that she should be the next president of the Bank of Alpine. Larry couldn't live with that. So Linda had to die."

For a few moments, Milo sat with his elbows on the table, mulling over my hypothesis. "I don't know. Maybe. I'll tell you one thing—Linda and Larry never could stand each other, not even when they were kids."

I nodded. "It's a family tradition. Marv and Elmer, Larry and Linda, Denise and her brothers. The Petersens may be one of Alpine's most beloved families—except by each other."

"Weird." Milo stifled a yawn. He pointed to his almost empty glass. "You want another one?"

"Why not?" I was winding down, leveling off to a comfortable plateau where only the scrape on my left knee still hurt. "I'll also have one of those." I pointed to Milo's cigarettes.

"Hey!" Milo held the pack far out of my reach. "No, you don't! What did you tell me about these things?"

I gave Milo my sweetest smile. "Smoking will kill you. But then, so will drinking. And driving. And banking."

Reluctantly Milo punched the bottom of the pack and shot a cigarette in my direction. Then, with a huge sigh, he lighted it for me. I sat back and puffed, puffed, puffed.

"What have you heard from Seattle about the Johnstons' car?" I knew that Christie and Troy had dumped their Nissan off at a sales lot near the airport on Saturday. Milo had had it traced through the Department of Motor Vehicles.

"It's got some front-end and axle damage," Milo said, after a nod to Oren Rhodes. "We can't prove that Christie tried to run down Andy Cederberg—or Dan Ruggiero, as she mistakenly thought. We'll settle for the charges we get from the state auditors. Of course, we'll have to extradite her. If we can."

Milo had already explained that the FBI wouldn't get involved unless the proven amount of theft was over a certain figure. There were also some extradition technicalities between the states of Washington and Michigan. Maybe it had something to do with the Rose Bowl football rivalry. I wasn't sure, and I didn't much care. Christie's embezzlement seemed pretty tame compared to fratricide. I puffed some more.

"What is *this*?" Vida was looming over our table. "Emma! Oh, Emma, you ought to be ashamed!"

I looked at her through the thin spiral of smoke. "I am, Vida. Deeply. What are you doing in the bar?"

"I . . ." Her eyes were still riveted on my cigarette. "I

came in here to have a bit of supper. There was some clam casserole left over from the dish I made for Marv and Cathleen, but when I heated it for myself, it seemed a little . . . off. Anyway, I heard you two were back here, so after I finished my prime rib, I thought I'd say hello. Tsk, tsk." Vida shook her head, the pink ears on her snow-bunny cap dancing. "You're both utterly disreputable."

Milo pulled over a chair from the vacant table next to us. "Sit down, Vida. Have a drink." The sheriff glanced at Oren Rhodes. "Emma and I are going to hell in a handcart anyway. We might as well get good and tight."

Oren, startled at seeing Vida anywhere but in the dining room, began to gush. "Something sweet, maybe, Mrs. Runkel? A nice liqueur, or a hot toddy or the first of our seasonal eggnogs . . ."

Vida had her cheek propped on her gloved hand. "I don't suppose," she said with a doubtful expression, "that you could mix a Singapore sling?"

Wednesday's edition of *The Alpine Advocate* was stuffed—with both news and advertising. Larry Petersen's arrest was a banner headline. Vida, bless her, had taken a picture of Milo reading Larry his rights in the middle of a snowstorm on Front Street. She had come out of the bank with Rick—and her camera—just after the sheriff cuffed his suspect. Fortunately, I was out of the picture, wallowing around in the snow on the sidewalk.

In the lull between the delivery of our advance copies and the public's reaction, I congratulated my staff on a productive workweek.

Leo was pleased; Ginny was thoughtful; Vida was subdued; and Carla was wan, having made a valiant effort to return to the office after only a day's absence.

She might still have been ailing, if, according to Vida, Peyton Flake hadn't made a house call to check on Carla's condition.

"I don't get it," Carla said, still mystified about the part her photos had played in solving the crime. "What did Big Mike Brockelman have to do with anything?"

I was sitting in Vida's visitor's chair. "We knew Mike was seeing Linda on the sly," I explained, avoiding eye contact with Leo on my immediate left. "When I saw his truck in Maple Lane in the first picture you took, he was sitting in the cab. In the second shot, on Alpine Way, the cab was empty. If he didn't kill Linda, why did he move his truck and where did he go? The only explanation was that he saw someone else go into Linda's condo first. It was her brother, Larry, but Mike might not recognize him. He probably figured that Linda already had a date. So Mike decided to change his dance card for the night. He drove around to the front of Parc Pines and spent the evening with Amanda Hanson, whose husband was out of town."

"You're guessing, babe," Leo said with an amused look.

I shrugged. "Maybe it was Marisa Foxx. It sure wasn't the guy Vida and I saw go into the sauna. I hope."

With a limp hand, Carla tossed her black hair over her shoulder. "I wish I'd seen Larry go into Parc Pines. Then I could testify at the trial. But what would I wear?"

"Your thinking cap," Vida snapped. "If you'd had it on the night Linda was killed, you might have seen Larry. He must have had to walk from wherever he parked his car."

Carla's hypothetical wardrobe was the least of my problems. I didn't relish the thought of Larry Petersen's trial. Judging from Vida's unhappy demeanor, she didn't, either. Having a member of one of Alpine's first families on trial for killing his sister was going to be very difficult for local residents to swallow. Maybe, between the ineptitude of the prosecuting attorney, Emmett Swecker, and the onerous task of picking an unbiased jury, the trial would be moved to Snohomish County.

It was Ginny who changed the subject. "Rick and I are going to dinner Friday night at Café de Flore."

"It's very pricey," Vida said.

"I've never liked French food," Leo remarked.

"You'll have to eat snails," Carla put in.

Obviously Ginny didn't care if she had to eat dirt. Rising from the chair, I meandered into my office. The irate phone calls would start soon. I sat down at my desk and lighted a cigarette from the pack I'd bought that morning at Safeway.

Ginny and Rick seemed to be reconciled. Carla was at least speaking to Peyton Flake again. Milo and Honoria had plans to drive to Bothell and have dinner at the Nieuw Amsterdam. Trying Dutch food was another concession that Milo was making to prove to Honoria that he wasn't just another narrow-minded, small-town guy.

"Unbelievable." It was Leo, standing in the doorway. "I thought you had more character, babe. How long have you been off those things?"

"Too long," I replied rebelliously. "I'll quit again on New Year's Day." Noting Leo's skeptical expression as he sat down in one of my visitor's chairs, I gave him a haughty look. "I will. I did it before, I'll do it again."

"Sure." Leo's face changed, sagging a bit with his brown eyes vacantly staring beyond my right shoulder. "I owe you an apology."

"For what? Smoking?"

He gave a little grunt. "Maybe that, too. But I've been a real dickhead."

"How so?"

"Ohhh . . ." He leaned back in the chair and reached around to close my door. "Before you invited me to dinner, I kept wanting to ask you out on a real date. I'd call and you'd answer and then I'd chicken out. I knew how you felt about fraternization."

The hang-ups came to mind at once. I realized that I hadn't had any since I'd cooked dinner for Leo. "That's okay. I thought it was kids."

The lines in Leo's face grew deeper. "You were right. A fifty-year-old kid. Maybe that's what my ex meant. I never grew up."

"Most of us don't." I grimaced, thinking of Tom, and how only the capture of a killer had kept me from dwelling on the possibility of his divorce.

Leo gave another grunt, this time of agreement. "Maybe. What I'm trying to say is that I didn't mean to push. I think you're a doll, but I really understand why you don't want to turn the office into a playpen."

"Oh. I see." I did, of course, but some perverse part of me wanted Leo to persevere. Or something. Maybe I merely wanted to be flattered. "Okay," I said lightly. "Then why don't we make Coffee Toss Two a group event? How about that Thanksgiving invitation? If Honoria doesn't go to Carmel, she and Milo will be there, along with my brother and my son and Carla and her roommate, Marilynn, and maybe Father Den from church."

Leo lifted his burnished eyebrows. "It sounds like an all-star cast. How many?" Before I could answer, Leo was ticking off the guest list on his fingers. "Ten, if I come. Would you mind making it eleven?"

"Huh? No, that's fine. I've already ordered a twenty-eight-pound turkey." I tried to act nonchalant. "Who are you bringing?"

Leo grinned, but sheepishly. "Delphine Corson. We've sort of been seeing each other for a while."

I should have known. Leo had been expecting to hear from Delphine when I called on Saturday. Leo had mentioned that the flu was going round, and I knew that Delphine had come down with it. Leo had been given a ride to work the day after his accident by Delphine. Leo had ordered the roses for Linda's funeral not because he'd been seeing her but to impress Delphine. Leo's expensive potted chrysanthemum wasn't meant merely to placate me but to . . .

"Sure," I said, hoping the pause hadn't been too lengthy. "Delphine's fun. Bring her along."

"Great." Leo stood up and slapped my desk. "She's got family here, but she says their holiday get-togethers are always a disaster. They fight a lot."

"How very Alpine," I said, but it was under my breath, and Leo had already strolled out of my office. The phone rang while I was still shaking my head.

"Larry voted for Bush," said the voice in my ear. "Serves him right. I'll bet he called Linda and told her to come up to our place to get together."

"Probably," I said to Elmer Petersen. It made sense. It gave Linda a reason to be on the Icicle Creek Road.

"I never liked Larry. I never liked Linda much, either. Marv's kids were as stuck on themselves as he is. But I think Linda voted for Clinton."

"Maybe so." The lights on my phone were now all glowing. *The Advocate* had hit the streets, or at least the delivery boxes of Alpine. "Excuse me, Elmer, I've got to—"

"It was him, you know." Elmer sounded unusually sanguine.

"Yes, it was Larry—"

"Not Larry." Elmer now sounded cantankerous. "I'm not talking about *now*, I'm talking about *then*. My father told me. It was back in 1932, when he still thought I was going to take over for him at the bank."

I had no idea what Elmer was jabbering about. "Excuse me, I—"

"Oh, he was a great one for the ladies, along with the gambling. A real rascal. The family was always in debt up to their snooty eyeballs. His missus wouldn't let on. Then he hit a lucky streak. Not that it lasted, but it bailed them out for a while. In fact, it was too good to be true, at least in terms of explaining to his wife where all the money came from, so he put it into the bank. My father was happy; so was Carl Clemans and the rest of them. They needed the capital. Lucky, too, that FDR came along and kept the country going."

It had finally occurred to me that Elmer was talking about the silent partner who had helped found the Bank of Alpine. "Who was it, Mr. Petersen?" I asked, keeping my voice bland.

"Who?" Elmer chortled. "Earl Ennis Blatt, that's who. Vida's old man. How do you put up with that Runkel woman? She drives me nuts."

A week later, life at the office had calmed down considerably. Because we had to work the Friday after Thanksgiving, I gave everybody, including me, Wednesday afternoon off. Adam and Ben were flying into Sea-Tac at six-ten. They planned to rent a car and drive to Alpine. Meanwhile, I had to run a dozen errands, which included a big stop at the Grocery Basket. It was almost five when I got home.

I checked the answering machine, but there were no messages. None of my guests had called to cancel. Adam and Ben must be on schedule. I hadn't heard from Tom since his call ten days earlier. He was probably caught up in preparing for the farce that would be the Cavanaugh Thanksgiving dinner. I guessed it would be catered, or that they'd eat out in an elegant San Francisco restaurant. Sandra hadn't been much of a cook even in the days before she boiled her purse in the soup kettle.

Next, I put away the groceries. I could barely squeeze the huge turkey onto the bottom shelf of my refrigerator. But its plump presence made me smile. I liked the idea of big holiday gatherings. It would have been even better if Vida could have joined us, but naturally, she preferred spending the day with her three daughters and their families. Maybe some of Roger's cousins would truss him up and roast him on a slow-turning spit.

Maybe I shouldn't have such evil thoughts about Roger. Instead, I should think kindly on the shattered Petersens. Linda was dead; Larry was in jail. They'd never share Thanksgiving again with their family.

But as far as I could tell, the Petersens' holidays had never been happy. The facade was there, but like so many of Alpine's secrets, the reality was ugly, and filled with rancor.

Finally I made myself a ham sandwich and sat down to look at *The Advocate*, which I hadn't yet seen in print. Leafing through the Thanksgiving special edition, I felt a surge of pride. The front page had a follow-up story on the Petersen murder, the second lead was the state auditors' request that criminal charges be filed against Christie Johnston, and our third big article featured interviews with the county commissioners regarding the proposed bond issue. There were plenty of ads, too, including a two-column-by-six-inch Buddy Bayard studio portrait of the munificent Ed Bronsky family, wishing that everybody in Alpine would get stuffed for Thanksgiving. I'm not sure if Ed meant what he said, but he was smiling in the picture.

At last I came to Vida's "Scene Around Town," which I hadn't yet read this week, and which she had proofed herself:

Rick Erlandson and Ginny Burmeister holding hands at Sunday's turkey shoot at the Overholt farm ... Durwood Parker spotted on a snowboard coming down Sixth Street and making an unscheduled stop under a mailbox between Cedar and Cascade ... Deputy Sam Heppner, on a well-deserved day off, displaying the eleven-pound steelhead he caught in the Tye River Monday ... Darla Puckett's lips were sealed when fellow members of the Burl Creek Thimble Club tried to get her to reveal her mouth-watering pecan pie recipe. ... That's newcomer Amanda Hanson waiting on the organized early birds who are already mailing off their Christmas parcels at the post office. ... Elmer Petersen suffering from scratches in a fight with his pretty Persian, Mamie Eisenhower. Did the cat get your tongue, Elmer? It should have. ...

How did Vida know?

That was one mystery I'd never attempt to solve. And I didn't dare ask. Vida's secret was safe with me. I had a feeling it would henceforth be safe with Elmer, too.

I went out into the kitchen to make the dressing and boil the cranberries. Back in 1911, the Alpine Lumber Company had started holding an annual Thanksgiving feast for the entire town. The dinners continued until the mill was shut down by Carl Clemans in 1929. I have two framed photographs in my living room. One shows the families gathered in the old social hall circa 1927, wearing their Sunday best and looking at the camera in a self-conscious manner. The other is of the mill itself, with snow covering the tin roof and the lumber on the railroad siding. Smoke is pouring out of the stacks. Across the valley where the highway and the river still run is Mount Baldy, with a huge gouge halfway up its flanks, mute evidence of where the loggers had stripped away the forest.

Baldy is now covered with second-growth timber. Many of the present generation of loggers and their families would have to get their Thanksgiving fare from the food bank. The environmentalists tell us we have come a long way since the reckless plundering of the woods. My head tells me that's true. My heart sends a different message.

The previous night, the wind had changed, blowing the clouds over the mountains into Eastern Washington. Looking through the kitchen window, I saw the vast array of stars, so close that they seemed to hover atop the snowcapped trees. A crescent moon was slung above Tonga Ridge. It tilted upward. My mother used to tell me that was a sign of clear weather. The moon held the snow in its cradle.

Somewhere out there, in the winter to come and the spring beyond, was the future. *My* future. I would grapple with it and fret over it and stagger and stumble and try to make the right decisions. As if there were any. There is only today, and getting through it without doing harm. Doing right, even doing good—those are bonuses.

For now, on the eve of Thanksgiving, a fat turkey in

the refrigerator and the smell of onions frying in butter
was enough. My menfolk were winding their way up
the Stevens Pass corridor to Alpine. At least two of
them were.

I wandered out into the living room. From over sixty
years ago, the faces around the table in the social hall
stared out at me. Maybe they weren't so self-conscious
after all. Studying them in the lamplight, I thought they
looked a little smug. What did they know that I didn't?
Was their Alpine different from mine?

Yes, it was.